Cresent Eagle

Cresent Eagle

A Novel

by

Joe Fontana

Joe Fontana
12/03

COMPANION PUBLICATIONS

Also by Joe Fontana
The Pentum Mission
Orchises Press, 1998
Alexandria, VA

Cover Design by Ross Feldner, New Age Graphics
Silver Spring, Maryland

Published by
Companion Publications
8844 Monard Drive
Silver Spring, Maryland 20910
301-563-6435 • Fax: 301-563-6438 • allied@toad.net
www.allied-bethesda.com

Printed in the United States of America

International Standard Book Number: 0-9668626-1-9

Dedication

To
Guido Columbo, Alfred von Escher
and Renato Serra
forever companions in all things good and generous

Preface

No author can honestly state that his work is his alone. It simply doesn't happen that way.

I first want to thank my editor, Michelle Meagher, a brilliant and sturdy young woman of immense composure who had ideas that strenghtened the novel and its organization.

Likewise with the publisher, Morris Cobern, who's indefagitable attitude and constant encouragement has made this a better book than it was when presented to him. Publishers are usually not easy people to deal with, but he is just the opposite—quiet, serious, precise, with a wry sense of humor, he made the final editing chore, not so much a joy (editing is never that), but worthwhile and sensible.

To the librarians at American and George Mason Universities, I owe another debt of gratitude for their help in finding sources of material with which I had to check and recheck the facts in the narrative.

To Jim Clear, a friend of long standing, who read the draft with wisdom and, in his own charming manner, suggested changes which helped smooth the plot line.

And, of course, to my wife, Barbara, who continues to see me toil doing something that she knows I enjoy and for that she is as happy as I am.

Author's Note

The origin of *Cresent Eagle,* its subject, treatment and every other motive that made me want to tell this story began when I was in London a few years ago. I was promoting my first novel, and received an invitation for dinner from a friend I hadn't seen for several years. We had taken different roads in life; I was surprised and delighted that he called. So, over dinner and good Beaujolais, we spent many hours talking of our youth in law and the firms in which we had practiced. He had the more interesting story to tell, so I went back to my hotel, immediately jotting down notes of our long talk.

As with all stories of international intrigue, it begins at an ending—death.

One

A dusty and tired stillness hung over London. The city was burdened with the unexpected heat wave that made the Parrot Restaurant's kitchen infernal, despite several fans whirling noiselessly overhead. The circulated hot air didn't ease the fatigue that Naomini Berganda was feeling, laboriously washing and cutting vegetables. A tall woman with a stooped-face, drawn and somewhat haggard, her long black hair held tightly in a bun covered by a black hairnet, Naomini felt that she had no legs or that the lower part of her body had gone to sleep. She was lightly perfumed—a feeble attempt to ward off the odors emanating from the kabob and onion meal being prepared for later serving. The heavily starched lime green serving dress she was wearing had lost its crispness and she could feel dampness in her armpits. Her feeling of weakness was increasing; and her doctor had warned her that she must quit her job or get one where she wasn't constantly on her feet. If she didn't make the change, she would not have long to live. The family needed the money she was earning and that was that.

She continued to work.

Using a six-inch stainless steel knife, her eyes red and her lips quivering, she rapidly pared the cucumber in thin, almost transparent, slices. Her skill was such that the knife barely touched the maple chopping block, making only the slightest sound before Naomini raised the knife again, repeating the action with the same dizzying speed. Frequently, she glanced over to the gray plastic-lined trash bin, squeezed between her preparation table and the oversized gas oven. It was there that she had placed the Harrod's package her cousin Kingsley had given her earlier in the day. She was feeling things. It was one of those occasions when one is planning to do something of a worrisome nature, knowing that there can be no turning back.

She shifted her large black eyes to the digital clock above the swinging door that led to the restaurant proper, a scowl crossing her forehead remembering her cousin Kingsley's warning as he handed her ten one-hundred English pound notes, "You must leave before six. Don't hesitate…regardless." She would not linger, everything would be calm, deliberate, not demonstrating any particular hurry. She could feel her heart beat quick and hard under her left breast.

"You're almost finished?" the chef asked loudly and testily, glancing at Naomini's salad plates as he passed her station. "No delay, Naomini. None. Everything must be perfect now…perfect. A very important man is here and there can be no mistakes. No mistakes, understand?" She didn't respond, but nodded as he hurried into the dining room, still muttering, "You must be neater, Naomini…much neater." He bent down, picking up a piece of wilted lettuce that had dropped to the floor and tossing it into the trash bin. The chef insisted on order and neatness, only he would have noticed such a small item. Except for this hypersensitive, fastidious habit, he usually seemed unconscious of the staff. Tonight he appeared to Naomini to be even more nervous, murmuring over and over again the name of the person being honored this evening. "This meal must be the best. It has to be the best for Mile Draculic."

The first tray of ten salads ready, she carried it into the dining room, freshly painted in sparkling white with chair rails and ceiling molding in a burnt gold. On the walls hung several mountain landscapes. Naomini felt chilly, lonely, and strange as she placed the salads on the tables as silently as her anxiety allowed.

A few people had already gathered at the small mahogany bar right off the street entrance to the restaurant. None paid Naomini the slightest notice. It was then that she saw Draculic. Tall, broad-shouldered, he moved and stood stiffly. He had olive skin and his hair was closely cropped. He smiled easily as he greeted those making their way to visit with him. The owner of the Parrot, a much shorter and heavier man, was engaged in animated conversation with Draculic and another taller man who was shaking Draculic's hand. As she passed the group, she heard the taller man wish Draculic a happy birthday. Draculic responded, "Thanks, Zoran, but where's my money?" All laughed loudly.

The dinner for about fifty people was to begin at 6:30 p. m. and a sign stating that the restaurant was closed for a private function had already been posted on the street entrance. On each of the fifteen tables, covered with brilliant white tablecloths over a skirt of rich gold, sat a small flag with horizontal bands of red, blue and white. Naomini had not recognized the flag, but earlier she had overheard a waiter say it represented a new country, Serbia. She wondered where such a country might be.

As Naomini finished placing the salads from her tray on the table closest to the entrance, she noticed that the taller man who had shaken Draculic's hand was leaving. In his hurry, he had brushed against her, excusing himself, then leaving through the front entrance, followed by two men.

She glanced at the clock above the door; it was now 5:45, time for her to clean up and leave. More people had arrived. All were still standing by the bar, trying to talk to Draculic, who was dressed in a dark blue suit, light blue shirt, and dark blue tie. In his lapel, he wore a small flag pin matching the flags on the dining tables.

She began cleaning up her station, glancing at the clock's digital numerals, which now read 5:50. She scraped the salad remains into a large colander and deposited then in the trash bin, placing the colander in the sink. Naomini didn't go to the bathroom to change her uniform. Pale, weak, the dark circles under her eyes more pronounced, breathing heavily, she left the Parrot through its rear door.

Tonight, she would tell her husband she would quit. After all, she had the money that her cousin had given her.

Naomini scurried up the alleyway behind the restaurant onto Eades Street, heading toward the Underground station three blocks away. She was thinking she would be home in Clapham Common a few minutes earlier than usual. Being home would do her good.

Just as she completed the first block, she heard a tremendous explosion, followed in close succession by two more. She turned and saw flashes of flame and billows of dark smoke in the sky. Could it be? Her eyes grew frightened as she doubled back, walking hastily. She didn't have to go any further to discover the sudden horror. The restaurant, where she had worked for the past few months, was no more. From half a block away she could see massive amounts of smoke and flame coming from the front of what had been the Parrot, now entirely blown away by the force of the blast. She stood, paralyzed, staring at the shattered remnants of tables, chairs, dishware, glass, and what appeared to be body parts, all grotesquely scattered along the street, some pieces just a few feet ahead of her. For some seconds she could neither think nor scream. She stared in disbelief at the pedestrians who, struck with panic, ran past her, their faces covered with fear and blood. Naomini placed her hands in front of her face, murmuring inaudibly, "Why, Kingsley? Why did you ask me to do this?"

At the end of Eades Street, three blocks from the Parrot, a dark gray Mercedes limousine was parked in front of Euston's Health and Pharmacy Shop. A tall, middle-aged, well-groomed man emerged carrying a small shopping sack. Upon seeing him, the driver immediately got out of his seat and opened the rear door.

"To the office, Mr. Hemmrich?"

As the man checked his watch, his thoughts were briefly disturbed by a booming noise emanating from the middle of the next block and by a fireball and thick black smoke shooting toward the sky. A slight smile flickered across his face as he observed the scene.

"No, Alan. Not right now. Take me to Farris' office."

Returning to the driver's seat, he slowly pulled away from the curb, making a U-turn and heading the limousine down Knightsbridge Road, away from the scene.

Naomini turned hopelessly, struggling to restore order to her mind. She began retracing her steps toward the Underground station, tears springing to her eyes. She felt baffled, betrayed. Trying to run, but failing, she finally rested against the side of a building, watching as a crowd began to surge toward the subway entrance. The wail of sirens in the background was getting closer. Naomini's head shook violently from side to side as fear and panic swept over her.

The train ride to her station at Clapham Common was fifteen minutes, long enough to calm down. Alex would be home, as would the children. She didn't want to appear frightened. The slow walk up the station stairs and the two blocks to her apartment would help her relax. She needed to do that. She was nauseated, sweat coming down her forehead, her body trembling, her throat raw.

The streets were uncommonly quiet, she thought. The buildings cast unusual shadows for this time of early evening. A terrible grayness was clouding her eyes. She noticed that no children were playing. She heard no cars. The first block seemed longer than usual. It would be but a few minutes now, she thought. A nice glass of cold water. She needed water. She felt heavy. As she made her way onto the second block, a crushing sensation in her chest now became unbearable. Only one more block. Just one block…one block….

In the distance, she saw Alex and the children. "My God. He is talking to Kingsley. I have to tell him what I did. I'm innocent of all wrong, Alex. Innocent." She tried to hurry her pace, but her steps slowed. "Alex, Alex, I'm here…come meet me. Can you hear me…? Alex, Alex, come get me…Kingsley asked me to do it…I did it for the family, Alex …one thousand pounds…Alex…the children, bring the children." Her arms extended feebly, she raised her voice one last time, collapsing on the sidewalk, sinking into unconsciousness.

Her husband did hear her, as did Kingsley and the children. But it was too late. She was dead.

Two

Of course he was irritated. Keiran Hogan had been dumped and he couldn't escape from the fact. It was, so to speak, a life sentence of sorts. She had been, he reflected, his love. Even the opportunity to go to his first London American Embassy function did nothing to disrupt his thoughts. He alternated between being furious and dejected at himself. Certainly he felt small and crushed. This isn't going to be any fun, he silently told himself as he checked in at the embassy reception desk, showing his passport and invitation to the clerk, a petite, delicate, boyish looking woman with green eyes who tapped in the required information into her computer. Barely looking at Keiran, she said, "You're late…and the last one to arrive. Fifth floor conference room. Please hang this pass around your neck and return it before you leave the building. Please don't forget. Security. You do understand, don't you? We need to know who goes in and out of the building."

"Sure," Keiran mumbled, and he walked to the bank of elevators and rode up to the fifth floor. "From that beginning, it won't be much of a trawling place here."

He was very much on edge. His weekend trips to Washington were for one purpose only, to try to resurrect his relationship with Allison. He wanted to believe that they still had a life together. He knew she was impressed with his persistence and his enthusiasm to be with her, but that didn't change her earlier decision. He wanted her to come to London with him, but she was happy at her own law firm and didn't want to leave. So, under the circumstances, she had left him. She had told him finally that he had no claim over her or any part of her life. That was it. Time wasn't the healer it should have been. What man accepts a failed relationship when he is in love? Or when he thinks he is love? At 31, Keiran thought he knew the difference between sex and in love, and now he was beginning to wonder whether he missed Allison or whether he simply missed the regularity of the sex they shared while living together.

Apart from the emotional worry, he needed sleep. He could not escape the effects of jet lag, despite all the books with pointers telling him to eat sparingly and drink plenty of water. He followed such advice, but with little success. Besides, he could seldom sleep on an airplane and spent most of the six-and-a-half-hour trip viewing in-flight movies until breakfast was served. No matter what he did, his biological clock was confused, so he had gone right to sleep after his arrival at Heathrow on Monday at 7:00 a.m. Rather than going directly to his law office, Keiran had gone instead to London's Royal Automobile Club, where he had been staying these past eight weeks. The meeting at the American Embassy was scheduled for 5:30, leaving him time to rest and have a swim beforehand. Despite an alarm clock he had set for 4:00, and a call from the club's reception desk, he couldn't get himself organized in order to arrive at the embassy in time for the start of the session. He was fifteen minutes late.

Keiran strode down the corridor and quietly opened the door to the conference room in the middle of the hall. The lights had dimmed for a slide presentation, and that pleased him as he eased himself into the last empty seat around the table. At the lectern, a speaker was talking in a slow, monotonous voice, flanked by two American flags and the seal of the United States prominently displayed behind him. At the speaker's direction, an aide changed the slides displayed on a large screen. Just as Keiran opened his briefcase to retrieve a note pad and pen, a dull, loud sound erupted, followed by an even louder, but similar, sound. The two chandeliers suspended from the conference room ceiling swayed for several seconds.

"Lights, please. Shades drawn," a voice spoke out loudly.

Instantly, the room was bathed in bright light, illuminating its stark white walls with an intense glare. The curtains covering the large two-story picture windows parted noiselessly, revealing in the distance a large, dark plume of smoke rising to the sky. Almost in unison, everyone rose from the table, heading toward the windows overlooking Grosvenor Square, their bulletproofing muffling the shrill sound of ambulances and police vehicles. Silence came over the group as they looked outside.

"Another IRA blast? I thought there was a cease fire," said someone in the crowd. Everyone began chattering as they jockeyed for positions at the windows.

"Maybe we should get out of here before panic sets in," said the middle-aged, gray-eyed man who had been sitting next to Keiran, adding, "Bob Grayson, Williams and Stevens. And you are?"

"Hogan. Keiran Hogan, Kenton & Ward." He looked at Grayson, a well groomed, closely shaven man with a kind smile. "Does this happen often?"

"You mean bombs going off in London causing dull meetings to end?" Grayson smiled.

"You think it was a bomb?"

"Oh, I don't know. Whatever it is, it caused those chandeliers to move. I say we get out of here." Grayson paused. "Anyway, I'm leaving. Want to share a cab?"

"Sure. My office is by the Bank of England. And yours?"

"Not too far from the 'gray lady.' Let's go."

As they left together, followed by two Marine guards, who shouted, "Hold the door! Hold open!" they brushed by a pasty-faced, slender man, his eyes shrunken into their sockets. With one hand, the man clutched a sheaf of papers, the other held onto the plastic identity card hanging around his neck, suspended by a blue ribbon on which was printed 'U. S. Department of State.'"

"Let's move, Hogan. They're going to close this building down. Those Marines didn't look happy and the gaunt-looking man is Jefferson Coborn, the admin guy for the ambassador. He's going into that room to grab the ambassador and tell him to leave."

"Why the rush?" Keiran inquired, hurrying along the corridor with Grayson.

"That blast wasn't too far from here. And who knows? Maybe they've received a bomb threat here. Not many people like Americans these days, so why not? Anyhow, Hogan, they'll shut this place tight, letting no one in or out."

They walked down the five floors in silence, reaching the lobby. Dropping their visitor passes at the reception desk, signing out quickly, they walked out the side-exit doors.

"It looks serious to me," Grayson said as he stopped for a moment and looked into the distance, where the dark and expanding smoke cloud still hovered in the windless dusk. "This way," Grayson directed. Crossing the street to a taxi stand, they swiftly got into a taxi.

"Experienced in this?"

"You mean bomb scares?" Grayson smiled. "Not much. Only watch action movies on the tube. You want a drink? Maybe we should get out of this traffic. You game?"

"I wish I could. I've got a meeting back at the office. Regular staff meeting, and Mr. Farris is keen on my being there. So I'd better hold off on your offer."

"No problem. And you've been in London for how long?" Grayson asked.

"This is my eighth week. These meetings with the ambassador—was he the speaker?"

"Yes. But don't worry. He never says anything. Besides, you'll have everything you need in the packet that was in front of you on the conference table. Did you pick it up?"

"Right in here." Keiran tapped his briefcase on his lap.

"There'll be a verbatim text of what the ambassador was droning on about. These sessions for the American law firm representatives are vehicles for the ambassador. Raise two million bucks for the President's political campaigns and you're Ambassador to England. No valuable information is passed on. But, hey, why not? We rub each other. Ask him for something, and it's a struggle, a real serious one. What do you expect from a Princeton graduate?"

"Not that," Keiran chuckled.

"Did you go to Princeton?" Grayson looked startled.

"Yeah. And most of us, I think, aren't like that."

"Me, in my old age.... Ah well...."

They both laughed.

"Let me get off the topic now while I'm behind," Grayson smiled. "I should tell you that the ambassador has a peculiar view when it comes to talking to us. 'Check with Washington' is his favorite response. He thinks we are all crooks fronting for our clients. You know, making what is illegal legal. Well, some of us are," he laughed. "By the bye—I've adopted this English phrase rather than 'by the way'—How is your man Farris these days?"

"I guess fine. You know him?"

"Just in passing and from these meetings at the embassy. You're enjoying the big city?"

"Yeah, as a matter of fact, I am. How long have you been in London?"

"On and off for a few years."

It took the cab about twenty minutes to navigate the evening traffic. Coming up to the Bank of England building, it was a few minutes after 6:30.

"I'll get out here. My office is just across the street. Thanks for the lift, Mr. Grayson."

"No problem. Here's my card. Oh...why not come over to our house this Saturday? Six or so. Cocktails. Okay? You may meet some interesting people. Take care, and my regards to Farris." Grayson smiled, shaking Keiran's hand as he exited the cab. "You okay? You sure you don't need a drink before heading to your office?"

"Yeah. Just hard to believe, that's all. I'll have a lot to tell the folks upstairs. See you Saturday. Thanks."

"Take good care of yourself. Saturday it'll be. My house. Six."

Keiran closed the cab door and waved goodbye to Grayson as the cab left.

Friendly guy, Keiran thought as he crossed the street. Bombs in London? He shook his head in disbelief as he hurried into his office building, noticing that the police were putting up barricades around the entrances to the Bank of England Building. It was close, Keiran Hogan. Very close. But why?

Three

The offices of Kenton & Ward were located at Number Two Lothbury Street in the financial district of London, just around the corner from the historic and stately Bank of England headquarters. The firm occupied the entire third floor of the restored turn-of-the-century granite-faced building, its mahogany doors led to a large marble lobby with two vintage elevators. Both were in working order, left by the owner to contribute to the ambiance. Despite the face lift, the granite-faced building still looked dirty, the gray overcast August late afternoon made it seem more so. Clutching his brief case in his left hand, the folder of information from the embassy stuck inside, Keiran entered from the elevator into the reception area of the office suite. Bold and bright gold antique lettering was centered on the paneled wall facing him like a shield of honor for everyone to see. Kenton & Ward wanted to be taken seriously and the entrance to the office suite gave the visitor an assurance of stability, reliability, and strength. The location near the Bank of England enforced the image.

There was no receptionist in sight as he entered the office, where indirect lighting gave the appearance of a hotel lobby. Large oil landscapes hung on the dark-paneled walls, and several cream and burgundy striped overstuffed chairs were carefully arranged into groups of three.. Hogan headed toward his office off the corridor leading to Farris.' It was still. As it was after six, the support staff had left and his colleagues were already at the staff meeting.

Inside his office, several files were piled on the floor—he didn't have a file cabinet. A note had been pinned on the computer monitor. "When you arrive, go directly to Farris' office. Important!!!!! HenHen"

Keiran placed his file on the desk, looked at some notes from lawyers who wanted to see him. A client assigned to him had called. As he lifted the phone, HenHen popped her head in the doorway. "Where have you been? We called the embassy and they said that you left a half hour ago." Keiran thought her horsy and her smirk annoying.

"HenHen, do you know where the American Embassy is? Try taking a cab from there to here and in this traffic. Anyway, I'm here now." He buried himself in scanning his files.

"Mr. Farris and the others are in the conference room waiting for you. It's Monday. Remember? Regular staff meetings. You should try to be on time, Mr. Hogan. The meeting began some ten minutes ago at 6:30."

"HenHen, you're worrying over nothing."

Keiran took the folder with the Great Seal of the United States on a glossy blue cover and walked briskly down the hall. He was silent, as was HenHen, who went in the opposite direction.

The white-walled, burgundy-carpeted conference room was windowless. The wall hanging depicted scenes of ancient London. Sitting around a rosewood table with flowers at its center was the ten-lawyer staff of the London office of Kenton & Ward. A strained silence permeated the room.

"Glad you made our regular meeting, Mr. Hogan," said Farris in a sonorous voice.

"Police were redirecting traffic because of the explosion in Mayfair." He stared directly at Farris with civil composure. His years of swim practice and competitive meets had taught him never to fidget, never to look uncomfortable, and never to give anyone the impression of being lost.

Farris didn't answer. Twisting his pen between his fingers, he turned his gaze away from Keiran. "In our third quarter, our profit projecting for this office is off by 8 percent. I don't like this at all. I want all of you to bill every hour to a client—I don't like seeing 'firm time' on your billing sheets. Until this year, we have always made our profit—and I intend to make it again. We may have to have an interim increase in hourly rates. There'll be no problem with getting increases approved by the Management committee, especially hourly increases for our associates. What is your rate, Keiran?"

"$200"

"Your rates are the lowest. Harper, your rates…" He turned to one of the two junior partners. "You and Goodrich are $385, right?"

"Yes, our rates were raised last year from $350 to $385. If you're thinking of raising our rates, Duane, I don't think our clients will stand another increase."

"Listen, Harper, I know what the market will bear and I don't want advice on that issue. The rates will be raised."

When he was nervous, as he was now, Farris had the disconcerting habit of bringing his hand to his bald head and patting down what few hairs he had left. He would do this almost as if he wished he had hair, feeling his head on the off chance that he would find growth.

For the next several minutes, Farris went over the client list and the workload of the office.

There would be no questions. Questions were never encouraged at these meetings. In fact, expressions of opinion were discouraged. Conversation was always complacent chatter. It was obvious that some would pad their time sheets and others would not, and Farris' comments were addressed to the later group. Keiran knew now that the pressure would be on him to follow suit. If he didn't, Farris would simply add to the bill in any event. No matter, he would let Farris make that decision. Keiran understood, and he hated the internal cheating of client billing accounts. Keiran's twelve hours per day would soon become fifteen hours, and few clients would complain. In the case of those who did, Farris would blame the associate for not knowing how to bill.

"Good. Now that's done." Farris closed the file in front of him. "Now Keiran, give us a précis of what was said at the embassy meeting."

Just as Keiran began to speak, three short phone rings broke the room's silence. Keiran knew the call must be urgent—HenHen would not have bothered Farris otherwise.

"Excuse me, Keiran." Farris picked up the receiver. "Yes, HenHen. Certainly, put him through."

"Zoran. You're a bit early. Downstairs. I'll be there in about five, no more than ten minutes. You don't want to come up to the office...? Fine. Okay. See you shortly." Farris hung up the phone.

"Keiran. Please begin. I have an appointment waiting for me, so we'll have to ask you to be very brief."

"No new information. The ambassador simply reviewed the embassy's offer to help U. S. business in whatever fashion it could and wanted to pass that info back to the firms so that they could then pass it on to the clients. I'll have a memorandum for you on your desk in the morning. That's it."

"Well…good." Farris paused. "We're finished. Thank you all for coming. See you tomorrow. Keiran, please join me in my office for a few moments."

Farris' office adjoined the conference room and was as large as it, on the corner with a good view of the Bank of England. Keiran sat in a gray leather seat directly across from Farris, who moved some papers across his desk before he spoke.

"Keiran, I want you to know I have been disappointed in your lack of promptness; I realize you have been going back to Washington these last several weeks for personal reasons. If your personal situation is such, I can arrange to have you go back to Washington, if that is what you want. We can't accommodate your tardiness. I'm about to assign you to a client—an important one—and this will require your undivided attention."

"Sir, I've never been late on any of my assignments. I always thought promptness in turning in the assignments was the important thing. If I were to be late in turning in client's work, I'd let you know. But I've never been late in meeting any of your deadlines, have I?"

Farris smiled slightly at his question. "Well now. My fellow partners in Washington told me that you were singularly independent, and you certainly are that. Normally, it's a good trait, but we have to adhere to some rudimentary rules in this office. So, if you're going to be late, and I don't mean in the assignments, I mean late to the office, call HenHen and tell her. We are a small office and it's important for HenHen to know where we all are. Agreed? Timely behavior is what I admire. Understood?"

"I won't be making any more trips to Washington on the weekends. If I do, I will certainly ask for the days off and advise HenHen."

"Good. We have an understanding. As for your work, it's superb, the best in the office, your writing is outstanding, and your analyses are on point. On to your new assignment. I know you'll continue to bring your best talents to bear on this new project."

Keiran nodded, but remained silent.

Farris opened a drawer in his desk and took out a large blue expandable file. "Here. Read it. We'll talk in the morning. Straight purchase agreement and financing documents for the purchase of cement. There are a few more files over at the side table for you to pick up. Background and so forth. All marked 'Benton Industries.' Remember, be on time tomorrow morning and make sure you read these tonight. Any questions?"

"None," Keiran answered.

"Good. Well…Good night, Keiran."

"Good night, sir." The meeting was over. Keiran walked over to the side table, grabbed the files, and left for his office.

Diana Peters, the associate who had the office next to his, poked her head into Keiran's office as he placed the Benton files on his desk. "Want to join me for a drink?" she asked.

"What are you carrying? Gold for the Bank of England?" Her briefcase bulged.

"Why not? So how about that mineral water?" she asked, standing in his doorway.

"Maybe something stronger," Keiran replied.

"And if you're nice to me, I may—just may—ask you to take me to dinner. But no meat. Just vegetables."

"God, I forgot you're into all that natural stuff."

"And you, a college champion swimmer. Look at you.... You need to firm up." She reached over, poking his stomach. "Ugh! You're fat." She laughed.

"No fat at all. Moderation, Diana, is the key."

"Moderation. Really? And what about sex?"

"Are you always this blunt?" Keiran gave a little laugh. "Well, part of my life plan is having regular sex."

"Regular sex? With whom?"

"Diana. Now watch it. You've obviously broken up again, right?"

"Yes. Last week, when I left Sebastian...."

"Sebastian? Great name Diana, great name."

"Don't joke about his name. Can't you see I'm in a state of complete depression? You must come out with me and have a drink and dinner. It's a matter of principle."

"I can't. I have too much work to do tonight. You know that. You were at the meeting. Not tonight. No."

"Keiran Hogan. You seem so rational all the time. No impulsive behavior traits at all. It's not worthwhile to fall in love with you." She leaned over and kissed him.

"Diana, stop. I have work to do. I'll see you tomorrow for dinner. I promise." Keiran pulled away from her, took her hand and led her to his office door, picking up her case and handing it to her.

"I'll be waiting. Don't disappoint me."

"Tomorrow. We'll go out tomorrow. Dinner."

"No changes?"

"None," he replied.

"See you and good night, Keiran Hogan. I'm glad you're with us. Don't let Farris push you down. Do you believe this about billing rates? That lecture was just a preview of what he will do—jack up our rates whether we like it or not. What a cold, greedy bastard. Frankly, I don't know how long I'll stay at this firm." She paused. "Rumor has it you've been assigned our most lucrative client, Zoran Hemmrich. There's a combination: Farris and Hemmrich. Two peas in a pod. Be wary Keiran."

"What the hell do you mean?"

"Dinner tomorrow may bring the answer to your query, *inter alia*." She winked at him. "You do understand Latin, don't you? You were educated at a Catholic high school, I assume they taught you Latin."

"You're something, Diana. Get out of here. Now. And how did you know that about my high school?"

"I know everything." She laughed loudly and walked away.

He saw her go down the corridor, struggling with her case.

Keiran went over to his computer to read his e-mails. Nothing needed answering tonight. The computer indicated he had two faxes. These he printed out, glanced at, and laid aside. He grabbed his case, the three file folders of Benton Industries, Ltd., the folder from the embassy meeting, and left, hoping he could catch the underground and be at the club in fifteen minutes. As he walked out the front door of the office building, he saw Farris get into a gray Mercedes limousine, its windows darkened. The chauffeur glanced at Keiran as he closed the door behind Farris and strode over to the drivers side of the car. In a moment, the car worked its way into the evening traffic. All Keiran was thinking about now was the inviting nature of the swimming pool back at the Royal Automobile Club.

Keiran let himself into his room. Not bothering to draw the oyster-colored drapes, he dropped his bag and briefcase on the floor, threw off his clothes, scattering them on the couch. He put on his bathrobe and walked the five flights via the back stairs to the pool area on the lower level of the club. The pool looked as it always did to him—an oasis of peace. It suited his body and his brain. The routine was always the same. The goggles tightly drawn over his eyes, he stretched his shoulders, shook his hands and arms, first one leg and foot, then the other. After three deep breaths, he assumed the start position, paused for a second or two, dove, swam to the other end, came back in backstroke, switched to breaststroke for the third lap, then into freestyle for 100 laps. After all these years—he had started to swim at three—he had what few of us have, watermanship—that ability to be at home in water, to become one with water, the ability to float, thrust, bend, roll, sink, rise, and spin in weightless suspension. Keiran swam for a full hour. He was comfortably alone with his thoughts as he glided through the water, without rushing or breaking records…just consistent, steady as his worries receded.

Four

The days since Monday's staff meeting had been spent, Keiran believed, in simple make-work. Nothing challenged him. All Keiran did was write and rewrite—first his memorandum on the embassy meeting he had just attended and then a proposed joint venture between a U. S. internet company and Lockwood, Ltd. of England, a file he had taken to Washington the weekend before. He composed a third draft of the documents for the new corporate client, Benton Industries, Ltd. Although bored, he took his job seriously, and as a result he was puzzled with Farris' proposed changes. It was probably too much to hope that any of Farris' suggestions would be relevant. Most seemed utterly gratuitous. The only good thing was the weather, which during the week had been hot, but turned seasonably cooler Saturday morning.

The first two memoranda had been finally 'okayed' by Farris, but he was still making more suggestions regarding Benton Industries "to strengthen" and make the narrative "tighter." All nonsense, in Keiran's view. So Keiran was angry, the kind of anger that comes to those who know there is nothing that can be done to alleviate the frustration that caused the anger in the first place. Because of Farris' penchant for delay and distraction, and in order to assert his authority over what he considers to be too independent an associate, the legal memorandum that he had requested on Benton Industries wasn't returned to Keiran for revision until late Friday afternoon. HenHen had noted, in a transmittal letter to Keiran, that he was to bring the revised memo by five o'clock Saturday evening to Farris' home in order that Farris could review the documents prior to leaving for Athens on Sunday.

Keiran had worked most of Friday evening and all day Saturday reworking the documents, taking into account the various notes and questions that Farris had asked be clarified. One lucky thing though, it was Saturday, and he would not have to listen to HenHen's burgling voice. She never came in to work on a weekend, unless Farris was there, and during the time that Keiran had been in London, Farris had never been in the office on a Saturday.

Trying to decipher Farris' script, written in green ink, was always a challenge. Many times, he would ask HenHen what it meant. She would always reply, "I don't understand, Keiran. It's clearly written." Today, he just guessed. Clipped to the returned documents was an envelope with air tickets and an itinerary for Keiran to go to St. Peter's Port, Guernsey on Monday to finalize the registration of Benton Industries with the island authorities.

He reviewed the revisions to the documents, scrolling down one page after the other on his computer screen. As he moved the cursor, he realized that these last assignments only reinforced his view that working with Farris would continue to be a succession of unnecessary efforts. Farris never seemed to be satisfied and appeared always apprehensive when it came to approving any documents. At times, Keiran had the distinct feeling that Farris was hiding something, keeping an important ten percent of the facts to himself.

Regardless, he had to take Farris the way he was, he had to be tolerant if he wanted to stay in London and work at this firm.

It wasn't until 4:30 that Keiran finished the amendments to the documents, proofread and made the copies, and placed Farris' copy in a red expandable folder. He insisted upon red for his copies, blue folders were for the firm copies and HenHen's desk, and Keiran's copies were in a green folder. Color coordination made for efficient filing, HenHen always said, and Keiran had to admit, she was right.

In the cover memorandum to Farris, despite the "X" Farris had scrawled on the earlier appendix, Keiran listed, in a summary fashion, his concerns about the proposed contract. He called into question the financing of such a large order—300,000 metric tons of cement for delivery to Singapore from the port of Alexandria, Egypt. In addition, he again pointed out that the letter of credit for the transaction was from a rather small privately owned bank, not a large commercial public bank.

Keiran wanted to be responsible. He wondered why his queries were of no concern to Farris. He needed to confront the realities of the deal…even if Farris held the answers in secret little holes and in the corners of his own mind. Keiran certainly didn't want to be like a trusting child whom Farris would abandon on a doorstep if something went horribly wrong with the deal. He had the suspicion that this is exactly what would happen to him if he were not forthright in listing his concerns. In the short time he had been in the London offices of the firm, he had witnessed Farris' insolent attitude toward others whom he felt had made mistakes, and he had mocked those individuals at the weekly staff meetings.

Although not specifically asked by Farris, Keiran had also run an Internet search on the owner of the Benton Industries and found precious little, but what was known was sordid. According to his search, early in his business career, Zoran Hemmrich had been charged in England with violating export trade restrictions for sales to Iraq of materials that could be used in the production of chemical weapons. The shipment occurred one year prior to the Iraqi suppression of a revolt by its Kurdish minority with the use of such weapons. Hemmrich said he was exporting chemicals for the production of pharmaceuticals and denied the accusation that he was aware of the intended use of the chemicals. In addition, there were charges that he was involved in money laundering. Despite a lengthy investigation by a Special Prosecuting Magistrate, the charges fell away for lack of corroborating evidence. In an interview with the *Times of London*, the Labor Party's shadow foreign secretary, Susan Meade, intimated that the real reason was the major contributions that Hemmrich made to the Conservative Party.

Hemmrich's lawyer was Duane Farris.

In a letter to the *Times* editor, he called Meade's suggestions libelous and suggested that he would file a legal brief against her. Beyond his words, however, he never took any action.

The original investigating London police officer in the case, Alan Simpson, retired and was subsequently hired by one of Hemmrich's companies as chief of security. More recently, just a year ago, the Belgian police decided to back off investigating Hemmrich's sale of pharmaceuticals, this time to Iran. The reasons why were never disclosed. Again, his spokesman was Farris.

Keiran reread his notes on Hemmrich's activities. Intelligence is often a foe to instinct. Yet here, he knew, in him, both had converged. "No faint sounds of purity there," he thought silently.

Keiran took the subway to Sloan Street Station and walked the five blocks to Farris' home at 20 Portman Walk, arriving just before 5:00. The house, a pleasant looking three-story red brick with bellying casement windows on each floor, had an appearance of meticulous upkeep, including the entranceway of white stone steps, which, to Keiran, looked freshly scrubbed. The shrubbery on both sides of the walkway was clipped and the small lawn was a luxurious deep green, neatly trimmed. As he was about to go up the stairs, his way was blocked for an instant by a modestly sized man, white haired, pasty-faced, slender, hurrying down the steps. He glanced at Keiran, his eyes scanning him for several moments, as if trying to recollect where he had seen him, then he continued down the street. Keiran did remember where they had passed. It was at the American Embassy earlier in the week. He was the man rushing down the fifth floor corridor toward the conference room as Keiran was leaving with Grayson.

Keiran climbed the steps quickly, halting before the door for a few seconds, looking alternately at the brass knocker and bell button, the latter prominently encircled by a highly polished frame with black lettering, "Please ring bell for entrance." With the option for the knocker foreclosed, he chose the bell, tightening his grip on his briefcase, which contained the red folder holding the documents Farris had to review. It was but a moment before the door opened.

"Good evening, sir." A thin, genial woman, her brown hair pulled back in a bun, dressed in a dark gray uniform and a brilliant white half apron greeted him.

"Good evening. Keiran Hogan to see Mr. Farris."

"Mr. Farris is expecting you. Do come in."

She motioned him to follow her through the vestibule down a long, dark green, carpeted corridor. At its end, she opened the door to a book-lined library where Farris was seated at his desk, the only light coming from a pedestal lamp, diffused through an antique white shade. He was reading some documents while another man, tall and with an olive complexion, looked over Farris' shoulders.

"Mr. Farris...Mr. Farris...do you wish to see Mr. Hogan now?"

Farris looked up, squinting in the dim light.

"Yes, of course. Good afternoon, Keiran. I'll be with you momentarily.... Anna, please take Mr. Hogan to the drawing room and make sure he has something to drink. Have you had lunch or did you work through lunch?"

"I had a sandwich," Keiran replied, surprised that Farris would make such a solicitous comment, but realizing it was said for effect in front of his guest, who continued to read the papers, turning over each page and placing them in front of Farris, not looking up at Keiran.

"Good. Anna, please take care of this young man."

Anna closed the door to the library and retraced her steps toward the front of the house, stopping in the middle of the corridor where she opened a set of double doors to reveal a pale yellow-walled drawing room, with furniture so exquisite that it reminded Keiran of what he had seen at an exhibition at Washington's National Gallery of Art. He was conscious of the feeling of wealth and power the room exuded through its furnishings. The drapes were open on ten-foot windows facing a side garden, letting in a soft natural light, and unlike the darkened library in which Farris had greeted him, enhanced by the shimmering radiance from two chandeliers dimmed to show off the portraits that hung on all the walls. A large gilded framed mirror hung over the regency marble mantle, on each end of the mantle sat silver candelabra. An aroma from the several flower arrangements filled the room. Everything seemed to be in order—perfect order, maintained and preserved by someone assured as to what his role in life was.

"A drink, perhaps, Mr. Hogan?"

"Juice or mineral water. Whatever you have on hand."

"No neglected beauty here," Keiran murmured to himself, as he wandered around the room, his briefcase clutched in his hand. Standing momentarily before each portrait, he looked for any similarity to Farris, trying to decide if any portraits were of Farris' family or if they were placed in the room by the decorator for an impression. Glancing at his watch, he knew he would be late for Grayson's cocktail party, and certainly there would not be any time for his daily swim. He realized that he would have barely enough time to change clothes and get to Islington, where the Graysons lived. He needed a haircut, and he had forgotten to shave today, unconsciously rubbing his chin, but his stubble was barely discernible. He probably wouldn't shave until Sunday. Some men would look upon shaving every other day as a blessing. Keiran thought otherwise.

"Mr. Hogan, your juice," the maid said as she placed a small silver tray with orange juice in a crystal tumbler. She had bought some sandwiches on a mint-green china plate and a neatly folded pale-yellow linen napkin. She bowed slightly and left the room, leaving the double doors to the room slightly ajar.

Keiran placed his briefcase on the floor next to his seat, then reached for his glass of orange juice and a sandwich. He marveled at how the British spent so much time cutting a sandwich into four pieces after removing the crust on the bread, rather than the more practical two pieces as is done in the United States. Probably sensible though, given that eating the smaller sandwich is certainly more gracious and neater. Holding his glass, he rose, and like an interested visitor to a museum, continued his viewing of the portraits in the room. Upon reaching the last and largest one hung by the entrance to the room he saw a small brass nameplate identifying the portrait: Sir Christopher Cradock, 1870-1914. As he gazed at the portrait, he heard a muffled conversation in the hall. Keiran turned, getting a fleeting glimpse of Farris ushering his visitor to the front door, and heard Farris say, "I worry whether it was a mistake,

Zoran…too much attention is not what we want. Naturally I understand, though."

"You worry too much Duane."

"Forgive me for being a bit late, Keiran. Last-minute business. No rest for us lawyers, now is there? I see you're looking at a distant relative of my wife," Farris said, casually coming into the room, and walking over to where Keiran was standing. "Sir Christopher Cradock went down with his ship sunk by the Germans near the Falkland Islands in World War I. He was fleet commander of five ships, and was facing the great German battle cruiser, Graf Spee, together with its squadron of five ships. Perhaps you have heard of the Graf Spee?"

"I really can't say that I have, Mr. Farris." Keiran continued to examine the full length gilded framed portrait of a sharp, yet sullen looking man with eyes like pale blue glass, in full dress white naval uniform, his left chest filled with various brilliantly colored military ribbons.

"Well, I probably wouldn't know much about the battle either if there were not a family connection. Cradock was criticized after the battle because he knew he was obviously outgunned by the much stronger German force. He knew he couldn't defeat this German armada, but he also believed he could sufficiently damage the German ship. Hoped help in the form of a British battleship group steaming to join his fleet would arrive in time to finish off the Graf Spee. But it was a deadly English defeat. Some at the time believed he was a fool to engage such an overwhelming force. Others thought him brave and courageous. I suppose, though, human behavior is such that Cradock probably would've felt shame if he didn't fight. The countries were at war and the enemy was present. Yet, Cradock forgot one thing. You fight to win, not to lose. Fighting requires not acting stupidly or mechanically, but carefully, with prudence. Good advice even in the law practice, wouldn't you agree, Keiran?"

"Sure, it's better to start from a stronger position than not. Yes, I agree. Certainly, if strength is not possible, then be clever. Even more preferable, I would think, is the combination of the two—strong and clever."

Farris lowered his head. A slow, odd smile creased his cheek.

"A wise reflection, Keiran. Very wise. Certainly, it's better to be both, but being clever is probably more important. Cleverness overcomes other weaknesses. No matter. Cradock was defeated and that is all that is important. Anyway, enough with history. Please sit down." Farris motioned to the chair next to the side table that held Keiran's refreshments.

"Thank you for coming to my home this late. You probably have better things to do. I know that it's an imposition, so I do thank you. Let's see what you have brought." Keiran placed his glass down on the table, and then picked up his briefcase, removing the red folder from it. Farris continued to gaze at the portrait. Keiran though he had detected a movement in Farris' lips as if he were silently talking to Cradock.

"Here is the Benton Industries file Mr. Farris. The memorandum is on top." Keiran handed the folder over to Farris.

Farris read each page of the twenty-page memorandum slowly and deliberately, and then briefly looked at a few sections of the appendix.

"Well, I believe that you have everything here. HenHen, I assume, has made plans for you to go to Guernsey on Monday to file these papers? This client is most anxious to get this corporation registered so the contract can be executed in the name of the new company."

"Yes, Mr. Farris, she has. I'll be on the 7:00 a.m. British Air Express flight to St. Peter's Port. According to HenHen's note, I'll meet David Leyden of Royal Trust Ltd. She said that he would take care of the registration. He called to say he looks forward to my visit."

"Call me from his office when you arrive on Monday, and I'll have some instructions for you at that time."

"Certainly, but before I leave, Mr. Farris, I wanted to highlight for you a few items—" Keiran interrupted.

Farris paused, his hands tapping on the file folders he was holding. "Oh! Well, yes, please...but I have read the entire memorandum and you have made all the changes that I had suggested. But, please go ahead, if you think that I have missed something."

"What is bothersome is the private bank that is opening the letter of credit for the purchase transaction for this amount of cement...it's a fairly small bank, minimally capitalized. I assume you know that and that its letter of credit's confirmed. I wonder if the letter of credit's a real document. Thirty five million U. S. dollars is a large sum for this amount of cement—in fact, my research shows that the price paid per metric ton is greater than the going rate. Do you think our client knows that?"

"I'm sure he does, Keiran. I'm sure he does," responded Farris, now obviously irritated. "Both banks are properly licensed, are they not? Capitalization of the banks is really not an issue. These banks have performed in the past on similar transactions."

"Why pay more than the going rate?" Keiran insisted.

"Probably to insure a long term contract with the supplier. At times, you pay a premium to insure a steady supply."

Keiran swallowed.

"Anything else of importance before I sign the transmittal letter to our agent in the Channel Islands? You're bright, Keiran, but don't get distracted. Stick to the issue at hand. If the client didn't like the banks, or if the banks were not comfortable with him, he would not have gone this far." He then took his pen and signed the cover letter with the client copies back to Keiran, retaining the remainder of the file. Keiran watched his face. There was now nothing to betray his mood. The earlier softness had been replaced with a hard edge in his voice. Keiran knew Farris didn't like questions; he was all cunning and deliberate.

"Thank you for coming. Enjoy the rest of your weekend. I'll talk to you on Monday while you're in Guernsey. He led Keiran out of the drawing room, down the corridor and showed him out.

"Goodbye Keiran." Farris put out his hand.

"Goodbye Mr. Farris. I'll call you Monday."

They shook hands. Keiran slowly walked down Sloan Street to the subway, trying to get into a frame of mind for the rest of the evening, but the short session with Farris had unnerved him. Maybe it would sort itself out in Guernsey on Monday. Yet, he was also now wondering if the deal was in fact a real deal. No, this can't be phony. My God, this is a reputable firm. Yeah. Been around for more than 100 years. It has to be legit. Now wasn't the time to get into a frenzied obsession about a client matter. Keiran gave a shake of his head as he rapidly walked to the subway entrance looking forward to dinner at the Graysons.' To have a good time, he knew that he had to blot out the workday. He was ready to accept the new experience of his first social occasion in London, as he accepted all that life gave him.

Five

It was half past six when Keiran arrived at the Grayson's three-story, brick and stone Georgian townhouse. The house was built on a corner across from a small park. It had a kind of simple grace disturbed only by the wild inconsistency of a turquoise-colored front door. Such a vibrant color—a hue more suited to a tropical hideaway, Keiran reflected, than a home in the fashionable Islington. A slight wind stirred the leaves on two oaks on either side of a stoned flagged walkway that lead to the entrance of the home, lighted on each side by two coach lamps. An ornate, tangled web of iron grillwork in the shape of climbing ivy, itself covered with the genuine article, enveloped the doorway. The moon was full; the air was fresh and pleasant. Keiran was looking forward to the evening. He stood at the top of the wide brick steps, a bottle of red wine in his left hand. He straightened his tie, glanced at his watch, and then lifted the large eagle knocker, hitting it against the brass.

"May I help you?" A diminutive lady, brown eyes, flat-cheeked face, her short brown hair showing touches of gray, dressed in a black uniform with a snow white lace collar, greeted him in a soft, friendly voice. Behind her, he heard the sound of many voices.

"Good evening. Keiran Hogan for Mr. and Mrs. Grayson."

Keiran heard the commotion as the maid led him down a long, uncarpeted, highly polished wood floor corridor which led to a large reception room shimmering in the light of a massive crystal chandelier and several wall sconces that matched the chandelier's tear-dropped crystals. Just as he entered, Bob Grayson, who was standing a few feet from the entrance, spotted him. Grayson had on a gray and white polka-dot patterned tie against a gray shirt and gray suit. He looked taller than Keiran had remembered from the embassy meeting.

"Keiran, glad you could come." Grayson shook Keiran's hand with vigor and eagerness as though he was welcoming a long lost friend. "I was worried that perhaps you would get lost. Getting to Islington's High Street may be a bit of a problem. Were my directions okay?"

"Perfect. The cab driver had absolutely no problem. Impossible to miss the front door, Bob. Sorry I'm late, but Farris had me work a bit this evening on a special project."

"The door. The famous front door in Islington. The color has caused a great deal of angst among our neighbors. But it certainly makes the house easy to find, wouldn't you agree?" He looked lightly and a little whimsically at Keiran.

"Yeah. It sure stands out." Keiran replied, a broad smile flitted over his lips.

"Good. That is why it's the color it is. Want to be able to be identified easily among all these lovely homes built so long ago. Master Farris handing out last minute assignments? What can I say? We never manage our assignments in our firm in that manner. We are a little more relaxed—actually go home everyday by about five. Want to come work for us?" Grayson smiled widely, placing his hand around Keiran's shoulder.

"Don't answer that unfair question, and don't believe that my colleagues and I go home by five. But we do try to organize the work so that at least the weekends are free. No matter, you're here and that is what is important. Come; let me introduce you to our guests. By the bye, I did say cocktails, but you'll stay for dinner. I simply forgot. Old age. Can you stay?"

"Sure. Sure. That'll be fine," Keiran replied.

Keiran quickly surveyed the guests—about a dozen people standing with drinks and in animated conversation. Grayson led him to the dining table where a chestnut-brown haired woman in a green mist cocktail dress was busily rearranging the flowers in one of the vases on the table.

"Dear, I hesitate to interrupt you…."

"Bob…these yellow roses. I asked for pale yellow, and what do they send…deep vibrant yellow. They just don't look correct in these arrangements, now do they?"

"Victoria, they're perfectly fine. The table looks lovely. Calm down now, and meet our final guest of the evening. Keiran Hogan, my wife Victoria. She is the chef this evening. Beautiful, as you can see for yourself, kind, and yet coercive when it comes to me, I must say. She is a superhuman chef. We'll all eat well tonight, won't we dear?" He leaned over and affectionately kissed her on the cheek.

"Kind and coercive. Now why would you tell Mr. Hogan that?" She extended her hand to Keiran. "Don't pay attention to Bob. He's the kind and coercive type. I'm just his cook." She and Bob laughed.

"You've just arrived in London?" she inquired.

"About eight weeks ago."

"Victoria, dear, Keiran is not only modest, but obviously a brilliant young man with the firm of Kenton & Ward. Why did I say brilliant…? I have no doubt, Keiran, that you're bright. The better description, though, would be shrewd. You came late to the ambassador's monthly briefings to the U. S. legal fraternity in London and asked the ambassador no questions." They all laughed.

"Why do you go to the meetings, Bob, when you tell me how boring they are? It's incomprehensible to me. Anyway, welcome to London, Keiran. I'm delighted you could come tonight," Victoria Grayson said with a genuine smile and wide blue eyes, as she took his hand and shook it. "I hope that you find the city as enjoyable as we do."

"What I've seen so far, I like."

"Now, Bob, make sure that he meets everyone. I don't want you to monopolize his time with all your legal talk. Right now, you'll both have to excuse me. I have to go to the kitchen to check on dinner and make sure Bob hasn't told the serving staff something different from what I have said. Again, welcome, Keiran. We are happy that you could come." She turned and walked away.

A waiter brought a glass of champagne.

"Have a glass, Keiran, or do you want something stronger?"

"Champagne will be fine. I haven't had any since my sister's college graduation this past June."

"Well, all the more reason to have one now and more later. If you're a connoisseur, which I proudly consider myself, you'll note that this is Krug. You won't have a headache in the morning, regardless of how many glasses you drink."

"One will be fine, Bob. I'm usually at the bar at the club, and the bartender says I'm one of the few who can nurse a drink for hours. I leave him a big tip anyway, so he doesn't complain too much."

Grayson laughed. "A disgrace to your Irish heritage, but certainly more sensible than a few here who will be guzzling this fine drink as if it were bottled water. Come, Keiran, let me show you around."

Keiran marveled at the elegance of the room. It was large and lofty, painted in a pale tint of yellow. Scattered throughout were a procession of different antique chairs and two divans, all in soft yellow, green, and peach tones. A large gold framed portrait of Grayson, his wife, and their three children hung over the unlit fireplace. On the gray streaked white marble mantle were placed an array of different colored crystal glass candlesticks with candles of varying length, each matching the color of the holder, all lit. There were sprays of yellow and white roses on several of the tables, with a large vase of similarly colored summer flowers on a grand piano at the far end of the room. The pale gray drapes were pulled back from the four six-tiered windows, allowing gleams of light to make their way through the panes and adding to the room's brilliance.

"Keiran, say hello to the man who will get you settled in an apartment. He owns everything there is to own in London." Grayson shifted his attention to a huge, stout, smiling man of square build, hair the color of ash, in his fifties, with a face of good natured wrinkles, a carefully trimmed beard, and a nose a little to one side. "A master of a man. The best real estate mogul in London, Jackson Iams. Oops! Sir Jackson Iams. Sorry for the slip, Jack. He was just knighted by the Queen for, what is it Jack, your contributions to the well being of Britain? Of course it helps being the Queen's personal real estate investment advisor, now, doesn't it?" Laughter ensued as Iams extended his had to Keiran, shaking it exuberantly.

"Bob...please...modesty. Please, just call me Jack, Keiran. That will suffice," he said with a hoarse, chuckling laugh.

"Nice to meet you...Jack," Keiran said.

"My wife, Alexandra." Iams put his arm around his wife. Before she could respond, however, he directly remarked, "Bob tells me you're at the RAC temporarily while you find a more suitable permanent flat. Come by my office. We have the best selection in the city because we own the best flats in the city. A young man...a young professional man...well, you must allow me to help you find a suitable place." He reached into his jacket pocket and pulled out a card, glancing at it quickly. "You're lucky. My last card."

"Jack, will you let me greet this young man? You introduce me and then ignore me. You should'nt be so rude. Please. Business later." Alexandra Iams interjected, her smile wide. A slender figure in a blinding white dress with narrow silver trim, big wistful brown eyes, golden blond hair that stood around her face like a halo, obviously joking yet shaking loose from her husband's arms which were draped around her small waist, she continued, "Dear Keiran Hogan, don't let my husband maneuver you at such a lovely occasion. He shouldn't be talking business here anyway. I am sure you're enjoying where you're staying now." She extended her hand to Keiran, who shook it.

"Glad to meet you, Lady Alexandra."

Before Keiran could carry on, Jack bellowed in, "My wife, young Keiran, is always trying to keep me straight...and won't let me discuss business at any social function, citing her verses from her own book on etiquette. You must buy her book. The title dear is...."

"Jack, stop!" She looked at her husband rather angrily.

"The title is: *Etiquette for the Single Person*," Iams persevered.

"Jack, you're hopeless. Absolutely hopeless," Alexandra said with a gesture of resignation.

"Dear, this lad needs a flat now. He can't have any women at the club. I have a rather vivid impression that living in the club must be awful because of that critical fact. You must have your own flat…and soon."

Alexandria Iams looked to the ceiling at her husband's comment, feeling totally helpless to respond.

"Your right on that score, Jack. Not having women around is a negative for staying at the club. Well, I do like the swimming pool, and the folks I meet at the downstairs clubroom are pretty solid fellows. The place is suitable for the interim, but I certainly will want to ask your advice about an apartment. It's awfully good of you to take all this trouble on my behalf."

"You must have them change the bloody rules, Keiran. Important to change the rules." Iams raised his voice. "And, after we find you a suitable apartment, we'll find you a suitable English woman to look after you."

"Jack, you're impossible!" Alexandra appeared mortified.

"Do you think you'll really need help finding a young lady, Keiran?" Grayson interrupted. "A young man like you will have every eligible woman in London after him. I guarantee that."

"Give me some time, Bob. I've only been here eight weeks. Maybe next week. We'll see."

"Correctly said. Alexandra, Jack, so, please excuse us. I should take Keiran to meet the others before Victoria calls us for dinner."

"I enjoyed meeting you both." Keiran smiled gently.

"Now, make sure you come by the office for a look at the available flats," Iams cautioned. "I'll be expecting you."

"Yeah. I'll call you next week," Keiran said, nodding his assent.

"Good." Iams extended his hand and shook Keiran's forcefully. "Good handshake, by the way. Very good."

Grayson placed his hand on Keiran's back and gently moved him toward a couple that were standing by the fireplace where a servant was refilling their glasses with champagne.

"Jack and Alexandra are pleasing to the ears, aren't they? He is a genuine person despite all the bombast, and his wife is a serious student of social mores. Her book is a bestseller here. Sort of a humorous, yet also serious, look on the decline of manners. Don't buy it though. I have a copy I can loan you—better still you can keep it. Victoria bought about ten copies for gifts, so I'll send one over to the club for you from my office on Monday."

"Well, that was thoughtful of him to help with an apartment."

"If he promised to help you, he will. You can be sure of that."

Grayson slowly made his way to the couple by the fireplace.

"Keiran, you should meet my good friends, Jennifer Berley and her fiancé, Craig Medill. Jennifer, Craig, say hello to Keiran Hogan, the new man in town for Kenton & Ward."

For a moment, Keiran just stared at Jennifer. Long, black, vigorous hair with just a hint of amber, delicate skin, deep black eyes with dark eyelashes, a soft olive complexion and a striking slim figure that was well shown in a short navy blue dress; her eyes with a half religious, half-erotic look. A sweet warmth overtook Keiran as he ignored her escort and blurted, "Haven't we met before?" Keiran smiled at his mouthing such a dumb line...but hell, why not, she did look familiar…that in a moment of self-realization—he put his hands to his face, laughingly answering his own question.

"You are the anchor on ITN news!"

"Yes, that's me. And, I'm happy you watch the show. Such an original line—'haven't we met before'." She smiled, speaking in a pretty, soft, crisp voice, extending her hand to meet his. He held her hand for a moment more than any handshake is suppose to last.

"Jennifer is the news reader. In the States, you call them call them anchors," Grayson said. "She holds forth on the six o'clock news every evening except on the weekend, I believe. I watch you all the time."

Grayson leaned over and gave her a friendly kiss. "Craig here has all the inside information about the best investments for you to make in the world. He's the rising young star at National Westminster…makes millions for his clients. Ask him for some advice. He'll make you rich. So with these introductions, you'll have to excuse me, I see my wife motioning me to come to the kitchen. Something must be burning—not that I'll be able to do anything about it. But when my wife, the chef, beckons, I must answer the call. Keiran, I'm leaving you in good hands. Now make him rich, Craig. He'll need some real money to rent one of Iams' flats." Grayson smiled and took his leave.

Keiran extended his hand to Medill, slightly shorter than Keiran, blue eyes, his cheeks rather high, dusty brown hair, a face heavily bronzed, an erect bearing, and when he spoke he barely moved his lips. There was just a suggestion of smugness about his eyes and his smile.

"Happy to meet you, Keiran—Bob is extravagant with his introductions. Twisty name you have. Irish?" They shook hands.

"Yeah. My great grandparents came from Ireland."

"Ah! An IRA supporter?" Medill said dryly.

"What is the IRA?" Keiran replied in mock disbelief. There was a small laugh from Jennifer.

"A defensive Irishman as well," Craig said.

"Don't listen to Craig. It's so characteristic of him to politicize everything and everybody."

"Jennifer, you never politicize anything? Come now. I've heard some of your on-air commentary," Medill replied, bringing his glass to his lips and finishing off the remains of his champagne.

"No matter. I took no offense, really." Keiran's eyes stayed on Jennifer.

Trying to change the subject gracefully, Keiran asked, "Jennifer, the copy you read on television, do you write it or is it written for you?"

"I have a hand in writing the final copy that I read, but of course we have writers who scan the news and write the basic copy. Generally I make those changes that would suit my presentation and at times I also make format changes—you know, what will be the lead story. That is where the discussions with the director come in. We disagree at times. Journalists do have some principles…accuracy and relevance are two major ones in which I believe."

"Principle is a luxury that is short supply these days." Keiran smiled.

"A solicitor believing in principles? A new beginning, I dare say," Medill said tauntingly.

"Well, some of us try to live by principles. I guess I belong to that school. You work for a bank. I suppose that your entire job is governed by principles of behavior, am I correct? You don't recommend investments in impermissible illegal activities, do you?" Keiran spoke softly.

"Good point, Keiran. Bloody good point. Yet, bankers have to bend at times; business would grind to a halt without a 'zig or zag' here and there. You know, passing along good, solid investment information to your favorite clients."

Keiran wished he could divert the conversation into more pleasant channels, but for some reason that option wasn't taking hold. So he continued.

"Craig, I guess you would agree with me that following principles doesn't mean one is timid or careless. In my judgment, it means just the opposite—one has a kind of independence, not collapsing to pressures. That is what I mean by following principles," Keiran replied, slyly winking at Jennifer as if to say, "I'm trying to be nice to this guy, but he's getting a bit bothersome."

"We're getting into heavy philosophical discourse," Medill remarked. "Reminds me of my days at Cambridge. I do want to point out, Keiran, that following principles can also be used for pursuing the wrong goals. For example, following principles just accorded your group to blow up a restaurant in Mayfair, now, didn't it?"

For a moment, there was silence between them, the silence of people groping for an understanding of each other.

Keiran slowly raised his glass and drank a sip, his eyes having a sudden fierceness and looking directly at Medill. Do I hit the fucker now or later? Keiran silently thought.

Quietly, almost inaudibly, Keiran said, "Perhaps you can define my group."

Jennifer lowered her head, a faint smile crossing her face. Medill was silent for a moment, nervously fiddling with his empty champagne glass, seemingly struck by Keiran's last statement.

"Touché, Keiran. Right on. Nothing like a feisty Irishman. I say, anyone for more champagne?"

"Yes, Craig, why don't you get me some?" She looked sharply at Craig.

"None for me. Thank you though," Keiran answered. Jennifer took a step closer to Keiran.

Glancing at Jennifer, Craig took his leave.

"Is he always such an asshole?" Keiran asked, incredulous that the words came out. "I'm sorry Jennifer. I didn't mean that. Totally out of line. Please forgive me."

She smiled. "Keiran, Craig is not very circumspect. One of his weaker points. He really doesn't mean any harm. You don't have to apologize to me. I wish he hadn't started that line of conversation, so maybe it's me who should be apologizing. Craig is just a bit nervous at times. I don't know why. So, please don't take him seriously on such a serious subject. He's a decent person. He really is."

"I should'nt have been so sensitive. I didn't mean to put you into an awful position," Keiran murmured.

"Not at all." She took his hand, holding it for a moment.

Perhaps, he thought, he was too touchy; too soft-tempered. But, with her deep looks at him, Jennifer signified understanding. He had been looking forward to a gentle night and now he was concerned it was rather beyond him. He looked again into Jennifer's eyes and he felt his heart beat rapidly.

In the background, a bell was ringing. Mrs. Grayson was in the archway between the living room and dining room ringing a small crystal bell.

"Dinner is now being served. Please bring your champagne if you wish and find your seats." She moved with nimbleness and airiness, greeting each guest as they passed her to go to their seats.

They were seated in a large dining room with a pillared recess and long windows opened to the warm evening. The table was uncovered except for lace placemats set with silverware, lavender flowered china, and three crystal glasses of varying sizes. Two four-candle candelabras provided a soft glow along with the dimmed chandelier. Down the center of the table were three circular pale yellow china vases in which were placed the re-arranged yellow and white roses. The room sparkled.

"I believe that I am sitting next to you," Jennifer said.

"I'm going to like that very much," Keiran smiled, instinctively taking her hand leading her to the dining table. Medill was already in the dining room standing by his seat at the opposite end of the table, chatting with Lady Alexandra, who was seated next to him. He looked over and his hand rose to greet Jennifer. She smiled back.

When you're seated next to someone that you can't take your eyes off, the evening goes by too quickly. During the meal service, Keiran and Jennifer spoke softly for a while. He answered her parade of questions about himself, about what kind of law he was practicing, about his firm, and about what he was going to do for a flat. He asked about her, where she lived, and what she liked about her Chelsea neighborhood. He listened intently to her answers, an assured method of continuing to get her attention…and he didn't want to lose it. Her face was bright during the conversation. She looked at him tenderly.

"You should come to the studios and I'll give you a tour," she volunteered gently.

"Yeah. I'd like that. I've never had a TV studio tour. I can offer you, in return, a tour of our offices. Our offices, I suspect, aren't as exciting as your studio, but perhaps you can come by for coffee or something after work."

"Or something. That sounds interesting, Keiran." She smiled. "Yes, I'd like that. Your offices are near Throckmorton Square…close to Craig's offices?" He glanced at the end of the table and saw that Craig was still engaged in an animated conversation with Lady Alexandra.

She continued, "That will be fine. If you wish, you can have a tour of the studios tomorrow. Not much of a crowd on Sunday. I have to go into work as I am doing the Sunday noon news show. The regular reader is off tomorrow. You can stay, if you wish, to see me do the broadcast. I'll be doing a special segment on the Mayfair incident. Awful death toll, Keiran, awful." She hesitated. "I don't want to open that line of discussion, Keiran. I'm just telling you what we have planned tomorrow at the studio. Will you still come?"

"Sunday would be fine. I have to leave for Guernsey on Monday, and probably won't be back for a few days, so a Sunday tour would be a treat. Can we have dinner Sunday night?" He was looking steadily at her.

"I don't think so. Craig has me engaged for the rest of the day as he also has a business trip on Monday. He is leaving for New York. But, I'd like to do it some other time. Perhaps later in the week. I'd like that, really. How about Wednesday?"

"Sure, great. You'll have to pick the restaurant, as I'm still not familiar with all the good places. By the way, when are you and Craig getting married? Bob called Craig your fiancé."

"Not really. We've been seeing each other for over a year now. Craig is anxious to make the relationship more permanent. We'll have to wait and see what happens. You might call me a committed career woman." She laughed. "And you, are you engaged back in the States?"

"No. I'm single. Nothing at all holding me down."

"Well, then, we'll have to make sure you meet all the eligible women that we know. I have a particular one in mind, actually," she said teasingly. "Now, would you excuse me for a moment?" Keiran rose from the table, and held her chair back while she got up. She walked around the table to Craig, whispered something into his ear, then disappeared into the hall off the dining room.

"Well, Keiran, you enjoying yourself, in between bites and conversation with Jennifer?" Grayson inquired. "I could barely get your attention, you were so involved with her."

"Yes, very much so, Bob. Jennifer is a fine and beautiful lady. How long have you know her?"

"Oh! For some time actually. Ever since we came to London and Victoria became active in the Brompton Oratory where we met her aunt and uncle. The aunt recently passed away—such a young age, around 55, of leukemia. A truly grand woman. Her uncle, Edmund Berley, is a currency speculator and investor. I'm sure you've heard of him in the States. Many follow his investment schemes. He is a brooding, silent man. Very wealthy, of course, and a philanthropist for children's causes. But not an easy man to get to know. He's very aloof. He and his wife raised Jennifer from the time she was three. Her own parents, her uncle's brother and his wife, died in an automobile accident outside Los Angeles many years ago. Tragic background really, but Jennifer seems to have weathered it all well. She is a balanced and beautiful woman. She was very close to her aunt Rebecca Berley and, of course, her uncle. I suppose now she feels obligated toward her uncle. I think that is why she hasn't yet married Craig. You're right. She is beautiful and, beyond that, intelligent. You know, she has a degree in Economics from Cambridge, her father's alma mater. I don't know how she got into television news, but she certainly is good at it. Maybe her uncle has some investments in ITN, I just don't know. You interested in her?"

"Hey! Who wouldn't be interested in such a beautiful woman? But she's taken, so why would I want to bang my head against a brick wall? Besides she says she's a committed career woman. I've been through that. I want someone to have a family with me and to do all those old-fashioned family things."

"Wow, you're in another century. And for such a young man. Keiran, get real. Women are different today. Very different."

"I suppose that you're right."

"You may be single a long, long time."

"Maybe."

"What about Craig?"

"He's pretty important at the Bank. He's the youngest VP in National Westminster's history. Lacks some discretion, and certainly not sincere all the time. The one thing that he has is Jennifer—and his sailing. He's an accomplished sailor and many weekends, he's off to the Isle of Man."

"Does Jennifer go with him when he sails?"

"Yes, but not always. She won't go on board when he is in a race. Only if it's a leisurely sail. She's not too keen on sailing, I don't think, but then I'm not sure."

"Bob, do you think…. Well, maybe…Jennifer would…."

"Do you think I think she would accept an invitation from you?"

"Yeah. That's it."

"Why not? She'd have married Craig if she were really interested in him. My wife must have had a plan if she sat you next to Jennifer."

"Well, she asked me to take a tour of the ITN studios. So, I'll start there. I have to say I feel pretty good toward her. I guess I'll just wait to see what happens."

"I think that you'll manage without any difficulty, Keiran. None whatsoever. By the bye what is Farris up to these days?"

"He's fine. Actually, I was at his home just a few hours ago going over a new project and I leave for Guernsey on Monday morning to finalize a new business arrangement for his client. He has me working 12-14 hours a day at the office these days. The work isn't difficult, just time consuming. I guess it's his way of initiating me into the office."

"Sorry I was so long in returning to my dinner partner," Jennifer interrupted. Keiran shot up, smiled, pulled out her chair. "No, Keiran. I won't be staying." Then turning toward Grayson, she added softly, "I'll not be able to stay for dessert—I have the show tomorrow and have to get up early to prepare. Replacing the regular Sunday reader has cut into my own weekend. You will forgive Craig and me, won't you?"

"Of course. The glamour of TV news. I have to say, Jennifer, I miss that show. I've my head buried in the *Times*."

"Now, Bob, tomorrow you'll watch it, okay? It's the noon Sunday news show. We have this continuing story about the Mayfair incident and I'll have to work on that presentation. Keiran, see you tomorrow for the tour and the program, okay?"

"What time do you want me to come?"

"I imagine you sleep late on the weekends?"

"No…not really. I'll be there. How about between 11:30 and 11:45?"

"Super! Well here comes Craig. Bob, it's been a real delight. And, Keiran, I've enjoyed talking to you tonight. Very enjoyable. See you tomorrow. Don't forget now."

"Thanks, Jennifer. I look forward to seeing you."

Craig came up, taking Jennifer's hand, saying, "Nice meeting you Keiran. Listen, I'd like to have you over for lunch and meet some of my mates from work. I'll give you a call. Also perhaps you can come sailing with me some weekend."

"Sure. I'd like that. Thanks."

Jennifer smiled at Keiran, went over and kissed Grayson on the cheek, then together they made their way around the table saying goodbye to the other guests.

Keiran looked steadily at her, envious of Craig, angry that they probably would be sleeping together tonight. He's never had this feeling of jealously or anger about a woman before—not even with Allison back in

Washington. He didn't know whether he liked the feeling or not. His heart was racing as he saw her take one quick look back at him and then she and Craig disappeared from the dining room.

Six

He wasn't really tired, and he was brooding. It wasn't that he was embarrassed or nervous about how the evening at the Graysons had gone. He actually had a good time and had left their home shortly after midnight, grateful for such a capital invitation. He had asked the cab driver to leave him by St. James Park where, for a while, he walked along the park side, then crossed over to Marlborough Street, the last curve of which brought him onto Pall Mall. The stealth of the early morning still lingered; traffic was light, there were few pedestrians at this hour as he made his way past the sedate yet handsome office buildings and shops of Pall Mall, and to the clubhouse. A light breeze had arisen and ruffled his tousled black hair. His hands remained thrust into his side pants pockets, his fingers toying with the loose change in one pocket and the cab receipts in the other. There wasn't a thing but his thoughts to distract him.

Along the way, he recalled who Marlborough was—an English military hero who had defeated either the French or the Spanish early on. No nation ever stops fighting, he thought, nor do individuals. Human nature never diverges and conflict is forever. A rather shaky and depressing thought.

My God! What am I thinking about?... And at this time of morning. He took a quick breath, shook his head a few times, stiffened himself, then quickened his pace toward the club. One thing he didn't want to do was to plunge suddenly into the dark wood of such heavy thoughts.

Yet, the confidence he felt had suddenly deserted him; he felt alone. Besides the excitement of the evening, meeting Jennifer stuck firmly in his memory and in his emotion. Jennifer Berley was a woman it did you good to look at, and not one you would likely forget. He kept thinking of her and the mystery of woman and of man—almost unexplainable. He missed her and he had only met her a few hours earlier. Fate and destiny can be either motley or helpful and he was unsure at this time how his meeting with Jennifer could be characterized. He knew that life had moments of rapture. He just prayed that his moment with Jennifer would last longer than a cloud's flight over the sun. Tomorrow, Sunday, she was going to take him on a tour of the ITN studios where she worked. She certainly wasn't under any pressure to offer the visit, and, more important, she had volunteered. In his heart, Keiran believed this was more than a courteous gesture. He certainly wasn't skeptical about his analysis, and he felt the familiar lift of expectation. Yet, right now, he found himself wondering what Jennifer and Medill were doing, and that, he honestly could confess, brought on a rush of jealousy and anger—feelings that bothered him.

I should not feel this way. He knew, though, he simply could not starve himself emotionally…that would be a mistake…but he was also afraid of another disappointment.

Keiran stayed in his room for only a few minutes. The maid had picked up his soiled laundry, which he had discarded in a corner by the clothes closet, placing them in a club laundry bag with a note: "Please verify count and initial." He stood for a moment taking on the familiar scene—an overflow bag of laundry on which the maid, for as many weeks as he had been at the club, had written the same message. He made a mental note to work much harder on that bad habit—discarding his dirty underwear, shirts, and socks on the floor rather placing them in the laundry bag provided for that sole purpose. Several messages had been slipped under his door. One from fellow associate, Diana Peters: "where are you?" Another from the club manager that he had to settle his weekly bill. One from his sister Aileen, who graduated from college in May of last year and was due in London in three weeks for a visit: "Keiran. Please call and can I bring a friend with me to London. Do you have room?" His sister's note reminded him that he had to get an apartment, and soon. The final message was cryptic: "Please call me tomorrow morning before 10:00 a.m. We must talk before I leave for Athens. Farris." The time on the Farris message was 8:00 Saturday evening. There wasn't a thing he could do about any of these messages at this early hour. What he knew he needed was a long swim to release the tensions of the day, but as it was a weekend, the pool had closed at 9:00 p.m.

Keiran understood his heart was troubled. He needed some quiet time. He turned the lights off, closed the door; and decided to go to the club library, which he knew to be open all night. Maybe reading the newspapers, or for that matter, perusing the books, would distract him sufficiently to reduce the tautness he now felt. There, he could get a cup of coffee, tea, or a cold soft or juice drink, even some snack cookies and crackers. Whoever thought of keeping the club library accessible probably knew there would be insomniacs as residents, and thus decided to keep it open throughout the day and night. The billiard room would have been a suitable alternative. There he could hit a few balls and otherwise attempt to practice a game that was intriguing him. But it shut its doors at midnight.

Also whirling in his mind was the peculiar late afternoon meeting with Duane Farris. The hushed swiftness of Farris escorting the client out without an introduction was particularly bothersome. Farris' strange behavior didn't appear rational, but then the whole project didn't make any sense either. He knew that there was something more to tell, and sensed something was wrong. But what could be wrong? The events of this Saturday had given him nothing but the unexpected.

The club was still at night, quiet even in this very heart of London, the thick stone and brick walls and double pane windows making any noise from the street unnoticeable. The few guests who had been in the reception area when he arrived from the Graysons, like him, had headed toward their rooms. Now, as he proceeded to the second floor library, only the faint sound of his slow steps on the long, gray, marble hallways and stairs broke the stillness. He had not changed from his suit, as the club rules made it mandatory to wear coat and tie throughout the common areas of the club save for the athletic section. Nevertheless, he did loosen his red paisley tie and opened the top button of his blue shirt.

The library, a two-story paneled room of silent grandeur, was somewhat gloomy at this time of night, despite the undraped soaring windows framing the back garden, itself lit up by several ground level floodlights. The lights revealed boxed shrubs kept rigidly pruned to construct an overall design with interweaving masses of flowers in their pattern, creating a painting of unusual beauty among the unfeeling nature of the library. One of the several double storied windows was opened, letting in the cool, calm, early morning air. Ten-shelf bookcases lined the walls, with portraits of earlier club leaders hanging above them. Across the top of the bookcases ran a rail from which a ladder was permanently placed, one that could be rolled along so the readers could have access to all the volumes in the upper shelves. If one looked closely at the cases, a great mist of dust was on the books. It appeared that many of them had not been recently touched. The coat of arms of present monarchy in England— The Windsors— was centered directly over the rich, intricate, wood carved mantled fireplace at the left far end as one entered the library. There was a scattering of brown leather chairs, divans, footstools, all neatly arranged across the length of the half block long room. At both its ends were placed several walnut wood writing tables with matching chairs, the tables veneered in elm and ebony with brass drawer pulls and brass pen and pencil holders, a neat arrangement of stationery and envelopes carefully centered on a black desk blotter. Several gray and maroon oriental carpets, threadbare in places, and obviously there for many years, covered the floor. Three overhead heavy brass framed chandeliers hung down from the mahogany paneled ceiling shedding a soft light in the room, the only other illumination coming from the many side lamps set on small tables beside all the reading chairs, the conical dark beige shades focusing the rays of light on each seat such like a spotlight does on a performer.

Keiran hesitated for a moment at the library doorway, however, wondering if he shouldn't just take another long walk, thinking through the evening, but quickly he realized that such pondering would only be expedient and solve nothing. No, better to stay inside and read, get his mind off Jennifer and certainly off Farris' unusual behavior. As he entered, the heavy library doors creaked closed behind him. He quickly noticed the only other person there was an elderly gentleman seated near the refreshment table, apparently asleep, a book laying upon his lap. He was about seventy, perhaps older. There was a suggestion of military bearing in the square set of his shoulder, the carefully combed thin white hair, the ruddy sunburn of his face, and the manner that he was seated very straight in the chair. The man made no move as Keiran slowly entered the room.

Keiran headed toward a large table in the room's center where the newspapers and magazines were displayed in an orderly fashion. A large sign sat stiffly upright in its brass holder proclaiming in bold, black script against a bright, white background: "Replace Any Items You Remove to Their Proper Position." He selected the *Guardian*, and walking over to a chair by the open window, laying the paper on the chair's seat, then returning to the far end of the library where the snacks and coffee were placed. He poured himself some coffee, took some cookies, grabbed some paper napkins. Returning to his seat, he placed his items on the table next to his chair. Before sitting down, he took off his jacket, folding it neatly and placing it on an adjacent chair, thinking to himself, that no one would notice, let alone the man who had not changed his position at all. A sound sleeper, thought Keiran. He loosened his tie a bit more and drew up his sleeve cuffs, glanced at his watch— it was now 1:30 a.m.— took a sip of coffee and began to read the paper. In the background the soft ticking of a large grandfather's clock broke an otherwise quiet room.

As they had been all week, the paper headlines were about the incident at Mayfair. The final death toll was now forty…all were supporters of the Serbian cause in the former Yugoslavia. No group came forward to claim responsibility and the government was provisionally convinced that it was a gas explosion. A spokesman for the police ruled out the involvement of the Irish Republican Army. Keiran wondered whether Craig Medill would now be convinced, but that would be asking too much, he reflected. Medill was biased. Silly shithead...just a silly shit, Keiran mused. But, Keiran admitted, it was a horrific terrorist attack.

And whoever did it was silent and unknown…the kind of attacker the police feared the most, he supposed.

A low faint cough now broke the silence.

"No vintage port tonight, my young man. No long fat Havana either. Miserable rules these are, young man. In the old days, that table over there—he pointed to the snack table with his walking stick—was filled with stock enough to spare. Now we have playthings such as crackers, coffee, and tea…and worst of all…no smoking. Why don't they keep the smoking lounge open rather than this…?" The old man who had been sleeping now stood in front of Keiran, speaking with a pleasant voice, yet with some weariness.

"This library. I guess the best thing here is that we have Sunday morning papers early Saturday evening." He laughed now, but without humor. He had violet circles under his eyes as if he had never really had a good night's sleep. "Vulgar, indolent, imprudent fools run the club now, but when the fool-killer snatches up the last fool, then we rogues will look to a better day, better port, and better cigars. Now young man, what do you say about that?"

Keiran abruptly stood. The man was trim, very straight with rigid shoulder and back, as though on parade, chin well up, not a quiver. He had gentle, slate blue eyes and a reassuring smile, his dark blue jacket enhanced with a small red carnation in its lapel, his big hands were folded on the top of his cane, which was a highly polished brass boar's head. He had few wrinkles and his tone was low and somewhat husky and deliberate, perhaps from smoking and drinking too much.

Trying to be polite, yet puzzled, Keiran said, "Well, I don't know sir." Keiran gave him a slow smile.

"You don't know?" The man reacted with shock and dismay but with a hearty laugh.

"Well, I thought…."

"Whatever you thought could be better explained if I give you a drop of this." He dropped his cane to the floor and pulled out of his jacket pocket a small silver flask. He opened it, and without a moment's hesitation, leaned over and poured a small amount into Keiran's cup of coffee, which sat on the table next to where he had been sitting.

"Sandeman's 1977 vintage port—one has to drink the whole bottle of that fine liquid when it's opened— and I try to do that principle justice. A little in your coffee will give it that special zing— better for you than sugar or cream, wouldn't you say?"

"Well, thanks, thanks very much. But I like my coffee straight up."

"Then, this will now be a great challenge for you. Drink up. See if the dollop of this elixir will enhance your spirit and protect your soul. You look as if you need something to pick you up. Must be women or money trouble. Nothing else should ever bother a real man. So, young man, whatever, I urge you to drink up. Cheers!"

Keiran lifted his cup and took a swallow of coffee. His drink benefactor took several swigs from the flask before screwing its top back on and placing the flask on the table between the two of them.

"Perfect. Wouldn't you say? Absolutely perfect. Now young man, what is your name?"

"Keiran Hogan. And you are...?" Keiran extended his hand, which was quickly grasped and shaken vigorously. The man's return grip was rough and firm.

"Oh! The swimmer every one talks about. An Olympic champ of sorts. I'm Runnard, to be exact, Sir Robert Albert Percival Runnard, and you should know that I have trouble staying afloat even with a lifebuoy attached to my body." He laughed boisterously.

"Happy to meet you, Sir Robert. But I have to correct you about one point. I was never in the Olympics, I went to many college meets though."

"I will stand corrected. Did you win any medals?

"A few."

"Ah! Modesty. Good quality in a young man. Well, I see you now have taken off your jacket and loosened your tie. Mind if I join you in violating the club rules?" His eyes twinkled and his smile was now wide.

"No. Of course not."

"You do know that if we are caught with our jackets off, we'll be fined. I believe it's fifty pounds. But, if you won't tell, I won't either." He laughed again, took both jackets and placed them on a chair the other side of Keiran, sinking into the armchair next to Keiran, resting his feet on an old-fashioned heavy dark four legged leather footstool. "Now, what brings you here to London? In reply, please delete personal matters or mundane professional ones." He again laughed loudly.

"Well, I'll try to comply with your instructions, Sir Robert. Okay, to begin with I was transferred from the Washington office of the law firm of Kenton & Ward. Tomorrow begins my ninth week. That's my brief. And you, sir?" Keiran sat down, pushed the reading lamp back to the edge of the side table so as not to interfere with his view of Runnard.

There was silence, much longer than necessary Keiran thought, making for an acutely uncomfortable period. Runnard had closed his eyes and he was rubbing his hands together. When he spoke, he did so quietly, his eyes opening slightly.

"Excellent, young man. Right to the point. No extraneous material. Only facts. I know you're a lawyer from the United States and with a very good firm, probably single or you would have mentioned you were married, and probably earning a handsome salary, or you would not be staying at this club. Now I consider that a good brief. Excellent perhaps. Yes…excellent." He opened his eyes wide as he continued, "As for me, well, young Keiran, I've been at the club for a few years. Permanent guest, you might say, since my wife met her maker several years ago. I'm a retired barrister and when I am in the city, I stay here. My real home is in Warwickshire village, a few miles from Stratford-on-Avon. Kenton & Ward…yes, a rather significant law firm. Now let me see…yes, you once had a partner in the London office…er, a man by the name of Duane Farris. Is he still in London?" Runnard asked, an ambiguous expression crossing his face.

"Yes. He is still in London and remains head of the office. You know Mr. Farris?"

"Yes, as a matter of fact, I do. Well, I have known him professionally…only professionally. This is indeed a strange coincidence. Funny how things happen. You ask how did this acquaintance with your Mr. Farris occur? It certainly wasn't planned. A few years ago, 1997…yes…the fall of that year, I was asked by the Lord Chancellor to come out of retirement. He appointed me to head a special inquiry into the government's role in the sale of arms to countries we don't like…such as North Korea, Iran, Iraq—and a few other miscreant nations. My wife had passed on, and the Lord Chancellor at the time, a friend from college days, was insistent that I head the inquiry panel. The study was extensive and lasted several months. Your partner represented the man, a Mr. Zoran Hemmrich, who, along with others similarly inclined, was the focus of the panel's investigation. You might say that Mr. Farris represented his client very well. He produced papers and other evidence that showed Mr. Hemmrich was merely shipping commodities—fertilizer, cement, wood products, and so forth— to these nefarious countries. As in all cases, there was other evidence to the contrary, but the government at the time declined to bring charges. I suspect Mr. Hemmrich is still making hefty political contributions, selling his commodities, and that your partner is still his lawyer. Yes. I met Farris many times during the course of the special inquiry. He has a pleasant enough face hiding, perhaps, a more secret and interesting aspect. Some solicitors and yes, even barristers, find it difficult to remain incorruptible, and many times, appearances can be deceptive, now can't they, young Keiran. You'll pardon me for making that bold observation. I'm sure you can learn a great deal from your Mr. Farris. My criticism comes as a result, no doubt, of too much vintage port or that I'm a barrister, or both. You'll have to forgive me for being so forward in my comments. Enough discourse on that topic, now what is your area of expertise?" He nodded toward Keiran.

Keiran was surprised at Runnard's frankness, yet knowing the clarity and sincerity of his remarks left little doubt about how he viewed Farris. Certainly he didn't get the impression that Runnard's comments were carelessly made—despite Runnard's assertion that drinking too much had freed up his tongue.

"I suppose that was an interesting investigation. Were the hearings public? Did you issue any reports?"

Runnard looked at Keiran and scowled, cleared his throat, and then spoke.

"Young Keiran. I asked you a question, and you're responding to my question with one of your own. Is this what they teach you in American law schools? Answering questions with questions?" He then laughed, took the flask out of his pocket, unscrewed its top slowly, and took a long swallow. "Ah! A necessary pause, while you collect your thoughts." He placed the flask and its top on the table next to his chair. "Just in case, I need another bit of liquid. Now, you wish an answer to your question…before you'll respond to mine. Were the hearings public and did you issue any reports? Spoken like a good prosecutor, which I don't believe you are, but perhaps you have the potential to be."

"I'm just curious as to…."

"Enough, young Keiran. I'll answer your query. As a matter of fact, the hearings were closed, but we did issue a final report to the Lord Chancellor. Unfortunately, the public version has redacted portions, but it does give the reader a flavor of the kind of arms activity between England and the unholy trinity. I don't know if the report is in this antiquated library— the vulgar fools who run this place haven't bought books since before World War II. In any event, I am sure you can get a copy from the Lord Chancellor's office. Perhaps your Mr. Farris has a copy. I would think he does. I've answered your questions, tell me about your area of expertise," he asked, again, now with a bit of weariness in his voice.

"Well," Keiran replied, "I'm concentrating on international business and finance. That's the area of law practice that I enjoy the most."

"That's very interesting. Good choice, given today's obsession with making money and making business deals happen. Antitrust laws? What antitrust laws? They don't exist other than in the deep recesses of abnormal government bureaucrats. So, young Keiran, you should make a great deal of money in your practice, now wouldn't you say?" Runnard smiled sardonically.

"I don't know about that. Obviously you have a strong opinion about corporate law. What can I say but that I do enjoy the work very much," Keiran answered.

"Have you ever done any trial work?" Runnard inquired.

"In Washington, I appeared before several administrative bodies on matters for clients involving international trade disputes. I didn't particularly like those forums, and I would have liked to have some training in trial work, but perhaps later. I do like London and my assignment here, so I suspect it will be a few years until it's decided that I get training for court appearances."

"That is a pity. A real pity. Nothing like trial work to bring out the strength in men. Battle lines are drawn in the pursuit of truth. One never, young Keiran, never snivels or whines in those battles, nor should one." Runnard laughed loudly.

"One should never snivel or whine in any battle, whether in the courtroom or any where else," Keiran added.

"Spoken like a true Irishman. Strong, unyielding, confident. I must apologize for telling you a short story about your Farris. I suppose that every lawyer has his reasons for his representations, now, doesn't one? My view is that representation has to be something with which you feel comfortable, otherwise the work becomes tedious and unrewarding. One should avoid having clients put their lawyers in a little hell of the client's own contriving. Would you not agree young Keiran?"

"Yes. Why would you want to represent a client who puts you into a little hell? It would be stupid." Keiran shifted in his seat, reaching over for his coffee and taking a sip, then continuing, "I could never be the sort of lawyer who would represent a client unless I believed in the client. I don't think I could ever represent someone who lied to me. No, I could never do that."

"To be young and have such innocent thoughts! I suppose, young Keiran, that a client can have a sort of badness in him, perhaps even a kind of ghastly selfishness, but one thing he must do is to tell his lawyer the full story. The client can never say no to whatever information his lawyer wants. The lawyer must be like a greedy child, always asking for more and more until he feels that he has the whole truth. You can represent a client with more kindness if you know the full story. A lawyer is always humiliated when he finds out his client has lied to him. That is something that should be avoided. Rather a horrible thought…to be humiliated." Runnard's voice rose to emphasize his last phrase.

Again, silence. Keiran looked straight at Runnard, wondering how to react to such a truism. What can be the response when what he just heard is a not-so-subtle hint that basically described his senior law partner, Duane Farris, as improperly in collusion with a client that lies and cheats, and is probably doing something illegal? It was as though all his hope for a professionally happy time in London suddenly melted.

"No. It is never pleasant to be humiliated, professionally or personally. Never," Keiran said softly, looking at Runnard directly, trying to understand him and his motives. He was perplexed as to Runnard's frankness in his views of Farris. Runnard seemed to shrewdly and deliberately want Keiran to know his impression of Farris. Maybe the frankness was more boldness. One thing though—Runnard did seem sincere—and knowledgeable.

"What do you think of the bombing at Mayfair? *The Guardian* says that it wasn't an IRA attack, but in all likelihood a faulty gas explosion. Horrific loss of life, though. Just horrible." Keiran smiled as he added, "I'm changing the subject."

Runnard turned real quick, his eyebrows arched, adding, "Young Keiran," he said slowly, as he reached over to get his flask, "changing the subject, as abruptly as you are now doing requires another swallow, now doesn't it? No, I am rude. You first…please place another few drops into your coffee cup, then pass it on to me." Keiran poured a little into his coffee cup.

"Here you go, sir." Keiran transferred the flask to Runnard. Runnard's big hands, now shaking a bit, took both items, quickly raising the flask to his lips and taking a long swallow himself.

"Ah! Helps the blood circulation, my doctor tells me…. Now young Keiran, so you change the subject. Good. When you know how to leave with something like a clean statement, there's no sense in messing it up by further discussion. I like that technique, young Keiran. I like it very much. Now, my view about the bombing at Mayfair. Well, the government," he continued, as he gave the flask back to Keiran, "please Keiran, place it back in my jacket now. It appears I will have to refill it. You see the top?"

"Yes," Keiran replied as he rose to take the flask, close it and place it in Runnard's jacket.

"My thanks. Yes, now the government explanation of the Mayfair bombing…well it's pure, unadulterated rot. Perhaps they want to hush the whole thing up because they know the truth and for some reason want to advise the public of something different. I shouldn't be a bit surprised if this is the real reason. The government can't be frank and tell the truth— which is that some one person or persons wanted to see whoever was in that restaurant dead. Now doesn't that make sense? Besides, some Serbian English supporter was in the place together with a number of his followers. Whoever took them out meant to and wanted to. It's that simple, and it certainly wasn't an amateur performance on the part of the perpetrator. Whoever did it was very, very skillful. Now, young Keiran. That is my take on the matter. Agree?"

"Well, it certainly is an answer. But lying to the public backfires."

"Innocents are no longer an impediment, if ever they were, to elimination of a target. It is clear that whoever did this dislikes the Serbs or the particular leader for whom the party was being held...thinks they're rubbish. I would presume it would be someone who was appalled by what the Serbs are doing to the Muslims in that sad nation, or, more likely, someone who wanted to hit the birthday party man. Was it a birthday party at the Parrot?"

"I don't really know, sir," Keiran replied.

"No matter. I would think it was that particular gentlemen the perpetrator was after. As I've said, collateral damage of the innocents no longer matters in this world of terror killings. Freelance murder has taken over the solving of whatever problem presents itself. That is my analysis. The vital question simmers down to this doesn't it? Follow the leader. Find out who he is, what he was doing at the restaurant, what he does for a living, who his enemies are and so forth. You answer those questions and you'll have the key to why and whom. Keiran Hogan, death...death the great simplifier, the great equalizer, neither rank nor station in the grave. You know the great American poet, Henry Wadsworth Longfellow, young Keiran?"

"Yeah. I took a course in American Lit and we had a sequence in poetry. Sure, everyone knows his epic poems, 'The Song of Hiawatha,' 'The Courtship of Miles Standish,' and 'Paul Revere's Ride.' He's one of the greatest. I can't say I've read him since getting out of college, but I do remember these. Yeah...one of our best."

"Well, here are two stanzas I've memorized…perhaps you know them also."

Where a star quenched on high,
For ages would its light,
Still traveling downward from the sky
Shine on our mortal sight.

So when a great man dies,
For years beyond our ken,
The light he leaves behind him lies
Upon the paths of men.

"I'll let you do some research in this great room, and find from whence these lines came. I believe that you'll be able to accomplish that task."

There was silence, and Keiran frowned, trying to figure out why Runnard was quoting these particular phrases from Longfellow. Runnard had lowered his head as if in deep thought. Then in a burst of emotion, he raised his voice, loudly proclaiming, "The curse of speaking my thoughts aloud."

"Pretty powerful lines, sir. Pretty powerful." Runnard didn't reply, but kept looking at the open window.

"Would you like me to close the window?" Just as he asked the question, the garden lights went off abruptly.

"Yes, that would be doing me a favor. Thank you. I feel a bit chilly, actually."

"Are the lights set on timers so that they automatically go off at this time? Sort of strange. It's about 2: 30," Keiran noted as he looked at his wristwatch.

"Vulgar fools run the club, young Keiran. What more can I say? Having lights in the garden is silly anyway and a waste of money. Time for me to depart. My doctor keeps telling me I need more rest and less drink…very boring. 'The ebbing of life is not for sissies' is what I tell the doctor. I hope we meet again, young Keiran. Perhaps we can have dinner, and you can tell me all about your new career here in London.

I hope, regardless, that it will involve a great many women and fewer lonely Saturdays— now it's Sunday morning— without the pleasure of the best creature God ever created— a woman. You will be careful in this big city, now, young Keiran. Would you be kind enough to get my cane. The cane…the curse of old age." He placed both hands on the sides of the chair and slowly raised himself.

Keiran rose, going over to where the cane had fallen, picked it up, and gave it to Runnard.

"Here let me help you." Keiran reached for one of Runnard's arms.

"No, No, that won't be necessary. I'm not that old…yet. But thank you, young Keiran. Thank you very much. One more thing. As you practice your law, you must promise me you'll remember this old Japanese proverb: 'The wise hawk hides his talons.' You will remember that now, won't you? It'll serve you well at your firm. Good night, young Keiran. A very good night to you."

Runnard seemed to hesitate for a moment, and then turned about rather awkwardly, brushing against a chair, then against a reading table, then passing through the library doors, which he opened with some difficulty. Keiran started to walk in the direction of the doors to help, but then stepped back, knowing that such help would probably embarrass Runnard. Those lines from Longfellow are about someone who wants to be remembered after he dies…pretty sorrowful really, Keiran reflected. 'The light he leaves behind him lies…upon the paths of men.' Runnard wanted to be a light.

Keiran picked up his newspaper, folded it back carefully, and sauntered over to the newspaper table, where he placed the paper back in its original place. Maybe, Keiran thought, maybe Runnard is bitter about his failure to convict Farris and his client—or quite wise about it—and he didn't care about his failure —but he did want me to know. Yet he seemed to have an eye for human values. Keiran lowered his shirtsleeves, put on his jacket, drifted toward the door. Yeah, he thought, he'd certainly take up Sir Robert Albert Percival Runnard—Keiran shook his head and smiled at the extended name. Keiran had listened to him and wanted to learn more from him. One thing he would do after his meeting with Jennifer would be to go to the office and try to hunt up a copy of

Runnard's report. It would be a necessary read. I'll join him for dinner. He seems so lonely…and that poem…strong stuff…strong stuff. Keiran closed the library door behind him and headed toward his room. The port had relaxed him a bit, and he looked forward to a sound night's sleep.

Seven

The knock on the door was persistent and vigorous.

"Mr. Hogan...Mr. Hogan...Your breakfast tray is here." In bed, Keiran turned his head a few times, then rose just enough to look at the door, his eyes wandering to the clock on his night stand, mumbling, "9:30...Damn! I forgot to set the alarm. Okay, okay, I'll be right there," he shouted as he jumped out of bed.

"Okay, okay...I'll be right there," he repeated as he headed toward the door, then turned back, realizing he had only his shorts on, grabbed the bathrobe at the foot of the bed, and put it on, tying the sash loosely around his waist, walking barefoot to the door, unlatching and quickly opening it.

"Sorry. Hope you didn't have to wait too long," Keiran said sleepily, holding the door open while the porter, a short man with a large bony face, resplendent in the club's gray uniform, ram-rod straight despite the weight of the tray he held high with one hand, alert and with a wide smile commented, "No trouble at all, sir. None whatsoever."

He placed the tray on the empty side of the desk. He moved the stack of files and loose papers that filled the other side over to the window and pulled open the oyster colored drapes, letting in a burst of sunlight.

"I believe the rain is gone sir—yes, a day of complete freshness—wonderful bright day," he said proudly as he handed Keiran the breakfast slip to sign.

"I hope it stays this way. This past week was dreary," Keiran reflected as he initialed the slip and returned it to the porter. "I left a little something on the slip for you," he reminded the porter.

"Not necessary, sir, but I thank you very much," he replied, but with such eagerness that Keiran wondered if he really meant that the tip wasn't necessary. With a grinning smile, he left, silently closing the door behind him.

Keiran went to the room sink, turned on the cold water, splashing handfuls on his face, toweling intensively, trying to stay awake and to avoid the comforting look of the bed. Farris' message had said to phone him before 10:00 a.m., so going back to bed would be out of the question. The call he now had to make to Farris weighed heavily on his mind. Runnard's comments early this morning in the club library made him wonder how many stale falsities Farris had told him. The problem is that Keiran now knew he knew way too little about Farris, the client, and the true intent of the client's project. He went to the desk, moved some books off the chair, placed them on the floor, and sat down, taking the paper cover off the orange juice, drinking about half, then putting it down on the tray. He put on his glasses, reached over and opened the Benton Industries file to the executive summary page, where he had listed his concerns about the project—concerns that Farris had said were not relevant. He was also thinking about the pasty-faced man who he had seen rush down the corridor at the embassy as he was leaving the day of the bombing. He had also seen him leave Farris' house the afternoon he arrived to discuss the Benton project. Uppermost was the early morning conversation with Sir Robert. A lot to think about, Keiran silently told himself, lifting his glass of orange juice and finishing it off.

He then lifted the phone receiver and dialed Farris' home.

"Good Morning. The Farris' residence." Keiran recognized the voice of the maid who had greeted him yesterday, now a little breathless, as if she had hurried to answer the phone.

"Good morning. This is Keiran Hogan, returning Mr. Farris' call. Is he in?"

"Yes. I'll fetch him. He is expecting your call." As Keiran continued to read the summary page over and over again, he was trying to figure out what could possibly be the problem—if, in fact, there was a problem.

"Good Sunday morning to you, Keiran," Farris said with great earnestness. "Please forgive me for disturbing you on such a fine day. There is an important point that I want to emphasize as you take your trip to Guernsey. I want to remind you to refrain from discussing any banking arrangements for the new company. I believe that I did mention that to you, but, in my old age, I tend to forget at times what I've said." Farris laughed. "Of course, I know that you will make sure the corporation is registered properly and that all the documentation is accurate for such registration. I have no doubt as to your attention to detail, but, perhaps, it's a fault of mine to be as overly cautious in reminding you again. I am confident you can understand this," he concluded.

There was a pause as if Farris was waiting for Keiran to respond. Keiran frowned, shaking his head in pensive silence, trying to understand whether this was really a serious talk, or an excuse for the real purpose of the call. Why would Keiran discuss banking details when his partner told him not to? Why wouldn't he follow the instructions of his partner? Farris' comment didn't make any sense. Besides, the registration of corporate documents on the island of Guernsey could not possibly be complicated, especially with the help of the firm's agent, who would escort Keiran to the appropriate government agencies.

"I would not have forgotten your instructions, Mr. Farris, not at all. Everything will be done properly. We have our agent in Guernsey waiting for me. No, I don't think anything will go awry," Keiran declared, his voice ringing a bit high, and it was plain that his indignation was beginning to overcome his sense of discipline in respecting his partner. Although he found it difficult, Keiran understood that it's a platitude that an associate in a law firm must learn to obey before he can command, which was the sole province of a partner. To Keiran, Farris' reminder was more malice than anything else—the conversation was really nothing more than that.

Sensing, perhaps, Keiran's restrained anger, Farris continued rather blandly, "My reminder is not a reflection on your good memory. This is such a serious matter for our client and under the circumstances, I hope that you appreciate my concern."

"Of course," Keiran spoke without emotion.

"I also wanted to apologize for not introducing you to Zoran Hemmrich, our client. The poor man was in such a rush, and of course, when you came into the library, I was totally immersed with him, and I simply forgot to make the proper introduction. Must be my old age. It was very impolite of me to ignore you in that manner. Totally inappropriate." Keiran felt his voice had a strange tenor, as if he were trying to sound more serious than he, in actuality, was. He found it hard to believe the generosity of the words coming from Farris' mouth. This had to be an illusory apology. He had never seen Farris apologize for anything to anybody—even when he was clearly at fault. No, this apology was deliberate, planned, and certainly not real, disguising something more significant. But why the charade? Nothing seemed to be making any sense.

"Nothing to it, Mr. Farris. I knew you were busy so it really wasn't of any concern. I know that at an appropriate time, I'll meet the client. In Washington, whenever we were assigned a client, we automatically met the client. It makes for an easier time for the associates—in case they need further information and so forth. Much easier for us. I certainly look forward to meeting Mr. Hemmrich." He heard Farris clear his throat.

"Certainly we do the same thing in London. We do introduce the clients to the associates who are doing work for the client. So we shall do that—perhaps over lunch after you return from Guernsey, as Zoran will be in London the later part of this week, I'll have HenHen arrange to have you meet us at lunch. You may even meet him on Guernsey. I'm not sure. In any event, you will meet him at some point soon. Now, I understand that you'll stay the night on Guernsey. It is a pretty island. See as much as you can. If you'd like, you can take an extra day there. You've been working very hard these last several weeks. I don't want you to think we in London are all work and no play. So, you have my permission to take an extra day to relax. A reminder though, if you do, make sure HenHen is aware of your decision. She can be a bear when she feels that she isn't aware of everything. Well, you've run into that already." He gave a humorous laugh. "Thanks for calling me back, Keiran. My regards to our man, David Leyden. He'll do a fine job on our behalf. Of that I am sure. Please notify HenHen when the registration is complete. She'll get a message to me in Athens. Anything you wish to ask me before I ring off?"

"No, Mr. Farris. And thanks for the extra day. I may take you up on that. Have a good trip, yourself, and I'll see you when you return."

"Goodbye, Keiran. And thank's for your help."

"Goodbye, Mr. Farris."

Keiran hung up. For several seconds, he stood silent, staring at the phone, wondering what the hell the conversation was all about. Farris wasn't a chattering man. Today his voice and manner were too mindful, too polite, too mushy, too unlike his true self. He was either the most cunning of men, or he was simply trying to make Keiran feel useful and important. As he pondered the conversation, he recalled the description of Farris Runnard had provided earlier this morning. "He has a pleasant enough face hiding, perhaps, a more secret and interesting aspect."

He pushed himself from the table, grabbed his coffee cup, taking it with him as he stood for a moment beside the window. The morning sun felt good. He looked down onto Pall Mall, which, this Sunday morning, was fairly deserted by pedestrians and cars. He had to forgo his hour swim and steam. Time was getting very short and he didn't want to be late for his visit with Jennifer. His thoughts had already moved on to her, thinking of her beauty, high spirits, and ever ready laughter which had so captivated his poetic, but at times, his more gloomy temperament. He couldn't wait until he saw her again.

The studios of Independent Television News were in a gleaming glass facaded building in central London, not far from the Houses of Parliament. Keiran, in casual olive slacks and a white polo shirt, arrived about twenty minutes before noon. The lobby was fairly large, with fifteen by twenty inch color photo blow-ups of the various ITN on-air personalities. He quickly spotted Jennifer's portrait. To him, her face was the most beautiful of all, eyes bright, smile serene and confident. Several people were seated in the off-white lobby. The furniture was done in black and gray leather throughout, with an abundance of plants in large silver colored containers, completing the picture of an efficient organization. Keiran approached the dark gray, curved marble top reception desk, behind which sat a pale, plump middle aged, fair, woman with thick golden hair and big gray eyes that stared at Keiran under half closed lids as he approached the desk. A large bouquet of red and white carnations sat in a crystal vase, the color matching her bright red suit. He approached the desk.

"Good Morning. I'm Keiran Hogan for Jennifer Berley."

Abruptly, she said, "Thank you for telling me that bit of information. But, first, please sign the register. Remember not only to sign your name, ducky, but also print it clearly. Some signatures are too difficult to make out and I have to have an accurate list to feed into my computer. Security you know. We have a clear record of who has come and gone. Don't forget to place your arrival time. It is now 11:50. Do you have any questions?"

"No, of course not," Keiran replied as he took up the pen and began signing and printing his name in the appropriate spaces on the register.

"Good. You'd be surprised how many people print first and then sign. No, it's sign first and then print. You're not making that mistake are you?"

"No. Not at all." Keiran smiled faintly.

"Fine. Now, I'll call upstairs for Jennifer's assistant. Jennifer is too busy right now preparing for her broadcast, so her assistant will come," she said curtly, rolling her eyes as she touched a button on her phone, talking into her head set. "Priscilla? Good. Mr. Hogan is here. He's here for the noon broadcast. So hurry down, ducky.

No courtly conversation here. Keiran marveled at the bluntness of the receptionist. This first impression of ITN certainly was different than what he had expected.

"Jennifer's production assistant will be down in just a minute to take you to the Green Room where you'll be able to watch the broadcast. You might as well stand here, but have a seat if you wish, although she'll be down in a jiffy."

"Yes. Of course…Sure…I'll stand here. No problem."

"Have you known Jennifer long?" the receptionist inquired animatedly, her gaze steady.

"Well, not really."

"She is our star presenter. Such a cheerful and bright person. Not like some of the others whose egos are bigger than this building. Can't stand people with egos. You know what popularity does to some people? It's like champagne with a heavy dose of brandy." She laughed loudly at her own statement. "You know what I mean?"

"Yeah, I do. Great line though," Keiran replied, joining in her laughter.

"Jennifer is the exception. A decent human being. Hope she doesn't go over to BBC. The rumor is they're asking her to come and offering her quite a bit of money. Do you watch BBC?"

"Sometimes. Actually, I'm so busy I don't have time to watch much television."

"Well, you're an American. So you probably watch CNN. Now, how did you meet Jennifer?" she asked, tapping her pen on her desk.

Keiran shrugged his shoulders, then responded quietly, "We met at a dinner party."

"Let me tell you, ducky, you're certainly nicer than her other friend. He storms in here, not even a hello and heads for the elevator. I've had to have security stop him. Security is very tight here. No matter who you are you have to wear one of these—a visitor's pass—here's yours—and it must be hung around your neck at all times.… Well, her friend," she raised both hands and made a gesture indicating quotation marks as she said friend, "he went by me. Well let me tell you, he learned the hard way and he was stopped by security as he tried to get on the elevator. Dennis over there," she pointed to a guard who sat behind a small desk in front of the bank of four elevators, "stopped him. He never did that again. Some men, well you know…they just don't like to take directions from a woman. You know what I mean?"

"Well....sure....Some don't like to take directions from a woman," Keiran repeated simply.

"Those kind of men are insecure. They don't like a powerful woman. Wouldn't you say? No one gets past me."

"That's good, I would think.... You know security." he smiled and bent his head.

"Especially with all these bombs going off in London. We do have terrorists...especially the IRA, so I have to be very vigilant. I carry not one, but two cans of mace, just in case, if you know what I mean. Just look at what happened in Mayfair. Now if you ask me I think it was the IRA. You know, they bomb everything. Crazy bunch. Don't you agree?" Before he had time to answer, she continued, "Priscilla...There you are. It's about time. You only have a few minutes to take Mr. Hogan to the Green Room, ducky. It's almost twelve. Hurry along now, folks. Enjoy." She again rolled her eyes.

"Mr. Hogan. I'm Priscilla Wetherby, one of Jennifer's production assistants. She is expecting you. Thank you Nancy. Thank you very much."

"Have fun, Keiran Hogan. Irish name, right?" the receptionist chimed in.

"Right, Nancy," he responded, with a broad smile.

"I guess I said the wrong thing about the IRA?"

"Yes, you did, but that's okay. You're British." He waved at her as he and Priscilla headed toward the elevator. Nancy laughed loudly.

"Okay, Irishman, I get your point."

Wetherby had long blond hair, her rimless glasses covering gray-blue eyes, a pretty figure, wearing a loose fitting plum dress, and several inches shorter than Keiran. She had a broad smile as she shook his hand.

"Nancy is a hoot, isn't she? Pretty well runs the place on the weekends. I suppose she obtained your life history in the few moments you were there. She actually had the Prime Minister sign it and gave him a security pass. He wrote her a thank you letter. She has an opinion on everything and doesn't mind telling whoever is in front of her what her views are.

Very efficient though, although she can be a bore at times." Priscilla laughed quietly.

Keiran smiled. "Yeah. She's something. No doubt about it."

"Have you been in London long, Mr. Hogan?"

"Please....please call me Keiran...Mr. Hogan sounds like my father. Been here about nine weeks. Great city you have. Without doubt, I'm going to like it very much."

"First visit in a TV studio?"

"Yeah. My first. Well, no. When I was a kid my parents took me on a tour of the NBC studios in New York. I was fascinated by all the equipment it takes to get a show on the air...all the cameras, lights, mikes. Really astonishing how a program gets put together."

"That's where we production assistants come in. We have to get the stories to the reporters, help write the scripts, locate the people the presenter wants to interview on air, do a great deal of 'drudge' work you might say. Keeps us busy. Well, here we are. Third Floor. Follow me please."

She led him down an off-white walled hallway, thickly carpeted in dark green, lined with glass enclosed cases displaying the awards that ITN had received over the years, to a room that was furnished like a home living room. One wall was entirely glass and looked down on the studio.

"Please make yourself comfortable. Jennifer will be up after the broadcast. I'll tell her you're here. Coffee, juice, and whatever else you'd like are on the table at the far end. Magazines and today's papers are on the table in front of the couch. If you do need anything while Jennifer is broadcasting, just pick up the phone and dial 2851. That's my extension. Okay? Hope we see you often." She smiled as she left.

Keiran went over to the window and looked down on the set—banks of overhead lights, several cameras, someone was placing a body mike on Jennifer, and a make-up woman was putting some touchups to her hair. She looked beautiful and serene. He saw Priscilla go up to Jennifer who then looked up, broke into a smile and waved. He waved back. He couldn't wait until the thirty-minute broadcast was over to see her. He watched the signage lights: 'Standby,' then 'On Air,' and he heard

Jennifer's voice come over the speaker system in the Green Room as her face appeared on the several television sets suspended from the ceiling.

"Good Afternoon, This is ITN Sunday's London Magazine. Today we will focus on the explosion at the Parrot Restaurant. The fatalities, at this point, number fifty, with thirty-five confirmed dead, and fifteen still in hospital. No definitive cause has as yet been established by the police, but the prime cause appears to have been a faulty gas connection into the building housing the restaurant. Our guest this afternoon is Thomas Fine, the Home Secretary, who will be followed by a panel of two distinguished journalists—Julia Lord of the *Financial Times*, and Frederick Collingwood of the *Guardian*. But first, we go for an update on the continuing police investigation to our correspondent, Robert Alderson, at the scene in Mayfair." As she concluded her opening comments, she was joined by Priscilla and another man, who were handing her papers that they all appeared to be reviewing.

For the next several minutes, Keiran listened to the now familiar facts of the explosion at the Parrot Restaurant. The number of dead and injured; the building completely destroyed as well as damage to the adjacent buildings. Some of the fatalities were innocent passer-bys. The cause was still undetermined. The reporter stated that the entire restaurant staff had been killed, as well as dozens of the patrons in the restaurant who had come to pay birthday tribute to a British citizen of Serbian origin, Mile Draculic, an outspoken supporter of the Serbian cause. He had been engaged in raising substantial sums of money for that cause. It was rumored also that several of his companies were conduits for arms shipments to the Serbian faction in the former Yugoslavia. Of course, such activity, the reporter noted, is contrary to British law and in violation of the embargo by the European Union, which called for a halt to all economic activity between the Union and the former Yugoslavia.

"Draculic," the correspondent continued in a studious tone, "had denied all such charges and had, in fact, filed suit against several newspapers that claimed he was engaged in money laundering and arms dealing. Despite his presence, the police continued to believe the cause to be a gas explosion. No other reason has yet been officially given.

"Government officials in Belgrade," the correspondent noted, "have charged that he was killed by or ordered killed by the United States CIA and the British MI5. Both governments denied such a charge using similar language: 'preposterous.'" The correspondent concluded with an interview with the spokesperson for the London Metropolitan Police Department who said that the investigation was ongoing and that the police were continuing their forensic review but could say nothing further than what had been announced earlier—in all likelihood, the explosion was caused by a faulty gas connection.

The correspondent signed off saying that his sources tell him that the investigation would take weeks more to complete as the police continue to sift through the debris, interview witnesses, and otherwise try to determine in a conclusive manner what exactly happened last Saturday when a birthday party for Mile Draculic turned into a horrific event.

Jennifer then asked Alderson for some final remarks. Keiran looked with pride as Jennifer looked directly into the camera, smoothly continuing the dialogue with the reporter. At this point, the screen split, with one side showing Jennifer, and the other side, the correspondent.

"Robert, do the police continue to rule out the IRA?"

"Yes, Jennifer, they're ruling it out, but not absolutely. They hedge their comments by saying that, as of now, there is no evidence that the IRA was involved, given the ethnic nature of the celebration at the Parrot Restaurant, and the history of attacks by the IRA, which is generally against British targets as opposed to other ethnic groups."

"So, the IRA is still under suspicion? Would that be your understanding of the police investigation?"

"No, I would say not. But, again, I want to underscore that the police don't believe at this moment, nor does the evidence accumulated up to now indicate, that the IRA is involved in this tragedy."

"Thank you Robert. That was our correspondent Robert Alderson at the scene in Mayfair. Now here to discuss this tragedy and give us some perspective, we have as our guest, Thomas Fine, the Home Secretary. Thank you for joining us, Mr. Fine. You have heard our correspondent's report. Do you still believe that the reason for the explosion was a faulty gas connection from the street gas main to the restaurant?" Keiran admired the way Jennifer got straight to the point, even though her voice had a soft, yet determined quality.

"Jennifer. I do wish I could give you a more definitive answer to the cause of this tragedy. The Metropolitan Police are doing an outstanding job and we in the government are doing all that we can to help. Nevertheless, it will be a somewhat long and tedious process to arrive at the final conclusion. It is my understanding, from experts in the field, that the debris damage, the force of the blast, and so forth, all indicate a gas explosion caused by the build up of gas from a gas leak."

"You're ruling out the explosion being caused by an incendiary device?"

"Well, it's not wise to rule anything out at this stage. I do believe that the police are looking into that avenue as well. Nevertheless, as your correspondent just pointed out, the spokesperson for the Metropolitan police, as well as the one for Scotland Yard, maintains the prime cause seems to be a faulty gas connection."

"Mr. Fine, do you believe that the cause will eventually be determined and with certainty?"

"No doubt on that whatsoever. Both the Police and the members of Scotland Yard have acted professionally and with dispatch. We must give them time to investigate this and to determine what the cause was and, of course, to take steps to prevent these kinds of accidents—if indeed it was an accident—from happening again."

"Are you ruling out any other terrorist group at this point?"

"Again, it's difficult to rule anything out until a final report is rendered by the authorities. It is remote that a terrorist group was responsible, but again, as the police have said, they're continuing their investigation and nothing is being discarded at this time."

"Mr. Fine, there appeared an opinion piece today in the *Times* by Sir Robert Albert Percival Runnard, the noted barrister, now retired, calling into question the government's opinion on the subject, stating that it certainly looked to him that the explosion wasn't gas induced, but rather a carefully planted bomb designed to do exactly what it did and probably planted by those who didn't like Mr. Draculic, and that indeed it may have been Draculic who was the target. Do you have a view as to his opinion?"

Sir Robert Albert Percival Runnard? Keiran heard the name, shaking his head momentarily, listening intently to the interview, but had trouble believing what he was hearing. The one who could barely walk he had so much to drink, writing an opinion piece on the Mayfair incident for the *Times*. Hard to fathom. Keiran reached over to the table in front of the couch where he was seated, grabbing the *Sunday Times* from the pile of papers. On the front page was bold lettering in a bordered box at the end of the lead article on the explosion: 'Sir Robert Percival Runnard writes explosion could be caused by a bomb. See Opinion Page A-12.' And he didn't even tell me. Son-of-a gun!

As he scanned the article, his ear continued to listen to Jennifer's interview with the home secretary.

"Certainly, Sir Robert is well respected and he is an eminent member of the bar. We have to respect his views, obviously. But, at this time, none of the evidence to date supports the opinion he has expressed in his article. This government is not engaged in any cover-up—and we are telling all we know as to the cause of the catastrophe."

"Runnard claims that the government is covering up the real evidence so as not to frighten the public that there may be a terrorist group or even an individual who will carry out this kind of activity again. Do you have an opinion on what Sir Robert has written?"

"I believe that it's preposterous to say something like that at this time. Again, none of the evidence points to the conclusion Sir Robert makes, and the government is not hiding anything. We have disclosed what we know to date. Nothing has been hidden from the public. Nothing."

"The Belgrade government has stated," Jennifer continued, "that the United States Central Intelligence Agency and the British MI5 are responsible not only for this matter but also for the unexplained and curious deaths of three other Serbian supporters in England. Would you care to comment on their assertion as to the governments of the United States and England being complicit in those occurrences?"

"I can emphatically state that the British government wasn't involved in any of these untimely deaths, and I am assured that the United States Government was also not involved. It is my understanding that they were simply accidents, two automobile accidents, and the other an accidental overdose of some medication. Certainly, the police reports were exhaustive at the time and the medical evidence clear as to the causes. No, I have no doubt as to the reasons for those matters, no doubt whatsoever."

"Lastly, Mr. Fine, do you have an idea when the investigation will be completed?"

"I wish I could give you a absolute answer. But all I can say is that all government agencies are working as quickly as is possible, given the circumstances, to come to a speedy conclusion. We want to be certain of our conclusion and not rush to any judgment that doesn't hold up to scrutiny."

"And, again, no IRA involvement?"

"Not that we are aware of. This, obviously, is not the kind of target that the IRA would be interested in. Besides, there is a cease-fire between the parties in Northern Ireland, and negotiations, difficult negotiations, are under way to resolve those issues. No, no responsible person has suggested that the IRA is involved in this Mayfair incident."

"Thank you Mr. Thomas Fine, Home Secretary. When we come back we will be joined by our two panelists, Julia Lord of the *Financial Times*, and Frederick Collingwood of the *Guardian*.

Keiran was mesmerized by Jennifer and the ease with which she handled the questions. The smile, the smile that was sincere. She looked up again to the Green Room and waved to him. He smiled and waved back to her. He saw her pick up the phone beneath her desk, and point to him. Shortly, the phone on the table next to his chair rang. Picking it up, he heard Jennifer ask, "Enjoying the broadcast?"

"Yeah. I'm learning a lot."

"I'll be up shortly. It won't be long, okay?"

"Sure...carry on Ms. Berley. I'm impressed." They laughed together.

"See you soon." She rang off.

He tried to pay attention to the panel discussion, but he just kept staring at Jennifer. Her confident manner, steering the discussion and watching the time carefully, obviously listening to the director on her earpiece, all without a trace of nervousness. Impressive, Keiran smiled to himself. Impressive, Jennifer.

At the program's end, Jennifer shook hands with the panel, took off her mike, placed it on the counter, looked up and waved to Keiran that she was on her way up. As he saw her leave the studio, a feeling of pent-up expectancy came upon him as he waited for Jennifer. He didn't want to show his anxiety for her, so he continued to read and reread the Runnard article in the *Times*, trying to figure out what Runnard was up to. Oh, shit. He probably just forgot to tell me, not that he had to. But he did tell me a great deal, so not pointing out his article is a bit strange.

"Well, Keiran. Did you enjoy the broadcast this Sunday morning?" He looked up to see Jennifer walking toward him, a wide smile on her face.

"Yeah. Very much, Jennifer. You're terrific. . . really...handling all those guests." He reached over and took her hand, leaned over and spontaneously kissed her on the cheek.

"Thank you. That was nice." She kept holding his hand. "Well let me take you on a tour of the studios. Would you like that?" He hesitated for a moment, his eyes meeting hers, her gaze falling on him in a wistful moment.

"It's such a great day, I thought maybe you would like to take a walk and go have a bite with me." He spoke falteringly. "Have you been at the studio for very long?"

"I had to get here around 9:30. There's a bit of rehearsal, to make sure the Teleprompter is fine; my script is revised, the editing of the correspondent's report, plus a brief review with the interviewee, Home Secretary Fine, and then get acquainted with the panel. The comments are spontaneous, but, of course, we have certain areas that we try to cover in the interview."

"Glad you set to rest the IRA involvement. Great question." Keiran laughed.

"Not sensitive about that, are you?"

"No, but everyone here seems to jump on the IRA…even when it's clear that they aren't involved."

"I guess it's the history of their involvement over the last several years that makes people jump to these conclusions. Not really necessary though, and you're right."

"So shall we take a long walk?" He held her hand tightly.

"Sure, I don't mind Keiran. You can come for a tour later if you wish. Yeah, I'd like to take a walk with you. Mind if I change into my 'walking' clothes?"

"No, of course not."

She took his hand and they walked out of the Green Room and down the corridor to the elevator.

"I'll meet you downstairs in five minutes in the lobby. Now, don't go anywhere or be distracted by anyone until I get there, and stay away from Nancy. She'll bend your ear. Okay?"

"Sure." She pressed the elevator and waited for him to get on, again he kissed her on the cheek. "See you soon, Jennifer." As the door closed, he saw her go down the corridor.

In the reception area, he noted the broadcast's panelists talking with Mr. Fine. Keiran overheard Fine say, "Please give me a ring and let's continue. My car is here and I have to go to another appointment. But, yes, in a nutshell, I think the government is telling the public all that it knows at this time. We have no hard evidence that this is a concerted program of eliminating the Serb supporters. The earlier deaths were just that—accidents. Please don't make this into something it's not."

Keiran stood in front of the displayed picture of Jennifer, pretending not to overhear the parting conversation. The woman panelist spoke to her colleague, "Do you think he really is telling the truth? And this bull about the IRA, they're so dead set against naming the IRA…probably want to protect the so-called peace process—something doesn't smell right here."

Her male companion commented, "No, I don't think it's the IRA, but I think it has to do with Draculic. That guy is steeped in arms buying and money raising, plus he's a genocidal killer himself. I'm going to dig into that for a while. I suggest you do also. Fine is smart, but has been known to float a balloon and watch it burst. Notice he always, says, 'Maybe…but…no hard evidence.' And Jennifer quoting Sir Robert…that guy's a has-been, an alcoholic recluse. I couldn't believe she did that. Does anybody believe that guy anymore?"

"Yeah. They do," the woman replied. "He's still got more brains that many others and his ability to analyze is still there. For God's sake, he believes what you do. Somebody is going after the Serbs, and the government is hiding the true nature of who that somebody is. He's still smart as hell and he ran that investigation a few years back on arms dealing with the nasties. Hey, I've got to get out of here. I have a deadline to make. Want to share a cab?"

"Sure, let's go." Keiran saw them both leave, hurrying to grab a cab in front of the building.

Jennifer looked too good. He'd be lying to himself if he didn't admit he wanted to take her home with him. His whole body trembled a bit as she came toward him. She had changed into black slacks, a loose short sleeve light gray blouse, a small gold chain around her neck, and flat black shoes. Without high heels, Keiran was a foot taller than she was. He walked toward her as she came out of the elevator.

"Well, I feel more comfortable now."

"You look great no matter what you're wearing…or probably not wearing." He laughed as he squeezed her hand."

"Keiran. . .Don't advance this too much now. Aren't you supposed to be a shy person?"

"That's a rumor that is not true. And who would have told you that anyway?"

"That's a secret that I'll never tell."

"Oh! I don't know about that, Jennifer. Shall we go?" He smiled broadly, squeezing her a bit tighter. They walked hand in hand past the reception desk. Nancy, her voice raised slightly, said, "Have a nice afternoon. And, remember you have a show tonight as well, Jennifer. Goodbye Keiran Hogan."

Jennifer turned and smiled, waving her hand. Keiran smiled back at Nancy. "I suspect everyone will know we were holding hands as we left?" Keiran asked quietly.

"I suppose so, but then you don't care do you?"

"No, of course not."

"See you about four, Nancy."

"You have to be back at four?" Keiran asked.

"Yeah. I have to do the six o'clock broadcast as well. We'll be back by then, won't we?"

"Sure. I just thought that maybe we could…."

"We have plenty of time, Keiran, okay?"

"Yeah, sure, okay." He had fallen in love with her so quickly that he wasn't sure how to behave or what to say. Her temperament and comliness chased his lingering memories of Allison to become a distant blur. As they walked together in the afternoon air his pulse quickened, but he had to continually remind himself not to push too hard or to seem controlling or possessive. He was happier than he had been for a long time and prayed to himself that she was happy as well.

Eight

Jefferson Coborn had a way of sitting at a bar that would remind one of a sack—slouching in the stool, seemingly crumpled up, his suit jacket all wrinkles and his tie bulged. He tightly clutched the glass, half filled with Glenlivet scotch, as if it were going to slip off and come crashing down on the pub's wood plank floor, creating a noise that would have humiliated him. He hated to be noticed. But he should not have concerned himself. In a crowd, he would not have been observed in any event. He didn't stand head or shoulders above his fellow men, was of medium height, pale, clean-shaven, slender. His brown hair was sprinkled with gray and closely clipped. One could see his type on the streets a dozen times a day and pass him without turning round for a second view. Regardless, usually he looked down when he walked and avoided the faces of others. When he did speak, his voice was flat and methodical.

He didn't look with interest at the few others sitting at the bar. He sat alone at the far end, silent and bored, making sure there were at least several bar stools between him and the next customer. His round gray eyes fixed on a large gold framed portrait of a woman hanging above the rack of liquor bottles, undraped except for one of her hands, which held a bouquet of red roses covering, in part, her intimacy. One rose, he noted, was wilted, drooping down from the rest. She was reclining on a maroon chaise lounge; her wide white face had a shimmering look, her breasts firm, yet her body appeared flaccid. There was something in her brown eyes that puzzled Coborn. Boldness, doubt, a hesitant appeal, perhaps wistful, certainly not happy. What did her look suggest? And, the one red rose, the edges of its petals that were a slight dirt brown, dejected from the others alert and fresh. What was its significance? She was no longer a virgin? Or a love gone astray?

He was a regular at this pub—some two blocks from embassy—and yet he had never been able to agree as to the meaning expressed in the nude's eyes.

"Means whatever you want to me, right mate?" the pub's bartender had told him once when Coborn had asked for his opinion. But that wasn't the answer Coborn wanted to hear. He wanted him to be more sympathetic and give an opinion. When that wasn't forthcoming, he never brought up the subject again, rationalizing that the bartender lacked understanding. He wanted to think her expression and the dead rose signified a love gone. . .like the one he had once had in his life. But even that, that love was probably fantasy. He and his wife had long ago parted company, and he could now truthfully say he had never loved her. It was a marriage that he selfishly believed would help him in his career in the Foreign Service. Memories can be bright and beautiful, but the memory of his marriage was heavy, sad, and distasteful. That was to be expected when the union is for reasons other than true affection. Regardless, to him, she was dull, petty, and worse, from his point of view, she believed him to be unsuccessful.

The only woman he saw now was a prostitute, Alleana, whom he financially supported by settling her rent every month for a small furnished apartment in Soho, as well as paying her handsomely for each of his many visits per week. He didn't mind that she had come from another world of 2:00 in the morning frenzies and much drink, wasn't fresh, vigorous or young. To him, her blue eyes were of the open air, she was kind, reassuring, her body always warm and inviting. She obeyed their natural impulses and made love to him, and the lovemaking was never stale. The physical excitement, repeated and repeated until both were exhausted, was all that mattered to him.

The nude's expression didn't concern him this evening. He pursued other thoughts, which always occur when one drinks alone. He chose to ignore the pub's television sets, which hung on brass poles from the ceiling on either side of the nude's portrait, blaring loudly the news events of the day, which, from the snippets he could not avoid hearing, still concentrated on the Mayfair explosion. Staring at his glass, turning it slowly in his hands, he pondered his life…a panorama….

Yeah. That's a good word for my life…a panorama. My life only differs in its details from others. But for luck, I could have been in that restaurant or close by and blown to bits. Everyone suffers. Sometimes we're lucky and sometimes not. His face looked tired; he was one of those men who lose their color quickly when depressed, and his paleness became sickly white, a color even he didn't like to see when he looked in a mirror.

Today he felt his life had been sucked out like an orange. He believed his double life had been discovered. The same young man who had accidentally seen him leaving Farris' home was the same person who had seen him rushing down the embassy corridor to see the ambassador. But why worry? he kept telling himself. These could be innocent arrangements. Certainly, he could be seeing Farris on behalf of the ambassador, or delivering a personal message. One had to make some sort of an effort to think of a proper excuse, didn't one? From such chance encounters, it would be ludicrous to jump to the conclusion that he was selling embassy secrets to Farris. He certainly wasn't going to go under because of the misfortune of an inopportune sighting. One had to be realistic. Maybe paranoia had set in. Dishonesty does that to a person. No one is trusted…perhaps one stops trusting one's own judgment. He lifted his glass, gulped it down in one swallow, then pushed it forward, raising his hand to get the attention of the bartender, who, anticipating what Coborn wanted, ambled over.

"Another one, mate?"

"Yeah, make it a double this time though."

"Still no ice?" he inquired.

"Yeah. No ice." The bartender placed the bottle down in front of Coborn, and took his small glass, placing it on a tray beneath the counter. Then he reached over for a large tumbler and began pouring.

"Tell me when mate."

When it was three-quarters full, Coborn said, "Okay. That's plenty." In a flourish, the bartender screwed the top on the bottle and replaced it on the rack behind him.

He felt chilly, lonely, and strange among the crowd now filling the pub—the professionals, lawyers, stockbrokers, bankers, successful people…. Successful like he was, until an unexpected event in Pakistan, where he had his last real Foreign Service posting, ended what had been an uninterrupted and highflying career. He gave his head a little lift again, looking at the nude now. Strangely, it looked sensuous and a part of him tingled. No matter what disturbs a man, anticipation of a woman's body makes whatever is bothersome quickly fade. He was still a slave to his male urges and now his body was anticipating excitement. In a few hours, he would be meeting Alleana and her flesh and tawdriness would remedy his sullenness. The warmth of the liquor was now having an effect. Glancing to the seats next to him, he noted that all were occupied by patrons. He no longer had the pleasure of having no one next to him, which to him was a signal to go.

It's such a stupid, jabbering world, he thought as he looked around. For him, he knew that he had no virtue anymore. He could do what he pleased and was able, because of his work with Farris, to pay for it in cash. Maybe, after all, fate had not been so cruel to him. Rather, it had been eminently kind. Perhaps the fact that his perfect record was now sullied and prevented him from ever being advanced in the Foreign Service was an event that Coborn should now welcome. Without that…well…he certainly would not have all the extra cash, and much of it sitting in a Channel Islands bank account…and Farris would never have known of 'Crescent Eagle.'

It was the innocent start of a quiet evening in Karachi, Pakistan, his posting as commercial counselor in 1995. He was having dinner with his wife at their home when a reporter, for London's *Financial Times* came by for an unannounced visit. He knew the reporter quite well, and asked him to stay for dinner. It would have been impolite to have done otherwise. What happened next was completely unexpected. Three members of the opposition leadership to the then government of Pakistan came to his home about five minutes after the reporter arrived. Coborn knew then that the visits were too timed to be a coincidence, and he joked about it to the assembled guests.

"You must all need a free meal." Everyone laughed. The Pakistani government at the time was very unpopular, and the opposition, getting stronger everyday, was calling for new elections. The reporter probably could have met the opposition leadership anywhere, and why he picked Coborn's home remains a mystery he has never been able to solve. Regardless, Coborn asked everyone to stay for dinner. It was a simple chicken stew and his wife extended the amount by serving less stew on more rice. During the meal, the conversation was social and virtually nothing was said about the political situation in the country. After dinner, the *Times'* reporter asked if he could continue the conversation alone with the three guests in the library. Coborn saw no reason to object and the group stayed for about three hours. First the reporter left and after a short while the others left.

Within a day or two, an article appeared in the *Financial Times*. No mention was made of the interview being conducted in Jefferson Coborn's home. Regardless, it wasn't long thereafter that Ambassador Geoffrey Baxter, appointed to the post just three months earlier, learned of the dinner at Coborn's house. In all likelihood, he found out from the Pakistani intelligence services who monitored the activities of foreign embassy staff as well as western reporters, among others. The ambassador was a man that Coborn knew, from the short time he had seen him function, would sooner talk than listen. Coborn's interpretation of the ambassador's attitude was correct, for when he confronted Coborn, his arms flayed and he screamed at Coborn, accusing him of "deliberately violating the rules of the embassy. Are you trying to get the good relationships we now have with this country tanked? You want me to believe that these people came to your house uninvited after a reporter came, uninvited? You're either stupid or you must think I am stupid."

When Coborn tried to explain that his report was being finalized and the week deadline for submission had not passed, the ambassador stormed out of the room, acidly saying he would not remain in the same place with someone so disobedient, and who had participated in a 'traitorous act.' All employees had to write weekly reports of any contacts with political and other leaders during the preceding weeks. The ambassador's anger became irrational and non- stop. Almost on a daily basis, he sent cables to the State Department claiming Coborn deliberately disobeyed the embassy's regulation and demanding his immediate withdrawal from the embassy—claiming that the host government now believed that because of Coborn's high position in the embassy, he actually was supporting the opposition group. Of course this was an exaggeration. Yet, the ambassador never would listen to Coborn's account nor would he even accept the contact report, which Coborn submitted timely but was returned to him, marked 'late.' Whatever the reason, the ambassador would not forgive what he termed a "traitorous act." The ambassador used that term…and it stung.

Within a few weeks, Coborn had his security clearance suspended and was rotated back to the United States. For two years thereafter, he exhausted himself, appealing the unfavorable rating and his abrupt dismissal, but to no avail. The strength of the ambassador's political friends, and his own lack of support in the department from career Foreign Service officers, prevented, in his view, a balanced inquiry by the Foreign Service Grievance Board. In fact, some of his friends urged him to accept his changed circumstances, telling him he should "Be reasonable. There is no need to be hurt anymore if you're wise." He read that to mean accept and apologize, which he could never do. Directly after the Review Board rendered its opinion upholding the ambassador's action, Jefferson Coborn's wife of twenty years asked for a divorce. The marriage had been over much earlier, and the stress of the appeal process was too much for her. A man in distress, as he was, is as appealing as a sick child needing comfort and help. She provided neither comfort nor help and made it clear she had no compassion for him or his problems. He was glad to see her go. He didn't contest the divorce proceedings, never saw her again, rarely saw his two daughters. He felt that he had been battered down to nothingness.

The Board, despite its bland commentary in its own report, did, however, strongly recommended that he be permitted to remain in the

Foreign Service, opining that the Pakistan matter was simply an aberration in an otherwise perfect record. How could they have done otherwise? Prior to this circumstance, his job appraisals were exemplary, including words such as "outstanding," "brilliantly analytical," "exceptional for his class." In fact, it was well known that he was on track to being nominated at some point to ambassador.

It wasn't, he sensed, as if he'd been left with something clean, something that really belonged to him. The feeling was more like having something killed in you. He felt utterly unworthy. Now, he was relegated to administrative posting...those that would ensure he didn't come into contact with political, economic, or military leaders of the countries where he would be—at the embassy in Ottawa, Canada, then the United Nations, and finally London. He wasn't in the least bit interested in these postings. To him they were demeaning. He didn't feel and didn't care. But above all, he was practical. At the time of the unfavorable rating, Coborn was in his late forties. He wasn't dumb enough to jeopardize his retirement income from the Service because of being stripped of his dignity by an incompetent ambassador. Besides, if he resigned in protest and made a public outcry, would anyone really be listening? Does anyone really care that a Foreign Service Officer was unfairly treated by a political hack ambassador? No. Unless some major fraud or scandal was in place. Certainly the inopportune meeting at Coborn's home was neither one of those. What was happening to him was a blow, but it would not be a blow that killed.

Among the duties in London were the mundane—to make sure that the building was cleaned, the trash taken out, the commissary was stocked with food and drink, the office supplies ordered, bills paid, payroll met, and the mail delivered—and the important tasks of seeing that building security was adequate and efficient, that the security regulations of the State Department were followed, that documents were carefully filed and monitored, the burn bags disposed of, the shredders in working order, and that the secure communications between the embassy and Washington worked efficiently. Of course he had staff, and they did most of the actual work. Yet, when he saw a meeting scheduled between the ambassador and political and economic leaders of Great Britain, the United States, the European Union, and others, his heart sank. He believed he had a great deal to contribute. . .after all he not only had a law degree, but also a Ph.D. in Economics from the University of Chicago...but no one was interested in his views. Insults, although unintended, were frequent. The ambassador often complained about the coffee and asked that a different make be purchased. Or, he complained when he believed the paper in the conference rooms wasn't 'crisp' enough. The humiliating nature of the requests infuriated him. . .and he could do nothing to change this behavior. But he could alter his own behavior and he did.

By the assignment to the administrative track, he felt his life's work with the Foreign Service had been betrayed. Certainly he wasn't grateful and his loyalty to his job began to crumble. He had been handicapped with that shameful report about his behavior in Pakistan, and the only way to remedy the evil was to become totally self-absorbed. It was clear there never would be any more hands to boost him in the Foreign Service. He would catch himself and continue. He would not consider the report a fatal closed door to life. He would not be like a plant crushed by clumsy feet. No, there were other ways to survive. Soon, he would be able to leave government service with a rich retirement and much, much more from his affiliation with the man to whom he had sold government secrets: Duane Farris.

Disloyalty is never planned. It depends upon chance and emotion. And when both those intersect, the result is preordained. It all started exactly three years ago when he met Farris at the first session of the monthly briefing of the American legal fraternity in London that was chaired by the new ambassador, Roger Davidson. He had been invited by the ambassador, as he was new to the embassy and the ambassador wanted him to make sure the administrative arrangements were in top form, "You also being a lawyer, come and meet some of those that attend these sessions. Will give you an idea on why it's important to have the refreshments not served in paper cups." He swallowed mightily at that comment. At the reception that normally followed such meetings, as he stood by the refreshment table, watching the two servers to make sure that everything was proceeding smoothly, he and Farris struck up a conversation. Farris asked about his background, and then ended with the comment, "When you're ready to leave the government, please give me a call. We're always looking for good people." The comment came as a surprise. He initially thought it was just social conversation, so he waited a couple of weeks before he called. Farris was gracious at their initial meeting and Coborn's job frustration became apparent at that session. Farris listened intently and his eyes expressed to Coborn an understanding of what he was saying.

"Perhaps I have been too open about my background, but I thought you should know that I am willing to leave government service if something interesting came along."

"Of course. Let's see what develops here in the London office in the next several months. Why don't we meet—let's say, next weekend. Why not come to my house Friday after work for some cocktails? We can continue talking then."

After that meeting at Farris' home, they began to have weekly lunches for several months. Finally, at dinner at Farris' home, Farris said he might have something of interest for Coborn. It wasn't so much that Farris was successful in cultivating Coborn as that Coborn happened to already have been motivated to become disloyal. And, when Farris quietly asked, "Perhaps you could help on some private matters, getting some advance information from time to time that I may need, and earn compensation accordingly. Can you do that? All I would need is information that may help me in my clients' representation."

"What kind of extracurricular work do you want me to do, and what is the compensation?" he asked. There is a line. Jefferson Coborn knew that when he asked that question, he stepped over, knowing that, in the final analysis, loyalty to oneself is more important that loyalty to one's country. Acknowledging this, and, of course, the money he would be making, made matters easier, giving him a kind of perpetual mental enchantment. All he had to do, from time to time, was to alert Farris of any matters, Farris had said that "involved arms dealing, arms transactions; those kinds of things. I certainly would not want anything that confidential…just a bit of a head's up on what is going on. You understand that we represent many clients who are in legitimate businesses, but sometimes, they may be the target...well...you understand what I am saying."

"Yes. Completely," Coborn replied. He knew this would be simple for him to accomplish, and he also knew that Farris wasn't limiting the request to inane information, but also to secret data. Other than the CIA communications room, he had access to the secure communication rooms in the embassy and, of course, he saw all the messages to the ambassador. Being an administrator had its advantages, especially when one is able to sell useful information. The posting now became meaningful to Coborn. Despite the restrictions imposed on him regarding the CIA security messages, he was able to discern bits and pieces of a project dubbed 'Crescent Eagle,' which he passed on to Farris. The project had to do with stopping the flow of arms to specified countries. Beyond that, he was never able to penetrate who was doing the stopping. Nevertheless, he passed the information on to Farris.

"Another one, mate?"

"No. No thanks. How much do I owe?"

"Ten pounds, thirty"

Jefferson Coborn put down a ten- and a five-pound note, slipped off the stool and headed toward Soho. Once outside, he reached into his pocket for his cell phone, punching in the number for Farris.'

"Yes."

"Duane. I'm sorry to bother you at this hour, but I thought I had better call you. There is something of which you should be aware."

"What is it, Jefferson?" Farris asked kindly, tolerantly.

"Well, the young man coming into your home last Saturday also saw me at the embassy the other day. He was leaving the ambassador's monthly legal briefing as I was coming down the fifth floor corridor. At that time, he looked at me, and of course, again when he saw me leave your home. Do you think it's something that about which he will be concerned? Am I overly worried? I certainly don't want to be exposed," he said anxiously.

"My young associate? Keiran Hogan? No, I don't think Keiran would be remotely interested in you or why you were leaving my home. Frankly, even if he did, it's none of his business. He has more important things to worry about at this point. No, you don't have to be upset about his seeing you."

"Okay. But, Duane, he did see me when I was going down the corridor to get the ambassador because of the explosion at Mayfair. As usual, we had some crank calls to the embassy threatening to blow the place up, so I was going up to get Roger to tell him about the calls, and to clear the building as quickly as possible. But I wanted his permission first, obviously."

"Well. . .allright. I just don't see this as a major concern. Really. I just don't see the alarm. No one knows of our affiliation and I doubt if Hogan would see your appearances at the embassy and at my home as some nefarious happening. Besides, you could have been coming to my home on embassy business. I am a friend of Roger's and perhaps it was a personal message from him. No, I wouldn't worry about this at all, you're simply getting too anxious, Jefferson. You must learn to relax."

"Yes, you're right. What you're saying makes better sense. Besides, if this Hogan were interested, wouldn't he ask you? Wouldn't he?"

"I would hope so. He works for me, and he will tow the line or be out. Anything else?" Farris said sternly.

" No. I'll see you upon my return. I'll have another delivery for you."

"Good. Call me any time, and please take it easy. I appreciate all you've done. Certainly I do and you know that. Oh. . .one other matter. . .any more news on the special project of which you alerted me?"

"No, sir. Not much more. Just the name and the target countries. Nothing further. I'll keep trying though."

"Of course you will. Well, good night, Jefferson." Farris rang off.

Coborn placed his cell phone back into his pocket, instinctively straightened his tie, and decided to walk the several blocks to Soho. How life changes. When he was young, he played life in his own particular way. He had originality, fierceness of purpose, belief in himself, and perhaps a touch of arrogance, even a skin that wasn't easily rubbed raw. Now look at me, he pondered, as he lowered his head, looking at the sidewalk, walking at a slow pace, frightened that he was now on the verge of being discovered. When he started his association with Farris, he was, he realized now, too flamboyant in his enthusiasm. His Foreign Service career in his mind over, he didn't care about anything but amassing money. He began to worship money—that would the legacy of his success—not promotion to an ambassadorship, probably to some third-rate country, he thought. He believed that meeting Farris wasn't only lucky but also clever. Now he understood that both are questions of degree.

It was bad luck and timing in Pakistan that ruined everything for me—and now this again—bad luck and timing. Now, though he would control the outcome. That's for sure.

He shook his head a bit trying to clear his mind of his worries and replacing those thoughts with those of Alleana. Maybe he would buy some flowers along the way for Alleana. Just thinking about her, his mood was now getting better as he begin to anticipate the pleasure of an evening with her. The streets were now crowded with evening rush hour pedestrians as he made his way toward Soho. No matter how hard he tried to cleanse his mind of his worries and to think of Alleana, he continued to have a nagging doubt about Farris' comments. Experience dictates certain instincts and his instinct was that Farris' interpretation of Hogan and the chance meetings between he and Hogan was simply not the case.

Nine

As he peered from his seat, Keiran spotted the man who HenHen had said would be his host. It would have been impossible not to notice him. Standing among the sparse crowd at St. Martin Airport, Guernsey Island, meeting the early morning British Air Express flight from London was a stocky, balding man, the lower part of his face covered with a shaggy gray beard. He was dressed in an absurdly tight, fitted, double-breasted, dark blue suit, which showed off his paunch well, his lavender tie providing a sharp contrast against an otherwise plain white shirt. HenHen had told Keiran to look for an immaculately dressed man, about fifty, with a trim, gray beard.

As usual, Keiran thought, shaking his head, a smile crossing his lips, in her constant state of anxiety, HenHen had the matter only half right. The man appeared somewhat clownish and his beard desperately needed a trim.

The plane was full. As he was seated in the middle of the cabin, it took him a few minutes to leave and descend the ramp to the tarmac and walk to the arrivals gate. The sky was a brilliant blue, the air crisp. Despite such an immaculate day, he knew he would rather be with Jennifer in London. The moments with her yesterday were the happiest moments he had had for a long time. It was remarkable. He no longer had that aching, awful feeling of loneliness. Clutching his briefcase in his right hand, his black overnight canvas bag hung over his left shoulder, his tall figure straightened as he sauntered over to the man who was now calling his name rather loudly.

"Keiran Hogan. . .Keiran Hogan?" he said anxiously, breathing hard and rapidly, smiling, as he stared at Keiran, his brown eyes wide with anticipation.

Keiran smiled as he held out his hand, "Yes. I'm Keiran Hogan. You must be Mr. Leyden," he said cordially.

"Right. David Leyden, Royal Trust Services," Leyden replied, the worried look now vanishing from his face, relieved that he had found Keiran. "I was told, by Duane's secretary HenHen, to be on the lookout for a tall young man with a distinct Irish look, thick black hair, blue eyes, and keen as a razor." Leyden, much shorter than Keiran, offered a stocky hand to Keiran and shook it energetically, continuing to smile. "And her description was perfect."

"Yeah. 'Keen as razor.' Hmm. . .What would we do without HenHen? I'll have to thank her for such a good reference," Keiran replied, shaking his head in mock surprise. "Anyway, sir, nice to meet you. I hope that you haven't been waiting too long for me."

"No, as a matter of fact, I arrived just a few minutes ago."

"I suppose she also told you to remind me to call her upon my arrival," Keiran replied, tossing his head and laughing quietly.

He could now see Leyden's face. It was curiously unwrinkled and firm, solid, a big jaw, rather like the face had been kept in ice. Keiran noticed immediately that his eyes, though steady, appeared disillusioned and hard. He seemed to be looking at Keiran with deliberation and care, probably wondering how Keiran would behave, and whether he would live up to whatever other description given him by Farris and HenHen or whether their characterization was overblown.

"You're right about HenHen's admonition. She did ask me to remind you. I've now reminded you to call your office." They both chuckled. Leyden motioned Keiran to follow him down the cluttered, narrow exit corridor, one side had a news and gift shop, a small restaurant, the other was a wall of floor-to-ceiling glass that overlooked the airport entrance and parking lot.

"Nice flight this early morning hour?" Leyden inquired.

"Great actually, Mr. Leyden, smooth and quick. Only a little more than an hour."

"Please call me Dave. Do you have a nickname or do you prefer Keiran?"

"Keiran will do."

"Interesting name, Keiran. You'll have to tell me its origins."

"Not much to tell, Dave. It's my mother's father's first name, and my mom and dad liked it, so that's all there really is to the story," he said with a shrug.

"Is there a special meaning to the name?"

"Perhaps. I've never done any research on it. My mom never told me it had any other meaning than that it was her father's name."

"Well, I guess that's the most important thing—carrying on your grandfather's name. Same with me. My first name is my father's name and before him his father's name. Even my son is named David Leyden, the fourth. Want to keep the line going." He laughed slightly, then continued, "Did you see much of the island as you approached?"

"Yeah. Actually, I could see the island coastline, the edge of sea. It is almost as if they melted together in a blue haze. Really beautiful. I couldn't take my eyes off the scene, Dave. I was thinking how lucky people are to live here, Mr. Farris is fond of Guernsey and suggested that I consider staying an extra day. I just may take him up on that offer."

"Yes, the folks who live here are lucky. A bit of paradise really… especially on a day as nice as it's today. On a cloudy, somber day, I may be encouraged to say something else, but today, with the clear sky and warm sun, yes…it's today a paradise. Certainly, though, you must remain and enjoy our hospitality. If you like sailing and you like seafood, well, you'll be home. And, when it's sunny, there's a certain sparkle in the air that makes me, I confess to you, want to take off and go sailing, my primary vice. Frankly, I like the feel of the wind and to be freed from the general madness of life. Once you succumb to sailing, no other sport compares for peace, beauty, and grace. There is a great deal of joy in sailing. I really believe that. By the bye, are you a sailor?"

"Well, not exactly. I've gone sailing from time to time, but I'm not a sailor as such. I can understand, though, if one lived here, that's the first thing to learn—how to sail. The second thing would be to get a good boat."

"If you stay a day or two longer, and the weather holds up, I hope I can interest you in coming aboard my little vessel. She has a simple name—'Play Fair'—sort of what we do, eh?" He laughed, his eyes twinkling at his own joke.

"It's a graphic name, Dave. Do you get any grief from your friends about it?" Keiran commented.

"As a matter of fact, yes. Especially from my wife. She doesn't like the name at all. Thinks I should have something more glamorous, like naming the boat after her—'Charmaine.' I told her I may do that when I retire. Right now, I like the name 'Play Fair.'"

"How long have you had 'Play Fair'?"

I got it a few years back, perhaps four, from an estate. A client decided to abandon her. . .as well as his life."

"His life. . .abandon his life?" Keiran looked askance at Leyden.

"He just vanished. Never heard from him again. His wife and three children had always been handsomely taken care of, and nothing changed after his disappearance, you know trusts and so forth—but poof—he just faded away never to be heard from again. She didn't want the boat, so she asked me to take it off her hands. She didn't want anything for it. Perhaps bad memories. . .so I took it as my final payment for services to her vanished husband."

"Strange story, David. Is she still trying to locate her husband?"

"For a while she did, private investigators, police and so forth. Nothing ever came from those searches. He's gone, period. Yeah. It's strange. I agree with that comment. Is this all your luggage?" Leyden interrupted the conversation as he looked at Keiran's hands, one holding a small briefcase, and the other the overnight black canvas bag.

"Yeah. For the day or two I'll be here, I just brought a change of clothes. That's it."

"So you think you'll stay an extra day?"

"I want to make some calls later and then I'll let you know. But, sure, I think I may stay another day. May even take you up on the sailing invitation."

"Good," Leyden said warmly. "Let's hope the weather holds together. Now then, I suggest that our first order of business be to take you to the hotel. You register, freshen up a bit and then head to my office. These early morning flights from London are a bear—you left at seven, probably had to get up around five or so, anyhow, do you want more time at the hotel?"

"No, I'm fine. Mr. Farris will want us to get started on the registration process, so…no, I don't need any more time at the hotel."

"You must be delighted to leave London for a few days respite, what with the explosion in Mayfair and all the police activity closing streets and so forth. One never knows when these terrorists will hit next. I don't believe for one moment that it was caused by a gas explosion, do you, Keiran?" Leyden expressed himself rather matter-of-factly as they hurried across the walkway to the parking lot.

"I just don't know really, Dave," Keiran responded. "You do feel for all those people who were killed, of course, and their families. A horrible tragedy."

"The principal person killed at the restaurant, Mile Draculic is, or better was, actually a customer of Zoran Hemmrich—our mutual client. Everyone knew he was an active supporter of the Serbian cause. So, well…. Who knows…. Someone must have been out for him. But to kill him and all those people…horrid case, I would have to say…appalling."

"This Draculic—a customer of Hemmrich?" Keiran commented, raising his eyebrows in surprise.

"Yeah, for several years now. He had sold Draculic tons of cement and loads of fertilizer, among other commodities. I've actually met him a few times. Quiet. He had a certain ruthless look though, not that should mean anything, I suppose. We all have our own looks. Made tons of dough, though, in the commodities trade."

"What did he do with all the cement and fertilizer?"

"Probably resold it. We never did ask. At least I never did. It wasn't my purview to ask. Certain matters are better kept than said. Zoran was the ultimate apostle of that creed, at least to me. I just made sure the corporations Farris had set up were the vehicles for the sale, the bank accounts in order and so forth. I suppose that Zoran is not happy now—a good customer has been lost."

"Won't Mr. Draculic's company continue as a customer of Mr. Hemmrich?"

"Probably, but then one never knows. Millions of pounds of business for several years with Draculic. Lately though, I understand that he and Zoran have been at odds over several large payments for commodities Draculic claims were faulty. Can't believe that he is dead. He traveled with bodyguards, lived an open life, didn't seem to be in contact with the wrong people. Everyone knew of his sympathies for the Serbs. Well, I suppose that we'll get an answer soon from the police. Maybe the leaking gas makes sense."

"Maybe so. But, if someone wanted to take out Draculic, why would they kill so many innocents with him? Whoever did this is a butcher—pure and simple." Keiran spoke quietly, looking straight ahead.

"I have no doubt you're correct, Keiran. All those deaths. Bloody awful," Leyden commented nervously.

They both walked in silence to the row of the parking lot where Leyden's black Jaguar was parked.

"Well, here we are." Leyden pressed a button on his key ring, electronically releasing the lock on the car doors. "Technology makes life so much easier. My second vice…cars. I just bought this last year. Just love it. Look at its elegance. Purrs as smoothly as…well…a jaguar." He laughed again, blinking his eyes and clearing his throat.

"Beauty of a machine, Dave," Keiran said, as he went over to the passenger side, placing his bags in the back seat, and sliding into the front.

"And you, what kind of wheels do you have?" Leyden asked, as he slipped behind the wheel, placing the key in the ignition with some flourish.

"Do I have a car? No, not yet. That's another thing I have to do apart, from getting an apartment. Driving around London doesn't make sense. You can take the underground almost anywhere. Yet, I'll need one to go into the country and generally see more than just London. So, I expect I'll get one soon," Keiran responded.

"I recommend, for someone your age, that you consider a BMW 321i. Bought one for my son. He works in Edinburgh—at a bank, naturally."

"BMWs. Pretty solid cars. Something to think about," Keiran commented.

Leyden slowly left the terminal lot, picking up speed as he swung out of the airport access road and onto the two-lane road leading toward St. Peter Port, the main town on Guernsey. The road ran into small loops and zigzags, the channel water appearing from time to time, glittering in the morning sun. They sped along, passing open green fields, then groups of houses that were dimly gray and white, many covered with ivy and blossoms of varied flowers that added a brilliant touch of color. Keiran's face turned this way and that, absorbing the newness a first visit always brings.

"The hotel that we booked you in—Old Government House Hotel—is on a hill with a sweeping view of St. Peter Port. On a clear day like today you can see, from your hotel, our neighboring islands: Alderney, Herm, Sark, and, of course, Jersey. I asked that you have a room with a view overlooking the harbor. The place was once the official colonial residence of the Island Governor. Now, it's a five star hotel. Can't go wrong staying here. A great heated swimming pool, bar, and restaurant. I hope you'll be comfortable. HenHen said to make sure you're comfortable and that you have access to a swimming pool. She said you're a swimmer of some fame."

"Dear HenHen. Knows everything or wants to make you think she knows everything. Yeah. I like to swim. Thanks for getting me a place with a pool." Keiran continued to look out at the passing scenery. "You have a beautiful place. Everything is so clean and green, and pretty peaceful. How long have you lived here?"

"I was born in Scotland, but we moved here when I was about ten or eleven. My father was a banker —at the Royal Bank of Scotland's branch here. We're actually Scottish, my father was born in Scotland, near Edinburgh. He loved to fish and when he was growing up, we went to every stream and lake within a day's drive. I'll tell you Keiran, those are days that I miss. He wasn't only a great fisherman, but also a good friend to me. I don't know if I can say that about my children and myself. I've been so damn busy all the time. I suppose my priorities aren't in order. And you, what is your background?" Leyden inquired.

"I was born in a suburb of Boston—Quincy, Massachusetts. Went on to school at Princeton and Columbia Law. Joined the firm in New York, but was transferred to Washington and now to London."

"London, Keiran, is the most civilized place in the world, I believe. Have you ever heard this little ditty:

Oh! London is a fine town
A very famous city
Where all the streets are paved with gold
And all the maidens pretty.

"It was written a long time ago, by George Coleman. He was a politician and poet of sorts. But the stanza sure is vivid. Wouldn't you agree?"

"Well said. There's so much to do and see in London. It's a great place, and right now, I couldn't be happier with the relocation from Washington."

"And you've been in the London office for how long?"

"This is the beginning of my ninth week."

"You haven't found the 'pretty maidens'? I can't believe it! Single, and in London. Farris has been working you too hard," Leyden said, a slight chuckle in his voice.

"Well…recently better…I've met my 'pretty maiden.' I've got to hang on to her now. Make sure she doesn't get away."

"Spoken like a smitten man." Leyden smiled.

"A bit, yeah. Well, maybe more than a bit."

"Good! Why not? Listen, Keiran, I have a strong feeling that Farris must think very highly of you to send you here. Sure, the registration of new corporate documents isn't an intellectual challenge, but it's a sign of the faith that he must have in you to trust you with Zoran's new company."

"That is a kind description, Dave, and I appreciate Mr. Farris' confidence in me. How did you meet Mr. Farris?" Keiran inquired quietly.

"I met him several years ago," Leyden replied, "like everything else in this business, through innumerable connections. There is this group of lawyers in London connected to people like me on this island, on our sister island of Jersey, and on other tax haven jurisdictions. The lawyers have clients who want to hide their money—you know, to lessen the tax burden, among other reasons. A harsh person would criticize this as basically stealing from the system that has been instrumental in their making money. What we do here isn't done with mirrors though. Basically, the island government passed laws to help the process along, and no one seems to mind. The rich, as well as the odious, who may also be rich, have enough money that they can buy the special privileges the island offers in the way of its tax and secrecy law. Sort of a silent acceptance by the authorities. Sufficient taxes flow in England so that Her Majesty's government is not too concerned if the rich and powerful hide some of their money here. Keeps me and others like me employed." Leyden again laughed loudly.

"Besides, Keiran, you should understand that half the people we deal with are in the game themselves. The other half don't know or don't want to know. Why do you think these tax haven islands exist? Because the powers allow them to exist. So we play the game now, don't we?" Leyden said soberly.

"Dave, I don't even know what the game is yet," Keiran replied gamely. "This Island must get some tax revenue from these transactions. How else would it survive?" Keiran remarked.

"Of course it does—registration fees and the like, and some modest tax on other transactions. But nothing like this would occur if the funds were held in accounts in London. There is always an aversion to paying taxes. . .especially among the rich. Taxes are to be paid by everyone but them."

"I suppose that you have to be predisposed to think that way. If it's all done properly and in accord with the island rules, I don't see how it can be legally impermissible, although it may be morally questionable," Keiran suggested.

"You're right of course. In all honesty, Keiran, you know, I've found practicing law to be a painful business. You're either practical in the business or you face extinction. Isn't that the case? I was a lawyer for a few years, but I'm happy that I gave up the practice a long time ago. My business is the investment advice and management, trust and offshore company formation, administration and accounting services—sort of a package deal for our clients, to whom we are very loyal. This whole process would come crashing down if betrayal of clients becomes the norm. Clients expect…no, they demand trust and loyalty. Betrayal can never be part and parcel of professional life." Leyden's eyes drifted from the highway to look at Keiran, who kept staring ahead.

"Betrayal and loyalty to clients. Two strong adjectives, Dave. Of course, unless the client is asking you to do something impermissible, you have to be loyal. What's the point otherwise? If a client is screwy enough to ask you to do something you legally can't do, then you don't represent him. I know some can avoid that decision by making adjustments in their thinking, but I couldn't get involved with such a client. Why would anyone want the headache anyway?"

"The puzzle of motivation. I've seen so much in my life that I can afford to be a cynic." Leyden laughed at his own statement. "Well now, Farris must believe you're pretty ambitious and the kind of flexible attorney with whom he feels comfortable—you know, someone young who wants to acquire wealth, distinction and power."

"Yeah, who doesn't want to acquire wealth, some distinction, independence, and maybe even power? But at what price, Dave? What price does one have to pay for those achievements? I'll tell you simply, though, that I never want to be part of a puppet show to achieve them."

"Simply put, Keiran, we are servants to our clients. Sure, we have to try mightily to be like the gods of Olympus—detached from our clients, above morality and as indifferent as fate. In truth, we can't achieve that loftiness because we aren't Gods, but humans with all the emotion that drives us."

Keiran remained silent, pondering what he had just heard from Leyden. Was he being genuine or just trying to test me out? Keiran wondered.

"You mentioned the word independence," Leyden continued, "but even being independent takes money. Regardless, what you and I do perhaps can be equated with your puppeteer. Our client holds all the strings. We simply ratify his decisions. The client wants us to do what he tells us to do. He's the big fellow who pays us…isn't he?" Leyden said earnestly, the tone of his voice indicating he wanted acceptance from Keiran for his statement.

"Certainly clients pay us for the services we agree to provide," Keiran abruptly said. "Regardless, I hope that what we're doing here, Dave, is not all part of a farce." Keiran was direct.

"Good attitude. Very good. My, for our first meeting, we have had such a heavy conversation, and so early in the morning. What we should be doing is drinking at one of our many pubs on the island to continue this discourse."

"Agreed, but it's a bit early for drinking."

"And you're Irish? I can't believe what I am hearing!" They both laughed.

"Well, here we are at your hotel, the Old Government House."

Leyden drove up the circular drive, bringing his car to a stop directly in front of the entrance of the large Georgian style hotel, its white facade sparkling in the morning sun. A vivid, carefully sown grass lay like a carpet spread between the driveway and the front entrance, it border filled with multicolored pansies.

"We'll be only a few minutes," Leyden advised the doorman. "Leave it in the driveway, if you can. Take good care. I just had it washed." He laughed.

"Don't concern yourself, sir. I'll do just that," the doorman responded as he closed the door behind Leyden.

They walked up the few steps into the hotel lobby, the far end of which opened out into a patio bedecked with flowers of various kinds and hues, a large swimming pool beyond it.

"Keiran, I'll wait for you in the coffee shop. Take your time getting settled. Make that call to HenHen. Otherwise, she'll be calling my office non-stop wanting to know if you are here. By the bye, I hope you like your room. Remember you're supposed to have a room with view."

"Okay. I won't be long. See you in the coffee shop." Keiran headed toward the reception desk to register, puzzling over the conversation with Leyden. He wasn't particularly happy, as he already missed Jennifer. Maybe that was the cause of his jumbled mind. It's hard to really sort anything out when one is in love.

Leyden hurried to the coffee shop adjacent to the reception area. He took a table by the window overlooking the pool, opened his briefcase and took out his cell phone, looking toward the shop's entrance before pressing in a number.

"Yes."

"Duane. He's here. Seems to be okay. Strong opinions."

"Oh? Well, we'll change those in due course. Not to worry about that. Have you taken care of his room accordingly?"

"Yes, I have."

"Good. Anything else?"

"No."

The conversation concluded. Leyden replaced his phone to his case, looked up and motioned to the waitress to come over. It was time for his morning coffee and roll…a sweet one at that. He looked over at the unoccupied pool, and across to the channel and thought to himself. This is a day I should be out on my boat. To be free of all these lies. All these damn lies.

Ten

Leyden delivered on his word. The third floor room, sparkling from the glittering sunlight and elegantly furnished with antiques did have a magnificent view of the channel from its small balcony. The walls were covered with a fine off-white wallpaper depicting small gray sea shells of varying kinds in repetitively patterned, parallel rows; the queen size bed's comforter and pillow sheaths were of a matching pattern—a place where one would not mind staying for a while and perhaps do nothing. He tossed his bags onto the bed and walked out the open glass doors onto the dark green-tiled balcony. On this sunny day, the other Channel Islands were clearly visible. The sun glistening on the water, the breeze mild, but steady, he gazed at several sailing yachts on the horizon heading toward one of the other islands, or perhaps even to Normandy on the coast of France. Overhead, gulls flew in their own special and graceful way. It wasn't a lifeless day. Rather than enjoy the scene to its fullest, he had to contend with the information that his client, Zoran Hemmrich, may not be all that 'clean,' that he was involved with the man, Draculic, whose body was in bits and pieces all over Eads Street in Mayfair, and that his law firm's London office partner-in-charge was probably corrupt. No, the only thing that would encourage him on this not particularly cheerful day would be to be with Jennifer. In these circumstances, the time he spent with her yesterday afternoon seemed so distant.

He had taken her on a boat ride on the Serpentine, in Hyde Park.

"You know, Keiran, I've never rowed on this lake before…and I've always wanted to. It's peaceful…the water so smooth…it's not at all like sailing where you bop up and down like a cork. You handle the boat like an expert. Are you enjoying yourself?" He felt her look at him intently, watching his every move, his hands gripping the heavy wood oars that barely made a sound as they dipped into the water.

"Yeah, rowing on a calm lake doesn't compare with tossing along the waves on a sail boat, but then, I've been sailing only a handful of times so far. I think I'd enjoy it actually, if I had the time and resources to put into it," he said, his voice soft and reassuring. Feeling for her deeply, he could not understand how she was attracted to Medill, a man who seemed to Keiran to have a vein of snobbery. Being peevish at this stage of the relationship, however, wasn't a particularly bright thing to do, so he swallowed hard, lowered his head for a moment, then pulled the oars harder, moving the boat faster as he navigated between the others plying the lake.

"Keiran, you didn't answer my question. Are you enjoying yourself?"

A broad smile crossed his face as he look directly at her, "Of course, I am, but soon, I have to take you back to your job, and I'd enjoy myself more if we could spend some time together this evening.. . .I mean for dinner, of course." She laughed as she stared at him.

"For dinner, of course", she repeated his words. "I'd like that, Keiran. Shall we plan on it when you return from Guernsey?"

"Sure, Jennifer." He gently responded, his eyes continued to be riveted on her. "I'll call you from Guernsey. I should be back on Tuesday, maybe I can even get back on Monday night. I'll let you know."

"I'll wait on your call, Keiran. You won't forget will you?

"No, I certainly won't forget. I promise you. How soon, though, Jennifer, do you have to be back to the studio?"

"Oh. About 4:00, 4:30 or so." She looked at her watch, then said, "We have a little more time"

"What if you played hooky?" Keiran asked mischievously.

"They would probably fire me and I'd be known for not being reliable so no other studio would hire me." She laughed. "I have to admit it's hard to do two shows on a Sunday, but this time with you has been pretty relaxing, so I'm sure I'll be in top form tonight. Besides, this will be the last Sunday this season that I have to work. The regular reader will be back and I'll have all my Sundays free, hopefully for a very long time." She reached over and touched his arm, her eyes looked lightly and a little wistfully toward Keiran.

"Maybe you can cancel your after-program appointment. How about it?" He smiled broadly. "What do you say about that suggestion?" he said softly, but provocatively, again his eyes not leaving hers.

"You don't give up, do you Keiran? You're making all sorts of suggestions that would get me into trouble. I'm now convinced that you don't like me, Keiran." She laughed, her smile wide and comforting. "You know I can't do that. Please. And, no, your question wasn't foolish, though. Just a bit over-eager. Besides, I think you're just teasing me."

"Well.... Perhaps.... Well, really no, come to think of it. I am not teasing you. I mean...what can I say? If you're having a good time with me now, why can't we continue it later?"

"Keiran, you're pushing this a bit too fast—and I don't mean the boat." She laughed again.

"I just thought that maybe...I'm sorry that I asked. It's just that.... No, forget that I asked. I understand. I was getting ahead of myself, I suppose."

"You do move fast, Keiran Hogan. A man of conviction, no doubt. I saw that the other evening at the Graysons' home."

"A good trait?" Keiran asked.

"Yeah. As a matter of fact, a very good trait."

"See, I've already passed your 'conviction trait' test, any other tests you have in mind?" Keiran smiled, winking at her.

She reached over again and squeezed his arm. "Take me back, Keiran. I'm also time sensitive."

Keiran didn't reply, but made a broad loop so that their boat faced the direction of the pier, slowly heading toward it. This time Keiran's strong sense of reserve had broken loose. He could not make any elaborate plans to hide his affection. This was a time that being too cautious or demonstrating self-restraint would not work. By asking the question, he told her of his true feelings and there was no turning back on expressing his emotion.

"You'll come back to the studio with me won't you?"

"I wouldn't think of anything else. I'll just mosey back to the club after I drop you off at the studio." Keiran's voice was muted.

"We've had a good day and I don't want it to end either. I'll think of you on your trip to Guernsey. That is another place I want to visit someday. Some folks from the studio spend their holidays there and they say it's a charming place. You'll have to tell me all about your trip when you get back"

"You don't think you can cancel your evening with your friend?" Keiran asked again, knowing he was pushing a question that had been answered already.

"Keiran Hogan. You're a most stubborn man. I've said that I can't. You surely have to accept my answer."

"Well, I just don't want to be the extra man in your life." Keiran said, his voice not disturbed in tone.

"Who says that you are? For a lawyer, you jump to conclusions too hastily. Now no more asking about this evening. I hope you'll watch the news program, though."

He looked at her quizzically, then chuckled, lowering and shaking his head. "I think that I'm continuing to handle this badly," Keiran said, grinning broadly.

Keiran brought the boat to the rental dock, secured the oars, throwing a line to a dockhand who held the boat steady as Jennifer got out first and he followed. He gently took her hand, holding it tightly. They walked in silence from the dock along the several food and beverage kiosks to the cabstand.

"Want something to drink, Jennifer?" She turned, and before she could answer, instinctively he leaned over, held her for a moment, and kissed her intensely. She didn't resist.

"I'm sorry," Keiran softly said as he let her go, "I should not be displaying so much affection in public—and in England, no less."

"Come here, Keiran." She took her hands to his face, fixed her eyes for several moments, then kissed him, holding onto to him.

"I'm for more," Keiran smiled.

"You've had enough for today."

"No, I haven't."

He held her hand tightly as they walked quietly to the cabstand, where a lone cab stood. Keiran opened the door, letting Jennifer in first, getting in behind her, still holding her hand.

"Please…the ITN studios," he said softly. She sat close to him, his hand holding her closely during the twenty minute cab ride to the studios, neither one speaking, their hands twisting and turning in each other, trying in some unstated manner to feel each other more intimately, yet holding back for reasons about which they remained mute. When the cab arrived at the studios, Keiran asked the driver to wait for him as he exited the cab first, Jennifer following, their hands still touching one another. He slowly walked her to the building entrance.

"I think I'd better say goodbye to you here or your receptionist will spread the rumor that I am your new friend…which, on second thought, would not be a bad idea. Yeah! Let's go in together." He made a motion of taking her through the revolving glass doors, and was stopped short by her hand grasping his and not letting go. "I'd be upset if you didn't take me in. Manners, you know."

She laughed as she went forward through the doors followed by Keiran. At the reception desk, Nancy, on the phone, appeared harassed.

"Thanks a great deal, Keiran, for a lovely afternoon. You know I enjoyed the whole time with you." She leaned over and gave him a kiss on both cheeks—not the passionate one given to him at the boat dock, but still a kiss. He held her hand tightly again.

"Now that was a real kiss." He smiled broadly, adding, "I'll call you from Guernsey. Have a good program. I'll be watching."

"I hope so," she responded as she went toward the elevator, where a colleague was holding the door open, waiting for her. She waved at him as the doors closed.

His slumbering virility seemed to stir. He wanted so badly to be alone with her, to feel and be part of her, to abandon himself to this new influence that had so suddenly and unexpectedly entered his life.

Keiran went back into his room, leaving the balcony doors wide open, the cool air a welcome relief from the humidity of London. He picked up the desk phone and dialed Jennifer's number in London. At this hour, he believed she would be at home, and wanted to hear her voice. A distressed look crossed his face as he momentarily thought that if she were not there, she would have passed the evening with Medill. The phone rang and rang; finally her voice came on the recording.

"This is 071-980-9987. Please leave a message at the tone, and I'll get back to you as soon as possible."

"Jennifer, this is Keiran. I'm at the Old Government House Hotel in Guernsey; the number here is 0481-24921, Room 301. It's about 9:30 in the morning and I'll be gone most of the day, but I'll try reaching you later. I'll be back tomorrow. Don't forget we'll see each other for dinner. Take care. I'll call you tonight in any event. I miss you very much." After he hung up, he felt uncomfortable wondering for an instant if he should have said the last few words. She had a fiancé, and he had to accept that. Take it easy, he told himself. He wanted the situation with her to be as smooth as silk, but he knew better. It was all so different from what he had expected it to be. He didn't think that he would be so passionate toward a woman, and so soon. Yet, Jennifer was unique in his eyes. She was at once playful and considerate. He now had the glow of love in his eyes—not the love that comes from sympathy, common interests, or intellectual community, but love, pure and simple. One thing though—he had ceased feeling on edge.

Rather than call HenHen, he decided to send a fax to the office. He just didn't want to talk to her or hear her washy voice. He sat down at the writing desk, drew out a fax form from the blue leather stationary folder neatly placed in the desk's center, and wrote briskly: 'HenHen. Arrived in Guernsey. At Old Government House. Room 301. Regards, Keiran Hogan.' He folded the completed fax form, put it in his side jacket pocket, took his briefcase, closing the door behind him. He walked slowly down the gray-carpeted corridor and towards the elevator that would take him three floors down to the lobby floor.

As the elevator door opened, he was startled to see Bob Grayson exit.

"Mr. Gra...."

Before he could finish his sentence, Grayson, momentarily surprised himself, interrupted robustly and with a smile, "Keiran Hogan. Now what are doing on this island?" Holding out his hand, Keiran grasped Grayson's.

"Hey! Mr. Grayson, what are you doing here?" Keiran exclaimed. A smile lighted up his face.

"Now, it's 'Mr. Grayson.' Who is 'Mr. Grayson'?" he joked as he turned his head to look behind, acting as if there was another in the corridor. "Please call me Bob. We did go through this name exercise at the embassy the other day, didn't we?"

Keiran noted that there was something in Grayson's eyes that puzzled him…something he could not define. The smile was on Grayson's face but not in his eyes.

"Okay. Bob, it's good to see you. What brings you here?"

"Are you implying that I cannot come to one of Her Majesty's dominions? Damn!" Grayson laughed loudly. "I should ask first—what are you doing on this tax haven island? Trying to hide one of Farris' clients' money from the tax authorities, I would suspect."

"Clearly, Bob, I must be missing something. All I'm doing today is registering a new corporation that Farris has set up for a client," Keiran said.

"Corporate registration. Good. That's the beginning of hiding income. Then, of course, there are trusts, and other vehicles to do the same thing, not to mention creating corporate fronts for the shipment of goods that aren't suppose to be shipped to places that aren't suppose to receive them. All of which I assume you'll learn in good time with an experienced teacher like Farris."

Keiran grimaced as he answered, "You're way ahead of me, Bob. Way ahead of me."

"I'm encouraging you to learn all you can while you're here. Farris, I am sure, sent you to this lovely island to absorb its legal culture. That's all I mean." Grayson grinned broadly, as he slowly mouthed the last few words.

"Yeah. Sure. Why not? The agent here, David Leyden, is to take me around to the registration offices and I guess I'll see the procedures in action, and then meet some of the people. Regular stuff. Can't be that difficult, I wouldn't imagine. By chance, do you know Mr. Leyden?"

"Sure, I've heard of him. Anyway, Keiran, I've got to run. Just don't find yourself caught like a fly in a spider's web."

"Now, what is that supposed to mean, Bob?"

Grayson shrugged. "Nothing really. Just a phrase that came to mind when you mentioned your agent's name. That's all."

"That's all? You wouldn't say it unless you were trying to tell me something via the riddle. I'm beginning to feel this is a part of learning puzzle."

"Not a bad comment, Keiran. Consider it a learning puzzle. Listen, I have to go. See you back in London. Leaving on the afternoon plane. By the way, how is Jennifer?"

"Great. I saw her yesterday."

"Good, so Saturday evening wasn't a total loss."

"Bob, hang on for a second. First, is Jennifer really that serious about Medill?"

"Well, didn't we go over this at dinner at my house? I just don't know. She keeps putting off the marriage, so I would suspect that she isn't so sure. Don't be so insecure, Keiran. If she went out with you on Sunday, she certainly wants to get to know you. She's a great girl…most sought after. You are one hell of a lucky fella. Did I answer your question satisfactorily, counselor?

"Yeah. I really feel good about her. I really do. Well, you know what I mean."

"Oh, to be young and single again! Those were the days, Keiran. Enjoy them while you can, or do I sound like an old, washed-up wispy man—which I hasten to say that I am not. I was just mouthing a truism, of sorts, of course."

Keiran laughed, replying, "Of course."

"Now what's the other item on your mind? You're full of all sorts of queries while we're standing in this corridor. Another woman? If so, good for you." They both laughed.

"No, no other woman. Well, I was going to call you in London about someone that I met at the club. Are you familiar with Sir Robert Runnard?"

"Sure. He's a retired barrister. In his day, he was the best around. Brilliant. He had the unusual gift of being both familiar and discreet. Took to drink though, and then just faded away until a few years ago, when he was called by the government to head a commission on illegal arms dealings and money laundering. The government needed a man of his high caliber for fear that any investigation, unless headed by someone like him, would be considered a whitewash. No one has seriously attacked him. Nobody of substance has ever accused him of being a back number. His humor, his charm, and his high sense of civic duty have rendered him sacrosanct to all. He is a man not to bother about trivialities…a class act. A very wise, eloquent man. I actually met him when I arrived in London a few years back and we had lunch from time to time. Then, as I said, he just disappeared. Is he at your club? You probably know that Farris and his clients were the subject of his investigation. Runnard wrote a report that was widely circulated, but nothing ever came of its recommendations. Why do you ask, Keiran?"

"Well, I met him at the club the other evening…actually, after I came from your party. He's a pretty interesting character. Told me I should read the report. Maybe it would help me to understand Farris."

"You should. I can dig out a copy in my office, if you need one. The classified version, of course, was never made public; only the sanitized version was released. Farris and his client slipped through the cracks—no action was ever taken, not because of the contents of the report, but for political reasons, I suspect. Because of the U. K. Official Secrets Act, the classified version cannot, as you may know, be released for at least 50 years, so we're left with the redacted version. Pretty devastating reading, though. Of course, Farris and his allies in the government spread gossip and joked about Runnard and his drinking habits. I never thought his drinking affected his brain though…but Farris called his abilities into question. As I remember, it wasn't a pleasant time for Runnard, who was only trying to do a credible job—which I think he did. Most of the editorial opinion supported him, so I think your Farris was using an age-old technique. When you're in trouble, attack the investigator. It sort of worked in his case, as nothing was done to him or his client. Of course, Keiran, many thought Runnard was called back by the government to write a whitewash report. You know, with his drinking and so forth, the government at the time thought they could control him. But just the opposite occurred. His report was devastatingly true and called for several people, including Farris and his client…ah...it's coming back now…a Zoran Hemmrich…to be prosecuted. Nothing was ever done, though. He wrote his memoirs, which were an instant best seller, but he refused to go on the book lecture circuit and just faded away to his place, I believe in Ireland, or maybe Scotland. I've forgotten. So you saw him. Good, Keiran. He is a great trial lawyer. Absolutely no doubt about that. Give him my regards. I'd like to visit with him, but I doubt he'll see me or anyone. How does he look?"

"Pretty Good, actually. What's he—about 70 or so?"

"Oh no, Keiran. He's a bit older than that. Probably 80—at least 80. If you have nothing to do someday, head for the library and look up some of his brilliant briefs or the news articles about him, even the several books he wrote on trial techniques."

"I had a great conversation with him. I told him I'd give him a ring when I returned. He seemed pretty lonely, actually. Bob. Is Farris described accurately in Runnard's report? Farris is still an honorable member of the bar and the firm—how could he be both if he is doing something wrong?"

"Farris isn't stupid. I'm sure you have found that out by now. Lawyers who are stupid are those that get into difficulty. So he's managed to, how do I put it delicately, stay free. Someone on your management committee must like him, or probably the profits he generates, to go along with his methods, wouldn't you say? Life is never that simple, Keiran. You're lucky to have met Runnard. Follow through with the invitation and see what happens. He's the greatest of the great in the English legal fraternity. If he can remember me, send my regards to him. You'll have to call me when you get back to London and tell me how everything worked out for you here on the island. Looks like we are on the same floor. Great view from the balconies. Okay, Keiran, have to run. Take care of Jennifer. See you again soon."

Grayson headed down the hall briskly, passing a maid who was rolling her cart slowly, stopping to let Grayson get by. Keiran watched Grayson stop at his room, noting that it was directly next to his own.

Keiran pressed the down elevator button. As the doors opened, he looked one more time down the hall. Grayson was gone, as was as the maid. The cart was standing solitary and, from Keiran's vantage point, nothing, not even the brooms, had been moved from the cart. He entered the elevator, pondering the conversation with Grayson—loaded with information and riddles. One thing was certain; his aspiration for a quieter personal and professional life in London was fast disappearing.

Eleven

Leyden asked Keiran, strangely and playfully, his smooth, large hands nervously twisting a tall glass of gin and tonic, "Well, what do you think? Any idle curiosities about the registration process or the people you met at the government offices? Difficult, or not?"He slumped in his chair, beginning to talk as if he was resuming a conversation that he had started long ago. His robust figure seemed to burst out of his suit, the middle button of the closed jacket straining with his every movement.

"No, not really. No questions. Pretty simple actually," Keiran said.

On this peerless early afternoon, Leyden had taken Keiran to a small restaurant directly across from one of the largest marinas in St. Peter Port, the major town on the island. The headwaiter, a man as large as Leyden, effusively greeted him, showing them to a corner table with a commanding view of the harbor.

"My table," Leyden commented rather proudly.

"Are you sure you shouldn't be on your sailing boat rather than squiring me around?" They both laughed.

The harbor water lay like a mirror that someone had breathed on, the water lapping softly on the many sailboats anchored in the harbor. It was a gentle day, beguiling with the scents of the harbor and the light breeze. Despite what could only be described as a perfect day for sailing, the marina was filled to capacity with all manner of sailing vessels. There were as many shapes and colors of boats as there were ships in the harbor. The sight was eye-catching.

"It takes real control, Keiran," Leyden replied, as he looked out at the harbor, "to stay in an office on such a day as perfect as today. A fair breeze and smooth water. What more can any sailor want? We are silly not to be on my boat and off into the channel. But, as you can see, we sailors on this island are busy bees, very few of us are out on the water today. For sure, I'd rather be on my 'Play Fair' feeling this gentle wind. On land I feel like a prisoner; sailing unlocks my cell. But I had this young lawyer from London who needed some help, so here I sit." Leyden laughed slightly. "Can you see the second slip on the main pier? Can you make it out?" Leyden asked, pointing to his boat. "See it, right next to the large white yacht with the radar poking on top?"

"Yeah, I see it. Looks pretty sturdy, not to mention beautiful," Keiran replied, turning his head to get a view of Leyden's boat.

"You should come sailing with me. Stay a few days, Keiran. With this weather, it would be a smooth trip. Nothing like the feeling of the sails, the rattle of the ropes, and a fair wind that would carry us wherever we wish to roam and wander. We could have the best of it today .. some good progress with this light, easterly breeze. What say you? But first, before you reply, a toast. Here, here Keiran!" Leyden solemnly raised his glass to meet Keiran's. "To continued success!" His little gray eyes were swimming and blinking as if a moth had gotten into them.

"Here, here," Keiran answered robustly. "Your invitation is tempting, Dave, really tempting. But I have to get back to London. I have a great deal of other work to do, and I think we've done everything that needs to be done here. I'd like to sail with you another time, though."

"Well, then, if you promise that you'll come back, I won't pressure you in staying now. I'm happy that you came and that it has been a very smooth day."

"What I don't understand, Dave, is that I could have sent over the originals to you by air express and had you register the documents. That would not only have been simpler, but cheaper," Keiran replied, a faint smile crossing his lips. "Certainly, I am happy that I met you and had the opportunity to meet your friends at the Royal Courthouse's registration office, but I think the actual paper work could just have easily been mailed to you."

"True enough," Leyden replied, his hands not resting for a moment, still encircling the glass as if it were about to spill or blow away somehow. "The corporate memoranda and articles of incorporation are drafted in a local firm and the time to form a corporation is generally one week. But, with you here, and me taking you to the registration office, it took a few hours. Having the client's London lawyer here adds a bit of importance to the registration and generally places you in the front of the queue. Impresses the bureaucrats…you can imagine that, of course,"

"Good try, but a pretty feeble analysis, Dave," Keiran added, "I think you wanted me to come so you could have company on your boat." They both laughed.

"Absolutely, Keiran. That was the reason," Leyden said with a sort of dreary passion.

"I did enjoy meeting every one at the Court House though, but I really don't think my coming had anything to do with getting the registration completed in so quickly. You knew everyone at the registration office. And it's pretty clear that they really respect you. So, I think you're just leading me on when you say I was important today to get the registration through."

"Thanks for the kind compliment. I think it's a compliment. But it has been my experience that bringing the client's counsel to the offices adds a bit of, what is the word you say, a bit of panache. The civil servants feel more comfortable when they meet folks like you. It gives them some sense of importance. Civil servants like to be treated as if they're important. In fact they are. If they don't feel comfortable with you, your papers can be lost, go to the bottom of the pile, or just take forever to be approved. They'll find little, insignificant errors if they want to delay. So there you have it. I hope you appreciate that mailing the documents may be what should be done, but it generally isn't what is done," Leyden concluded.

"Frankly, though, I think you're the more important of the two of us. I don't doubt that for a minute. So why not tell me why am I really here?"

"Well, now, brother Keiran—in England we can call our fellow barrister and solicitors brother, so with your permission, I'll anoint you with that designation, unless of course you take offence."

"No offense whatsoever. Be a friend and tell me why I'm here." Keiran took the last swallow of his diet Coke and then placed the glass down on the table.

"Okay, okay. You must realize, of course, that Farris sent you first to meet me and second, to get acquainted with the island's legal procedures and court personnel. Candidly, I don't see anything wrong with his decision to send you. You're bright, articulate and—shall I conclude by saying wise?"

"I agree with every attribute you've given me," Keiran's smile was wide. "Maybe I should have that beer now?"

"A very wise decision." Leyden raised his hand to get the attention of the waiter, who came over quickly. "A beer for this young man. Kind?"

"Guinness. What else?"

"Best choice." Turning to the waiter, he continued, "Bring me a refresher for my drink. Don't mix it though. I'll do it myself. Okay, now that the important business has been taken care of—Farris. Sure he knows that I can handle everything for his clients. After all I am the registered agent for all of his clients' companies. Those forms you filled have nominee directors, so the true owners of the company are unknown to the general public. Of course the true owners are protected because the nominees, like me, have to sign a blank share transfer and letter of trust in favor of the true owner. I maintain the registered office on the island and file all the required annual returns and reports." Leyden's words now came spinning out like the beaten-up white of an egg. "Your anxiety to get back to London can only mean that there's something much more interesting to do in that city than to go to the office and write more legal memos. Merry maidens of London town? Am I correct?"

"Yeah. Maybe. Here come our drinks." Keiran laughed.

The waiter came over, placing Keiran's drink in front of him, pouring the Guinness from the bottle, being careful to protect the foam from overflowing. He then put a glass half full of gin in front of Leyden, leaving a bottle of tonic for him to adjust the strength of the drink for himself.

"Ah ha. I thought so. Men are so damn nervous when they think of a woman. Go back to London. You should. Anyway, did you learn something on this trip?" Leyden asked, his voice turning serious.

"Yeah. I know who you are and where the registration office is. And that the island is a pretty interesting place. Farris had his reasons for sending me here, and for meeting you, so I shouldn't complain."

"Well, I guess you can say that comprehending Farris could be the work of a lifetime. And, sure, it can be looked upon as a misuse of the client's money," Leyden replied. "Nevertheless, Farris wanted you here and here you are. Listen, Keiran. I can't catalogue Duane, or postulate his reasons for doing things, or predict his reactions, or fasten upon any system of behavior that is easy and obvious. What I can say truthfully is that it's my belief that he is a man of great practical experience who never says anything unexpected, and who insists that we look upon him as a man of authority. Farris quite clearly wants to observe whether you can work within his system. Directly, when he spoke to me about your coming, he described you in very laudatory terms…a young man he feels he can groom for greater things, I would suspect. That is why he sent you here. To see how you would handle the situation, my reaction, and those you met at the registration office. And I think he should not worry about you at all. You have all the makings of a pretty solid partner in his firm."

Leyden turned his chair slightly, now looking down at his second depleted drink.

"He did point out that you're a singular independent mind, which he admired. Now, clearly, he knows that the trip is clerical in nature, yet he wanted you to take it and that should be sufficient, now shouldn't it? I've enjoyed having you with me and getting to know you, so now at least I'll place a face with the voice at the other end of the telephone. So, from my standpoint, it has been a good beginning. You should give Farris the thanks he deserves for sending you here."

"Yeah! I should give him thanks." Keiran's eyebrows arched. "I still want to get to London today, if possible."

"Well, before you do that—there is a plane that leaves around 4:00 or so—we have to call Farris in Athens. He did tell you to call him, didn't he?"

"Of course he did. Do I have to call him from here? From this place?" Keiran inquired.

"It would be preferable. He may want to talk to both of us."

"Before we make that call, though, I have a question. Are all these companies you have registered, like Benton Industries, are they for real? Or are they all shell companies? Will they have employees and actual activity, or do they just exist on the paper that you and I filed today?"

"Certainly," Leyden replied matter-of-factly, "they're not just paper companies. Benton Industries will have contracts for the purchase of cement in its name with the funds flowing through its own bank account. It's true, though, that the actual work of purchasing the cement for Benton Industries may be done by a member of Zoran's staff in Geneva or Beirut. There's nothing illegal about that. Companies are always formed for specific and sole contracts always. I'm sure you know that. The companies for which I'm the registered agent are for real." Leyden gave him an embarrassed look that Keiran noted quietly.

"But how do you know if they're real? And if they were not, what would you do about it?"

"Oh, they're real all right, Keiran. No doubt about that. The money flows into the account once the contract is completed, or in this case, the money will flow out to the seller of the cement to Benton Industries, and funds come into Benton from the customer who is buying the cement. Benton pockets the difference. I can understand your concern. My advice to you, though, is that you would be wise to understand that the business we are in is not pure and certainly never simple, at least in the way you think it may be. One has to be flexible in international business. Flexibility is the key to success. You have to be willing to make a deal. You have to be enterprising if you want to be effective. It's hard for me to believe that you, as intelligent as you are, don't understand this basic principle. What do they teach you in law school these days?" Leyden said, a quick smirk crossing his face as he continued, "There are reasons why tax havens such as Guernsey exist. The island's main source of revenue is the fees it generates both for agents like me and for the government by authorizing these companies to transact business, to have bank accounts, and to do those things that ordinary corporations do. Farris' companies buy and sell commodities. The island is a perfect place for those inclined to take advantage of its laws…and to do so legitimately."

"I know what you're driving at and it's all correct," Keiran replied. "I guess what you're really telling me is that to be successful in this business, you need plenty of guts, no scruples and no conscience. Well, then, maybe I won't be successful in this kind of practice. But hey, why worry. As you say…everything's legal. The true nature of the company is hidden; the owners are hidden; and the bank accounts are secret. What more could any reasonable person ask for? You have a great combination—the greed of man dressed as velvet. Perfect way. Why change it? I wouldn't if I were you? But then, I'm not you."

There was silence.

"You're direct, aren't you? And do you really believe you have the right to advise me of what is right or wrong?" Leyden's tone changed. His voice rose in a shrill anger as he continued, "I'm trying to be a good host, but you make it difficult. No matter, I've finished my drink. Will you now join me in a real drink or do you want to have another beer?"

He stared at Keiran, admiring the confidence and strength in the young man, thinking back to when, yes, even he had those traits. But once you feel the temperature of the water and like it, you take the plunge. Money talks. It always has. Keiran will take the plunge. It's only a matter of time, Leyden thought silently.

"I'd better stick with the one beer. Didn't mean to offend you." Keiran looked away toward the harbor. "You do have a beautiful boat, Dave. You're real lucky on that score. Real lucky."

"Hogan. A-okay. You know how to change the subject to one dear to my heart. My boat." Leyden called over the waiter and ordered another round of drinks. "We'll also have lunch. Please bring a menu," he ordered.

Abruptly, Leyden reached into his pocket, saying, "It's time that I call Farris in Athens. You know that he's in Athens? Of course you know he's in Athens. What am I thinking? See, Keiran, you're making me nervous. Really, I don't like being nervous. There is no reason for me to be nervous," Leyden said, trying to convince himself of the validity of his statement as he took out his cell phone and punched in Farris' number.

"Duane, Good evening. Are things going well in Athens…? Well, good. I'm happy about that…Keiran. Well, this young man is a quick study. He knows more about the registration process and the documents than I do…. What did you do, lock his office door until he read through our entire code? Duane, you have to give this young man a break."

There was laughter on Leyden's part. But Keiran was appreciative that Leyden was giving him a thumbs-up to Farris. Not that it mattered, he told himself. In the recesses of his own mind, he was wondering about Farris and whether he was a partner with whom he wanted to work.

Leyden continued. "I introduced him to the bureaucrats who run the registry office and they were suitably impressed. We're about to have lunch now, so I though I'd give you a jingle to see if you needed anything further…. Well, no, we have not met Richard Ellis. It was my understanding that you wanted Keiran to have a visit with him another time…. Of course…. Certainly. I'll suggest that to Keiran…. What time did you say Zoran would arrive on the island…? Oh, not until then, 7:00 or so. Of course I'll pick him up at the airport. Certainly…. Yes…. His office made his reservations at the Old Government House…. Yes, the same as Keiran. Of course you want Keiran to meet him…. Here, let me pass you on to him…Keiran, Duane Farris for you."

"Hello Mr. Farris. How are you?"

"Fine. I understand from Dave that your trip is going well, and that you're enjoying yourself. I wish I were there with you, as it's very warm here in Athens and the cool breezes you're probably getting on Guernsey are more refreshing indeed. Keiran, our client, Zoran Hemmrich will be coming to Guernsey to meet with his banker, Richard Ellis, this evening. I'd like you to stay and meet Zoran, perhaps his banker as well. Have dinner with them and get better acquainted. I believe that you planned on staying the night? Correct?"

"In a way sir, I was. But the registration took so little time, I was trying to get back to London late this afternoon, as I have a great deal of work to do at the office."

"Of course. But Zoran will be on the island, so you must stay and visit with him. He's our client. There is no other alternative than for you to remain on Guernsey and visit with Zoran." Farris' voice was firm, yet soft, but Keiran felt it was as cold as stone. "Dave will be at the dinner meeting as well. If you wish, you can leave for London first thing in the morning. The weather is fine on Guernsey, so enjoy the rest of the afternoon. Is there anything further you wish to discuss with me?" he asked.

"No, Mr. Farris. Not at all. I look forward to meeting Mr. Hemmrich. Let me pass you on to Dave."

"Thank you Keiran. I'll see you when I get back to London."

"Duane.... Certainly.... It will be taken care of. Yes, I'll be at the airport to meet Zoran. I'll call you after the meeting tonight. Goodbye, Duane." Leyden flipped the cover back onto the cell phone and placed it in his jacket pocket.

"There you have it. He wants you to stay the evening and to have dinner with Zoran. You will do that, won't you?" Leyden looked imploringly at Keiran, with an expression in his eyes that bordered on pleading. He just wasn't sure of Keiran's reaction and was somewhat afraid of Keiran's independent attitude—or was he envious?

"Putting aside, Dave, for the moment, the registration process, I now know the real reason I'm in Guernsey. It's to meet Hemmrich. You and Farris both knew he was coming here the entire time but didn't want to tell me, for whatever reason, or am I to believe that Hemmrich's visit's just one of those strange coincidences in life that we are to accept as unplanned? Hell, how do you keep all your games straight?"

Leyden tried to avoid Keiran's stare. Lowering his head, he said, "Keiran, that's good insight. Insight can be an advantage in certain cases, and, of course, a disadvantage in others. But you're missing one point, and that's because you're not yet familiar with our client. He is secretive about all his movements, and makes changes at the very last minute. So, yes, I knew he was coming this week, Keiran. Not necessarily today. He still may not come. I don't know. I've been through this before. You have to understand the client and his behavior regarding security."

"But what's the logic behind all of this secrecy?"

"I just don't know. But that is the way he is. We can't argue with his belief that security is all-important. After all, he's a well known businessman—a possible target for kidnappers and so forth."

"Sort of makes you wonder what's going on…what's really going on. You see my point?" Keiran said with conviction.

"Well, of course, I do. But you also have to understand that all clients aren't the same. Zoran acts in this manner and we have to accept his method of operation. Besides, you'll find that you will enjoy his company. He is very charming," Leyden responded. "Time to order, Keiran. I'm starved. No more conversation about business. I want another drink and some food. And you...?" Leyden asked, his eyes again blinking wildly.

"Sure. Why not? I'll have that other beer now," Keiran said, realizing he was now getting deeper into a situation that he had yet to understand. The situation seemed as smooth as silk but in reality, Keiran understood, it wasn't. All of this was different from what he had expected it to be when he got to London weeks ago. There was nothing lurid or embarrassing that he could point to as yet, but his mind told him the story was just unfolding.

Twelve

The two beers he had with lunch probably didn't help. Keiran was tired. Maybe from the beer, but, he believed, more likely from a feeling of discouragement—the excitement of coming to London to a new office and what he believed would be an intriguing practice no longer seemed quite real. Quickly changing into his swimsuit, he threw on the bathrobe and slippers provided by the hotel and made his way to the pool area.

As he came to the end of a twisting path, geranium pots along its sides marking the patio fronting the pool, he was surprised to see Grayson along with two other men, one of whom he recognized as having been at Grayson's party.

His partner. Yeah, Keiran remarked to himself, his law partner, John…what was his last name…? McPherson? No, it was McPeek—yeah, that's the guy."

They were seated under the white pillars of a pergola covered with climbing red and white roses, providing some needed shade on this sunny day. They appeared to be deep in conversation and didn't notice Keiran as he entered the pool, climbing down the short ladder at its shallow end, away from where Grayson was seated. He decided to go over and greet Grayson, but only after he had concluded his swim.

It was 3:00 in the afternoon. As he swam his usual laps, the stress of the day began leaving him slowly. The sun was still bright, the sky cloudless. Gradually, the routine took over and his mind became quiet of thought, the only sound being the soft splash of his hands as they effortlessly and steadily propelled him forward toward one end of the pool, then a quick reverse to the other. Apart from a mother and her two small children who were playing at the shallow end, Keiran had no one to bother him as he methodically swam laps. At the end of his hour swim, he lifted himself up in one swift push from the pool ledge, walked to the lounge chair where he had placed some towels, his bathrobe, and his slippers. As he dried himself, he looked over to where Grayson had been seated. The only activity there now was a waiter who was clearing off the table. Putting on his bathrobe and slippers, he reminded himself that he would call Grayson later…if he had any time. Leyden had said that he would come by the hotel around 5:30 or so to pick him up for the dinner meeting with Hemmrich. Enough time for a quick nap, clean up and a call to Jennifer. Keiran smiled…especially the call to Jennifer.

When he arrived in his room, he saw the blinking light on this phone signaling he had a message. The wind had picked up slightly, billowing the sheer curtains covering the open balcony glass doors, casting soft, yet sunny streaks of light dancing in the room. He picked up the phone, pressing the button on its console for messages. The voice was Jennifer's.

"Keiran, I got your message. Sorry I missed you…. We're on for Tuesday. Will you call me when you get to London? It'll be hard to reach me this evening. I want you to know that I had such a great time on Sunday. I really did. I know you're working hard, so do take care of yourself. Can't wait until you're back."

Her voice was soft, whispery. He replayed the message a few more times, savoring each word. The manner of her speaking meant, to Keiran, she really cared for him. Even though he knew she would not be at her home phone, he didn't want to bother her at work, and he dialed it anyway, leaving his own voice message.

"Thanks for calling Jennifer. Work here is pretty simple, the island is great, though, and the view from my room is beautiful. Wish you were here to enjoy all of this with me. Take care of yourself. I miss you."

He wanted so badly to love her passionately, wholeheartedly, and naturally. He decided to leave Guernsey later, after the dinner with Hemmrich, if he could get a flight out.

As he hung up the phone, there were a series of knocks on the door.

"Keiran, it's me. Leyden. Open up, I have to see you."

"Be right there.... Hang on.... be right there." Tightening his robe sash, he hurried to the door, opening it to find an out-of-breath and very distressed man.

"What's wrong Dave?" Keiran asked as he held the door open for Leyden to enter.

"Things have changed. I went to the pool and the attendant said you had already left. Then I tried calling you from downstairs but your phone was engaged. Sorry to disturb you.... Zoran will be landing in about thirty minutes at the airport. He called from his plane. He will stay for dinner tonight and perhaps stay overnight at the hotel. Can you get ready and come now?" His words came out in a stuttering fashion, stumbling over many, anxiety written all over his face.

"Well...sure...of course, Dave. This guy really changes his mind, doesn't he?"

"Yeah, he does." Leyden said, his voice indicating resignation.

"Okay, okay, Dave. I'll see you downstairs. It won't take me long to shower and dress. In the meantime, calm down."

"Make it quick Keiran. I don't want to keep him waiting." Leyden left hurriedly, as Keiran, shaking his head, slowly closed the door behind him.

It took Keiran only ten minutes to get ready and get to the hotel lobby, where he found Leyden pacing back and forth like a figure trapped in glass, his face flushed with anxiety, repeatedly looking at his watch. Seated nearby in a corner of the lobby, Keiran recognized Grayson, Grayson's partner McPeek, and another, tall, heavy-set man. This time Grayson looked up as Keiran was coming toward Leyden. He made a quick raise of his hand, waving at Keiran.

"You know him?" Leyden asked suspiciously, his lips trembling, his eyes darting between Keiran and to where Grayson was seated.

"Yeah. Met him at the U. S. Embassy—at one of the ambassador's coffee klatches. Why do you ask?" Keiran inquired.

Leyden didn't answer as they both hurried out the hotel, walking briskly to Leyden's car, which was parked directly in front. The doorman held the driver's side open as Leyden got in, muttering a brief, "Thank you," then repeating to himself, "We have to hurry…can't dawdle." Keiran settled in, placing his briefcase in front of him on the car floor.

"Maybe I should drive," Keiran suggested. "You're pretty nervous. Why is that? Does Mr. Hemmrich scream and threaten if you're late?"

As the car picked up speed, Leyden didn't respond to Keiran's comments, nervously saying instead, "Why do I ask about Grayson? Oh. I'm surprised that the ambassador would ask him to the monthly meetings. You probably know that although his law firm has a grand sounding name, in reality they have only a few lawyers in London, and not many more in Washington. Some even wonder if he is really a lawyer and if his firm is really a firm. Just came in about five, six years ago, and with plenty of money."

"Are you serious about that? I don't think you can practice law in London without being a lawyer. Besides, I don't suspect that the size of the firm has anything to do with the ambassador's invitation. I suppose any American law firm with an office in London that wants to come, can. I don't imagine the ambassador would keep anyone away. It's a P. R. thing. The meeting I went to was fairly bland. The ambassador wants a good audience, and from what I saw the only time I've gone, he gets what he wants…lawyers milling around him making conversation."

"Well, I wonder what Grayson really does. He's on the island frequently, and I've met him. But I know of no company that he's ever registered."

"Why would you know, anyway? There must be hundreds of companies registered every month."

"That's true. That's true. I don't know who his island agent is, though I thought I knew them all."

"Next time I see him, I'll just ask him and let you know," Keiran joked. "Now, you tell me about Zoran Hemmrich and why he changes his schedule so often, and why he unsettles you. Last time I saw him, he was racing out of Farris' home. The man seems to be in a hurry all the time."

Leyden fell silent for a moment, the cheek that was visible to Keiran began to quiver like the movements of a fish caught on a fisherman's hook.

"You have to calm down, Dave. You'll be all over this road if you don't. Hell, you're driving the middle of the road. Slow down and stay cool."

Again, Leyden ignored Keiran's admonitions.

"I didn't know that you had already met him…or, at least seen him."

"Okay, Dave. Stay in the right lane, or whatever lane you use here. I don't like this driving down the center of a two-lane road. Now do it, or let me out. Now. You're annoying me by being so agitated. For God's sake, the client will wait. Where in the fuck will he go? Back to the airport?"

There was silence for several moments. Leyden slowed the car down, driving now in the appropriate lane.

"Sorry, Keiran. I do get a bit carried away. Zoran is a bit much if I am late. He can always change the time; but once he tells you where he wants you to be, you'd better show up and at the right hour and minute. Pure shit, I know. So you saw him?"

"Yeah. But what I saw was a blur. Farris later told me it was Zoran. So, it'll be interesting to meet him in person. Now what about him? I did do an internet search and it turns out he's had several government investigations into his companies. You probably know all about them."

"Investigations? Yeah, I know about them. He's clean though. Farris keeps him clean. You want to know personal things about Zoran? Well to begin with, he is about my age, around 50, married, one son died in a boating accident off Venice, a daughter is in school, college actually, in London. I've forgotten her name. He rarely talks about his family…and I wouldn't advise you to bring it up. Wants to keep that part of his life separate and secret. Business interests? Well your internet search must have brought up what he does. He's into sale and purchase of commodities—cement, fertilizer, petroleum products, and so forth. He has several offices, mostly, however, he operates from either London or Cairo. Moves a great amount of these products and, of course, makes a handsome amount of money. That's about it really. Not much more, but he does want to be taken care of…and, on his timeframe. Never ours."

"And all these charges about arms dealing? True ?"

"Oh. I suppose there may be something in that. But, honestly, Keiran, I just don't know for sure. All the contracts are purchases and then resale of commodities. You know that from working on the Benton Industries matter."

"Well, you've got a point. No one has ever proven he has shipped arms. So unless there is proof, we have to believe our client," Keiran noted, looking at the speedometer of Leyden's Jaguar, now hovering over 140 kilometers an hour. "I think you should slow down, Dave. Please. You've got a valuable passenger." There was laughter.

"Hell. I forgot. Okay, okay. But I can't slow down. We have a client who will have our heads if we don't get there pronto."

"The guy sounds nutty. How in the hell did Mr. Farris get him as a client?"

"Zoran may have strange idiosyncrasies, but he is not 'nutty.' That I can assure you. How did Farris and Zoran connect? You know I really don't even know that. Through networking, I suppose. That is how most of our business is obtained."

"Certainly provides a great deal of business for my firm's London office. I think he is one of our biggest clients. And I bet that Mr. Farris spends more than half his time on Hemmrich's corporate, and maybe even personal, legal matters. Had a strange occurrence the other evening. Met an old gentleman at the club, Sir Robert Albert Percival Runnard. How's that for an English name?"

"You're kidding. You met Runnard?"

"He's the guy who told me about a special commission he headed to investigate arms dealing and money laundering. Well, you probably know this. He wrote a report implicating our client Zoran Hemmrich. You know about the report?" Keiran inquired, noting that Leyden was now sweating.

"So, you met Runnard at your club?" Leyden asked, surprised, his hand gripping the steering wheel. There was now silence. The subject of this question startled Leyden.

"Yeah. Is there a reason for your surprise?" Keiran asked.

"He's still alive?"

"Yeah. Very much so. Why, is he supposed to be dead?" Keiran replied.

"Well, frankly, I thought that he had passed on a few years ago. Some say he was an alcoholic and that was the reason for his death. Maybe it's someone else I'm thinking about. Okay…yes, he did an investigation of arms dealing. But no action was taken on his report by the government, and he just faded away. Some politicians, even a few in the media claimed the report wasn't worthwhile because of his addiction to alcohol, and some also said to drugs. Of course he denied the charges, but then, one never knows."

"What did Farris and Hemmrich do to merit an investigation?"

"Unfortunately they, along with others, were targets of a government inquiry into arms dealing and money laundering. But, even though the report recommended certain additional investigations and queries, nothing was ever done by the U. K. politicians. That whole period—I believe it was about six months or maybe even longer—is a sore point with Duane and Zoran. I wouldn't mention that you know about the report to either one. They both believe they were targeted because they didn't contribute to the Conservative Party, the party in power at the time."

"But why did the government include Farris as a subject of the investigation?" Keiran asked again.

"I don't know really. Probably because he had been Zoran's lawyer for some time. You know lawyers are always tied to their clients, now aren't they?"

"The report—do you have a copy?"

"No. The government released a version of the report to the public, everyone quickly forgot about it. You know these things are sometimes done just to cover someone's behind. Runnard actually accused the government of aiding in the export of certain arms—prohibited arms—to the several countries where these sales are embargoed. Zoran was investigated because he shipped commodities to those countries, many times in a roundabout way, but it was always perfectly legal. Farris would make sure of that. A word of caution. You may not want to even mention you've met Runnard. He would...." The ring on his car phone interrupted Leyden's comments. Leyden pressed the speaker button on his console, allowing him to speak without taking the phone from its cradle.

"Yes. David Leyden here."

A low, steady voice came over the speaker. Keiran thought it considerate and calm.

"David. We are already at the restaurant. We landed a bit earlier than expected. Favorable winds, you know. You are now on your way and Mr. Hogan is with you?"

"Of course, we should be there in about five, maximum ten minutes. Keiran is with me."

"Good. See you soon, then."

"Goodbye, Zoran." Leyden switched off the phone.

"Now, why didn't he call you earlier to say his plans had changed again so we wouldn't be heading to the airport when we should be going to the restaurant?"

"Oh, I don't know Keiran. He is constantly shifting his time and place. I suspected this would happen in any event. That's life, Keiran. If you work with Zoran you'd had better get used to his erratic behavior, at least insofar as schedules and times are concerned." Leyden made a sharp u-turn in the lightly traveled two-lane highway, and headed in the direction of the restaurant.

Neither Leyden nor Keiran noticed a van bearing the logo of Guernsey Telecom following at a distance. A cluster of three small antennae was positioned in the center of the van. The conversation that Leyden had just concluded had been overheard by the three men in the van, two of whom had uniforms of telephone repairmen, one was in a business suit.

"Don't get any closer than this, John." The driver nodded as he also made a u-turn, following Leyden's car.

Mallard's Restaurant was on the outskirts of St. Peter Port. A large swinging sign boasted fresh fish dinners every day. It was about 5:30 and the dinner crowd had not yet arrived, so the parking lot adjacent to the restaurant was fairly empty. Leyden pulled his car into the space closest to the entrance. Keiran reached for his briefcase.

"I don't think you'll be needing that. You won't have to take any notes. Leave it here. This is just a social visit."

"Sure." Keiran left his case in the car and got out. As he waited for Leyden to come around from the driver's side, a Guernsey Telecom van came into the lot and drove around to the back of the building. The late afternoon sun felt good and the wind was picking up, slightly swaying the trimmed field of asters on either side of the restaurant.

The interior of the restaurant was pleasant. Pale yellow and white-checkered tablecloths covered the thirty-odd dining tables. A small bar was at the end of the room, off the restaurant's entrance. To the left side of the bar were swinging doors leading to the kitchen and the back door exit. A bank of windows, which overlooked the channel visible in the far distance, as well as the restaurant's front, let a great deal of light into the richly paneled dining room. Fish trophies were placed on all the walls interspersed with photos of fishing boats and their crews. As Leyden and Keiran entered, Leyden spotted Zoran seated alone at a corner table facing both the front of the restaurant as well as the channel. The table was no more than three meters from the reception desk. He appeared to be engrossed in the menu. At a table directly next to him sat two men, also looking at their menus. Leyden hurried over, reaching out with his hand as Zoran stood up.

"Zoran, good to see you...good to see you...beautiful day...beautiful day," said Leyden, shaking Zoran's hand effusively. Keiran noted that Leyden's forehead was covered with droplets of moisture. As soon as he had finished shaking Zoran's hand, he reached into his jacket pocket, pulling out a tissue and patting away the sweat, then crumpling it into a ball before putting it back into his pocket.

"You still look prosperous, David. Always prosperous. Yet a bit harried. Must be unreasonable requests from all your clients." There was laughter all around.

"No. No. No unreasonable requests, Zoran. Please though...please meet Duane's new associate, Keiran Hogan. Keiran...Zoran Hemmrich."

Keiran held out his hand and strongly shook Zoran's extended hand.

"Mr. Hemmrich, it's a real pleasure to meet you, sir." Zoran's eyes were dark, prominent on his face. There was no expression as he met Keiran in a friendly and cordial manner. Keiran noted Zoran was almost the same height as he. His large, olive complexioned face out delicate looking for a man, with the strangely adolescent look of a figure in a religious icon. On the small finger of his left hand glittered a gold and diamond band.

"Please be seated gentlemen. Mr. Hogan, Duane has told me a great deal about you. Are you enjoying this fine island?"

"Yes. It's an interesting place. Certainly, we could not have asked for a more flawless day. Dave, here," Keiran looked at Leyden for a moment, "is a great host as well as good promoter for Guernsey."

"Of course. Dave is a promoter. And, I would think he would want to be sailing today. Of that I am sure." Zoran replied.

"You've read my mind, Zoran. We should all be sailing."

"I wish we could do that, but business calls. I appreciate your interrupting your visit, Mr. Hogan, to see me on such short notice. I did want to make your acquaintance, as Duane has said that you will be working somewhat closely with us on the legal monitoring of my companies, and of course working with Dave." Zoran's narrow black eyes constantly shifted, he head moving ever so slightly as if he were surveying this surrounding constantly, a strange, inscrutable smirk crossing his mouth.

They were interrupted by a waitress. She was short, her brown hair tied back with a pale yellow ribbon, which matched her uniform.

"Would the gentlemen like to order a beverage before dinner?" She asked, pulling her pen from her pocket tapping her small pad.

"Zoran, what would you prefer?" Leyden asked.

"Mineral water with lemon, please."

"Keiran?"

"The same for me, Dave. Thanks."

"I'll have coffee with cream. Give us a few moments and we'll be ready to order," Leyden said.

"That's two mineral waters, both with lemon, one coffee with cream."

"Correct," Leyden answered.

"Keiran…that's a unique name. Duane says that it's Irish," Zoran commented.

"I'm named after my mother's father, my grandfather. Your name is a family name as well?"

Leyden sat quietly, giving Keiran a quick glance suggesting he should answer Zoran's questions but not ask any.

"My name is also a family name. Zoran means strength. I was named after my father's brother, who died during World War II, actually fighting in Libya for the British against the Germans." There was silence before Zoran continued, his voice lowered. "War? To some it offers nothing but horror, to others a way of living, a business. Do you know why Rommel lost the desert war in World War II, Keiran? Dave? I'll tell you why—not because he wasn't the best tactical general around on both sides. The problem wasn't the bravery of his men or the superiority of his tanks. He lost the desert war, finally, because he could not get petrol. The winners were the British who could and did get unlimited amounts of petrol. Eventually, Rommel's tanks could not go anywhere, nor could his planes. Supplies, unlimited supplies, decide which party wins a conflict."

Silence again. Leyden kept looking back and forth from Keiran to Zoran, every once in a while indicating agreement with Zoran by uttering a slight "uh-huh."

The waitress came, placing the coffee in front of Leyden, the mineral waters in front of Keiran and Zoran.

"Have you decided on dinner yet?"

"A few more minutes, please. Thank you," Leyden responded.

"Conflicts are good for business, gentlemen. Always good for business. I like to think of myself as providing those supplies…you know, it's like our customers are going to a supermarket to buy milk and bread. We're the supermarket. The victor and the vanquished are, many times, reversed depending upon what period of history one is examining. Victors eventually become the vanquished and *vice versa*. Business remains, however. We have to adjust to the needs of both. Dave, you would agree with me on this?"

"I don't see it any other way," Leyden responded, "No other way."

"And Keiran Hogan. Agree?"

"Well, I don't know about that. There is always another way," Keiran answered, turning directly to face Leyden, then turning to Zoran. "Certainly, circumstances change and businesses change as well. That is the one constant in life…change. I would think, though, that one has to have a solid idea of what is right and wrong, even in business. Why would anyone want to do business with a leader who is brutalizing the people of his country? That would be stupid. You would make money selling supplies to him, but how could you live with yourself, knowing that what you're selling was helping him to kill his own people, or maybe even others?"

"Spoken from the inexperience of youth in international business," Zoran said dismissingly. "International businessmen, like myself, aren't members of a religious order. We are businessmen, and as such, can deal with whomever we wish. Some will deal with the one doing the brutality and others will deal with those being brutalized. Some will deal with both. It's all business. As for right and wrong, only God knows and we don't hear from him often. And, of course, you Americans, you always know what is right and wrong, not understanding that what you may think is right may in fact be wrong. We have only to observe the shifting alliances among countries during the last century."

"That may be, and, sir, I respect and understand your opinions. I just happen to believe differently," Keiran remarked.

Trying to put an end to what he perceived as Keiran's lack of manners and respect for Zoran, Leyden interrupted, "I think Keiran, Zoran, we should order. I know that you want to get back to London tonight, Zoran, and I believe that Keiran also plans to leave."

"Good, perhaps he will honor me by coming on my plane. We can continue discussing the differences of our philosophy at that time. Perhaps I may be able to change your mind. Agreed Keiran?"

"Sure, why not?" Keiran smiled. "About changing my mind though…."

"Not so sure?" Zoran interrupted with broad smile.

The Guernsey Telecom repairman entered the restaurant from the kitchen carrying his box of tools, which he carefully placed on the floor by the reception stand. He took a small cloth package from the toolbox, untied it, carefully lifting the four flaps and revealing several small chrome implements. He then knelt down, unplugging the phone and disconnecting the wires from the phone jack fastened on the floor in the molding.

"How long will you be?" asked the owner's wife, a plump lady dressed in dark brown, a loose white scarf around her neck. "We have to have our phones working for reservations," she said, irritated at the disruption. "I don't understand why you couldn't have come earlier. It's simply a maintenance call. Our phones are okay except for the static on the line." She walked away smartly, not waiting for any reply.

He continued his work, undeterred by the lecture. Working rapidly, he first inserted a small metal point which looked like a Phillips screwdriver into the front of the one inch diameter metal tube, itself about sixteen inches long. Then he inserted a similar metal section, six inches in length but slightly smaller in diameter at the back and placed a small square black rubber grip handle at the end. The entire assembly took about thirty seconds. The dart gun was now ready. Pulling the grip slightly backward would cause the firing pin to ignite a powder charge in the tube's center section, which in turned propelled the poisoned dart, no larger than a sewing needle, toward its intended target.

Bending down, the phone technician scanned the room one more time, noting that the two waitresses were not in the dining room, and that the owner's wife was at the bar talking to her husband. Nothing prevented his clear view of Zoran. His hands moved quickly. He held the base of the tool steady with one hand, pointing the device toward the table where Zoran, Keiran, and Leyden were seated, then pressing a small button at the base of the tube. A slight breath of a sound—silent, yet discernible, like the soft breeze on a summer's night—came from the tube as the dart hurled toward its target. It would take just two seconds to cover the three meters to where Zoran was seated.

Leyden started to rise, bending forward, saying, "Excuse me. I have to use the facilities. When the waitress comes over, Keiran, order me the fish and chips special, okay?" The sudden sharp pain on the left side of his neck was all he felt as the dart penetrated the skin. Its poison was a synthetic derivative of curare; only one-tenth of a millimeter touching the skin would cause instant death. Leyden stared at Zoran for a second, then fell back on his chair, tipping it over, collapsing on the floor, hanging onto the table cloth which, as he fell, he pulled from the table, spilling over the coffee cups, water glasses, silverware and plates.

Keiran jumped up, leaning down, taking Leyden's arm.

"Dave, Dave…what's wrong?" He leaned over closer to Leyden's face, trying to hear any breathing. There was none. "Zoran, He's not breathing. I think he…he's not breathing at all."

Zoran motioned to the two gentlemen who were at the other table, indicating to them by a movement of his hand that they should remain where they were. He didn't rush over to Keiran, but slowly got up and walked over to where Leyden lay crumpled on the floor. Calmly, he looked at Leyden, commenting, "We must call a doctor. Looks like he's had a heart attack. You have your cell phone, Keiran?"

"Oh. Shit. Excuse me, sir. I left it in my briefcase. There must be a phone here."

By now, the owner's wife rushed over, as did her husband, and several patrons.

"Where is the phone?" Keiran asked.

"On the reception desk. I'll get an ambulance. My God, poor Mr. Leyden…poor Mr. Leyden." She turned and shouted to the repairman, who was closing his tool case. "Are the phones working?"

"Yes, they are. I'll call the emergency services for you. He picked up the phone and spoke for a few minutes. "Should be here in about three minutes," he said in a raised voice to the owner's wife, who was still shocked, looking at the body of Leyden. No one noticed him packing and quietly walking into the kitchen and out the back door.

"Can we step aside for a moment, Keiran?"

Zoran backed away from the table and the small crowd that had gathered around Leyden's body. Keiran likewise stepped back and joined Zoran by the table where the two men, now standing, were waiting.

"My assistants," Zoran mentioned casually. "I will miss him a great deal, Keiran. He was a loyal man. Very loyal. There is not much more I can do here. I have to be in it London for a meeting this evening. Can you handle everything here?" he inquired of Keiran.

"Well…yes. Sure. I would think, though, that perhaps you would want to stay and see Mrs. Leyden…or…."

"I'll call her from the plane. If she does come here, please tell her that I'll take care of whatever she needs. We shall help her. Here is my card—my personal card with my personal cell phone number. You can reach me at any time on this number. Thank you Keiran. I enjoyed meeting you and will see you again. Come, gentlemen. We must go." He turned to his assistants who followed him out, not looking again at the body of Leyden, who lay crumpled untouched on the floor.

The Guernsey Telecom van left the restaurant parking lot and stopped at the crossroad before heading onto the main highway for St. Peter Port.

"Well?" Grayson asked.

"We got the wrong man. Someone stood up at the last minute."

"Not to worry. We'll try again. Soon, we'll try again." Grayson calmly said.

Thirteen

Keiran stood calmly by the window, his eyes fixed on the channel, which continued to shimmer in the late afternoon sun. He held Zoran's business card in one hand, turning it around every so often, finally placing it in his jacket pocket. His other hand held the phone listening to Farris' words, broken only by the mild static coming over the phone. His words, although gentle, were as cold as ice. Leyden's body remained only a few meters away, crumpled on the floor undisturbed. All the restaurant patrons had now gathered by the bar, drinks in their hands courtesy of the restaurant owner, very few conversing. Death brought a chill in the air; their earlier chattering was silenced.

"This is very unsettling information you have just given me. Dave dying of a heart attack. Very disturbing. Very surprising. Keiran. Alarming news," he repeated slowly. "I would suggest that you hitch a ride with Zoran back to London. There really isn't much you can do on Guernsey. I'll call Dave's wife to express my condolences and that of the firm and I'll arrange my schedule so that I'll try to be at the funeral, which I assume will be later this week. This is a difficult time for me as well. Dave was a loyal partner, Keiran, a very loyal...a very trustworthy partner. I shall miss him." Despite the considerate words, Farris' tone remained indifferent, almost uncaring, emotionless. Keiran noted he used almost the exact language that Zoran had used earlier in describing his own relationship with Leyden.

"You're not anxious? Frightened? Are you all right?" Farris asked in rapid succession. Keiran shook his head in disbelief. Even when Farris tried to be solicitous, the words came out unkind. There was never any feeling in Farris' utterances. His try at being sympathetic succeeded only in being stupidly tactless.

Keiran fell silent for several moments.

"No…not anxious," he finally replied. "Just pretty stunned. Maybe a bit fatigued. A lot has happened today. I had not expected this. Hard to believe that Dave is now gone. Very hard. But, I'm fine. As for taking Zoran's plane, I don't think that is going to be possible. All of us who were in the restaurant are waiting for the police—just a formality according to the restaurant owner. He tells us they'll want to interview everyone including, of course, those at our table."

"The police?" Farris interrupted, the pitch of his voice indicating surprise. "Zoran is not there now, I assume." As he listened to Farris' own uneasiness about the matter, Keiran had to admit that his heart was beating in a strange way. Maybe he was frightened.

"No…No, he is not. I thought he was going to call you from his car or plane. Hasn't he called yet?" Keiran asked.

"He's not called yet, " Farris responded quietly. "I'm sure that I will hear from him soon."

Why the fuck is this guy lying to me? Keiran asked himself silently. He knows I know that Zoran must have called him upon leaving the restaurant to tell him of Leyden's death. That is the sole reason Keiran waited several minutes before calling Farris…to give Zoran a chance to do so first. Farris, even when he tried, was a miserable liar, Keiran thought.

"The police will probably want to know who was as at our table. I will tell them that Zoran was with us when Dave had his attack. Zoran did say, Mr. Farris, that if the police needed him, he would come back later in the week, or provide them with a statement from London. There are other witnesses here who saw us all together. So again, I don't think his being gone will pose any particular difficulty."

"Keiran," Farris quickly broke into Keiran's explanation, "Have you given the police Zoran's name…his real name?"

"I haven't given them any name as they have yet to talk to me. They're not even here yet. Do you have a problem with giving Zoran's real name? You want me to give a false one? Why?" Keiran testily asked, his anger now increasing because of a sense of dreariness. He didn't care if his voice took on the sound of defiance and yes, even insolence.

"Well, you must know that Zoran's business interests are controversial, and he would not want to be dragged into any police investigation. It would simply be prudent not to give his real name."

"That would be a bit difficult as he was at the restaurant first," Keiran replied. "He was here when Dave and I arrived. He must have given the *maître d'* his name."

"Oh. I don't think so. He probably said that he was there waiting for Dave, and if he had to give a name, it would not have been his own. Our client is very sensitive about his movements and business. It would be uncomfortable for him to be part of whatever police investigation will be undertaken over Dave's untimely death."

"Mr. Farris. You want me to lie to the police? I'm to tell them that the man I was with wasn't Zoran Hemmrich, but someone else? That is what you want me to do…lie?" Keiran wasn't surprised at his own boldness; his ire was now becoming clear in the tone of his voice.

"You make up your own mind," Farris replied, his voice rising harshly. " I hope you clearly realize who is in charge of the client's matters and I also hope you'd have enough sense and be restrained while you're talking to me from the restaurant. Listen and listen carefully. I strongly urge you to think this matter through, mindful only of what our client's need is, which at this time is anonymity. We have to protect him, we are his lawyers…you do understand this fact don't you? I don't wish to argue with you, Keiran."

"Mr. Farris, don't ever remind me who is in charge. I fully comprehend your role; I also know mine. I understand about protecting a client's interest and candidly, I don't think that lying about a client's name is the way to protect the client. You're treating Mr. Hemmrich as if he were a criminal bracing himself for inevitable detection. You're not protecting the client with that kind of advice, sir."

For several moments there was no conversation. Keiran heard only heavy breathing over the line.

"Certainly, Zoran is not a criminal," Farris' voice now became collected as he continued, "and in our dealings with him, or with anyone on his behalf, we don't ever want to give that impression. Enough. We have a disagreement, a strong disagreement, Keiran. I see nothing wrong with giving the police, should they ask, a different name from Zoran's. That to me would be…."

Now Keiran interrupted. "What you're asking me to do is imprudent. You're simply ignoring the facts. Zoran was in here with two of his assistants, which I assume were his bodyguards. Everyone here knows what he looks like. If, by chance, the police had to reach him and interview him, and just so you don't forget, he said he would not mind being interviewed by the police, they would have to reach him. Understand? This whole conversation is nonsense. Dave is dead on the floor—dead right in front of me—and you want me to lie about someone's name. I'm ringing off, Mr. Farris. I'll see you in London. Sorry, sir. I won't lie. Period." Keiran's voice was quiet but firm.

"Keiran…Keiran Hogan," Farris' voice was, almost inaudible as he proceeded, "it's best that we discuss this when you're less tense. You have been through a great deal, which obviously has been stressful. If Zoran said that he would be available, I simply misspoke. Thank you for correcting me. I'm sure that you have everything under control. You believe that Zoran is on the plane now?"

"Mr. Farris, I want to ring off," Keiran curtly said, "I've told you that. Zoran left not so long ago—maybe fifteen minutes—for his plane, so he should be there by now. The airport is not too far from the restaurant. We agreed that he should not wait for me, and that I would see him in London. And to conclude, sir, my tenseness has less to do with what has just happened here, than with what you have asked me to do…."

Again, Keiran could not complete his thoughts as Farris stopped him in mid-sentence.

"Well, there is not much more to say, now is there? I'm sure you'll be able to handle the police interview quite well and in an orderly fashion.

Given the circumstances, I'm leaving for London immediately. I'll see you sometime tomorrow then. Stay in touch and call me or HenHen directly upon your arrival in London."

"Goodbye Mr. Farris." What a fuckin' idiot. Pure stupidity.

As he thought about Farris' request, two emergency personnel dressed in stark white coveralls with the words 'Guernsey Emergency Services' stenciled in red on the back of their uniforms briskly came in, pushing a gurney. They were followed by two police officers. Keiran looked at his watch. He thought an hour had passed since Leyden had died, but in reality it had been only about fifteen minutes. The room felt horribly still and airless. The restaurant owner came over to join the emergency staff as one of them bent down, picking up Leyden's left hand, pushing slightly back his jacket and shirt, trying to feel for a pulse.

"Nothing," he said as he turned, looking up to his colleague. "Nothing at all." He then placed his right hand over Leyden's eyes, and closed the lids. Methodically, they placed a light blue sheet over him, slowly lifting his body, placing it carefully on the gurney, and snapping the restraining straps across Leyden's covered body. Keiran, who had been standing a few feet away from Leyden, stared at his shrouded body, following the procession as it noiselessly weaved its way among the tables and chairs, and out the front door.

Despite all the discipline Keiran knew he had, small droplets of water began appearing on his forehead, and his body now felt damp. He was sweating profusely. He wasn't one to be afraid, yet seeing someone die makes one fearful. To think otherwise, he knew, is absurd. For a moment, all Keiran's Catholic religious training regarding death vanished. Maybe there is really no next life. There is no immortality of the soul. Death is final. The door is never opened again. Life is a game and death is always the winner. There is no Lazarus; there is no rising from the dead; death is conclusive; it's irreversible. Alone with these thoughts, regardless of a cynicism he didn't want to have, he lowered his head and prayed, looking down at the spot where Leyden had collapsed. The memorized words he would intone as an altar boy, so many years ago, with the priest at a funeral mass now came automatically to him.

He quietly mouthed the words now, his lips barely moving, You are worthy, our Lord and our God. Death will be no more. Mourning and crying and pain will be no more…for the first things have passed. . .you're the Alpha and the Omega…the beginning and the end. He wanted so badly for Leyden to hear the sound of a trumpet pealing a great reveille from an Almighty God. As he looked at the debris filled part of the floor where Leyden's body had collapsed, he wanted to put aside his bitterness, and believe. He wanted so much to believe. He continued to stand by the window, turning his eyes down, gazing at the debris on the wood floor, the soiled tablecloth, dishes, cutlery, still scattered and untouched. Tears came to his eyes. He needed to cry badly, but he knew he had to wait for another time for his emotion to crack and when it did, he wanted to be alone.

A small puddle of coffee and water had settled in a pool where the floor took a slight dip, unnoticed until the combined liquid found a place to settle. The emergency attendants had straightened the chair, but that was about it. Everything remained as it was when Leyden keeled over. Finally, after the police had taken photos of the scene, and after getting an okay from one of the policemen, a waiter came over, efficiently putting as much of the debris as he could in the tablecloth; folding it as if it were a sack and carrying it away. Another came with a broom and mop and it didn't take long to obliterate any evidence of Leyden's collapse. The table was reset quickly with a sparkling new bright-yellow tablecloth new china, glassware, and cutlery were placed appropriately. Keiran watched all of this, alternating between sadness and anger, not understanding either emotion with regard for a man he barely knew, and wasn't particularly fond of, but it was the final scene that death brings. Even when his mother's father died, it was different. Keiran didn't actually see him die. When next he saw his grandfather, he seemed to be in a deep sleep in a sturdy mahogany coffin, his hands clasping rosary beads, flowers everywhere. He looked as if he were already in heaven. But, now, here, the swiftness of Leyden's death brought the finality of life in all its rawness and it was hard to believe that an afterlife awaited him.

Keiran wanted to go outside to throw up. The restaurant owner, seeing him alone, came over and handed him a shot glass.

"Here, young man. Drink this brandy. It'll steady your stomach."

"Thanks…thanks very much."

Keiran drank it in one gulp. Too much was happening and it was happening too soon. He needed some time to think, to organize himself. He needed to be by himself, to put all of this in some order, to gain some perspective. How did Zoran know it was a heart attack? How does anyone know if it was a heart attack? And Farris. The jerk. Wants him to lie and if anything goes wrong with the lie, it's Keiran who'll be disposable.

One of the two attending police officers finally came over. The interview with Keiran was perfunctory: name, address, a description of what happened. Was anyone else present? Keiran mentioned Zoran by his real name, noted that he had waited as long as he could, but had to leave as his plane was waiting for him at the airport to take him to London. Keiran was told that the police might, at a later date, want a statement from Zoran. Keiran assured them they could get it. He was Zoran's counsel. He gave the officers his business card and wrote his club phone number on the back, at the police officer's request.

Keiran stepped over to the bar. He would get another drink and ask the owner to call a cab to take him back to the hotel. The several patrons who had been in the restaurant when Leyden had died were still all gathered there, drinking and talking more loudly now.

"Young man. I'm very sorry. I'm Thomas Bodkin, the bloke who owns this place with my missy. Want another shot?" Keiran tipped his head to indicate yes. Slowly pouring brandy into Keiran's glass, Bodkin continued, "Poor David. You know my wife and I were quite fond of him. He was a good man. Brought a great deal of business here. Were you working with him?"

"Yeah, I was." Keiran answered as he took his glass and quickly emptied it. "I just arrived today as a matter of fact. We had finished our business and were meeting with our mutual client. Everything has happened so quickly…a bit strange actually. Do you know if Dave had a history of any heart problems?"

"No, not really. More brandy?"

"No. No. Thanks though"

"We used to tell him to slow down on the drinking and the eating. He sure liked both of those—plus his boat. Oh, did he love that boat! 'Play Fair,' yeah, that's what it was called…not 'Fair Play'…not for him…he reversed the name. I guess it meant that he played fair. And I believe he did. Now, he's gone. We'll miss him."

Keiran shook his head, a slight smile came across his face as he said, "Mr. Bodkin, please forgive me. I didn't introduce myself. I'm Keiran Hogan from London. Dave was my law firm's agent on the island. When I can't remember to tell you who I am, it's time for me to go to the hotel."

"Keiran Hogan. Good Irish name. Why not stay a while, mate? Have more to drink and eat some of my missy's good cooking. Everything on the house, okay?"

"No, I'd better go. You're generous and I appreciate that. But I need to get back to the hotel and try to get an evening flight back to London. Can you call a cab for me?"

"I understand, mate. I understand. Please, though, have another drink while you're waiting." He placed a bottle of brandy in front of Keiran, then left, going toward the phone at the reception counter just inside the entrance.

"What the hell." Keiran poured himself another shot glass of brandy, drinking it in one gulp. This last drink was having an effect. His internal shaking was ceasing, but emotion was taking over. Again he felt he wanted to cry. I can't. Not in front of all these people. I have to get off this island tonight. Keiran would get on the evening plane. This island wasn't a paradise for him. He wanted to get home and to Jennifer. He really needed her now…very, very badly.

Dr. Jamie Gard had the least glamorous position in the medical profession on the island, and he intensely hated what he was doing. Being the island medical examiner wasn't what he had dreamed about when he went to medical school in London. He graduated at the top of his class at the University of London's Guy's Hospital Medical School in 1990, taking thereafter a surgical residency at the most prestigious private hospital in London, The Dennison Clinic. Then, during his third year at Dennison, something went horribly wrong. He could blame it on the fact that on that morning his wife had calmly asked for a divorce, telling him she was in love with another man, and would not be home when he returned that evening. She said she was sorry, but that she needed to be happy, and wished him happiness as well, but together there was no hope of achieving any kind of close and lasting feeling. In a fit of impulsive rage, he hit her hard with his fist, sending her small-framed, 110-pound body plummeting to the ground. He reached a wooden kitchen chair, bringing it down on her head, knocking her finally unconscious, repeatedly beating her with the chair, all the while screaming, "You bitch.... You bitch.... Having all those abortions so I couldn't have children.... I hate you.... You sick bitch.... You sick bitch.... You sick...." He fell down on his knees looking at her, the blood oozing from her head, her skin torn from her face, he knew she was dead.... He started to sob...burying his face in his hands "You sick bitch.... You made me do this.... Why did you marry me? Why? You never loved me.... You were hateful.... Why, Lorrie.... Why?"

It was 8:00. and he had to get the hospital by 9:00 to begin his operating schedule. This morning Sir Avery Malting, the West End theatrical producer, would be his first patient. It was a fairly routine operation to remove a gall bladder. So he realized he had just a few minutes to remove any evidence of his involvement with the bludgeoning death of his wife. Or did he? Why couldn't he have his fingerprints on the chair? After all, he had been home earlier in the morning and had breakfast with her. Yes, that is what he would tell the police. He left shortly after 8:00 or so and that was the last he had seen of her. They would buy that. Why not? He was Dr. Jamie Gard, a socially prominent doctor. Young, handsome, well liked, a beautiful wife.

Dr. Gard left everything as it was, including the breakfast plates on the table. He hurried upstairs and changed what he was wearing as some of his wife's blood had splattered on his shirt, pants, and tie. He carefully washed his hands, removed all the clothes and even the towel he used to wipe his hands, placing them in a plastic bag, stuffing them in a large briefcase that he would carry to work. He would discard the plastic bag in the incinerator container at the hospital. As he left his home, he was shaking. He had just killed his wife, and was exhilarated that he had done so. A funny feeling of profound peace came over him, a peace that he hadn't felt for years. The silent monster he carried with him was no more.

Operating Sister Melonie Charles first noticed his shaking hands.

"Are you fine this morning, Dr. Gard?" He looked up to see Melonie staring at his trembling hands. "Of course, why do you ask?"

"Well, I just wondered. Your hands seem to be shaking slightly. Are you cold?"

"Oh…they'll settle down soon. I don't know why, but I'm sure they'll settle soon."

Assistant Surgeon Joseph Settemen and Assistant Surgeon Sylvia Harrison also noted the shaking hands.

"Jamie…. You want to go through with this...? Your hands…."

"Of course, I do." Both surgeons stopped him as he attempted to make the first incision. He was furious….

"You can't go on, Jamie. Let's call in Dr. Keys. He's free until noon. Please?" His hands continued to shake as he dropped the incision knife on the floor and stormed out of the operating theater. He knew as he left, his job was finished, over, done. The mild tremor in his hands never stopped. He would never operate on a live person again. He went to several specialists in neurology, but no one could understand or diagnose the tremors in his hands. It wasn't caused by any known disease. The last specialist he consulted suggested that it was a psychological matter—"perhaps you should seek some counseling. That may help." He refused to believe this suggestion. He knew it was physical damage to his hand brought on when he murdered his wife. A punishment so to speak, he thought, from God, whoever that might be. The shaking would remind him forever of the hateful scene of violence the morning he murdered his wife. Hate had led him, he understood that and complaining about an infirmity would accomplish nothing. The truth terrified him, and his trembling hands obliged him to remember.

The police never caught the killer. Although he remained a suspect for some time, the police finally decided to close the case without charging him. He stayed for a few months at Dennison, but only to be assigned as the Assistant Hospital Administrator with minimal duties. It was clear the Board of Directors at the Clinic wanted him to leave. A friend from medical school told him about the position on the island of Guernsey. It paid well…and a slight tremor in hands would not be a bother—he would cut up only dead people. He would become the island's medical examiner, a job that was neither taxing nor desirable. He needed to get away in any event and it was here that he started a new life of calm and of freedom.

"Dr. Gard. Another one for you. Heart attack." Anniston Harren, the chief ambulance driver said, as he and his colleague rolled in the gurney bearing Leyden's body, still covered with the light blue sheet.

"Place in File 3. The others are full. I'll get to him in due course."

"Three bodies already. Sort of a busy day," Harren laughed heartedly.

"Yeah. One auto accident, one drowning, and now this. Won't take me long though. File 3, okay?"

"Sure." Harren and his assistant rolled the gurney forward, stopping by the refrigerated storage drawers, pulling out the stainless steel tray, then carefully placed the body on the table and slid it into the cabinet.

"We left his clothes on. Nothing touched. Not even his pockets, okay?"

"Okay, I'll get to it. Thanks." From experience he knew that Harren and his assistant had probably looked in the wallet and taken some of the dead man's money. When he looked in any of the wallets of the decedents brought in by Harren, there was never more than a few pounds in the wallet or a few coins. Over the few years he had been on the island, that the dead had so little money made him wonder. But, then, he had gotten away with his crime as well. So he said nothing to them or to the authorities. It would have been pointless anyway; he had no proof. He only surmised that not everyone dies with only a few pounds on their person.

Bob Grayson walked down the long corridor of the Guernsey Central Hospital, stopping at the door marked 'Medical Examiner.' He walked slowly into the sparsely furnished office, its only unique feature being a large faux palm tree set directly in front of a window that overlooked the hospital's rear parking lot. Two large maps of Guernsey hung on opposite walls. There was no one at the reception desk; it was bare except for a computer terminal, calendar, and phone. Behind the desk was another door marked 'Authorized Personnel Only.' Grasping his small brief case, Grayson went through the door. The room he entered was large, bright lights shone from the ceiling. Two large stainless steel tables and assorted stainless shelves and cabinets lined the room. The air was cool and smelled of disinfectant. A man hovered over a body, his hands making several cuts in the cadaver's chest. An assistant stood by. Soft music played over a speaker. The floor was tiled in white ceramic. Grayson's leather shoes made a sharp noise as he entered the room.

Dr. Gard looked up, startled and half angry.

"You should not be in here. The patients' family waiting room is off the entrance foyer. Please leave."

"Dr. Gard. I am not a family member. I have come to see you on an important matter."

Flashing through Gard's mind was his wife's murder. Had they finally come to get him? He lived in such fear that he would be caught some day. This well-dressed man could be a private investigator hired by his wife's family.... Maybe. Gard's hands began to quiver even more as he laid down his scalpel.

"Tim," he addressed his assistant, "take over and finish. Let me see what this man wants. Mr....?

"Mr. Bernard Edwards." Grayson smiled.

"Yes. Mr. Edwards. It'll take me just a moment to clean up. Please wait. I'll be...I'll be right there," Gard said softly

"Fine," Grayson said. "I'll wait in your reception room. It is urgent that we talk."

Grayson slowly made his way through the door connecting the morgue and the reception room. He sat down, placing his brief case on his lap, and waited. Several minutes later, Dr. Gard came out dressed in a new white starched smock, the sleeves of which fitted tightly over his arms, his plastic identity badge pinned on his uniform.

"I apologize for taking more than a few minutes, but, because of the work I do, it's necessary to clean up fairly thoroughly."

"Of course," Grayson replied gently. "I do appreciate your taking the time to visit with me."

"We normally have a receptionist, but Barbara is on vacation, so we make due." Gard commented, showing Edwards into his private office next to the reception area. It was small, square, and well furnished with a large table that Gard used as his desk. Several bookcases were filled to capacity, a computer terminal was behind the table, a multiple-line phone sat on the table, which was piled high with papers. Two guest chairs faced the table; several books were piled on the floor as well; enlarged photos of the seashore were on the office walls.

"Please be seated. What can I do for you, Mr. Edwards? Is it about my wife? I haven't heard from the police in over three years. Do you have any information about her killer?"

Grayson had to bluff. He had asked his office if they had anything on Dr. Gard. They had told him by phone of the unsolved murder, and that Gard had always been a suspect, that he had to resign from the hospital because of an infirmity, and that the murderer had never been caught. One thing Grayson had to do was prevent any autopsy of Leyden. An autopsy would reveal that the reason for Leyden's death was poison. An investigation would naturally have been opened.

It is oftentimes luck that makes the most intelligent plans succeed. Grayson's instincts told him he had drawn the lucky straw in Dr. Gard, who was obviously nervous and in painful hesitation at meeting him.

"Yes. Certainly, I do wish I had some information about that tragic and brutal murder. I'm sure that you're suffering a great deal…and that you continue to suffer. Horrible…."

"Yes, I do miss her so much. . .life has never been the same without her. What office do you represent?"

"I'm with the security services of Her Majesty's government. I've been sent to ask you to assist the government in a pressing matter. Dr. Gard, you have in your morgue David Leyden, who recently died. . .we believe of a heart attack. He was one of Her Majesty's government's best agents on this island and an autopsy would be inappropriate, given the security nature of his position. Do you think that is possible?" As he said that, he opened his briefcase and took out a large manila envelope and placed it on the table. "I am authorized by Her Majesty's government to give this to you, for your helpful cooperation."

"Do you have identification?" Gard inquired, his voice soft and hesitant, the expression on his face submissive. He was afraid, and was asking the question because he felt he had to.

"Of course." Grayson took out his wallet and slipped out a plastic card with his picture and position, Director of Operations, Foreign Office. He passed the card over to Gard who looked at it casually, then handed it back.

"This is not your true identity, am I correct?"

"You can call that number and they will verify my position. Feel free to call now, if that would make you feel more comfortable."

"What if I don't agree to do what you wish me to do?"

"Oh?" Grayson feigned surprise. "Well, I suppose that is for you to decide. It would be a shame to disturb your peaceful life on this island and reopen your wife's murder case. So much time has passed. Such a shame. One never knows what a review of the evidence will show when old suspects are now more thoroughly scrutinized."

Gard fell silent. Gazing at Grayson, a sense of weariness overcame him. He took the envelope.

Gard swung his chair around so that his back was now facing Grayson. He tore open the flap, peered into the envelope, then took out its contents. He counted thirty 1000-pound notes.

"All this just not to conduct an autopsy?" he said as he swung his chair around now to face Grayson.

"Yes. And Her Majesty's Government will be most thankful if you can be of assistance at this delicate time."

"What if the Leyden family wants me to conduct an autopsy?"

"I don't think they will. But, if they do…then you can indicate you will, but, of course, you won't undertake such a procedure. Correct?"

"Well…."

"Dr. Gard. You have taken the envelope; we certainly won't give the information we have regarding your wife's true murderer, whom I suspect you know, to the police. Do not hesitate. We expect you to cooperate. This is an important security matter for the government. You can be assured that, should your cooperation be full, the file we have on your wife's untimely death will be closed. I must have your assurance that there will be no autopsy of Mr. Leyden's body. Agreed?"

Gard, his lowered his head, suggesting he was looking at the papers he was shuffling on his desk.

"The file will be destroyed?" Gard asked, still looking down at his papers.

"Permanently," Grayson answered. "No autopsy on Mr. Leyden."

"Agreed." Gard finally looked directly at Grayson.

"If you don't mind," Grayson continued to talk softly, "I'll wait for a copy of the death certificate. Will that be a problem?"

"Well, it will take me a few minutes."

"I'm confident that you'll be accurate as to the cause of death."

"Certainly. Very accurate," Gard said as he turned slightly to log onto his computer. "We do everything by the computer. The forms we use are on the computer. I'll need some information, height, weight, and so on. You'll have to excuse me, as I'll have to go to the preparation room and take these measurements. It'll only be a few moments."

"I have that information here." Grayson smiled, reaching into his side pocket and drawing out a small piece of paper. "Here are his vital statistics. From looking at him in your mortuary, I believe they're still valid. I certainly don't mind waiting."

"You have come well prepared, Mr. Edwards, very well prepared"

"You are kind to say that. So many times, the intelligence services are criticized for not being so well prepared. We do try…from time to time, we do try." Grayson's smile broadened as he handed the paper over to Gard. "Please, does this information help?"

Gard glanced at the statistics on the sheet. "Yes, these seem to be correct. The deceased is very heavy and not too tall…yes seems correct." Gard took but a few moments to enter the data into the computer, printing out the form, which he quickly signed, passing it on to Grayson.

"The original? No, I'll take a copy. I assume the original will go to the family."

"Yes. Of course. You can understand why I'm a bit confused. This is so irregular, must have been thinking of something...." Gard let the rest of his words drop as he rose, went over to a small copy machine on a side table, made several copies, and handed one over to Grayson.

"Thank you, Dr. Gard. Untimely death for Mr. Leyden. The destinies of men, Dr. Gard, are unaccountable things, now aren't they? You have been most helpful to Her Majesty's Government. Goodbye and, again, thank you. We are most pleased that you have been dignified throughout this discussion. Most dignified."

"Goodbye, Mr. Edwards."

Grayson turned, and without haste opened the door and calmly walked out.

Fourteen

The light in the room was very bright moonlight filtering through the windows of Jennifer's bedroom. He lay quite still in bed, Jennifer naked in his arms, her head resting on his chest, her breathing signifying deep satisfaction. He felt as if he was submerged into a half-conscious depth of velvet contentment, in which all kinds of agreeable thoughts floated around like lazy fish in a warm sea. It was a happy time for him, at peace and rest. He wanted this feeling to remain always. This picture to him was exact. It was all so different from his earlier relationship. Only now he understood it to have been a pretense. He wondered if what was happening to him was happening much too fast, and yet perhaps not. He was completely taken in by Jennifer, and he knew it wasn't a boy's romantic passion. Softly stroking her silky black hair and realizing that every beginning has another beginning, he closed his eyes, pleasantly tired, and soon returned to a deep sleep.

The previous day on Guernsey was beginning to blur—all unreal and yet too real. The day tore him rather badly, certainly not in his body, but in his soul. The death of Leyden, the discussion with Farris about Zoran, the request to lie about Zoran's real name, the retreat of Farris from pursuing Keiran when he said he wasn't going to lie. Keiran always wanted to live life's game in his own particular manner. But to be able to play a game in this way, a man needs strength and discipline. Keiran had this history. But now he was frightened.

He was now into his ninth week in London and he understood that his relationship with Farris had become less than noble. He believed that now, after his direct conversation with Farris, he would be about as welcome in the London office as a firecracker let off in the middle of his Quincy parish church mass. He knew that Farris would be waiting for him at the office. Farris, a man with an insecure disposition, though clever, was waiting for him with a verbal club, probably now calling him 'a damn young fool' or more harsh words, all the while thinking in the back of his mind that Keiran was trying to destroy his relationship with his client. Farris probably felt insulted, and well he might. He should not have asked me to lie, Keiran told himself. Yet, again, he didn't want to be wearing too much of a halo. He wanted to be practical, but honest and was beginning to feel that just maybe those two attitudes were not, in reality, compatible.

When he left Guernsey, the sparkling sun had disappeared behind gathering storm clouds, and the sea was as gray as lead. Arriving in London, the evening sky was clear, the air balmy. It was as if the day's weather on Guernsey had been reversed with that in London, normally soggy and wet in spring. The cab drew up to 54 Cliverowe Mews, a large, dark, rustic, brick townhouse with weathered black shutters clearly in need of paint. The mild wind troubled the foliage on the sole oak tree sitting squarely in the centered of a modest, yet neatly trimmed, lawn that abutted the worn, matching-tinted brick walkway. He had arrived at Jennifer's apartment, anxious and wanting badly to be with her. He had called her at the ITN studios believing that she would be there after her evening program. But she had already left. He had then called her apartment but she wasn't there, so he left a message: "Jennifer, I'm on my way to London. Should be there around 9:00 or 9:30. I'd like to see you this evening, so I'll come by your apartment. I hope this will be okay. If you're not there...well...then...well...then, I'll head back to the club. A lot has happened today and, well..." Keiran hesitated for a moment, but then continued, "I'd like to be with you." He was disappointed when he tried again upon his arrival at the London airport, and she was still not home. He didn't want to think about the fact that she may now be with Medill. Still, Grayson said to him at Saturday's dinner party that Jennifer seemed to be putting off the marriage, encouraging him to make a play for her. He wasn't inclined to be in the competitive process of winning her over. He wanted to be accepted by her, totally—and now. A man gets confused thoughts when he is not only tired from a day of the unexpected, but also knows that he wants to be with a woman with whom he is falling in love.

He hurried up the brick and stone entrance steps, stopping to read the directory of residents, encased in a small glass-covered, lighted, brass shadow box attached to the right side entrance wall, next to the double black door. 'J. Berley. No. 4A.' He pressed the buzzer next to her name, his heart pounding. She has to be here.... Calm down, he kept telling himself, calm down. If she is not there...so be it. That's life. Yeah, shit...that's life. One has to have a detached resignation at times. He frowned as he pressed the button again.

"Yes...?" His heart raced more as he heard her voice.

"Jennifer, Jennifer...it's me, Keiran."

"Great, you're here! Come up," she said, her voice enthusiastic, beautiful and soft. "Take the lift. It's down a bit and in the middle of the corridor. I'll be waiting for you. I'm happy you're here, Keiran. I was worried about you."

"Be right there," Keiran replied.

He didn't wait for the elevator, but hustled up the stairs, taking two steps at a time. At the stop of the steps, the door stood open, Jennifer waiting outside in the corridor, her black slacks and black and white stripe silk blouse showing off her figure well. Her smile was wide, her brown eyes sparkling.

"Keiran.... Somehow I knew you wouldn't take the lift." She laughed as she took a few steps to meet him. Keiran dropped his briefcase and overnight bag, put his arms around her, pulling her close to him, kissing her ardently. She didn't resist, holding on to him tightly, her body feeling his hardness, then playfully pulling herself away.

"Do Americans have any manners? Aren't you suppose to at least say hello before you grab me and get, well you know...get so excited?"

Her smile was wide as she leaned back, looking up at him, her hands holding on to his arms.

"Yeah, we normally do. Hello..." then he grabbed her again, kissing her, his hands exploring more of her, his hands unbuttoning her blouse, one hand slipping behind, trying to unsnap her bra. "Keiran. Please...I'm...I'm happy you're here, but shouldn't we go inside?"

"Oh! Sure...I'm sorry. I've just thought of you so often since Sunday, and I just...well, I need to be with you very badly.... That wasn't said right. It's been such a day, Jennifer. I want to stay with you tonight." His words came out rapidly, as he was afraid he would forget them if he didn't speak quickly. "I didn't really mean what I was thinking to come out the way it did."

He slowly removed his hand from her breast, and was beginning to re-button her blouse when she reached up and stopped him.

"You should get your cases, Keiran and we should go inside." He reached down and picked up his briefcase and overnight bag, slowly walking into the apartment, placing them down on the floor in the vestibule.

Jennifer closed the door behind him, all the while looking at him, his eyes so weary, his large frame a bit stooped. From the moment she had met him, he had touched the woman in her. She admired him, not only his originality, but also his fierceness of purpose, his belief in himself, perhaps a touch of arrogance, and a skin that wasn't easily rubbed raw. Certainly, he wasn't flamboyant or radical. So unlike Medill, who had a jealous disposition and a proprietary nature. Right now, Keiran was like a child—big, solid, boyish, lovable, and so lonely.

"Come here, Keiran." Her hands rose to his face, tenderly stroking his cheeks for several moments, pushing his locks of black hair that had fallen over his forehead. "I am very fond of you Keiran...very fond of you...but you know my situation...." she said, putting her head on his chest, holding him tightly.

"I don't care, Jennifer. I know that I love you and I believe you love me."

"Keiran, we just met.... You know this...."

"Jennifer, don't you understand? I don't care about whatever he is…I'm not going to give up." She looked at him, his voice the sound of the sea on a lonely night.

"I…. But I'm…. This is so soon, don't you understand…? This is so soon…yet, I feel so different about you. I really do. When I heard your voice messages, and how unhappy they sounded, I was worried about you. For the first time, I actually cared enough about a man to worry about him."

It was nine in the morning before he woke up. Jennifer still had her head on his chest, but she was awake.

"You know, Keiran," she spoke softly, her hand reaching up and brushing her fingers through his hair, "you need a haircut." He laughed softly. "You've also made my life very confusing." She leaned over closely and kissed him, "very confusing."

"What do you mean?" he asked softly. She kept her head on his chest, hearing his heartbeat.

"Oh, nothing really. Keiran Hogan, do you realize that you have a very slow heart beat?"

"Well, no. Is that bad?"

"I don't think so. I think it means you're healthy. Very healthy."

"Good. Come here. Let's get closer."

"Keiran, do you have a tendency to brood?"

"In a questioning mood? Brood. Yeah, maybe at times…I think of things too deeply, perhaps. I try to offset those moments by the swimming routine. Do you think I'm moody now?"

"No. I was just inquiring." He wondered why she asked that question, trying to quickly examine what he had said or done to indicate any moodiness.

"Meeting you and now being with you has muddled a great deal in my life that I thought was certain. What I mean is Medill has asked me to…."

"Marry you. I know. Grayson told me. But, you're not married, so in my mind you're free...and you know I'm more than just fond of you. The minute I met you, something inside me.... I've never felt this way before for any woman. I knew then you were special to me. So that is all I can say. Unless you tell me to go away, I'd like to be with you, Jennifer, for as long as ever means. And, if you wanted to marry him, you've would have a long time ago, right?" Keiran spoke softly.

She stared at his face, noting the air of innocence about him, his blue eyes now taking on a luster, boyish eyes in a man's face, she thought. She didn't feel that she was the kind of woman who could be sentimental about a man just because he had an air of innocence. No, she felt for his essential kindness, his candor. She was falling in love herself and knew she was listening to the same music that he was.

"I know. I know. Right now, though, I should get up and get us some breakfast. Don't you have to go to work this morning?"

"Yeah, I probably should have been there over an hour ago, but I'm not worried about it. I'll have to call them though. Are you happy about my staying, Jennifer? I mean, did I...."

"I've never been happier, Keiran. Let me get up and get us something to eat. You must be hungry."

"No need to, really. I'd just like to clean up and then go on to the office. I still have my overnight bag, so I don't have to go back to the club. Would you like to join me in the shower?" He laughed and pulled her even closer to him.

"You never stop Keiran. Of course, I want to, but then if I do, you'll never leave, you'll get into trouble with your firm, and then you'll blame me for getting you fired."

She rose from the bed, reaching for her robe, on a side chair.

"You don't have to put it on for me. I like what I see." Keiran jumped out of bed, grabbed her, hugging her closely.

"Keiran! You've got to get ready. Now go!"

"Can I come again tonight?" he asked, looking at her again with the eyes that seemed so lost and wistful.

"Don't be silly. Yes, of course."

"I'll probably have to work late tonight, though. You have the evening broadcast?" Keiran asked.

"Yeah. I'm through by seven thirty. Why don't I meet you at Rumours on Sloan Square around eight or so? You know where the restaurant is?"

"No, but I'll find it. You have my cell phone number, Jennifer, don't you?"

"I don't think so."

"Can you remember 233-57890?"

"No, write it down by the phone. Now go clean up."

"So you're not coming with me. You do have to wash up, don't you?"

"No, not now, stop tempting me. You're awful!"

He rose from the bed, grabbed her again, kissed her and then went off to get ready for what he expected would be a difficult day at the office.

He wanted to take a long shower, but realized that he couldn't. Farris was probably at the office already rehearsing, in all probability, what he was going to say to Keiran. HenHen was probably anxiously calling the club, leaving messages for him. He was sorry for both, for he believed that they were doing things that had ceased to be worthwhile, and they were merely messing about with idle work and words. They must know by now that he didn't jump when Farris barked.

Jennifer's eyes rested on Keiran as he entered her dining room. He walked over, kissed her lightly on the cheek, his hands reaching into her robe, feeling her warm breasts.

"Keiran. You have to stop. You'll never get away from here, and you'll make me spill the orange juice." She smiled and kissed him back. "Now, sit down and eat."

The table was set beautifully for him. There was toast, cereal, strawberries, juice, coffee, and even pale orange sherbet linen napkins.

"You didn't have to do all of this for me"

"Notice, everything is healthy."

"I'm going to like living here," he laughed.

"Now don't get any ideas, Keiran. I have a great deal to sort out. You do understand, don't you?"

"Yeah, I do. I guess so," Keiran replied.

He pulled out his cell phone from his jacket pocket and punched in his office number. He noted the time indicated on his phone was 10:00. God, he'd have to talk to HenHen. The firm's receptionist, a young girl named Trish, answer cheerfully.

"Kenton & Ward."

"Hi! Trish. This is Keiran. I'm on my way to the office."

"Mr. Hogan.... Wait, wait, don't hang up. HenHen wants to talk to you. She told me to put you through. I think Mr. Farris is angry; they've left several messages at your club. Where are you?"

"Trish, now don't become a younger version of HenHen. Listen, I'm on my way. So don't worry, okay?"

"I'll have to pass you to HenHen. She did say...."

"Trish, I'm in a hurry, so please tell her and Farris I'm on my way." He hung up.

"Everyone waiting for you?" Jennifer said as she poured Keiran some coffee. "You seem pretty angry in your tone. Why are you so angry?"

"Oh, the firm's chief secretary is always bugging me to let her know where I am all the time...just so they can reach me. I suppose they thought I was at the club and tried there and I didn't answer the page, so I suspect they think I'm stiffing them. I told them from Guernsey that I would be in the office in late morning. So here is late morning. Yet Farris's secretary can get so excited about the silliest things. I guess she means well, though."

"She's probably just trying to do her job. I have to notify the studio where I am, just in case there is a breaking news story and they need some help. I guess it's part of both our jobs."

"Yeah. Maybe." Keiran gobbled one slice of toast, gulped his juice, and began to eat the cereal and berries.

"You never told me what happened on the island, Keiran. You sounded so distressed actually. By the way, Keiran, do you realize that you talk in your sleep?"

"I do?"

"Yes. But I couldn't understand what you were saying. Once I kissed you, though, you never said another word and I went back to sleep."

"There you have it. I need you to get my sound sleep. The island. Well, the agent we use for all our work on the island died of a heart attack while we were at a restaurant with our client. Pretty upsetting, actually. I had spent most of the day with him doing all our client's work, and then—poof—he's gone. The client thought it was a heart attack. Maybe it was. I'd never seen someone die before. It makes you think about a lot of things, actually."

"My God. How sad. Did he complain about anything before he died?"

"No, he just got up to go the bathroom, and then just bent over and fell to the floor. What is strange, though, is that when I talked to Farris, he told me to lie to the police about the name of the firm's client who was at the restaurant table with me and the agent."

"Lie? Why on earth? And what were the police doing there?"

"I guess that it's standard, when someone dies so suddenly. The police are called just to interview any witnesses. But Mr. Farris didn't even want the client to be interviewed by the police. That wasn't a problem, though, because the client had already left to board his plane back to London."

"What did you do?"

"I told Farris I wasn't going to lie. I think he was pissed. Really pissed. I just don't think anyone gets anywhere lying. These were police. There were other witnesses in the restaurant. Can you imagine where my credibility would be if the police found out the real name of the client? Then I'd be in trouble for misleading the police. I wasn't going to take that chance. No way."

"Who is your client?"

"Zoran Hemmrich. Ever hear of him?"

"Can't say I have. What kind of business is he in?"

"Cement. Other commodities such as wheat, fertilizer, some oil. Very successful man. Jennifer, I just can't be the kind of lawyer that Farris wants me to be. I don't think I can really work with him."

"Farris should understand the situation. I agree it would have been ridiculous to lie about your client's name. Stupid, actually."

"Agreed. Well, I'd better go. Thanks for the breakfast. Next time, I'll get it for you."

He rose from the table, went over to Jennifer, kissed her lightly, holding her hands for several moments, softly saying, "Thanks, Jennifer. I really love you. See you tonight."

"I love you too, Keiran. Now, don't get angry when you get to the office. Promise?"

He hesitated.

"Promise Keiran."

"Okay, Jennifer. I promise."

He kissed her again, holding her tightly, feeling her warm body and wishing like hell he could stay with her forever.

Fifteen

Diana Peters poked her head into Keiran's office, her smile and blue eyes wide, wearing a perfume that smelled like white lilies, her green dress form-fitting, suggesting to Keiran a sensuousness about her that was a little inflamed. "So you're back."

"Keiran, if you're at all interested, rumor has it that Farris is going to have your head this morning. What did you do on that favorite island of his? And when are you going to organize your office? All these files on the floor and on the chairs." Before sitting down, she reached over, took a stack of his files off a guest chair seat, and dropped them to the floor aside her chair, scattering a few.

"Well, hello to you, Diana, and watch what you do to my files. Valuable info in them." Keiran looked at her, his eyes moving quickly, surveying her figure. "You're looking pretty good this morning. Sophisticated, nice…or are those sexist comments?"

"Do I look like a lady that doesn't like favorable comments from men, sexist or not? I wore green in your honor, and only in your honor, you fink," she countered seductively, giving Keiran a look as if shocked by his question. "At least you're noticing. A good start on renewing our relationship."

"Renewing our relationship? Did it ever start? Another myth shattered." Keiran laughed. "To answer your queries: one, I don't have a file cabinet yet. HenHen says it's on order; two, absolutely nothing happened on the island. So how have you been?"

"You are an absolutely horrible man, and I still love you. Fellow associate Hogan, you call the death of the firm's agent on the island nothing? Come on Keiran, show a little remorse and sadness. Or is keeping inside information to yourself part of your persona?"

"Diana, watch it now. More importantly, how did you know that?"

"HenHen has a loud mouth…especially when she goes all over the office asking where you are and drops hints about this that and the other thing. The depth of her information can be infinite. I don't think she likes you very much, Keiran."

"What a shame! God Almighty, what a laughable shame. HenHen doesn't like me. I won't get my file cabinet. I'll beg her forgiveness. You have to be joking. You think I care? Come now, Diana. Get serious. Yeah, your 'inside info' on what happened on the island is true. What happened wasn't only unexpected, but also a bit strange. Never had someone die right in front of me. Right now, everything is a cloud. A bit confusing."

"My God. How dreadful. And then what…?" Diana sat up slightly, pulling her chair to Keiran's desk, so as to be closer, as if secrets were about to be passed between them.

"I really can't tell you much more, at least not now. Maybe later. So, Diana, how was your weekend? Calm and uneventful I trust."

"You're not going to take me into your confidence and tell me all? Always ignoring me, Keiran Hogan. 'Fink' and Keiran Hogan are now one and the same. You ask how my weekend went. Are you making small conversation or are you really interested? Don't even try to answer that. I'm going to tell you anyway. Well, 'fink'…."

"Diana, I'm trying to be pleasant to you…so no more name-calling. It's unseemly from someone as nice looking as you."

Diana feigned shock; she tossed her head back, her hand went up to her breast, and she began laughing hilariously, "Two compliments in one morning. I can't stand it. Enough already, okay? Since you ignored me all last week, this weekend I went back to my friend Sebastian. Actually, he called, and said that he needed me…and I never turn down a man in need. Those demands bring an obvious reply from me. You know how warm-hearted I am, and besides, it's not ladylike. And where were you last night? Not alone, I suspect?"

"Good for you. Never turning a man down. I'll remember that when I'm in need." He winked at her as he rose from his desk. "I better go. I know Farris is waiting for me—panting like a dog ready to pounce on my every brilliant word."

"Sure. Sure. I'll have the headache powder ready in my office, so drop by after he gives you a migraine for the week. And, Sir Keiran, you didn't answer my question. Did you sleep alone last night?"

"Well, actually, there were several in my bed. So I'd better not divulge my vices…at least to you, and certainly not now." His smile now wide, he waved a file at Diana, before flipping it over to a pile on the right side of his office. "There, I made it, and all the paper stayed in the file." He got up and clapped his hands together lightly.

"Keiran Hogan. Did anyone ever tell you that you're absolutely horrible?" Diana said as she rose from her chair, taking Keiran by his hand, leading him to his office doorway.

"Yup. You just did. That's okay. I like you anyway." Diana leaned over and kissed him on the cheek.

"Do you think Farris will kiss me like that?"

"No, I don't. Be careful, though. Promise. Oh! What the hell, you'll promise and then do exactly what you want to do."

"You think Farris is upset at me...? Well, let me tell you something, he should be worried about how upset I am about him. One thing is certain. He'll know that I'm not some hack lawyer in a Mafia movie who's supposed to keep his mouth shut. Anger is a minor definition of how I feel about him. I'm disgusted."

They both walked out the doorway, arm in arm. She spoke softly now, "Keiran, remember you're an associate. You're suppose to grovel…g-r-o-v-e-l. That's an English word for 'crawl on your knees.'"

"Thanks for the advice. I may kick him instead of licking his boots."

"Take care of yourself, Keiran…and please be careful…you know Farris can be a snake, a peculiarly cunning, withering creature." Her voice was concerned as she stopped for a moment at her office entrance, still holding Keiran's hand.

"Don't worry. If anyone should worry, it should be Farris. See you later. I owe you lunch," he said, squeezing her hand for a moment. "Hey, thanks for your concern."

"Promises, promises…I'll wait."

As he hurried down the hall toward Farris' office, all the office doors along the corridor were opened and he heard several phones ringing. Busy place, he said to himself, trying to organize his mind so that when he saw Farris he would be respectful, even though his thoughts were to be otherwise. The guy's dishonest, an unstable, tipsy fool, he silently told himself. Lying about a client's name to the police. For God's sake. How stupid is he and how stupid does he think I am? He better understand I wasn't employed to be a messenger of his deceits. Fuck it. If I start down that pathway, he'll soon treat me like some character out of *Alice in Wonderland*. I'd be left scurrying down the rabbit hole again and again, He's such a fuckin' jerk.

HenHen barely looked up from her computer, her fingers flying across the keys in a frenzy. She looked something like a chicken whose head had just been severed and was flaying around aimlessly.

"Good morning, HenHen."

"Good morning to you Mr. Hogan. Mr. Farris was expecting you over an hour ago. He will see you now," her lips were barely moving, her face having a stubborn immobility, keeping her eyes glued to the monitor. Her face was, to Keiran, like a mash of white wax with two black motionless eyes. Her attitude, he thought, always reflected Farris, so Keiran knew from looking at her that the meeting with Farris would be difficult.

"Did you have a nice weekend, HenHen?" He asked the question to show he was ignoring her tightness of voice.

"Yes, and you?" Her voice was somewhat petulant.

"It was fine, actually, but different." Keiran responded, a slight smile on his face.

"Mr. Hogan. Mr. Farris is waiting for you, so we shouldn't keep him waiting now, should we? Please go in his office." She finally looked up at him, then tilted her head toward Farris' office door.

"We shouldn't keep Mr. Farris waiting. Absolutely not," Keiran responded.

She glared at him, knowing that he was mimicking her. He smiled back. As he walked into Farris' office, he was feeling both hot and cold. He was angry with himself for feeling that way. It was absurd for him to feel this way. He wanted to be contemptuous of Farris but knew it would be futile. Yet he could no longer help feeling this way about Farris. One thing though, he wasn't about to let Farris play emotional tricks with him. Keiran had no intention of surrendering. He had come to London bent on making a success of his profession…and he had now fallen in love. As he walked into Farris' office, he rallied himself; he would express himself without being a fool…and he wouldn't cave. He no longer felt the need to dispell the notion that he is not an unimportant young man.

When he walked into Farris' office, he was astonished to see Zoran there. HenHen made no mention of his being with Farris. She didn't want me to know. Figures. This is not going to be graceful, he reflected silently.

"Good morning Mr. Farris, Mr. Hemmrich." It was a few moments before Farris, sitting stiffly in a padded black leather chair, lifted his eyes from the document he was reading to reply to Keiran. Zoran was seated in one of the two overstuffed gray leather wing chairs that faced Farris' desk. Keiran paused for a moment.

"Good to see you here in the office, Keiran," Farris looked up from his reading. "Thought you would be here much earlier, but I suppose that you needed the rest," he said, looking at Keiran, his eyes with a brittle darkness, he continued, his tone that of a stranger, "what with all that went on in Guernsey."

"Can't you see he has been with a woman?" Zoran laughingly interrupted, with visible relish, as he glanced at Farris, then his eyes fixed on Keiran. "He has the look of satisfaction in his eyes. Come now, Duane, this signal only comes when one is with a woman. I know it all too well. In fact, I'm sure he wishes he were with his lady friend rather than here. Am I correct Keiran? And, good morning to you Keiran." Zoran's smile was wide, his tone indicating that he was certain of his comments about Keiran. He rose and extended his hand, which Keiran shook. Farris looked at both without comment. Keiran didn't reply, wondering if the disreputable like Zoran are more amusing when they act as if they're reputable, but he wasn't about to argue the point Zoran made. Keiran bowed slightly to Zoran, broke into soft laugher, and strolled over to sit in the empty chair next to Zoran, who after shaking Keiran's hand sat down, was looking again at his file folder and continuing to flip through the contents.

"I didn't realize, Mr. Farris, that I had to be here meet you at a specific time," he replied, staring directly at Farris. "You mentioned over the phone that you would see me sometime this morning, which is when we're now meeting. If I knew you wanted me at a specific time, I would have made every effort to be here." Keiran's voice was steady and calm. His cheeks reddened with a flush brought on by restrained anger.

"Keiran, I understand what 'in the morning' means. I believe that we have had a discussion about timeliness," Farris replied, his utterances sounding even and firm, much like a banker who has just notified an owner that he was foreclosing on his property…a certain smugness that clearly indicated, 'and you can't do anything about what I just said, don't even try.'

"The problem is that we obviously disagree. When I say I'll meet you in the morning, it means first thing in the morning. You think otherwise. No matter, in private, we can have as extensive a discourse as you would like on that subject. Regardless, our client Zoran seems to have analyzed the reason for your tardiness. I just don't believe, Keiran, that personal matters should inhibit our professional work. I'm positive you agree with that, but we need not get into that discussion either at this time. We have a more important matters. We have been waiting for over an hour for you, and now that you're here, we can begin." A shade of dark displeasure crossed Farris' features as he continued, "Coffee, Keiran? Zoran, more coffee?"

"Yes, I'll have some. Black." Keiran replied, his voice soft and calm.

"Certainly, I'll have another cup." Zoran added. He looked quickly at Keiran, a slight smile crossing his face. He quickly gave Keiran a wink of his eye, then lowered his head, continuing to scan the file he was holding.

"Another item, Keiran...."

"Before 'another item,' Mr. Farris," Keiran interrupted, his voice now elevated in tone, "it would be best if you were precise about when you want me to attend a meeting with you. I don't understand vagueness. You want me here at 7:00, 8:00, or whatever time and I'll be here."

"Naturally, naturally," Farris gazed at Keiran, his lips barely moving, as he continued, "we'll add that to the list of items we shall discuss privately later." Farris pressed the intercom button, repeating the coffee orders to HenHen who, later brought in a tray, placed it on a side table, and set the first the cup for Zoran.

"Fresh coffee for you, Mr. Hemmrich." HenHen delicately handed him his cup. Turning to Keiran she smiled, then gave him his cup. "Nothing in your coffee, right, Mr. Hogan?" She spoke, her voice sugary yet unconvincing in sincerity. Keiran wanted to laugh at her serving him, calling him Mr. Hogan. He realized that her manners were not directed at him, but at Mr. Farris and Zoran.

"Fine. Just black. Thanks, HenHen." She smiled, then quietly left the room.

"Now, to business." Farris opened a folder in front of him looking at the first page, which he fingered carefully. "First, Keiran, I want to say again how much I appreciate the manner in which you handled David's untimely death. It's still difficult for me and for Zoran to understand this sudden turn. His wife tells me that he had no history of any heart problems. She asked that an autopsy be performed, so perhaps we'll have some answer after that. It's very sad, however. He was a modest fellow; accommodating to Zoran, a solid, moral man, a man who felt rather happy about his life. We'll miss him." Farris looked hesitant. All his comments were given in a monotone while he watched Keiran's face, like a lion ready to pounce.

Keiran gave a slight and restive shake of his head.

"I only met him yesterday," Keiran replied, "he was gracious to me in the short time I was with him he told me a great deal about the island, its registration protocol, and of course, about his boat. I think, if he could, he would have spent all his time on that boat—you probably know the name—'Play Fair.' He was an easy fellow with whom to talk and he certainly knew his business."

Zoran looked up from his file, but said nothing, returning to the intimacy of reviewing whatever papers intrigued him in the folder in his lap.

"Yes. Yes. Yes…he did admire his boat," Farris answered in a casual, uncaring manner. "We, unfortunately don't have the time, however necessary and appropriate that would be, to dwell on his death. We move on, as we must. Keiran, you were upset yesterday when I asked you to provide the police with a false name for Zoran. I must say in all candor that your feelings of dishonesty were misplaced. There is a serious reason for my suggestion. I wasn't, to coin a metaphor, asking you to be a mason, building a wall of lies around Zoran on the…."

"Then what were you asking me to do?" Keiran interrupted, his stare now making Farris uncomfortable. He avoided Keiran by again looking at Zoran and then returning to his cursory review of a file on his desk, turning the pages slowly, before raising his eyes to meet Keiran's steady gaze.

"Keiran, you must let me finish. Are associates this rude in Washington? Always interrupting?"

Keiran restrained his impulse to make a mockery of the excuses he now knew would be coming from Farris. He remained silent.

"You will recall the untimely explosion at the Parrot Restaurant in Mayfair just a few days ago? Zoran left that restaurant just a few minutes before the blast occurred. As you most assuredly know, the police continue to say that it was leaking gas that created the explosion. I'm not an expert, and the police may be right, but I don't think so. Zoran arrived about an hour before to meet the guest of honor, Mile Draculic, with whom he has done business over the years. Mr. Draculic wanted Zoran to stay for dinner, but Zoran left. He is alive today because he left early. He believes that the perpetrators were also after him. Virtually all of the Serbian support group in London was wiped out in that event."

"Why would Zoran be targeted?" Keiran countered, thinking to himself, this whole story seemed incredulous…but then, the Runnard report, arms dealing…maybe…just maybe….

"There's a show of reason in your question, Keiran," Zoran intruded. "As you know, I sell products, commodities, cement, oil products, fertilizer and related materials. I have sold to companies owned by Mr. Draculic, who was, perhaps, among his other activities, a prominent supporter of the Serbian cause in England. As I have had dealings with him over the years, I was invited, but left, before the explosion. I was very, very fortunate to escape death." Zoran's voice was mechanical and emotionless, like someone giving a report on budget numbers before a corporate board of directors.

Keiran turned to Zoran but didn't react.

"So you can understand, I hope," Zoran continued, "why I try always to be practical in my movements. Sometimes I have the instinct that something is not to my liking, so I change. I leave. I had the same feeling on Guernsey when I saw Dave fall over. Perhaps it was a heart attack, perhaps not. Perhaps someone was after me and hit him instead. Who knows?"

"I was with you and saw the same thing that you did. Dave rose from his chair, then keeled over and dropped to the floor. How would anyone have killed him right in front of us?" Keiran remarked.

"One never knows for sure, Keiran. Never. I'll be interested in the autopsy, though," Zoran responded.

"Why would anyone be after you anyway?" Keiran queried, shaking his head slightly. "People are after businessmen who sell cement?"

"There are many strange people in the world, Keiran," Farris added. "Even in business, competitors—especially jealous ones—tend to take harsh measures against one another, including murder in the form of accidents. That may be hard for you to understand, but it's true."

Again, Keiran turned to Zoran, asking, "Are you sure that you aren't selling something else? Or maybe those after you may think you're selling something that is not helping whoever they represent. Is there something that your competitors know that we don't know—or at least I don't know?"

There was a long silence.

Farris opened a file in front of him, trying to appear preoccupied, while Zoran merely stared at Keiran, his face darkened in obvious displeasure at Keiran's suggestion. He made a furtive glance to Farris.

"Smart, Keiran Hogan. An excellent question," Zoran finally responded. "My enemies may think I am doing something wrong, but on my honor, I tell you I am not!" He looked at Keiran with steady eyes, a slow smile crept across his face, the darkness fading quickly from his face. "That is it, Keiran. That is it." After a few moments reflection, he returned to reading the papers in his file. It was Farris who then responded in a slow, frosty voice.

"I agree with Zoran that the question is an excellent one. The answer is fairly simple, though. What Zoran's companies sell is in the public domain. It is no secret...none whatsoever. The letters of credit, purchasers, all are on the record. To be precise, Keiran, Zoran is not selling a product that he is not legally entitled to sell. Zoran is only giving you his impression of events. He has been in business for over twenty years and has dealt with many different kinds of personalities, some of whom don't take kindly to him...wouldn't you agree with that, Zoran?"

"Yes. I believe I am a tough negotiator for the purchase of my products and, many times, those who buy the products are in positions that require strict confidentiality and different methods of product delivery, therefore my costs are much higher than normal. When the customer balks at the costs; I tell them they can go to another supplier. I have an overwhelming appeal to some and am totally disliked by others. Yet, all my business arrangements, as you know, are in conformance with the law and the tax regulations of Guernsey and other locations where I operate. Duane sees to that. I just want to sell what others may want—and at a price commensurate with the risk of that sale to that particular customer. Over the years, Keiran, I've built my business wisely, developing complex relationships between others and myself. Most assuredly, I don't share the attributes of a Joan of Arc. That should be clear to you. Unfortunately, therefore, those who think of me adversely have no qualms about retaliating, including threatening my life. I believe you understand?" His voice dropped and he spoke quietly, like someone who believed what he was saying.

Keiran could have told Zoran many things—especially about the Runnard report, the arms dealing and money laundering—but he knew that emotional interference now wouldn't be wise.

He restrained himself with difficulty, expressing himself quietly, "That is one way of describing events, I suppose. There are probably others…."

"Spoken like a true lawyer. Always options, other methods, other ways. I believe that I will like this young man and will like working with him. He doesn't have the look, or ever could have the look I don't suppose, that anything would frighten him." As Zoran spoke, Keiran looked at him and had the feeling of being sized up by a man who was articulate and acutely conscious of hiding his true business nature.

"Keiran, unless you object, I intend to have you work with Zoran on his many business arrangements. You will liaise with Dave's assistant on the island—we certainly will still use Dave's company, at least for a while—and generally be available to do what is required, legally, to effect the various contracts in which Zoran's companies are engaged. In other words, you'll be assigned to work with Zoran full time. This may require more travel and longer hours. I'm asking our Management Committee in New York to authorize me to give you a raise, which we normally give to an associate after six months in London. Does this interest you?"

Keiran wanted to say no. He was silent and turned to look on the faces of Farris and Zoran, trying to collect their sentiments on what had just been said.

"I have no objection, Mr. Farris. How much travel?"

"Zoran is going to Dublin to start negotiations with a new client. He'd like you to help him in those negotiations."

"Fine," Keiran tersely said.

"It'll be good to have you on our team, Keiran. You, I know, will be very helpful. You are perceptive, skillful and intelligent—all qualities needed in this kind of work. I won't, however, need help in the actual negotiations. But for the paperwork, the documents and so forth, I do need someone. In the past, Dave came and took care of those details. In the interim, you don't mind helping me, do you? I need your services; they will be necessary on occasion and therefore nothing will be concealed from you."

"Thank you for your kind words, Zoran. I'll do what I can to help you."

What else could he say? His head told him that the assignment to Zoran would be difficult. Yet, if he said no, he knew he would be packing his bags home. . .and he had just met Jennifer. No, another time, on his own schedule, he would leave.

"When do we leave for Dublin?" Keiran inquired.

"Tomorrow. Only one day though. We'll fly up and back in one day. I appreciate your coming with me to help me out. We will be starting another Guernsey Island company, so you may want to alert Dave's assistant to that effect."

"Satisfactory, Keiran?" Mr. Farris asked.

"Yes."

"Thank you, Keiran, for helping me out. I promise you that it won't be all work. Duane here is a workaholic, so once you're out from under him, we'll have some fun." Zoran smiled, then burst into a laugh as he looked at Farris, who also broke into a smile.

"I'll miss Dave, but I suppose that I should have suspected something untoward would happen. I believe in dreams," Zoran said, his voice taking on a sharp, yet nervous edge.

"Dreams?" Keiran looked askance for a moment.

"Yes. Do you?"

Before Keiran could answer, Farris said, "There are times I have dreams, but I forget them. Keiran?"

"I don't have dreams. I just sort of sleep…probably too soundly." They all laughed.

"True enough, Keiran. True enough." Farris responded, his voice now lighter and friendlier.

"A man of innocence, Duane, clear innocence! How lucky you are Keiran. Lucky, indeed." Zoran looked at him a bit admirably. Then he continued, his eyes closing partially, as if to concentrate on his narrative.

"Well, let me tell you that the night before I arrived on Guernsey, I had a dream. I was in Scotland fishing with Dave, which is odd, because, although he enjoys fishing, he loves sailing much, and would generally excuse himself from my fishing ventures. While fishing not too far from Inverness, where I have a country home, I encountered a strange presence, a ghost-like cloud, but the cloud had the form of a human, without eyes, a shrouded figure, yet very bright. I can't describe it any better. Fear? Perhaps. Suddenly the specter, making an unaccountable sound, turned on me and began to come toward us. We dropped our poles and fled from the water. I ran faster than Dave, and when I looked back, the presence had swallowed him. A cloud denser than anything I had ever seen simply enveloped him, and he was gone. I now know that this meant that Dave wasn't going to live…not going to live." Zoran lowered his head, and his hands began to tap quietly on his file folder. Farris swiveled his chair to a sideways position, his face staring out the window. The room fell silent.

Keiran didn't know what to think now. Was Zoran a stable man or not? Dreams? Well, maybe people do believe in them, he silently told himself. He then spoke calmly, "Well, I'd better get back to my office, Zoran. I have a great deal of work to do. Let me know when you want me to go to Dublin." Keiran stood up, as did Zoran.

"Thank you, Keiran. I'm sure we will have a good time together." They shook hands.

"Goodbye, Mr. Farris." Farris swiveled his chair back to the point where he was facing Keiran. He scowled for a moment, an ugly expression crossing his face.

"Goodbye, Keiran. We'll talk later."

"Just give me a call," Keiran said, and he left the room.

Keiran walked slowly down the corridor to his office. He had a look of distress in his eyes, wondering to himself, how did I get into this sleazy place which calls itself a law firm headed by a veritable deceitful man with an equally devious client? He didn't want to be in the firm's dark corner for such clients. He believed in holding on to certain decencies, but now he was confronting the realties he didn't like. Maybe it was tragic farce. Most likely though, he knew it not to be. What was clear from the meeting he had just left was that what was said in Farris' office and what was true were utterly different things. There were bonds that held Farris and Zoran to each other in ways Keiran was only beginning to faintly understand. Whatever it was that made them act the way they did, there wasn't a thing he could do.

Sixteen

Farris watched Keiran leave, his eyes fixed on him compulsively, as Keiran silently closed the door to Farris' darkened office. At his insistence, when the offices were being renovated, no ceiling lights were installed. He didn't like to have a brightly lighted room; it hurt his eyes, as he would remind HenHen. This morning, dim natural light came from the corner office's large windows, the overcast London sky portending heavy rain. Often he would wear glasses that were slightly tinted blue-gray to avoid being exposed to any harsh, and what he considered 'blinding' light, which was, in reality, normal room illumination. Maybe it was to avoid having anyone looking at his eyes, which appeared to be like those of a melancholy toad and so ruined an otherwise flawless face.

"You seem irritated with your new associate," Zoran commented, his voice giving a little grating crack, as he rose from his chair and went over to the corner window, looking at the Bank of England building, gloomy against the gray sky. Zoran turned to face Farris, who had swung around in his chair as Zoran slowly walked around his desk so that he faced the same view. Farris spoke, his lips barely moving, his words scratchy like a kitchen spoon and began scraping off crust hardened on a baking sheet.

"Did you watch Keiran staring at me and you? It's hard to forget that stare which, is obviously weighted with meaning. I can't decide whether its respect for us or not."

"It is clear that he is certainly straightforward in his comments, not one to deceive, I would imagine," Zoran returned to his seat, then turning the chair next to him around and placing his legs on its seat. "Excuse me, Duane. This isn't rudeness, but my legs, at times, have a tired feeling."

"How long have you had this problem? This is the first I've heard of it." Farris said, his voice taking on a more distressed tone.

"Not long, not too long. I'm okay, Duane. Please."

"You'd better be examined, Zoran. I know you don't like doctors, but I suggest you see one and have this tiredness checked out. Do you want HenHen to make an appointment?"

"No, not at all. I'll take care of this in due course, Duane," Zoran responded sharply. "Please, don't be so concerned. Now, about Hogan. Whether being straightforward…too open…whether that is a good quality in our business is another matter. He seems to be the sort of young man who, even if civilization were visibly collapsing in front of him, would remain calm and even-tempered. He handled the matter regarding Dave's death very well. He was calm, a bit arrogant, and yet efficient. I haven't made up my mind if he is the one we need for the long term. Certainly he is an independent person. Doesn't appear to me to be an ordinary silent man. Clearly speaks his mind. If he's troublesome," Zoran continued, "we can always get someone else. Can't you Duane?"

"Yes, we can," Farris answered sharply, dismissing Zoran's worry, resuming after a slight pause. "Let's not worry about him now, though. We have a more critical matter to review. You know what it is and I'm concerned, Zoran. What you did last week has bothered me," his voice sounding a faint bitterness and disappointment, "greatly, Zoran…greatly."

"For God's sake, Duane. Not again. That matter is over. Nothing will happen to me, or to you. Stop your eternal concern, please, I'm getting annoyed. Besides, who will ever know?" Zoran looked at his watch, glancing at the time. "I don't want to spend another moment on your worries. . .and I only want my worries to be yours when and if I am concerned about a matter. Right now, I'm not concerned or confused about what happened. I'm happy it has turned out in the way it did. No complaints. No regrets. Understood, Duane?"

Farris remained motionless while he gazed at Zoran. After a pause, he spoke.

"You may be right, Zoran. I sincerely hope so. You should be aware that our man at the Embassy tells me that the U. S. is providing the Brits with help in trying to find out who blew up the Parrot. What you thought was containable may not be. Draculic had been a relatively good customer for several years now. There should have been another way to collect."

Zoran sneered. "You're becoming a nuisance on this subject, Duane. I'm disturbed that you're disturbed. This is about the third, fourth, or maybe even fifth time you've deliberated on this. This repetitive discussion reminds me of a bird's cry in the desert, piercing and insistent, and I hate a bird's cry in the desert. Understand the metaphor? Listen, and listen carefully. You must know, after all these years, that I don't believe in reacting. Purposes have to be served by those who work with us, not those who attempt to betray. He had paid us about half for the weapons we had sent him, claiming that a majority of them were old, rusted Russian personal arms, not the surface-to-air missiles that he had wanted. I know he was lying. I had the shipment checked. He was holding us up. By doing that he showed his true colors as scum, a shit-face scum. He owed me twenty million dollars. You know this—you were present when I told him I would not tolerate any more payment delay. He had the weapons he had ordered. I wanted what he owed us. To me that is a simple enough proposition. Don't make it more complicated by wringing your hands now. Of course, he didn't believe me and set off making all sorts of threats—including going to the police and tax authorities unless I gave him more time to pay me. In my world, what he threatened to do is called blackmail. That was his mistake. I couldn't be content with that kind of threat—period, Duane. I simply could not." He took his legs off the side chair, pushing the chair back, muttering, "there, my legs feel much better, much, much better." He stood up, shaking both legs slightly, then sat down.

Farris kept silent, his hands continuing to fiddle with the files on his desk.

"And who knows," Zoran continued, staring intently at Farris, "he may have taken out a contract on my life. If he could get away with not paying twenty million, why not? I know my customers, Duane, very well. No, it's clear to me that he would have caused pretty serious problems. Going to the police? Maybe he had done that already by the time he spoke to me. You'd have to be blind not to see that his activity would have hurt us. I don't like intimidations, either transparent or hidden. It wouldn't be prudent for me to take the chance. He was too unstable, in my judgment. And you know…the sudden death of David, perhaps that was meant for me. Whoever he hired may still be after me."

Zoran rose from his chair and began pacing slowly in front of Farris' desk, his head slightly lowered but looking directly at Farris, leaning over and placing one hand on the file that Farris had opened.

"No more reading or making believe that you're reading the files, Duane. I'm talking to you. And when I do, you listen. Understood?"

Farris pulled the files from Zoran's grip. "Watch it Zoran. I'm your lawyer and friend, not your lackey. And don't try to intimidate me. Do you understand?"

"Duane. Don't cave in on me. I don't like that attitude."

"Draculic may have turned to the police and cooperated with them," Farris responded, his voice monotone, hiding the resentment that was inside him. He knew he was a lackey and he had accepted that for many, many years, and that was the only reason he was rich, no other. "But we don't know that," Farris continued, "and, in my judgment the chances of that are pretty remote. I know you couldn't take that chance. I also know he knew too much of our operation. I also understand that to take him out alone would have been more difficult. He has more bodyguards than you do. But all those others who were killed…just to get rid of him. That is the tragedy, Zoran. It's not him; it's the death of the others that will propel the police and government to not let go of this for a long while."

"Oh, shit, Duane! I feel I no longer know you. When did you, of all people, get moral? Please, please, get off this morality kick. These theatrics of yours sicken me. Frankly, I thought it was pretty clever—killing him and his supporters. No one will suspect us and everyone will suspect the Americans or the British intelligence services. In point of fact, I was probably doing those countries a favor. They may even agree that it was an accident and forget doing anything further. It is in their interest to continue the lie…even if they ever, and I doubt they would, find out the true nature of the explosion."

"Please sit down, Zoran. This pacing is bothersome. Killing all the innocents, though, Zoran. Just too much. Simply overreaching," Farris softly said.

"Duane, if I want to pace, I will pace. End your supercilious comments now. Those 'innocents' as you call them have no right to be defined as such. They are all guilty. You know it and so do I. Look what the people they're supporting have done to the Yugoslavia. There is more blood on their hands than you or I can ever contemplate. None of them had any compassion. They were bloodthirsty jerks who would just as soon kill as talk. What do you think that Draculic's birthday bash was? A fundraiser for the Red Cross? No, it was to grab more money—maybe to buy more arms, more likely to steal more, placing it in their Swiss bank accounts. Scum, Duane, pure scum, and although I have to deal with scum, I don't have to deal with scum who don't pay their bills. Period. End. Closed." Zoran said as he sat down, rubbing his hands together as if he were drying them with an imaginary towel.

"There is no way," he continued, "absolutely no way the police will ever trace that 'accident' to me. None whatsoever. I used one of the best people around and he is not one of us, and you don't even know him. And believe me, Duane, it was all luck…and very last minute. I'll never tell you the full story, but believe me, it was all luck." Zoran sat down, taking his coffee, commenting "It's cold," placing it back on the side table. Farris ignored the comment.

"I pray, Zoran," Farris answered gravely, "that you're right and I'm wrong. That's all. Better to work in the shadows than in the daylight. What happened at the Parrot has brought the daylight that we—I, particularly—have structured all of your operations to avoid. I don't believe that the police will stop. Maybe you should go under for a while."

"In due time, Duane. In due time. It's necessary to complete the deal with the special friends we will be meeting in Dublin. You are coming with Hogan?"

"Yes, I'll come with you…but I don't want him to be part of any of the meetings or to meet any of the principals. I don't have good vibrations about him. He is bright, but he is too independent…just too independent. He'll stand by while we negotiate and he can do the paper work. Frankly, is there much to negotiate? Haven't you already decided on the price and delivery date?"

"I'm beginning not to understand your relationship with Hogan. If you have 'bad vibrations' about him, why not replace him now? Why wait?"

"I just told you, he is bright. He's here in London. Let's see what he does in the next few days. If he doesn't work out, then we'll decide. Now, the price and so forth," Farris countered.

"Your employee. Not mine. Okay, terms. Yes, I've set them. But they have a special request that we will discuss in person. I don't have any idea of the special package they want; I have my suspicions, but I'm not certain."

"Zoran, we should be careful at this stage, and perhaps slow down additional sales until times are more calm. No need to rush into any more deals…especially if the 'special package' contains what I think it contains."

"My aren't you frightened, Duane. I've never seen so much worry on your face. Your forehead looks as if someone has drawn lines across it with a sharp, dark pencil. Relax. Please, Duane, be more confident. I know you have that ability. In our business there is never a good time; only a productive time," Zoran said, jutting out his jaw for emphasis.

"That may be so," Farris replied, "I also don't like tempting fate. Leyden's heart attack has made our team more vulnerable…."

"What makes you think," Zoran interrupted, "that it was a heart attack?"

"I'll ask the same question that Keiran asked: Who on earth would want to take him out?"

"I was there. Again, I think someone is trying to take me out, not Dave. No, whoever did this wasn't after him; they were after me."

"Good God! How paranoid can you get? Telling Hogan that you left the Parrot because you were afraid that someone was after you is a good cover, but don't go forward with the idea that Leyden died other than by natural causes. Disabuse yourself of that nonsense."

"Perhaps, for the present, this may be a mere suspicion, but like a dictator, I'm always inclined to paranoia and suspicion, and most often what I believe to be true is true. I haven't forgotten how to handle a situation…and people. I'm well aware of how to survive. Why do lawyers always feel they have the superior advice and intelligence? I've made you a very rich man—not only by paying the jacked up fees you send my companies, but also giving you a cut of all the business deals paid to your own front company. Don't lecture me. I needed your respectability behind which to operate, and you like my money. End. Finish."

Farris kept his eyes resolutely on his file papers. He knew that Zoran was right. He was ashamed and it wasn't a pitiful thing that brought on this feeling; it was exactly what Zoran had summarized: money. Zoran spoke the truth, and it was anathema to Farris. Early in his youth, he had cultivated a passion for money. When the opportunity came, he became the prostitute most favored by Zoran. He reached for his shaded glasses, putting them on quickly, to hide the moisture now entering his eyes.

Zoran again rose and walked to the large window behind Farris, glancing again at the fortress-like Bank of England building. His eyes closed for several moments, his face still looking at the scene, he asked, his voice wistful, "Duane, how may wars—both economic, military, real and imagined—have been started to save the pound? That almighty currency. Do you know, Duane?" He turned and took hold of the back of Farris' chair, swinging it around so that Farris now faced him. "Duane, are you listening? Why the dark glasses in a dark room?"

"Zoran…Zoran. What the hell are you doing? I can turn my own chair around if I want to. Now what is it?"

"You weren't listening."

"Zoran, what is it you want?" Farris asked, his voice now indicating exasperation. He sighed, and said, "something about the Bank of England?"

"Yeah, counselor," Zoran's voice took on a sarcastic tone. "How many wars have been fought to protect the pound?"

"You're kidding." Farris replied. "I don't know, perhaps many. What I do know, Zoran, is that I don't have to be reminded by you about our relationship. It's been mutually beneficial. I admit that. With the high fees you have paid, you've made me influential in the firm; I also admit you've made me a rich man. That's not as important as what else I know, which is that you made a terrible mistake on how you took out Draculic. It's that kind of thing that will attract a great deal of attention. I don't want both our lives crashing down. I don't want that to happen."

"Duane. Good old worrisome Duane. I don't want to go over this again. You're turning a simple accident into a nuclear event. What happened," Zoran countered, his voice now bitter and acerbic, "is that there was a gas leak; an explosion occurred; people are dead. End of story, Duane. Besides, remember Runnard's shit investigation? Well, he never found anything and what he did find, the government didn't pursue. You know the reasons for that as well. No, I'm not worried at all. The police will never find out the truth, unless you or I tell them."

"Zoran, why are you even suggesting that?"

"Naturally," Zoran cracked a slight smile, "I know that you, Duane would never jeopardize our relationship. Enough. What about your source at the embassy? Wouldn't he tell us if the Brits or the Americans are on to anything? We pay him handsomely…and for what? Is he worth the money we give him?"

"Probably. You've criticized me about having him on the payroll. I like having someone inside who is pliable and has access to information. You pay just in case someday you need the source to obtain critical facts. It's called insurance, Zoran," Farris said, his voice now taking on the tone of self-satisfaction, "and, as you also know, we pay a high premium for this inside source. Here, read this." Farris passed on a blue file folder toward Zoran who took it and slowly returned to his seat. Farris swiveled his chair around, following Zoran as he sat down.

"What is this?"

Zoran scanned the three pages in the file. "How did he get this information?"

"I don't know and don't care. You can read that the U. S. has offered its help to the Brits and is sending over a skilled team to help the police come to a resolution of what really happened. It is worrisome, Zoran. You have to appreciate this."

"I don't know about that. It'll be a miracle if they ever trace anything to us. An absolute miracle." Zoran handed the file back to Farris. "Don't worry. It'll never happen. No one will ever find out. Never."

"One never knows when bits of information are important…and useful."

"Don't we both kneel at the altar of deceit? And I like that, frankly," Zoran smiled.

"Information is the beginning of power…and with information, I can see more clearly," Farris said.

"You said I'm paranoid. Well, Duane, so are you."

"I like that, 'kneel at the altar of deceit.' Good phrase. Good phrase," Farris replied. They both laughed.

If one looked carefully, one would have noticed small bits of moisture coming down Farris' cheeks, making their way from underneath the bottom of his glasses, slowly crossing his pale cheeks. Smoothly, he reached for the brass holder on his desk, pulling a tissue from it, padding his face slightly.

"Warm in the office, isn't it Zoran?"

"A little, just a little."

"Now about Dublin. That deal is something very different…not your regular order, I would say."

"Hogan understands all of this?" Zoran asked.

"He's seen most of the documents. Not all. I still feel, though, that beneath his open behavior, is someone we can turn in our favor."

"If you're worried, Duane, why you don't change the personnel right now? You seem to be spending a great deal of time wondering about this new man of yours."

"Perhaps. Yet, I have no doubt that with time, his independence will turn to a more practical approach. After all, I was the same way when I was young. We all change. Some more rapidly than others. But we do change. Money effects change. It will happen to him as well."

"Perhaps, Duane, perhaps."

"Your customer will be in Dublin tomorrow? For sure?"

"Yes. I have heard nothing to the contrary."

"At times, people from that culture may be unreliable."

"Duane, you're such a racist. Must be the American in you. Yes, they will be there and on time. They need the product we have to sell. Why wouldn't they come? I don't suspect they will change their minds."

"Good."

"And will you come to the airport with Hogan?"

"No, he'll have to make his own way. He knows how to get to Gatwick."

"We should have a successful meeting, Duane."

"And a very lucrative one."

"Yeah. I'll think even more seriously of taking a sabbatical for a while. Your advice on this may be something I will follow. Go to some quiet location. No sense in taking more risks at this stage."

"I don't believe you'll ever stop, Zoran. Not you. Too much money comes in from the deals. Regardless, I still think you made a mistake with Draculic."

"We shall see, Duane. We shall see. Time to go. Talk to you later. Relax, Duane. Besides, you have all this information coming in from your source at the embassy. We'll always have advance notice for when to run away." Zoran laughed loudly as he rose, shook Farris' hand, and left.

Farris sat down, turning his chair so he again looked at the Bank of England building.

I wonder how many wars have been fought over protecting the almighty English pound. Interesting question. I'll have to look into that. He took off his glasses and placed them in his lap. The tears swelled up. I'm losing it, God. Fuckin' losing it. All those people killed. Too much…way too much…He cupped his hands over his eyes, trying unsuccessfully to stop the tears. Zoran's a fuckin' brute and a fool, he told himself silently, yet vehemently. But it has always been so with him. I've always felt that way. It's folly to think otherwise, Duane Farris. Zoran's not the real fool. It's you. He knew what life he wanted and is living it, impulsively, coldly, mechanically, but living as he wishes. And me…nothingness in me. I'm a skeleton sitting here with flesh and blood and trying to believe, to make believe that I, too, am living as I wish. God I want out of this hell. God don't leave me…fuck it…don't leave me."

His glasses fell to the floor as he doubled up, trying to stifle the sounds of his sobbing, cloaking his mouth with both hands, shaking his head. Please…God, don't, don't ever leave me."

Seventeen

The wind blew faintly. It seemed to pluck with invisible fingers the varied summer flowers planted in the large, round, concrete cisterns positioned on either side of the club's dark-stained wooden double doors, the trembling of the flowers emphasizing the solidity of the old gray stone-faced club Keiran still called home. He scurried up the steps, his mind on the day's events, trying to be tolerant of his new assignment. His only distraction and escape from these thoughts would be this evening and the time he would spend with Jennifer. Once inside, he headed toward the reception desk to get his messages, and then headed to the swimming pool.

"Mr. Hogan, Sir Robert left a package for you. He told me that he was going downstairs to the Turkish Bath area. That was about half an hour ago. I've placed your other mail and phone messages on top." Vanessa Anderson gave Keiran an amusing smile, quickly blurting out all the information she had stored to tell him in a breathless voice as she handed him his package, everything held together by a large rubber band. "Did you have a nice weekend?" she asked.

"Yes, thank you. And you?" Keiran, undoing the band, quickly scanned what appeared to be advertisements for upcoming club events about which he really didn't need to know, and old phone messages from his office. He repositioned them all on top of Runnard's sealed package, twisted the band around, and then slowly slid the bundle toward Anderson.

"So, you had a nice weekend?" he repeated.

"Mr. Hogan, you're not paying any attention to your mail and messages. My weekend? Very well thank you. I went to one of Mr. Nigel's health seminars at University College. You know, he is the one who has the series on television about keeping healthy. Have you forgotten that I already told you about him? You should really listen to his program, Mr. Hogan. Do you realize how important pure oxygen is?"

"Pure oxygen?" Keiran's brow furled, a smile crossing his face.

"Yes. Dr. Nigel says we should inhale pure oxygen at least once a day."

"Once a day. Where would you get the oxygen?" Keiran asked, slightly interested at the seriousness of her comments.

"Well, you can order it from one of the medical supply houses. I'm looking into it. I think that the club should have several canisters both for the staff and for the residents. It is important, oxygen, very important for one's health. Keeps certain of our systems, you do understand…? Certain of our systems need a great deal of energy."

"Our systems?" Keiran noted she had lowered her gaze to his package of mail and messages.

"Yes. Our very important systems. Pure oxygen is required for optimum results." She spoke slowly and her eyes downcast as if she were a shy teenager on her first date.

"Well then, I'll support the club having these canisters of pure oxygen. It'll be good for us, for our 'important systems.' I must be off now. Keep the stuff here. I'll pick it up when I finish my time downstairs, okay?"

"Yes, Mr. Hogan. Last time you said that, we had several days worth of mail for you. You should learn to remember these administrative details now. Important to keep up with your mail and messages. I believe it would be wise to have the porter take them up to your room and leave them on your desk. That would be more efficient, wouldn't you agree? You would be able to review them before you retire for the evening."

"Perfect suggestion, Vanessa. Right on point. Thanks."

She giggled as she responded, "Mr. Hogan, you're just teasing me. I like the compliment though."

Keiran smiled at her, then quickly walked down the few steps from the reception dest to the main corridor. At its end were oversized highly polished mahogany doors, above which, on a matching arch shaped wood trim, were engraved in gold the words 'Turkish Baths.' Keiran entered, smiling silently at Anderson's code words for the sexual organs, 'important systems.'

It was just after six in the evening. There was a bustling crowd of men at this hour in the brightly lit, dark wood-paneled locker room, bantering with one another, all eager to swim, play squash, go to the exercise room, or do nothing but sit in the lounge area taking an evening cocktail. He hurried to his own locker, placing his briefcase and his overnight case in it; he changed quickly, showered, and headed toward the pool. He would find Sir Robert later, after his swim. Certainly, a quick scan of those seated in the several gray wood, white padded pool lounge chairs that lined two sides of the pool, didn't reveal his presence here. He was probably sleeping in the steam loom.

The stress and the worries of the day left him as the routine of his body cutting through the water took over. It had been a moody, gray day at the office, starting with the meeting with Farris and Zoran. There was, he reflected, a certain rawness in Zoran, and maybe even in Farris. Zoran was boasting, in a curious way, that he had tempted fate and won—at least it was his view that if he had stayed at the Parrot Restaurant when the explosion went off, he would not be alive today.

To Zoran, even Leyden's death was suspicious. In Keiran's view, Zoran had the impulses of a paranoiac. Farris now had a vague hostility toward Keiran, a watchfulness that held him with obvious anger. Diana was right. An associate doesn't talk back. And Keiran had done just that. The whole atmosphere now with Farris and Zoran was rather dim and strange. It was puzzling to him. Farris wanted him to work with Zoran but not in the way Keiran believed he should. Farris wanted a subservient associate—bright, not honest and slavish.

The hour went by quickly. He rose from the pool, put on his club-supplied terry cloth bathrobe and slippers and walked swiftly through the double door entrance from the pool into the steam bath area. Three separate rooms fanned from a large, central, high-ceiling, airy, white colored chamber, well-lit, with gray tiled floor and several gray-speckled marble Corinthian pillars supporting its ceiling. Each individual steam room was successively warmer than the previous, the first being the least uncomfortable in terms of its temperature. Many called this initial room the 'seniors room' as all of those that went there were older men who could not tolerate the two other, hotter, rooms. All were identical in size—about 25 feet by 35 feet, with lounge chairs along the walls and the center area free. Large circular clocks and temperature gauges with oversize numbering were positioned on all the walls. In each room's center was a square gray marble stand, from which steam emitted from vents at its base. Over half the chairs in the 'seniors room' were occupied, and everyone appeared to be asleep, all wrapped tightly in their robes and towels as if there were a chill. No one moved. It appeared to Keiran that sleep had set up its kingdom here for all eternity.

Keiran walked in front of the row of chairs, searching for Sir Robert's cane, its top a polished brass boar's head. Without that signature piece, he would have found it difficult to find him, as even the faces of the men in the steam room were substantially covered with towels. It wasn't until he reached the end of the row that he spotted the cane propped up against the wall behind the last chair. Sir Robert appeared to be napping, his head slightly back against the side of the chair's top.

"Sir Robert…Sir Robert…?" Keiran leaned over and gently tugged at his sleeve. "It's me, Keiran Hogan."

There was a slight stir, a mumble; one eye opened, followed by the other.

"Did I not tell you not to disturb me for at least an hour? Now what is it?" His hand reached for the towel surrounding his head, slowly pulling it aside so that his face was revealed.

"Sir Robert. I'm sorry to wake you. It's me. Keiran Hogan. The receptionist, said you wanted to see me. I can come back another time if you wish."

There was a long period of silence as Runnard grabbed both sides of his chair, his face twitching for a moment as if in pain, and he pushed himself up from his resting position, reaching for his cane.

"Then you're not the attendant. Well, those blokes never follow instructions anyway. I shouldn't sleep so much. It's not good for the circulation, and at my age, circulation is very important. Wouldn't you agree, Keiran Hogan?"

"Sure. Circulation is very important. You should go for a swim, sir, it's good exercise."

"Me. Swim? Are you daft? Why would I want to do that when I have my own circulation booster right here in my pocket? Here, take this. It's an annoyance and I need a free hand." Keiran took hold of his cane while Runnard pulled out his silver flask from his robe pocket.

"You shouldn't be drinking that…especially not in here. Heat and liquor don't mix, sir. Besides, club rules…."

"Rules?" Runnard interrupted, his voice sarcastic and raspy. "Here…look around you…everyone in this room is half dead or waiting to meet their maker and all because of the rules. Always, 'Don't do this, Don't do that.' When someone reaches old age, or whatever it is, all of a sudden everything becomes forbidden—as if one were a child again. Well, I was never a child who followed any rules, so I'm certainly not going to do that silly thing now. Enjoy Keiran. Have a swig. It'll bring color to your face. You look as if you've seen ghost—or is that your natural color all the time? You're as white as the caps on the waves of the Irish Sea." Runnard took a swallow from his flask, passing it on to Keiran. "Here, you definitely look as if you need it."

Keiran paused for a moment. Not wanting to offend Runnard, he took a swallow. The warm liquid was good, actually, he silently told himself. He passed the flask back to Runnard who, after taking another swallow, placed it back in his robe pocket, patting it several times as if to make sure it was secure in its place.

"Now, Keiran Hogan, why are you so pale?"

"I don't think you have your glasses on, sir. I'm not that white. I actually did get a little sun on Guernsey."

"Where in the blazes are those infernal things? The infirmities of age. I don't hate the age, but its infirmities."

"Try your other pocket, sir," Keiran suggested.

"Right. I wouldn't mix my glasses with my life's medicine," he replied, again patting the pocket holding his flask.

He pulled out his wire-rimmed glasses, slowly putting them on his face, which was moistened from the steady heat in the room.

"This is nonsense. I can't see in here. Let's go. I'll put them on when we're out of this place of the living dead."

"Your cane, sir," Keiran reminded Runnard, who by now had come closer to him.

"Ah, I see you have gotten some sun. Of course, Guernsey. Not that it matters. Even being exposed to the sun for fair people like you and me is a no-no now. Disgusting." He looked down for his slippers, found and slipped into them, all the while steadying himself with the cane.

"Okay, young man. I'm ready. Lead the way." He thrust his cane toward the exit, but only after lightly hitting Keiran on his right leg. Keiran turned and walked alongside Runnard as they slowly made their way to the exit. Although Runnard walked with a slight shuffle, he still kept his posture erect.

"You're stooping a bit, Keiran. Stand tall!" Keiran smiled and straightened his back, even though he knew that he walked very straight and did so all the time.

When they were midway to the exit, Jefferson Coborn rose to follow them. He had been seated directly next to Runnard, his face partially shrouded with a towel, eavesdropping on the conversation. He was annoyed that Keiran had interrupted, at least for a short while, the plans he had made for Sir Robert. A disruption of plans was, to him, like almost slipping off a ledge. He'd have to inch back and rethink what he had schemed.

"Have you been here very long?" Keiran asked.

"No," Runnard replied, his gait slowing as he leaned on his cane more forcefully. "Just arrived about an hour ago, maybe less. The heat helps my bones…as does my medicine." Again, he patted the pocket containing his flask. "Oh. That is a good feeling to know that my medicine goes with me everywhere. Did you know that Caesar, Julius Caesar—you do know Julius Caesar don't you? Do they teach Roman history in your country?"

Keiran laughed softly. "Yeah, they do, but…I only had a smattering of it in a course called 'History of Western Civilization.' I do know about Julius Caesar, though. We did learn about him."

"Just like the Americans. Everything has to be a summary. Nothing in depth. All summaries. What a waste of the educational process. Anyway, young man, Julius Caesar believed in wine as the elixir of life and never went a day without drinking some, including that fateful day when a traitor killed him. Beware of traitors, Keiran Hogan. Always beware of traitors."

Keiran listened carefully to Runnard's voice. It was pleasant, and though slow, it was deliberate, still having the quality of bright steel. His smile was less now, his thinning white hair was glossy from moisture brought on from being in the hot room. His good temper, however, remained.

"Well, tell me about what you've been doing since last we met."

"I've been in Guernsey Island. Met my client for the first…actually the second time."

"Guernsey. The tax haven. Tax avoidance island. It's a place about which we think we know a great deal, when in reality, we should know that we don't know what goes on in that serene little place. Did you like the island named after a cow?"

There was light laughter.

"Yeah. Pretty nice, actually. The weather was beautiful, so that probably accounted for part of my positive attitude toward the place. I now know how to register a corporation, which was fairly simple. I met our agent, and he was generous with his time and introduced me to all the folks at the government house. Then, later in the afternoon, Sir Robert, an incredible thing happened. Right in front of me, we were at his favorite restaurant with our client, as he rose from the table, he just collapsed. Died, just like that. It was an awful sight for me. I still can't get over what happened."

"Get over it. People die. I'm going to die, as are you. It's life's unending circle. Yet, not a pleasant introduction to the island."

They had arrived in the lounge area, where Sir Robert headed toward a large gray overstuffed chair, one of several in the large windowed room, the early dusk light casting a delicate glow throughout. There were two other club residents in the room, one dozing, the other engrossed in a magazine. Runnard immediately sat down, exclaiming, "A soft and not inappropriate seat. Can you drag over that footstool? I want to place my bum leg on it. Infirmities. Hate them. Hate them all."

Not far from where Runnard had seated himself, Keiran picked up a small footstool, its top padded in gray puffed fabric, its wood legs stained dark.

"Here you are, sir."

"Good. Don't bother going over to the bar. There's nothing there but juice, water and sodas. Boring. These fools who run this club. Someday, Keiran Hogan, we revolutionaries will take over. That we will. Now, your agent, the one who dropped dead in front of you, his name…? Oh, stop looking at me as if I have no sympathy. Of course I do. When you're as young as you are, death comes as a shock; when you're old like me, it comes as a blessing. Now, your agent's name."

"David Leyden, sir. David Leyden." Keiran spoke softly, looking at Runnard a bit quizzically, realizing he should not be doing that. He thought to himself, this guy's been around the block so many times, he knows what life is and what it's not, and he knows when to show his emotions and when to hide them. Shouldn't you feel sorry when someone dies? I mean you have to feel some remorse. Isn't that what you were taught by your parents and your teachers? Here's Runnard dismissing the event much as he would swat a mosquito that landed on a patch of skin, something irritating to be struck away.

Neither Runnard nor Keiran looked up as Coborn entered the room and headed for the bar. Once there, he poured himself some tomato juice, walked away from the two others who were in the lounge seated by the bar, and sat down in a chair parallel to the windows. With just a slight twist of his head, he could see Runnard and Keiran easily. His towel still remained swung loosely over his head. He avoided looking toward them, sipping his juice, staring out the window. Soon he'd be the hero he had always wanted to be. Farris would be indebted to him, and he'd be set for life. And to think I worried about a promotion in the Service. You stupid shit, Jefferson. You know that you were a stupid shit.

"David Leyden. Yes. Yes. The name is familiar. Of course, a complaisant partner of your Mr. Farris. I believe that one of my Commission investigators interviewed him when we were looking into the arms dealing and money laundering issues involving Farris and Hemmrich. Never found much on him, though. Just seemed to be doing what he did for all his clients on that island—registering phony companies and getting paid for his services. Heart attack?"

"Yeah, he just keeled over. It was awful. Farris says that Leyden didn't have a history of heart trouble. Strange tragedy."

"I assume they'll have an autopsy. That should provide an answer. This ticker of mine will give out some day and I'll be history as well. That's a long way off, and my medicine will make sure it's a long way off. Now tell me, young Hogan, what do you think of your client, Zoran Hemmrich?"

"Very friendly towards me. He's obviously a successful, traveling in his own plane with bodyguards he calls his assistants. Paranoid though. When I met him again in Farris' office this morning, he said he wasn't sure that Leyden, in fact, died of a heart attack. The conversation was a bit odd. Zoran also mentioned that he had left the Parrot Restaurant just before the explosion. Apparently, he had business dealing with the guest of honor at the restaurant. I got the impression he believes that someone's after him. He told me that he felt uncomfortable at the Parrot and that's why he left earlier than he planned."

"An observant man. I'm sure people are after him, and why not? A man known for his dishonesty and greed, a man of a thousand lies. He had reneged on so many arms deals, took his customer's money, and provided them with inferior equipment. I'm not surprised that someone out there would want to get rid of him. Lucky man so far. Now, young Hogan, how's that for trashing your client…? And don't blame my comments on my drinking too much of my medicine."

"What's odd is that Farris agreed with Zoran's interpretation of both events, Leyden's death and the luck of Zoran's leaving the Parrot."

"What did you expect? A disagreement between two look-a-likes? One has the gentle veneer of being a lawyer, the other an ungentle manner of a business thief—those are strong words. They need one another."

Runnard shifted slightly in his chair. "Damn chair pads. Not as soft as they used to be. Some fool bureaucrat in this club probably bought them at the Portobello flea market. You know about the flea market—everything for sale except people, and if you look long enough, maybe a few of them too. God, we've got to get better cushions."

"Are you okay, sir?" Keiran asked, his voice expressing concern.

"I've told you I'm okay. So let it rest, young Hogan." Runnard closed his eyes. "What will you do, Keiran? Stay around Farris and his client?"

"I just don't know yet. With Leyden no longer around, I've now been assigned to Zoran sort of permanently to monitor his corporations and so forth. I leave for Dublin tomorrow to meet him and to work on some matters."

"You'll be the spoke in their wheel of fortune." Runnard opened his eyes, blinking them a few times, before they settled on Keiran. "Damn light. Too much light."

"Wheel of fortune? I don't think so, sir. Not at all. While I was at the restaurant, the police came to the place to interview all the patrons; it's standard, I gather, for these kinds of happenings. I had called Farris to tell him of Leyden's death, and he told me…hard to believe he really asked me…to lie about Zoran's name. I'm still upset about that. He later apologized of sorts, but I didn't misrepresent, and I won't. Farris has a perverted notion of dealing with the authorities. It made me think about my future with him and the firm."

"So Farris wanted to hide the true identity of Hemmrich. Well, why not? He spoke like a good lawyer—protecting his client. What's wrong with that?"

Keiran looked at Runnard, trying to figure out if he was serious or not. Then he smiled, "You can't be sincere in your comment, not you. No, not you."

"And, pray young Hogan, why not? What are you supposed to do for your client?"

"For one thing, you don't just lie to the authorities about something as basic as your name. Secondly, it would be stupid, as the police eventually would find out the person's true identity. I can't believe that you would ever agree with what Farris asked me to do."

"You make me wonder, Keiran Hogan, if you're naive and ridiculous or brave and smart. The latter I believe and I'm happy with that. Of course, you can't lie when it comes to giving your name. That was an absurd request by Farris. Yet, I will tell you, that solicitors—yes, even barristers—do often shade the truth and might even cross the line to protect the man who is paying the bills. Not a pretty picture. Not a pretty one at all. My hope is that there are many more practitioners of the law who are honest than those who aren't. I get discouraged when I see what is now happening to the practitioner. Enough. I left you an unexpurgated copy of my report. It is my copy, so don't lose it. Of course, I have all the appendices at my country home and didn't want to bother you with all that reading. The report is slim, so it won't take you long to read. Now, when are you coming back from the homeland of your heritage?"

"Thursday. I should be back by Thursday. Dublin is a city I would like to spend more time in, but I have to get back. I have a great deal to do here."

"Spoken with a gleam in your eye that indicates you have found a woman. No one hurries back to work on legal briefs. You have a lady friend then?"

"As a matter of fact, I do. She's a great girl…really great…I know that you'll like her."

"Good. If you're free when you return, let's have dinner. Bring your friend along. I hope she is interesting and bright. I assume she is, or you wouldn't be seeing her. Physical attraction can only go so far, if you understand my drift."

Keiran smiled broadly, "You'll like her, sir. She's great. Dinner is fine. We'll settle on the time and place when I call you when I return from Dublin."

"Assuredly, we shall meet. A woman at dinner makes for a more productive and worthwhile conversation, not to mention having someone who's lovely to look at. In the meantime, read the report. Learn. And be careful, young Hogan. Farris may suck you into something that is difficult from which to extricate yourself. Read my report. Come visit with your friend and we'll talk later over a good meal, and of course, a great deal of after dinner port. Don't be so healthy. You're going to miss out on too much of real life."

Keiran rose and extended his hand. Runnard shook it firmly, saying, "I assume you're rushing off to visit your lady friend. Understandable. Now go. Read the report"

"I will. Take care of yourself. Keep your hands off the flask. I'll call you soon."

"I won't keep away from my medicine. Now get out of here. And remember, the report."

Keiran walked to the door, took one last look at Runnard, who had again closed his eyes, and thought silently as he exited into the corridor, I love that guy. What a teacher he must have been to his associates. What a great teacher.

Coborn watched Keiran leave. He looked at the other two men in the lounge, one was now sleeping, the other was engrossed in a magazine. Both were in chairs that faced the windows and away from Runnard. He rose quietly, his hands reaching the towel that drooped over his head, adjusting it slightly, tucking its end into the top of his robe. For a flash, a doubt crossed his mind as to what he was about to do. Just as it came to him, it vanished, much like the roll of thunder—frightening for a moment, then calm. He approached Runnard from the side, pretending to trip on Runnard's extended leg, which rested on the footstool. Runnard's eyes opened just as Coborn caught himself by placing his hand on Runnard's chest, slightly made visible by an opening in the robe. In his hand, Coborn held a small palm-size instrument that looked like a cell phone.

"I'm so sorry. Very clumsy of me. Very." He pressed a button on the instrument, sending a quick charge of 100,000 volts of electricity—sufficient to disrupt the signal from the brain to the muscles and to cause a complete collapse into unconsciousness in one second. Runnard's eyes closed immediately. Pretending to rearrange Runnard's robe and towel, he reached into the pocket of his own robe and took out two small rubber plugs, which he inserted in Runnard's nostrils. Then, taking out a piece of medical tape, he placed it over Runnard's mouth. Not his own idea, he mused to himself. He had borrowed the idea from a program he had seen on television. Closing the towel across Runnard's face, Coborn retreated to his chair. Finishing his tomato juice, his eyes gazing again out the window. His own heart was now racing. This was the first time he had planned and carried out a murder…and Farris would pay handsomely for this, very handsomely. Coborn slowly counted the seconds in his mind. When he reached 300, he rose, passing Runnard again.

"Sorry, old chap. Really I am. Hope the rest of your evening is peaceful." He reached over, removed the nose plugs and tape and placed them in the trash bin as he left the lounge. He slipped the 'stun' instrument in his pocket. That he would dispose of later. It wasn't so bad. Easy, actually. Yeah. Very easy, he quietly told himself as he left the room.

Eighteen

Keiran glanced at his wristwatch, and then peered out the cab window at the traffic jam by Buckingham Palace. He probably had overstayed at the club talking with Sir Robert, but it was worth it. Jennifer would understand. He'd explain it all to her, Keiran thought to himself as he tried to relax in the slow-moving cab.

"Sorry mate, the Queen must be leaving, so the police have stopped the traffic. Shouldn't be but a few minutes and we'll be on our way."

"I hope so," Keiran responded, realizing that he left his cell phone in his briefcase back at the club, so he couldn't call Jennifer to tell her he was going to be delayed. He wanted to be in high spirits when he saw her. He didn't want to appear as if he were sucked dry or was in some deep melancholy. When Farris asked him to lie to the police, he had wanted Keiran to follow, grin, and bow. He had laid something of a whip across his shoulders in order to see whether Keiran would shrug it off or succumb to its pain. He shrugged it off. Probably made the bastard a bit angry, but who gives a shit, Keiran silently thought.

The waiting area at Rumours was crowded with people and greenery. There were plants everywhere, including several palms that looked up toward a ceiling that was enclosed by curved Plexiglas. The lighting was bright, the atmosphere frenetic with waiters jostling for space at the long, open kitchen counter, waiting to pick up their orders. Keiran moved quickly through the line of about thirty patrons waiting to be seated, finally seeing Jennifer seated in the bar area, dressed in a soft red pantsuit, reading a magazine, a glass of water in front of her. He hurried to her side. "Jennifer, sorry…I hope you haven't been waiting too long…Really sorry…." He hesitated for a moment, looking into her dark eyes, then leaned over to her and kissed her on her lips, holding her for a moment tightly, oblivious to the throng at the bar.

"You're allowed to be late only once. Promise?" He gazed at her, so taken with her beauty, her smile lighting up her face, her mouth alluring and even provocative. He loved her totally.

"Yeah, I promise. I ran into Sir Robert. We had a not-so-brief conversation, that's why I'm a bit late. I could also blame it on the traffic. It's awful." His brow wrinkled as he spoke softly

"You're scowling, Keiran. You must be angry at something. I don't think it could be me. I even thought of you a few times today, and to answer your question, it was a normal, good day." She laughed as she rose from her seat, taking his hand and squeezing it tightly. "Let's get our table…before they give it away."

"I'm scowling?" Keiran replied.

"Yes, you are. What happened to you today to make you scowl?"

Keiran broke into a soft laugh, his eyes brightened, his brow began to rest, his hand tightly joined with hers. "No. Nothing untoward happened today."

"I don't believe you," Jennifer declared. "Anyway, the reservation is in my name." She smiled at him as they approached the reservation stand, where a middle-aged short man dressed in a pale orange shirt, black tie, and black slacks stood guard, his voice rising slightly as he told the couple in front of Jennifer and Keiran that there were no tables—"Unless you made a reservation early this morning, you're out of luck," he told the hapless pair.

"Reservations for Berley." Keiran announced.

"Certainly, sir. Ms. Berley, happy to have you with us again," announced the *maître d'* as he crossed out Jennifer's name on his list with a flourish with the large red pen that hung from the corner of the stand on a brass chain. "I had to do this," he explained, "people were actually taking my pens! Would you believe it?"

They smiled at him as he took them to the last vacant table alongside a wall covered with photos of news celebrities.

"Is your picture here?" Keiran asked, scanning the wall.

"Well, as a matter of fact…yes," Jennifer remarked after a pause. "Can you find it among the others? Look carefully now."

He slowly let his eyes run the length of the wall, which had at least seven rows of photos hanging between the chair rail and the top of the twelve-foot ceiling. "I think I need my glasses," he said, reaching in his side pocket, taking them out, and placing them on. "Wow. You're at the very top…tenth one over." Keiran pointed to the spot where her photo was hanging.

"At least you found it. It's not that easy. Not in the most desirable location on the trophy wall, as that space is called."

"What does having your photo on the wall mean? Do you get free meals or better tables?" Keiran asked with a wry smile. "Is this a better table?"

"Neither. How tables are allocated depends upon the temperament of the man who just showed us to our table. My photo on the wall certainly doesn't mean I get a table whenever I want it. I have to call for reservations like everyone else."

"Better than not having your picture hanging at all," Keiran answered. "When did it go up?"

"A few months ago, on the anniversary of my third year at ITN. I suppose the restaurant owner believes I'll be around for a while. Or maybe the ratings were good. I just don't know. As far as that goes, it really isn't that important to me, really. You had a good day, Keiran?"

"Yeah, it was okay. I was told that I have to go to Dublin tomorrow. Only a day trip, I think. I hope it won't be longer than that. Farris' client is a bit strange in his habits, as is Farris. I'll go and draft whatever documents they want for their meetings."

"You don't sound cheerful about the trip."

"Well…no. I'd like to see Dublin again, though. It's been a few years since I've been there. Went with my family when I graduated from Princeton. It's just that working with Farris…well, it's different. That's all I can say. Different. Before I forget, though, Sir Robert has asked us to join him for dinner at the club this Friday. Interested in coming?"

Despite his smile and the brightness of his eyes, he appeared to her to be tired and troubled. She had never worried about a man before, at least not in this way. She had known Keiran for such a short time, and yet she knew, not exaggerating in her feelings, that she was falling in love with him. She believed in him without yet understanding him fully. She was feeling different, different than ever before, thinking of him all the time, every day since she had met him, anxious always to see him.

"Sure. Be a treat for me. Runnard is a classic icon to many barristers in England. Probably one of the greatest barristers of all time. On Friday, though, I have the evening broadcast plus a special, which is a follow-up on last Sunday's segment on the Parrot Restaurant explosion. Saturday would be better for me. Do you think he'd be free on Saturday?"

"You can't come after the broadcast?"

Jennifer hesitated before continuing. "No, I can't. Craig is returning from New York that morning. He called me and asked that we meet for dinner Friday evening, after the broadcast."

"You're going to see him?" Keiran asked, his voice soft. "I'd be upset if you did, Jennifer. I mean, what's going on here?"

"I have to see him, Keiran. I do."

"Why? I thought you were seeing me, that you wanted to be with me."

"Please, please. If I didn't want to be with you, I wouldn't. I'm falling in love with you and you must know that. Last night wasn't some spur-of-the-moment thing. I've been thinking of you since I saw you at Mr. Grayson's house. I've thought of no one else. And, if you're wondering, no, Craig didn't stay with me that night. But I can't just drop him with a phone call. I have to see him and explain my changed emotions. There's no other way. You understand, don't you?"

"You know how I feel about you. I mean...."

"Keiran Hogan, listen. Before you came, I was with Craig. I can't help that history anymore than what you did back in Washington. You weren't celibate. I don't know what more to say. I'm trying to be honest with you."

"I've only known you a short time, and I know my feelings—which I don't fling around easily either. What does last night mean? Just another warm body. Is that what you're telling me?"

"Keiran, don't talk that way to me," Jennifer replied softly, reaching across the table and placing her hands on his, holding them tightly. "I didn't stay with you last night because I had nothing better to do. If I wanted to have warm bodies in my bed, I would have no trouble getting them. I don't do that. I'm taken with you. You know that. Be realistic. I can't call him on the phone and say, 'Things have changed, we're through. I'm no longer going to see you.' I have to tell him in person and in my own way."

"So the answer is no. You can't see me Friday night?" Keiran replied, his eyes resting gently and sadly upon her face.

Her whole nature told her everything was different since she had met Keiran. He was thoughtful and strong, yet she knew his heart was soft. She also knew that he needed her in more than just a physical way. As she listened to him speak, she understood his feelings, almost felt what he was thinking. Her relationship with Craig was so very different. She never felt as if he needed her. Craig would constantly take her to social events, checking on what she would wear, always wondering how she looked, commenting on whether she should stay in the news business, even telling her directly, "It's a bloody silly job, reading a teleprompter, isn't it?" and never trying to understand what she really did. She brushed off his entreaties, and it was his lack of understanding of her career that made her hesitate over marriage. Keiran was a man of conviction; he obviously loved her; he treated her tenderly. She wanted to be part of him, to be there for him. She enjoyed talking to him, hearing about his work, his life. She never had that feeling with Craig. She always had felt empty with Craig.

"Keiran, I just believe that I should see him and be mannerly about the whole thing. I want you to stay with me tonight, and every night thereafter. I want to be with you. But..." she paused, holding his hands tightly, "you have to understand my feelings as well." She looked at him, saw the sadness in his blue eyes—so expressive of his mood—the same look he'd had when he came to her apartment just the other evening. She let her hands slip from his, rose, and walked around the small table where they had been seated, brushing against its crisp white tablecloth, to where Keiran was, leaning over, and kissing him gently on his cheek, then taking his head in her hands, kissed him on the lips for several moments.

"That is a public display of affection," she smiled.

"I like these displays," he replied, rising from his seat, kissing her in return. "Hell with dinner. Let's go to your apartment and get comfortable."

"You're hopeless…completely hopeless." Jennifer gently broke from his arms and returned to her seat. "Then, you do understand about Friday? I'll call you directly after dinner. I should be finished about ten or so."

"What more can I say, really? I believe you. I shouldn't be so proprietary, I suppose. It's not the way I should be. You know I love you, Jennifer. Sorry to have a tantrum. I'm sure Sir Robert will see us on Saturday, if he can."

"Anytime but Friday is fine. If not Saturday, then another weekend will be fine with me. We also have to plan on your visiting my uncle at this country place. I've told him about you, and he would like to see you."

"Your uncle?"

"Yes. He raised me when my father and mother died years ago. He's alone now; his own wife passed away a few years ago. You'll like him. I know you will. And he'll like you too."

"I'd like that. I'd like it very much. By then, I hope I'll be in better humor. What about your news special? Any info as to what really caused the explosion at the Parrot? Or is it still thought to be a gas leak?"

"We're trying to make some headway but the situation is getting more complex. First of all, there's some evidence, which the police aren't yet releasing, which may indicate that the explosion was set deliberately…that it wasn't an accidental gas explosion. One of the police officers, off the record, told one of our producers that the preliminary analysis of pieces of wreckage showed traces of semtex—the plastic explosive. They were not absolutely sure, but some evidence point in that direction. If that's the case, the police obviously have a different condition on their hands."

"Maybe my client, Zoran, isn't so wrong. He thinks it wasn't an accident. Crazy. Why would anyone be so cruel? So many innocent people lost, even if there is a political agenda somewhere. Have they finished identifying all the bodies?"

"Almost. No one who was in the restaurant survived. Of course, there were wounded bystanders. What is interesting is the police found a computer list of the names of the people that had been invited to the party among the debris. We'll lead off the special with this new piece of information."

"All bad guys?" Keiran asked.

"All bad guys…if you're on one side of the argument regarding the former Yugoslavia. On the other hand, if you're on the other…well, maybe you think you're a good guy. Your client, Zoran Hemmrich is on the list, but he is still alive, as you saw him on the island. I wouldn't be surprised if the police aren't now trying to contact him."

"Zoran is on the list?" Keiran now voiced surprised.

"Yes. His name is there. If he suspected that the explosion was set and not an accident maybe he knows more about it. You just told me that he said something…? Or was it just his opinion that the explosion may not have been an accident?"

"Just this morning he said that it may not have been an accident, but a deliberate attempt, and this is what is scary, he believes it may have been a deliberate attempt to kill him. I didn't believe him at first, but maybe he was also targeted as part of the group—he did have a business relationship with Draculic. In fact, Jennifer, Zoran left the Parrot a few minutes before the explosion. He said to me that his instincts told him to leave earlier than he'd planned. I guess his instincts were right."

"It would be great to interview him for the special—the only one who was present that survived. What a coup for the program. Can you…."

"Jennifer. No. Answer is no. First of all, even if I asked, he'd say no. I can assure you he's not going on television to broadcast his views. Period."

"Stupid of me, I guess. The news scoop in my blood. It makes sense. Why would he want to go on a news program? What's the advantage for him?"

"None that I can see. He has a reputation, and it's not the best, as I understand. Those who were taken out were pretty solid financial supporters of the Serbian cause. Maybe Zoran feels a certain sadness for Draculic's death, but I doubt it. They were in a business deal together. That's about it."

"A disaster, Keiran. Awful. More than 40 people dead and many wounded. Whether Zoran goes on television or not, the police will be after him sooner or than later."

"Well, when that happens, Farris will make a decision and I'm sure it won't be to cooperate."

"If he has information, he should tell the police what he knows. I just can't understand anyone killing innocent people, regardless of the problem they're trying to solve. I've interviewed some of the survivors in the hospital and it's so unreal. The suffering. So cruel." She lowered her head for a moment, and Keiran thought he saw tears come to her eyes. He reached over and touched her face, bringing his hand down lightly on her cheek.

"You okay, Jennifer?"

"Yes. I shouldn't get emotional about such things, I suppose. It's that the people who did this, if indeed it wasn't an accident, don't they care at all about the innocents that get murdered just because they have a gripe against something or someone?"

"I don't want to sound uncaring myself, but the answer is probably not. It's the bigger issue they're attacking, and if someone is in the way, well, that's just too bad. Life is never fair. In fact it's probably unjust. The list with his name on it, is that common knowledge?"

"No, no, our police source told us and we have a copy. We'll have to decide whether to use the information or not. Part of the decision is whether to advise the police that we have the list and if so, whether we can use the names. We want to be careful. So we'll tread pretty gingerly with this material. If the police say not to use the info, then we probably won't—at least for a while. No interview with Mr. Hemmrich then?"

"You don't give up. Certainly, he'll talk to the police if they call, but even that will be with his lawyer present, which I guess will be me or Mr. Farris, or both of us. Zoran is a suspected arms dealer and I know that Farris will limit the time he'll spend with the police, and he'll certainly restrict the content of those conversations. Farris will probably try to avoid a face-to-face interview and see if he can get away with answering written questions with the excuse that Zoran's travel schedule is so tight that he can't possibly take the time to talk to the police in person."

"Mr. Farris does know," Jennifer's voice softened, "that there is a U.K. and European Community as well as a U.N. embargo on selling arms to anyone in the former Yugoslavia? So your client, an arms dealer, if he was dealing with Draculic, may have been violating that embargo."

"Now you know my problem in working with these guys."

"I still want to interview Zoran, and I'm going to ask for your help later…later this evening."

Keiran laughed loudly now.

"Man, you're something. No matter how much fun we have, the answer will still be no."

"I was only kidding, Keiran. Just kidding," she responded.

Keiran chuckled, his eyes brightened. "Besides, we won't do much talking tonight, especially about Zoran, work, and other crazy things. We've more important activity." He looked at her with a gentle malevolence.

"You're terrible," she responded, "and I love you deeply."

Nineteen

The sky was laden with rain clouds as the Centurion jet, its engines straining against the wind, broke through the clouds and reached the smoother altitude of 37,000 feet as it made its way from London to Dublin. Keiran sat on one side of a small white and green speckled Corian top conference table that extended from the side of the front cabin. Facing him were Farris and Zoran. Zoran's two assistants remained in the back, slouched in their dark brown leather seats, apparently dozing. Farris was opening document folders, glancing at the contents of a page, passing a loose sheet to Keiran, asking him repeatedly, "Now, do you understand this section, Keiran?" Keiran would answer wearily, his mind on the small black-bordered article on the front page of the *London Times*—'Noted Barrister Dies. Sir Robert Albert Percival Runnard, dead at the age of 82. Full Obituary, Page 16.' Keiran didn't want to go on this trip; he wanted to rush over to the club and talk to anyone who knew about the death. It was hard to believe that he had been with Runnard less than 24 hours ago. Runnard seemed vibrant and eager. Keiran had only met him a few times, and yet he felt as if he had known him for an awfully long time. He stared blankly at the papers in front of him, thinking silently that when he got to Dublin he'd give Jennifer a call. Maybe she'll know more. Maybe she'll know....

"Keiran, are you paying attention?" Farris inquired, appearing to be more nervous than Keiran had ever seen him. Zoran said nothing, his eyes glued to the window and watching the dark rain clouds below the jet, his hands folded neatly in his lap like a priest patiently waiting for his turn at the pulpit, obviously bored with the speaker he would be following.

"Yes, why do you ask?"

"Well, you don't seem to be reviewing the documents carefully." He spoke slowly, breathing audibly, probably believing that his words needed time to make an impact on Keiran, like medicine takes time before its effects are felt.

"I know what's in these documents, Mr. Farris," replied Keiran, taking the sheet that he had just been handed and flipping it back to Farris. "I've reviewed all these documents several times. It isn't that I am not interested. I'm just know their contents. The sale documents are for thirty million dollars worth of cement to be paid for, in this instance, by a wire transfer of funds in three stages, one third upon shipment, one third upon transit to the half-way point to the cargo's final destination, and the remaining third upon delivery at a port selected by the customer. This change was made at the last minute at Mr. Hemmrich's insistence. The letter of credit would not be needed for this transaction. Mr. Hemmrich wants the proceeds from the sale deposited directly into the Benton Industries account in Guernsey. The buyer is Northern Sun Construction, Singapore. The matter, sir, is not that complicated."

"Very good. I just have the feeling that your mind is elsewhere."

"Perhaps on his lady friend, Duane," Zoran interrupted as he looked over, laughing slightly, and added, "I'm sure he'd rather be with her." Zoran's low voice crackled as he looked at Keiran. "Am I right, Keiran?"

Keiran grinned, picked up his pen and begin twisting it between his fingers, finally placing it back on the table. Did his inner thoughts announce themselves by his facial expressions, or did Zoran just guess?

"I'm thinking about a great many things," Keiran answered. "Most important of all, your contract. Everything is in order. I think we're all set. A lot of cement, sir. What's the customer going to do? Build some highways?"

"Superhighways somewhere. I don't know where, though. Not really my interest. My only interests are that he is buying what we have to sell and that he is paying a premium price," Zoran replied. This time Farris also smiled, a quick thin smile that vanished as quickly as it had crossed his face. He lowered his head like an errant boy who wanted to avoid the gaze of the person he'd lied to. Keiran didn't miss the change in expression. His instincts told him there was more to the story than either was letting on.

The graceful driveway of Dublin's Berkeley Hotel unfurled itself like a scroll and at its center a doorman was waiting at the bottom of a flight of steps leading to the lobby entrance. Masses of green foliage and lavender impatiens filled several large cisterns on either side of the entrance.

"Welcome back, Mr. Hemmrich. You have had a good flight?"

"Yes, thank you, Phillip. Always good to be back at such a lovely place." Zoran shook the hand of the doorman. Farris and Keiran followed Zoran and his assistants as they walked rapidly through the reception room where the hotel manager was waiting.

"Welcome again, Mr. Hemmrich. This way, please." He turned smartly, leading them to the to the elevator, its door held opened by another hotel functionary. They all rode in silence to the second floor, where the manager walked stiffly, slightly ahead of the group, leading them down the corridor to the conference room suite where he swung open the door.

"I trust this will be satisfactory, Mr. Hemmrich. Your guests are already in the conference room waiting for you. They arrived about ten minutes ago."

"Oh? A bit early I would say. Good, good, thank you. I'm sure you made them comfortable?" Zoran asked as he extended his hand to the manager.

"Without a doubt. As you requested, we've set up our coffee service and light breakfast—both here and in the main conference room. If you need anything, Mr. Hemmrich, please advise me directly." With a slight bow, he then excused himself.

"Duane, will you and Keiran stay for a moment while I go in and greet my customer? I'll call you when the need arises."

"Certainly. We'll stand ready for your call," Farris replied as he placed his briefcase on one of the several blood-red leather chairs.

Zoran, followed by his assistants, opened the connecting door and disappeared into the main conference room.

Keiran placed his briefcase down on a side table, and then headed toward the breakfast buffet set up alongside the window that overlooked the street fronting the hotel.

"Coffee, Mr. Farris?" Keiran inquired.

"Yes. Do they have decaf?"

"Yeah. Cream? Sugar?"

"A little of both."

Keiran followed Farris' direction. Then he walked over to where Farris had sat down, noting the persistent worried look on his face as he placed the cup and saucer on the small black marble top table next to him.

"Do you think we will be waiting for some time? I'd like to make some calls, if you think we have the time." Keiran asked.

"I don't believe it will be but a few minutes before we'll be called. In due course, we'll be there. Learn to be patient." He then closed his eyes for a moment as if in deep contemplation.

Keiran sat at a small writing table a short way from Farris, facing the connecting door. He took out his papers from his briefcase arranging them in order, just in case, he mused. He also took out the *Times*. Just as he opened the paper to read the obituary, the connecting door opened, and Zoran poked his head in, saying firmly, "Duane. Can you come in?"

Farris jumped up, grabbed his briefcase, hurrying to the slightly opened conference room door. As he passed Keiran, he said, "Stay put, Keiran. Don't leave the room."

Keiran nodded, then returned to his reading, page 16 of the *Times*.

The article, a half page that recounted Runnard's entire career, listed all the important cases that he had handled, including a full discussion of the investigation he had conducted for the U. K. government on money laundering and arms dealing that had involved several members of the government, among others.

What became known as the Runnard Report is still, in major part, classified. No one investigated by Sir Robert and his team was ever brought to the bar. He retired shortly after the report was issued. His autobiography, "A Barrister Who Tried" was on the Times *bestseller list for over a year and half.*

He is survived by his sister, Amelia Strathope. Services will be held Friday at noon, Brompton Oratory, Peter Cardinal Vechery, officiating. Burial will be at the family estate located at Braemore, Hampshire. Burial will be private. Expressions of sympathy should be addressed to the Runnard Fund, Greater London Legal Aid Society, 45 Tansel Rd. SW5."

Keiran took out his cell phone and dialed Jennifer's home number. After a few rings she came on the line.

"Hello," she answered, her voice soft yet cheerful.

"Jennifer. Sorry to bother you so early in the morning."

"Keiran. It's not that early. About nine I think. Are you in Dublin?"

"Yeah, and I already miss you. I just want you to know that."

"It's great to hear your voice. Where are you?" she asked.

"At the Berkeley Hotel. The meeting has begun, and without me. I guess I'm here just in case they need me to do something, I'm still unsure what. Anyhow, have you read your morning paper?"

"Yes, I get the both the *Times*, and *The Independent*. Why do you ask?

"Look at page one of the *Times.* See the box at the bottom of the page? Sir Robert has died."

"My Gosh. Didn't you just see him yesterday?"

"Yes. Can you find out anything about what really happened and let me know? Maybe you'll have more information at the studio. Will you report it tonight?"

"Of course we will. I'll check when I get to the studio. This is so sad. You really got to like him."

"Yeah. He had some good sense and was decent. I so looked forward to having you meet him. This is so unexpected. So much is happening that is so unexpected. Sir Robert was such a good person. I really had that impression. Even the obituary confirms that. He helped so many, many people. What a tragedy. Really bad news." The phone on the desk near Keiran began to ring. "Hear that ring? It's the room phone. Maybe they need me now in the meeting. Maybe they need coffee or something important like that. I have to go now, talk to you later, love you."

"Take care Keiran. Don't worry, now. I love you too."

The ring continued—short bursts of sound followed by silence, and then short bursts of sounds again. Certainly the sound wasn't loud enough to hear outside the room, and if there was an extension in the conference room, no one was answering it there. Something useful for me to do, Keiran thought as he picked up the phone.

"Keiran Hogan. May I help you?"

"This is Marge Rackline, the hotel operator, Mr. Hogan. Can either Mr. Han or Mr. Ho-Lee take an overseas call from Singapore?

"Did you ring the conference room, Ms. Rackline? The meeting is being held in that room. I am in the anteroom. You should try ringing directly into the conference room."

"We can't ring into the conference room at the moment," she responded briskly. "We have been asked to have the phone disabled so there can be no disturbance while the meeting is being held. These are our instructions."

"Certainly. Fine. Mr. Ho-Lee or Mr. Han. I'll see if they will take the call from...."

"Singapore. The call is from Mr. Koo in Singapore. He said the matter was urgent."

"Okay. I'll be right back and let you know if either gentleman will take the call."

Keiran pressed the hold button on the phone and walked over to the door connecting the two rooms. He knocked twice, then opened the door. Seated around an oblong mahogany table were two Asian gentlemen, Hemmrich, and Farris. Zoran's two assistants were seated behind Zoran, four other Asian men were seated on the other side of the table behind the two men who were busy looking at documents.

Keiran walked into the room and went over to Farris. He spoke softly and quickly.

"Mr. Farris, there is a call for Mr. Ho-Lee or Mr. Han. The phone in this room has been disabled, so the call has to be taken outside, in the anteroom."

Farris looked up from his file, calmly responding, "Thank you Keiran. Tell the caller one of them will be right out shortly." Keiran closed the door and walked swiftly to the phone table.

"Operator?"

"Yes, Mr. Hogan?"

"One of the gentlemen will be here shortly to take the call." Accompanied by one of the Asian gentlemen, Farris followed Keiran within a few minutes, his face showing obvious annoyance,

"Keiran, let me introduce to Mr. Ho-Lee." Keiran placed the phone on the desk as he extended his hand to a short, immaculately groomed middle-aged man, his deep black hair streaked with gray, slicked back on his head, so shiny, it appeared to have been plastered on his head. His wore a dark gray Nehru-style suit. Keiran noted his shoes were so highly polished it was as if someone had painted them with glossy black paint.

"Nice to meet you Mr. Ho-Lee."

Mr. Ho-Lee shook Keiran's hand, then bowed slightly. Farris smiled, adding, "Mr. Hogan is one of our finest young associates. He has worked very hard on the matter we are discussing this morning. We are most grateful to have him in the firm." Mr. Ho-Lee simply nodded, bowing slightly again. Farris picked up the phone and passed it on to Ho-Lee. Farris looked at Keiran and took him by the arm, gently and slowly walking him to a corner in the room, where he whispered to Keiran: "Keiran, please see that the phone in the conference room is working. I want this accomplished immediately. I don't understand why it's not working. If it's broken, the hotel managers should have had it replaced before we arrived. This is very embarrassing for me to have our phone disabled. See to it at once."

"Sure, I'll see what the problem is. Do you want me to disturb your meeting to let you know?"

"Yes, as a matter of fact, yes. Call me out of the meeting. I do want to know." As Keiran left, he noted that Mr. Ho-Lee was looking up and motioning Farris to come to him. If anything, Keiran though, Zoran's customer Ho-Lee seemed pretty interesting, even if Keiran didn't understand what was going on at this point.

He walked down one flight of stairs to the lobby floor to see the manager and get the phone problem solved. Keiran smiled and shook his head as he thought, what a gentle word 'disabled' is compared to the harsh word 'broken.' He walked toward the concierge's desk, where a tall reed-thin man sat pouring over what appeared to be a tour book. The name on the placard on his desk said 'Mr. Nicholson.'

"Mr. Nicholson, I'm Keiran Hogan. We have a client session in a Conference Suite on the second floor. One of the phones in the room is not working. Can we get it fixed promptly?"

Mr. Nicholson looked up, obviously annoyed, and asked, coldly, "Have you tried calling the events manager? Patricia Redman handles all of our events. Go down the hall and her office is in the Executive Office Suite. Or, you can go to the hotel phone and ring '666,' which is the number for the events office. I'm sure she will be able to help you. Anything else?"

"No. Thanks for the information." Keiran silently told himself that even though the guy was Irish, Nicholson was a real prick. He headed toward the hotel phone, which was located in an alcove right off the reception lobby and adjacent to the cafe. Keiran picked up the phone, pressed in the triple six phone number, and waited while the phone rang several times.

"Patricia Redman here. May I help you?"

"Yes, Ms. Redman. I'm Keiran Hogan and, as you may know, my firm, Kenton & Ward reserved Suite 200, The Mayoral Suite, for our meeting today. Unfortunately, the phone in the conference room is not working. Can you have that phone repaired immediately? We need access to its use on an urgently."

"Mr. Hogan. Suite 200…the phone is not working? This is strange. Are you sure you didn't ask that it be disengaged?"

"Well, there is some confusion about that at this point. I will be checking with my office to see who made the arrangements for us. In any event, we need the phone to be operating properly…and the sooner the better. Can you attend to it?"

"Certainly. It shouldn't take very long. I'll notify the operator to remove the number from the disengagement list. By the time you get back to your meeting, the phone will be operational. I'm sorry, Mr. Hogan, if we misinterpreted the instructions from your office. We are very careful to send confirmation notices of all such instructions to the office of the reserving party. I'm positive that we did this in your case as well. Nevertheless, I'll certainly check it out and let you know."

"Why don't I stay on the line while you call your operator and tell her to disengaged the phone in our suite."

"Certainly. I'll be right back."

Keiran passed the time by toying with the phone cord, and was about to turn to face the cafe, when a hand slapped his back.

"We meet again. What, my *confrère*—that's French for colleague just in case you don't understand that language—are you doing here in Dublin?" Grayson smiled broadly as he kept his hand on Keiran's back. Certainly, we don't have the same client, do we?"

"I can't tell you what I'm doing here in Dublin. If I told you I'd have to swear you to secrecy. Fair to say, I'm carrying Farris' files. You know the role of associates in large law firms. Right now I'm trying to get the phone in the conference room working. And, what are you doing here…not on some pub tour…?" They both laughed.

"Mr. Hogan…Mr. Hogan?"

"Yes, I'm here. Just a moment, Ms. Redman." Placing his hand over the phone's mouthpiece, Keiran turned to Grayson, "Bob, I've got to take this call. Are you staying in the hotel?"

"Yes, but I'll be leaving shortly. I'll give you a call in London. Take care and stay out of trouble."

"I'll try. And, Bob, stop following me." Keiran laughed.

"Okay," Grayson, smiled back. "Your life is dull anyway." Grayson walked away, waving goodbye to Keiran.

"Yes, Ms. Redman?"

"The phone is now working properly. Again, I regret that the instructions were misunderstood. Now, I have the file in front of me. A Ms. Rogers of your office verified the information about the needed amenities. Everything else in order in the Suite?"

"Yeah, sure, thank you for the information." He hung up. He knew of no Ms. Rogers in the offices of Kenton & Ward. Something wasn't working out here…not at all.

Keiran hurried up the stairs to the second floor, and quickly went down to the suite. He opened the door, no one was in the anteroom, and the door between the anteroom and the conference room was opened. That room was also empty. A large piece of yellow legal paper was propped up by the phone in the conference room. He recognized Farris' scrawl:

We decided to change our meeting venue. Please take care of the hotel statement with your firm credit card. You can take a commercial flight back to London. There is no need to stay here any longer. I'll be in touch with you later tonight. In any event I'll see you early tomorrow morning. Try to be on time. Thanks. DF

The desk was clean. Not a piece of paper remained; all the chairs were placed back into their proper position around the table. The day's newspapers, which had been placed on a side table, were now in the trash. What a way to practice law. This is crazy.

He went into the anteroom, picked up his briefcase and headed toward the stairs. As he walked down the flight to the reception room, the his cell phone rang.

"Keiran Hogan."

"Keiran, I've got some information on Sir Robert. Are you free to talk now…or do you want me to call you later?"

"No, now is fine. Actually, the meeting is over so I'll get back to London sooner than I thought."

"Great! Sir Robert—well, it's believed that he did, in fact, die of a heart attack, although the police can't find any medical history of any heart trouble. Drinking too much, yes. But heart problems, none. They are trying to locate any witnesses who were in the room at the time.

They have found two other club members, they can't locate two others, you're obviously another. Who would be the other one?"

"There were three other gentlemen in the room besides Sir Robert and I. But with their faces covered with towels, it'll be hard to identify anyone. Anyhow, I'll be back this afternoon, and I'll go to the club. I'll call the police from there."

"Do you want to have dinner tonight?"

"Dinner and more."

"Can't wait until I see you. Dinner will be at my place. After my broadcast, about 8:30 or so. Good for you?"

"I'll be there. See you tonight. I love you and miss you."

"Lots of kisses, Keiran. Take care of yourself. I'll be waiting for you."

Twenty

It was shortly before 8:00 a.m. and Farris had come to Keiran's office.

"Good morning, Keiran, may I sit down?" he asked in a bland, yet smiling voice.

Keiran looked up from his reading, surprised at Farris' entrance in his shirtsleeves, his red and navy striped tie loosened at his neck, trying hard to give a casual look. Seeing him brought no sudden cheerfulness to Keiran. He wondered if this was an appearance to check on whether he had arrived on time, or whether it was going to be another corrective lecture on how to behave as an associate.

"Appears as if you need a file cabinet," Farris noted as he took some files off a chair and placed them on the floor.

"Yeah, I expect to get one soon. HenHen has ordered one. Once that arrives, I'll have my guest chairs free of paper. Truth is, though, I like my files out in the open. Easier for me to get to them."

"Good thought. Whatever makes you comfortable in the way of office furniture, we'll make sure you have. Check again with HenHen. Perhaps there is a piece of furniture that will accomplish what you want. Well, now," Farris spoke slowly, continuing his forced smile, "I have to apologize on behalf of Zoran and myself for leaving Dublin so hurriedly. Crude, very crude behavior. You know by now of Zoran's anxieties. If certain pre-determined matters aren't followed scrupulously, he leaves, believing that the unexpected is an omen of an impending event over which he has no control. I know that it may sound strange to you, but that's how it is. When he believes he has lost control, he panics…but that's between you and me. He thinks he's being prudent, and perhaps from his standpoint, he is."

Keiran looked at Farris, noting that the apology was certainly an abrupt change in personality for him. Keiran understood that for Farris, expression of regret would be a sign of weakness. So even though the apology was uttered, there was darkness in his statement that made his words seem contrived.

"Probably frustrating for you," Keiran replied, "not being able to plan anything in any meaningful way if Zoran changes his mind all the time. I suspect anxieties can really make life difficult."

"It does make one have to understand that flexibility is a key element of representing Zoran. He changes his program pretty regularly." Farris answered.

"No need to have rushed off, Mr. Farris. By the time I got back to the suite, the phone was fixed. Apparently, there were instructions from our office that the phone in the conference room be disabled, as you didn't want to be disturbed. According to the events manager at the hotel, a Ms. Rogers from here passed on that information. I don't believe we have a Ms. Rogers, unless it was a temp."

Farris didn't reply immediately. He nervously brought his right, then his left, hand to the top of his bald head, straightening the few remaining strands of gray hair, trying to cover what could not be covered, an obsessive habit that Keiran had seen several times before. Finally, Farris commented. "I certainly didn't give any instructions to HenHen to stop any incoming calls into the conference room. Interesting information, Keiran. So that is why the phone wasn't working…the orders came from us. HenHen took care of all our arrangements in Dublin. I don't think, even if we had temporary help, that she would have turned over that assignment to such a person. Get HenHen on the line. Let's find out what went on with the preparations for the meeting." Farris now spoke in a low murmuring voice, speaking to himself. "Bad…Bad…Get HenHen," he repeated. "If Zoran hears that it was our fault…Oh my…Bad, bad."

"Sure." Keiran pressed into the phone the interoffice phone number for HenHen. After a short ring, HenHen came on the phone with an abrupt "Yes?"

"HenHen, this is Keiran. I'm with Mr. Farris and he would like to speak to you." Keiran passed the receiver over to Farris.

"HenHen, we don't have a Ms. Rogers in this office, do we? That's is what I thought. No. Must be a mix up. Certainly. Did you make all the arrangements with the hotel in Dublin? Yes…All right. Thank you." He returned the phone to Keiran, who replaced it in its cradle.

As he spoke, his voice faltered, his face pale as if he were close to fainting.

"No Ms. Rogers here and HenHen alone had all the dealings with the hotel. It must have been a mix up from the hotel's end. Perhaps Ms. Rogers is with another office and another meeting was going on near ours. We've never had any problem with that hotel, so this is very, very strange. Please follow up. Check again with the hotel and get back to me immediately. This is quite serious. An imposter from our office…I can understand why Zoran alters plans so readily. I just hope it was the hotel's fault and not someone else who knew of our meeting and was going to do us harm."

"It's certainly bizarre," Keiran replied. "Someone claiming to be from our office. Why would anyone do that?"

"No idea whatsoever. Let's hope it's the hotel that made the mistake. I don't like to think that someone in this office is interfering with our client work. That would be very disturbing…very disturbing. I don't like this at all. Not at all." Farris rose to leave, his face still white with worry. Zoran continues to be pleased with your work and I know you'll get to the bottom of this soon."

"Before you leave, Mr. Farris, I want to thank you for introducing me to Mr. Ho-Lee. I'm sorry that the meeting ended so abruptly. It would have been interesting to talk to him. What's his nationality?" Keiran asked, ignoring Farris' comments about Zoran being pleased with his work. He'd heard that remark before.

Farris nodded, without first speaking, as if he was in deep thought. Then he looked up, his face showing displeasure as if this new query was idle chatter not warranting a reply. "What did you ask?"

"Mr. Ho-Lee. His nationality?"

"Of course. Mr. Ho-Lee. He's Korean. Sorry, I'm distracted by concentrating on our earlier deliberations. Anything else?"

"No. Nothing at all."

"Well now, Keiran, get to the bottom of the mess that occurred in Dublin. I'd like an interim report by close of business today."

Farris rose, making his way toward Keiran's office door, when he paused for several moments. He turned around, both hands now in his pockets as if he wanted to put an end to the annoying 'hand to head' habit. His eyes wandered to the front of Keiran's desk, then closed as if contemplating what he would say. Farris' manner reminded Keiran of Professor Haroldson from his law school days, who had the unsettling habit of leaving long pauses between his sentences in his lectures, giving the impression that either he didn't know what he wanted to say next or he was carefully choosing his words. No one could ever figure out which it was, but the student consensus was that he was figuring out what to say, as he probably hadn't prepared for the lecture. In Farris' case, it was probably the alternative—he knew what he was about to say, but was searching carefully for the right words.

"A few more matters. I'm sorry this conversation is so disjointed. The information about the disabled phone in the conference room now preoccupies me. I totally forgot to advise you of my view of your performance." Farris' voice now trembled as if he was uncomfortable with what he was about to say. "As I indicated a few days ago to you, I'm impressed with your work, but I also told you that you have to work on your discipline and promptness, although, frankly, I see that improving a great deal. You were on time today. In fact you were early."

"Well, I'm trying, Mr. Farris. Trying. I've never been late with an assignment and to me that is more important than arriving at the stroke of 7:00 or, as today, 8:00 in the morning."

"I understand your view completely. And, you, of course, understand my position. When you came from Washington, your references from the partners there and from those in New York were all of the highest quality—partnership track is what everyone said in their reviews. Earlier, frankly, I had trouble understanding how they had arrived at that opinion…now I am inclined to agree with them. You are a poised young man with solid intelligence. You handled yourself well after the tragedy on the island. Zoran was impressed with your demeanor and with how you conducted yourself and dealt with people. He admires your composure greatly, as do I. Also, HenHen reports that you're advising her of your whereabouts when you leave the office, and I must say that she is happy about that change in behavior on your part." Farris laughed. Keiran smiled, wondering silently, what the fuck does he want now? This guy is all over the place.

"So we have arrived at a platform of understanding in a very short time." Farris continued, "That merits my continued confidence in you. Any comments?"

Keiran hesitated for a moment, then spoke. "No. Thank you for your kind observations about my performance." Farris gazed at Keiran, waiting for more words. Keiran didn't elaborate. He had said all he wanted to say at this time.

"Well, good. You do understand what I am driving at. One last thing, and I promise that this will be the last request this morning. Zoran would like to visit with us this evening. Will your schedule permit this?"

"What time do you want me there?"

"Eight. Dinner tonight at the Connaught Hotel restaurant. Are you familiar with the place?"

"No, but I'm sure I can find it."

"Come earlier if you can. We'll be in the lounge having a drink before dinner. Are you enjoying working in London?" Farris said, almost as an afterthought.

"Yes, I like London." Keiran looked at Farris, thinking silently, why is he asking me if I like London? Small conversation from a sinister S.O.B.

"Oh, I almost forgot my mind, where is it this morning? Old age is creeping up on me, and the worry of what you have told me about the phone mess. Most important item, Keiran, is that Zoran leaves for Venice this weekend. He wants you to accompany him. It'll only be for a few days. I gather he wants you to meet some of his business associates and discuss some new business ventures. This is a good sign of his confidence in you. A very good sign."

"I'm pleased. Frankly, though, I have weekend plans that I can't change. I can join him on Sunday."

Farris returned to his habit of stroking his head, smoothing over the few strands of hair on his head, which he was now shaking slightly.

"You have plans?"

"I'd prefer not to go. I can leave early Sunday morning and be in Venice later that day. I'm sure there are flights that can get me there by mid-afternoon. Certainly, I can stay for several days thereafter, if he wishes."

"Let me see what I can do. I'll call Zoran and we can discuss it this evening over dinner."

"I can't change my plans, Mr. Farris." Keiran repeated.

Farris just stared at Keiran for a long time, as if trying to communicate to Keiran without speaking that he did have to change his plans. His hands dropped to his side as he turned away; his lips barely moving, saying, "We'll see, Keiran. We'll see."

Keiran turned around in his seat and looked up across the alleyway to see a sliver of a cloudy sky making the day dim as a gray sea. Second thoughts aren't healthy, he told himself. Maybe I should have called Jennifer and told her about Venice…? Shit, no, the client can wait. What's one more day? He had accepted Jennifer's invitation to visit her uncle this weekend, and he was going to stick to those plans. Luck had intervened when he had met her. The chances of life and the influences of destiny were strange, he knew, and not to be foreseen. Everything with Jennifer was so natural, so unpretentious, so beautiful. His private life was tranquil, but calmness still eluded him in his profession. Farris always used the term 'law game,' never 'law practice.' It can't be a 'game.' No, I don't believe that. I won't believe that it's a game. No, shit, it must be the dark day that's making my thoughts too deep. Enough of this moment of selfish sadness.

The phone rang. By its tone, he knew it was an outside call. He debated whether to have his voicemail answer the call, but decided that everyone knew he was in the office. He picked up the receiver.

"Keiran Hogan here."

"Keiran, this is Zoran. Farris just told me that you have to delay your departure until Sunday. I was hoping you could come Saturday as I have planned a dinner party. You would be able to meet my wife and my family and some of my business partners. You certainly can bring a friend with you if you wish. There's room on my plane."

The invitation sounded real. His voice was gentle and kind, actually.

"Thanks, Mr. Hemmrich."

"Please, Keiran, please call me Zoran."

"Sir…Zoran, I do thank you for the invitation. But I really can't cancel the plans that I have this weekend. I'll only miss Saturday though. I can leave Sunday afternoon and be in Venice by early evening, if the flights permit. I can stay longer if you wish."

"Well, fine. We'll have another dinner party then on Sunday. My wife will punish me for making that promise, but I'll keep her in good humor." He laughed.

"Thank you, Zoran."

"Goodbye, Keiran." The line went dead.

Farris, back in his office, was still angry at Keiran's continued and insistent independence. He began to worry that his own patience with this new associate was already at its end. But Zoran liked Keiran. Maybe it was that streak of independence that attracted Zoran to him. In the dark recesses of his mind, he knew that he had been the same, at one time. That was all buried now beneath an avalanche of experiences that culminated with his taking the less honorable road. The only salvation in the decision he had taken years ago was to look at Keiran and wonder how long that independence would last before he followed the path.

And he will, I have no doubt about that. Farris threw his pen on the desk, watching it bouncing around until it came to rest by the picture of his wife. I've done all this for you, Laura…all for you. He liked the power that the money he brought into the firm gave him with his other partners. How he loved that respect. He was one of the top three billing partners in the firm. And he was rich. No, Keiran would feel the taste and want to follow.

He has to follow if he wants to survive with me. Farris felt no sense of confusion or pain in believing Keiran would follow in his footsteps. "He's not a fool," Farris quietly said, "no, he's not a fool."

HenHen walked in with a sheaf of messages.

"Mr. Farris, Mr. Coborn from the embassy called and said it was urgent that you call him. Do you wish me to get him?"

"No, I'll do it myself. Thank you, though. HenHen, I'm concerned about this Ms. Rogers who canceled our phone in the conference room in Dublin. Are you sure no one here would have played that kind of trick?"

"Absolutely. I've already checked our phone records and the only calls to Dublin were by me, to make those arrangements. Even Mr. Hogan's line had no calls to Dublin…although he is calling ITN frequently."

"ITN?"

"Yes, Independent Television News, Channel Five"

"Oh!" Farris arched his eyebrows.

"Rumor around the office is that his friend is the presenter on the six o'clock news. I don't suppose you watch the program. Her name is Jennifer Berley."

"I'm happy he's found someone here. Those trips of his back and forth to Washington were beginning to interfere with his work here. You know I spoke to him about that. So, in a way, this is good news. Maybe he'll be more stable and less arrogant. Anyway, I've asked Keiran to work with you on finding out exactly what happened. We'll get to the bottom of this. He is to join Zoran and me at the Connaught for dinner at eight. Make sure he doesn't forget."

"I'll leave a message at his club as well as on his computer. Should I make reservations for you?"

"No, Zoran's office will do that. Unless it's Zoran, hold all calls. I need some private time."

"Certainly, sir." HenHen lowered her head slightly, her grimace showing a bit of annoyance that Farris wasn't telling her why he needed the private time.

It must be Coborn's call. He must be concerned about that, she told herself silently as she left the office.

"Coborn. He's beginning to be a bother. I've told him to limit the calls to this office and call me at home. Now the bastard is doing just what I asked him not to do," Farris muttered to himself. Before placing the call, he went through a mental list of possible problem areas, trying to sort out what his response would be. He knew Coborn was reaching the end of his usefulness. Coborn was sometimes irrational; he was drinking too much—and when that happens, the tongue is loose and mistakes are made. Farris was worried about his stability. Farris picked up his phone, twiddled with the cord for several moments, then punched in the direct dial number for Coborn.

"This is Jefferson Coborn"

"You called?" Farris inquired.

"Yes. I haven't heard from you in a few days, and wondered what you thought of the recent death."

"Recent death?"

"Yes. Page one of yesterday's *Times* and other papers."

"Oh, you mean Runnard?"

"Yes."

"Well, I don't have any feeling for that event one way or the other."

"We should see one another, Duane. We should see one another soon. I have something for your library." When Coborn used the word library, Farris knew it to mean that he information he intended to pass on.

"It is now about 9:00. Please join me for coffee at Greystone Gardens Hotel. I'll see you in about a half hour, in the coffee bar."

Farris hung up, not waiting for a reply. Certainly, Coborn's instability was taking hold. Coborn would soon make mistakes. Mistakes have a habit of dragging down all those associated with them. Farris didn't like the tone of Coborn's voice. He had enough on his mind right now and he didn't need to add an unstable informant to those worries.

Jefferson Coborn sat alone in the last booth, waiting for Farris. Each booth was separated by a dark green wooden planter, in which ferns were placed to obscure the view from one booth to another. One had to walk down the center aisle of the coffee house and look in each booth to find whomever one was looking for. He was sure Farris would be happy with what he had accomplished. Coborn knew it would mean infinitely more money for him, and the real possibility that he could retire much sooner. Sure he did it on his own, but then he remembered Farris saying that he wished Sir Robert dead.

Sir Robert had caused great problems for Farris...and now he was making friends with one of Farris' associates. He was probably passing on information to that associate, Keiran Hogan. So Farris should be happy. Of course Farris will be happy, thought Coborn.

Farris walked in promptly at 9:30.

"One sir?" The waitress asked, holding several menus in the crook of her arm.

"No, I'm actually meeting someone here."

"Certainly. Please this way." She led him down the aisle where Coborn sat, looking intently at the menu.

"Your menu sir." As he sat down, she placed the menu on top of the plain yellow placemat, already set with utensils and a coffee cup and saucer.

"Thank you. This is fine. Jefferson, good morning to you." Farris and Coborn shook hands.

"Would you like coffee, sir?" The waitress directed her question to Farris.

"Yes, please—decaf—and some toast, whole wheat toast and a cup of fruit as well. Jefferson, will you join me?"

"Yes. I'll have the same."

"Be right back with your order, gentlemen."

"Now, Jefferson, what is the urgency? You are well, first of all?"

"Yes. I'm going to leave for holiday in a week or so—Majorca."

"That should be fine. Relaxing spot."

There was a moment of silence. Coborn's head was bent down, his right hand fiddling with the cutlery. Finally he spoke, taking up his fork and poking it into the cloth napkin that still remained folded

"Remember when you told me that you wished Sir Robert dead?" Coborn blurted out, his eyes wide, his voice shaking and anxious.

"I don't recall specifically. A few years ago, he did cause me and my client some difficulty."

"I did tell you that he and your associate, Mr. Hogan, had been meeting, that they have had a few meetings. My own source at the club told me that."

"Hogan and Sir Robert?"

"Yes."

"Well, that's their privilege. The club is small and I suspect that everyone runs into one another from time to time. So what?"

"The other day, he left Mr. Hogan a package. I think it contains information about you and your client."

"How do you know that?"

"Let's say I have my ways."

"Let's say you do. Are they as trustworthy as you are to me?"

"Yes, yes, of course."

"What is it that you want to tell me, Jefferson?" The waitress interrupted with their order.

"Thank you. Thank you very much. This will be fine," Farris said.

She left a few extra napkins on the table, explaining, "Just in case, you need a few more. The toast is a bit crumby this morning. Bread is fresh though."

Farris smiled. Coborn said nothing and didn't look up from the table, not touching his drink or food.

"Now, Jefferson, what is it?" Farris spoke softly.

"I killed Sir Robert, and I want you to pay me for what I did. I want to be paid a great deal. I want to retire. I hate what I am doing, Duane. Hate it. I've been maligned enough. I want out. I remember you asking me what I could do get rid of him, but you never wanted to know anything. Now you know. I want the money, I want a million dollars."

Farris lifted one piece of toast to his mouth and bit off a chunk, slowly chewing it, then reached for his coffee taking a sip, placing it gently back on its saucer.

"Are you talking to me or to the table? Look up when you're speaking to me. Now, Jefferson, how do I know you not making this up? You have had some strange moments lately."

"You don't know whether I'm making the story up or not and I don't like your comment about having strange moments. I don't have such moments. I know exactly what I am doing all the time. Don't patronize me. I hate it when people do that. Hate it."

Farris took another sip from his coffee cup, then reached over to bring his fruit cup closer to him, taking a spoon and lifting a small amount of the fruit to his mouth, chewing it slowly, finally silently swallowing it.

"You should eat your breakfast before it gets cold, Jefferson. Toast loses its warmth quickly despite being so nicely covered in this basket."

"I want the amount I asked you for." Coborn looked directly at Farris now, his voice no longer shaking, the tone higher than normal.

"Jefferson, please, I'm right across from you. No need to raise your voice. Please," Farris said softly, and continued, "Why should I pay you for what has happened if I don't even know you accomplished what you have said you did?"

"Because you have no choice."

"We'll see, Jefferson. We'll see."

"You're finished if you don't give me what I want. And you know it. Goodbye, Duane."

Coborn rose and threw a small white envelope on the table.

"Read this. It tells you where to send the money. Listen, Duane, don't try to fuck me. Be a smart lawyer, okay?"

Farris continued eating from his fruit bowl. "You should finish your breakfast, Jefferson."

"Instructions are in the envelope. Follow them," Coborn answered, then he rose and walked toward the exit, his head visibly shaking.

Twenty-One

Farris finished his drink in a gulp. Hemmrich nodded as Farris ended his tale about Coborn's wasting of Runnard. "I just don't know whether to believe him or not. I've never thought him capable of murder, let alone blackmail." They sat in the lounge of the Connaught Hotel, with its unusual period pieces, large and comfortable armchairs. Hemmrich's two assistants sat close by. Separating Farris and Hemmrich was a pie-shaped table, its rim of scrolls shaped like the tops of undulating waves. Farris placed his empty glass down on the table. Hemmrich had yet to touch his drink of scotch over ice. "Either way, Coborn has us...."

"You mean 'you,'" Zoran interrupted, pointing a finger at Farris.

"Yes...yes, he has me at a disadvantage. I know I can't tolerate what he is trying to do. Lately he has been giving me good information. Some messages have been going back and forth from the CIA chief here in London and Washington regarding a project dubbed 'Crescent Eagle.' Fairly cryptic. Only that the undertaking is ready to be concluded. He doesn't know what it's, but he believes it has something to do with finding who was responsible for the Parrot explosion."

"Look, Duane, this guy is nuts. No one will ever find out. Never. Repeat after me, Duane: 'Never will anyone find out about the Parrot.' It's over. Done. Period. Now how do you think you'll handle this idiot mole of yours?" Zoran said, his voice indicating annoyance.

There was silence as Farris nervously brought his hands to his head, again fingering the few strands of hair. He kept his composure for several moments, finally bringing his hands down to his lap, and said, "No sense in dwelling on the issue. When this latest deal goes through, you've said that you will be taking a break from other deals. I'm thinking of doing the same. We've had a good run, Zoran. Time to close the show down. My law partners will complain about the loss of income to the firm, but if I'm not there to hear the complaints, what does it matter? Besides, they're all jack-off moralists." Farris commented, now reaching for his drink

"It's empty. You need more scotch," Zoran reminded him. "And for Christ's sake, stop being so nervous. You're making me think you've lost your cool, just like your bloody mole. Clearly, we can't afford to have any difficulties at this time," Zoran continued, "But who would believe him if he did go to the police? Did you leave any footprints in terms of your payments? You were creative, I assume, in those payments?"

Farris finally looked up at Zoran. The expression in his eyes was of a person on the point of saying something untoward, but held back by some unknown frightening sensation. He spoke quietly. "Only phone calls and they're rare. Even those calls can be explained because he is the administrator of the embassy. There would be professional reasons for me to call him. As for the funds, nothing traceable. All moneys are sent from one of my offshore companies to one of his. Nothing goes through his own bank account here. In fact, there is no record of my even paying him. Company to company—no individual names are used. No traceability at all to me or to anything we have done together."

"Still, Duane," Hemmrich noted sharply, "people like him can raise eyebrows and get security people interested—especially if he decides to spill what he knows. You'd at least have to answer to an investigator, and who knows what documents they would want. Who knows what documents he has kept? No, this is not good news at all. Not at all. Just doing what he did and then telling you about is…let's face it, he can cause harm all over the place."

"What would you say if I call upon your own special operative," Farris paused, " to…to attend to an appointment for me. Possible?"

Zoran picked up his drink and drained it. "Ah! Nothing like good scotch. You were saying…my special operative. These things have to be planned carefully. Why not wait and see if your Coborn brings up the subject again? Let's give it a few more days. We have had many good years together and I would not want everything to begin to unravel. I don't think anyone will benefit, including Coborn, if he decides to go forward with his scheme. See if you can talk to him and get him to rethink the matter."

"I don't think he'll change his mind. He's clearly lost his balance. He's flipped. He won't change."

"Then that answers my question. Well, we can continue this debate on the future, if any, of your mole. Your associate, Duane, he's at the entrance," Zoran said. Farris turned toward the entrance of the lounge to see that Keiran had just arrived. "Come to a rapid conclusion, Duane, about Coborn. A rapid conclusion."

"That would be prudent," Farris replied. "Hogan is a bright young man. We have to watch him. Too independent." He shifted his eyes toward Keiran, who was walking toward them.

"Duane, you're as paranoid as you accuse me of being. You come with problems tonight and now you're creating another one. I won't have it. Enough. Done. Period. Leave Hogan alone. He's just finding himself. He'll come around in due course. Be patient. Between the healthy imagination and intelligence of a young man, is ambition, and ambition, and as you know, includes making money, a lot of money. Or let him go. Don't agonize. It's bothersome and I'm tired of these repetitive conversations. Sometimes I think you have gone a bit mad." Zoran laughed heartedly.

"I'm not amused," Farris replied, his face taking on a dour expression as if he was a child who had been admonished in first grade for misspelling a word.

Keiran stood in the entrance to the lounge for a moment, his eyes surveying the crowd, looking for Farris and Hemmrich. Finally recognizing them seated in the far corner, he strode briskly through the evening throng, heading in their direction. They seemed, he noted, to be in earnest conversation, nursing their drinks. He chuckled to himself. Man, am I going to like this or what?

"Good evening, Mr. Farris, Mr. Hemmrich." Keiran spoke with cautious politeness as he extended his hand first to Farris, then to Hemmrich, who spoke first.

"Good evening to you, Keiran. Almost on time." They all laughed.

"Nice to see you again," Farris added.

"It seems as if I am getting the reputation of being tardy. In reality, something always seems to come up as I am about to leave. I don't know if either one of you're aware of the death of Sir Robert Runnard. He lived at the club, and I met him a few times. He died of a heart attack. As I was one of the last people to see him, the police wanted to interview me just as I was ready to come here. I have to tell you, two heart attacks, Leyden and now Sir Robert, and two police interviews in a few days is not something that I ever expected. I thought London would be exciting for me, but not in this way." Keiran smiled, tossing his head slightly.

"The police?" Farris asked anxiously.

"Yes, sir. The police wanted to know what we had talked about, whether there was any indication that Runnard was ill and so forth. A very short interview."

"Good. I don't need one of my associates' name in the newspaper or being a suspect for anything." Keiran laughed.

"Interestingly, though, I hadn't seen a notice of Runnard's death," Farris now responded innocently.

"It was in yesterday's *Times.* He died the evening before." Keiran knew Farris was lying. The paper was on Zoran's plane yesterday as they flew to Dublin.

"Of course. How forgetful of me. I did glance at the short notice in the *Times,* but never read the full story, we were so busy."

"I believe it made the major newscasts as well. Anyway, the obituary in the paper laid out his long career. Services, according to the notice at the club, will be at Brompton Oratory tomorrow at noon. He had no children. He was a kind man and I enjoyed talking to him. Did you know him, Mr. Farris?"

Farris cast up his eyes at Hemmrich before answering.

"Oh, I may have met him from time to time. He was, I believe, a barrister, so our paths would not have crossed much. What I remember about him is that he was an excellent trial attorney. Disappeared several years ago and the rumor was that he liked to drink and had gone into some form of rehabilitation. How did he look to you, Keiran?" Farris asked, now speaking rather easily and softly.

"Fine, actually, fine. It's a surprise that he died so suddenly. Hard to understand," Keiran lowered his head, thinking to himself, what a liar this guy is. An accomplished liar and does it so convincingly.

After a pause, Hemmrich asked nonchalantly, "You've been through a great deal in a short amount of time, Keiran. This trip to Venice will be just a bit of business and mostly vacation—on me. That's if your partner here will let you take some needed time off. Duane, what do you think?"

"Certainly it matters that he gets some time off. Keiran, why not take the entire week in Venice? Visit the art galleries, museums, and so forth, take a break and relax. How does that sound?"

"Actually, not bad...."

"And, if you want to bring a friend you're welcome to do so. We'll only spend a day on business—you're arriving on Sunday—we'll discuss some business, then the rest of week is free. I'll have my office arrange the tours and everything will be on me. There, it's finished. You'll stay in Venice."

Keiran looked at both of them, trying to figure out if they really agreed on this suggestion. He knew both Farris and Hemmrich didn't generally proceed without some serious discussion before such a decision, although this time, it did look spontaneous. He also knew he could not say no, having told them both that he had made other arrangements for the weekend.

"I don't know if I'll stay the whole week, maybe a few days though."

"Good, my office will make all the arrangements. They'll leave word at your club. Now let us drink to a good trip with no heart attacks." Hemmrich reached over for his glass, then replaced it saying, "Keiran, how can I toast when you don't have a drink?" Everyone laughed. "And you need a refill, Duane." Zoran continued.

Farris motioned for a waiter who came promptly. "Keiran, you will have…?"

"Amstel Light," Keiran answered.

"Another scotch on ice for me," Farris added. "Zoran...?"

"Sure. Why not? A refill for me as well."

The waiter bowed slightly saying, "Right away, sir."

"What, no Guinness stout?" Hemmrich exclaimed. "Where is the Irish in you?"

Keiran smiled lightly, responding, "I like Guinness, no doubt about that. But I thought I'd try something different tonight."

"Sticks to his own decisions regarding drink! That, Duane, is a singularly determined man. And, I say, a stout-hearted one, as the Brits say," Hemmrich bellowed. Farris looked embarrassed.

"Now we need food," Hemmrich added. "Would it please you both to stay here, have some appetizers, good wine, and relax for a few hours? What is your pleasure?"

"I suspect that Keiran wants a good meal. I know that when I was a bachelor, I ate pretty haphazardly unless I went to dinner with friends. Same with you, Keiran?" Farris asked.

"The food is passable at the club. You probably know that there is a reserved table where you can join others who are also alone for the evening meal. A great way to meet new people. Everyone introduces himself; some revert to their evening papers, others though are kind in conversation. I don't mind having a bite here. Whatever you two decide is fine with me."

"An important query, as you lawyers like to say," Zoran turned and looked directly at Keiran, "Is your new lady friend a good cook? Important issue in a relationship." He laughed heartily.

"She hasn't cooked me a full meal yet, so I don't really know. Enough about me, though. Mr. Hemmrich, what is the status of the business contract we were supposed to work on in Dublin before everyone broke and left?"

"So you don't want me to delve into your personal life. Good man. Fine. You want to talk business. The conscientious attitude of youth! Well, now, we continued our discussions on my plane back to London, and signed the appropriate letter of intent. We'll meet the customer in Venice on Monday. It is my intention to finalize everything then."

"Were there any changes to the documents I had drafted for you?" Keiran inquired.

"No, not really," Farris interjected, raising his hand slightly indicating to Hemmrich not to answer. "One or two minor items, but nothing of any real substance."

"As I told Mr. Farris, Zoran, by the time I returned to the suite, the phone was working."

"I understand that some, perhaps even you Keiran, feel that I am too anxious about events that don't go according to plan, but that's the way I am. What, by the way, was wrong with the phone?"

Farris looked askance at Keiran, a pleading look in his eyes suggesting that Keiran not tell the truth about the office instruction mix-up.

Keiran observed his look, responding, "We're still trying to find out. The hotel events manager is looking into it. Perhaps some mistaken instructions when the order to reserve the suite was made."

"Mistaken instructions from your office?" Hemmrich asked, his head turning toward Farris.

"That's still to be determined. Highly unlikely though," Farris answered, his voice quivering slightly.

"I would hope so. I would find it hard to believe that instructions from HenHen would be misinterpreted," Zoran added.

"One Amstel Light for you, sir," the waiter put a frosted beer mug in front of Keiran, then he began to gently pour the beer. "Gentlemen, two scotch over ice. Can I get you anything else?"

"Yes," Farris replied. "The appetizer menu. We intend to eat here. And notify the *maître d'* we won't need our table. The name is Farris."

"Certainly, sir. I'll take care of that for you." The waiter bowed again and briskly went away.

"Well now, a toast to the bright young man who will make sure that I don't do anything illegal. Cheers, Keiran! Cheers!" Hemmrich lifted his glass as did Farris, each touching slightly Keiran's. They all took a quaff.

"Cheers to both of you. This has been a roller coaster ride, Mr. Hemmrich, lots of twists and turns," Keiran answered, his smile slight as he looked at them.

"Makes your young life interesting, though. Life should be interesting, wouldn't you agree, Duane?"

"Of course." Farris nodded eagerly.

"Working with you, Mr. Hemmrich, I have a distinct feeling, is never going to be in slow motion. I can get to Venice and you could have already left because of some perceived event."

Hemmrich laughed heartily. His hands circled his drink rapidly, and he took a long swallow. "Ah! Nothing like good golden clear scotch that's being paid for by your lawyer!" There was laughter all around as Zoran continued, "Venice? Possibly things could change. I doubt it. That's where I spend a lot of my time. My family is there from time to time and should be there now. Yet, Keiran, on a more earnest note, as you well understand, we were engaged in Dublin in serious and sensitive negotiations. And when I am told the phone in the conference room is not working, that, to me, is a bit unsettling. The phone doesn't just become inoperable while we are meeting. I'm sure the management checked everything out before my arrival. Besides, it's a simple task to unplug the inoperable phone and replace it with one that is working. I can't believe that the wiring was broken. No, the whole episode makes one wonder if there wasn't a third hand involved, someone who wanted to know about the deal. We are learning to trust you, Keiran, but even you were not in the room, and you had drafted the documents. No, something untoward happened, and I, frankly, doubt that you will ever find out the real story."

"You understand, Keiran," Farris added, his voice now taking on the authoritative tone used in the office staff meeting, looking directly at Keiran, "multimillion dollar business deals have to be, of necessity, carried out in confidence. After all, this is a competitive business. Zoran is not alone in the world selling commodities. There are many others. They aren't as reliable as he is, but there are others. And the profit on commodities is constantly changing; everyone wants to know the prices Zoran is charging. Zoran's pricing is always held closely—only he and I know. In fact, you'll notice that in the contract document you drafted, the pricing for the product was left blank—to be filled in at the last moment during the final negotiations."

"I realize all of this, Mr. Farris, Mr. Hemmrich. It is just that I can understand certain unexpected events being disruptive and calling for a change in plans, but an inoperable phone?"

"You have a point, Keiran," Hemmrich replied. "Normally, my assistants carry equipment that advises whether there are any listening devices in the room, or taps on the phone. But because the customer was already in the conference room, this sweep wasn't done. In my view, something must have been done to the phone between the time we walked into the room to meet our customers and when we began our session. That is what is bothersome, wouldn't you agree?"

All this was new information for Keiran—the assistants taking a scan of the room, checking the phone for listening devices. If that was true, then Hemmrich had a point. Someone, some third hand, as he said, was interested in finding out what was going on in the room. But who could that person be? Certainly, Keiran silently told himself, Hemmrich and Farris must have an idea of who might be behind such intrigue. They could not be totally in the dark. Or, again, was this all a ruse, some sort of strange initiation into working with them? There was no logic to what was happening.

"So, the phone not working means to me that the third hand wanted to do something more dramatic than just listen in. We may have all been a target for assassination," Hemmrich said, now whispering his words.

There was silence. Keiran begin to feel uneasy. Were these unstable men, or did they have a realistic view of their business and its perils?

"Menu, sir." The waiter returned, giving each of them a leather-covered placard in which the menu had been inserted

"Now we must eat. All this serous conversation has made me hungry. Perhaps we should go into the dining room, Duane?"

"What ever you wish. I'm certain we can get our table back."

"Keiran," Hemmrich asked, "Would you like a full dinner?"

"You mean you're changing your mind…again?" There was laughter all around. Even Keiran joined in, realizing what he had just said.

"Actually, this menu looks pretty good. Let's stay here," Keiran answered, aggravated at how quickly Hemmrich altered his decisions, even a simple matter like dinner.

"We must obey the young man, Duane. He has made a command decision." Hemmrich laughed as he spoke.

"I guess we will stay here." Farris looked at Keiran with eyes that Keiran could not misunderstand—don't ever disagree with the client. If he wants to change his mind, it's his prerogative.

"I'll make the menu decisions for us all," Zoran remarked. "Bring us all petite fillets, medium, french fries, and a cup of fresh fruit. There, done. Any complaints?"

"Perfect order," Farris replied. "Keiran?"

"Fine with me."

They would remain in the lounge. A small victory. Yet, he knew that Hemmrich was right about the phone. He'd have to find out—and soon—who had told the hotel to disengage the phone.

As Keiran handed back his menu to the waiter, he viewed for a short instant three men sitting about five tables away, closer to the windows that overlooked the street. He thought one of them looked like the telephone repairman on Guernsey. And the back of the other man, his hair, speckled gray, could that be Grayson? Silly. Too far away, and besides I don't have my glasses on. Can't tell someone from his back. Keiran reached for his glass of beer and decided that he'd better settle in for a few hours.

Twenty-Two

The rain fell in torrents, hitting the roof of his black BMW sedan mercilessly, making visibility difficult despite the wipers at high speed trying to keep the window clear. Kingsley Abidoun sat alone in the front seat of his car, his face hardening as he reviewed his next assignment. His two silent companions sat in the back. The car was parked at a corner on a side street perpendicular to the street that fronted the U. S. Embassy. From his vantage point, he had a good view of the embassy's front entrance. The target was an official at the embassy. He fingered a small photo in his hands—not that he needed it, as he had identified and followed the target his apartment to the embassy earlier. It was a habit of his to carry a small photo of the intended hit —a strange superstitious habit for which he had no explanation. He had to admit that he felt a strange bit of uneasiness, unusual for him. He never liked to have that feeling. It wasn't helpful to be distracted by an emotion he despised. Anxiety is for the weak, not for the courageous.

He generally insisted on detailed planning for such assignments, but he was told to get it done before the weekend was over. This left him little time in which to carry out any test run, which is what he always liked to do. His last assignment for this particular client had taken two months of intricate preparation and a dose of luck. His cousin worked in the very restaurant where the target would be eliminated. Although he recognized that good fortune is an ingredient in virtually all successful hits, luck didn't matter much to him. Even in that earlier assignment, if the restaurant hadn't provided the proper cover, he would have thought of something else—he knew that there was always another way, and he had a string of successes in his lifetime to prove that rule. His skill: untraceable assassinations. Yet, he had to admit, this hit was being done far too quickly. And when that happens, things can go wrong. He thought all of this silently, still confident that this mission would be accomplished.

Kingsley had Jefferson Coborn's home address, several photos—including the small one which he kept twisting among his fingers—and a brief run-down of where he usually went, including the three weekly visits to a prostitute's apartment near Piccadilly. It was from here that one of Kingsley's boys had followed the target back to his apartment, parking his van across the street until Kingsley and the others came to relieve him. Some of this information came from the man who had hired him, whom he knew only as Mr. Alain DeLattre, a dark skinned Frenchman. He was more likely from the Middle East as his accent wasn't that of a Frenchman despite the French name. Kingsley really didn't know. In itself, it wasn't strange; he never knew the full story behind any of his employers. He had done several jobs for this man—all successful—and they had added to Kingsley's already sizeable fortune that sat nicely in a Zurich bank.

The call had come from DeLattre around 10:00 Thursday evening. His instructions were explicit: "You have to accomplish this hit this weekend. This man is unstable and we no longer trust him. You must act quickly." Today, late Saturday afternoon, he decided he would strike. A few hours of planning replaced a week; there was no time for rehearsals. This will be simple, though. One person. Easy, Kingsley told himself. Now it was time to stage the 'accident.'

The heavy rain, he thought, would make it easier; there would be fewer people to observe. Rain keeps many indoors. This is good. The rain. A good omen, he shook his head slightly as he repeated the words quite to himself. Now, however, he was faced with a timetable that he didn't particularly like, but accepted. The rest, he thought, is up to God.

"Are my boys ready?" Kingsley turned to look at the two men in the back seat.

They replied in unison. "Yes. No problem. Ready, boss."

Jefferson Coborn desperately needed some peace of mind. He had killed a man he barely knew, and only because he believed it would make him more important to Farris, who, he hoped, would be more generous to him. When he found the opposite to be true, for a few days he refused to believe Farris' outburst towards him was real. I'm sure he'll call to apologize, Coborn thought. But the call never came. Coborn could not believe that Farris was unhappy, not appreciative of what he had done. Farris was now reminding him of Geoffrey Baxter, the unskilled and incompetent U. S. Ambassador to Pakistan who had ruined his career. Why don't these people listen to me? Coborn thought. Farris should be delighted that I got rid of someone who he's despised all these years…and I did it on my own! Besides, that old man, Runnard, was meeting one of Farris' associates. Who knows what information he had given that young man. Hah—if he gave him too much, I'd have to get rid of him too.

Coborn smiled to himself, one of those quirky parting of the lips that is less a happy grin and more a strange and appalling smile which would make anyone seeing it to believe the devil is not yet dead.

Yeah, watch it, Mr. Farris. I'm not some insignificant man. You'll have to pay me—pay me more than you have—you'll beg me not to reveal secrets about you. No, sir, I'm not someone to toss out to the wind like a leaf, waiting to be stepped upon when it lands. No sir. You are history, not me.

He sat at his desk, staring at the clock over his office door, waiting for the magic time of 5:30, when he would leave, regardless of the amount of work that needed to be done. Coborn reviewed in his mind what his doctor had advised him at his last annual physical just a few weeks ago. At that time, he told the doctor that he was having trouble sleeping and asked him for some medication to help him get through the night. He also told the doctor that he had a loud ringing in his ear and, at times, when he was trying to sleep, he would hear voices—soft distant voices—but he could not distinguish what the voices were saying.

The sounds were what one would hear approaching a room filled with chattering people, the noise of people talking, but impossible to make out any words. Toward dawn, the voices and the ringing would stop. Even after he had sex with Alleana, the ringing and muddled voices would come back…but only at night. His doctor suggested that he was probably under a great deal of stress.

"You're working too hard. You should take more time off. Go on a vacation, then come back, and we'll see where we go with this. I do, however, want you to go to Dr. Berenson for a psychiatric evaluation. He is one of the best in London, and he'll be able to pinpoint what is bothering you. In the meantime, I'll give you a prescription for a mild tranquilizer. That should help. Now, make the appointment with Dr. Berenson. You must do that. I'll see you in two weeks, and we'll take it from there."

Coborn didn't feel much better after that meeting. It was a struggle to accept what he had just been told. Somehow, he believed that the doctor's recommendation would get back to others at the embassy. Of course, when Coborn would be reviewed for his security clearance, he would have to put down that he had a psychiatric evaluation and perhaps undergone psychiatric treatment. It would be another negative that, along with the Pakistan mess, would mar his record. "Records," he said to himself, "that outlast life." No, it was time to retire with his money to someplace safe, quiet, away from everyone, maybe on the island of Mykonos. He had been there once and abandoned himself to life…it was one of the few times he loved life. Yeah. I'll go there. Why not? No one cares where I go anyway. No one.

First he knew he had to make more money…much more money. The only manner in which to get the amount he needed was to get it from Farris. He would surprise Farris with his ability to carry out the ultimate mission, killing someone regarded by Farris as the enemy. No, he would not do it in some bloody fashion. After all the man was in his eighties. He had seen him at the Royal Automobile Club where he also went, lulled into dreams while he took the steam, hoping that the voices would go away. It was a strange thought that crossed his mind. He had never killed anyone before, and at one time considered himself a pacifist.

Now, though, his mind had changed. He was thinking of himself—self-absorption became his guide. He would have to figure out how to do it and then surprise Farris with the results. It never became part of his thinking to get Farris' permission. No, he would do this on his own—a manly decision, proud, brilliant, a strong decision.

He was happy that Farris didn't appear to be angry when he told him of what he had accomplished. In fact, Farris seemed calm. It was only later in the day, about two or three hours later, that Coborn received a call from Farris. Good he'll give me the money. I know he would, Coborn silently thought as Farris came on the line. He was mistaken. Farris shouted at him.

"How dumb are you? You're on your own, Jefferson, totally on your own. I never want to hear from you again. What you did was stupid. Do you understand me…? Stupid." He hung up before Coborn could say anything.

There would be no bonus…and no more money.

Did Farris really call me those names? I think he really did. No matter. Okay, we'll see. I've got other things up my sleeve. I know how to hurt you, Mr. Duane Farris. I know what you've been doing. Okay, watch and see how dumb I am. Just watch. Well, sir, you don't understand how smart I am. I was just trying to help you. Why are you abusing me? You're treating me just like that shit-head ambassador in Pakistan. He screwed me. I'll make sure you don't. I'm right. I'm just trying to help you. Don't you understand? Why don't you understand? You'll give me all the money I want…much more money. I'll ruin you, asshole. I'll ruin your life.

As the clock over his office door reached 5:30, Coborn immediately rose from his desk. Methodically, as he did every evening, he checked his file cabinet safe to make sure it was locked, noted that he had put whatever security material he had away in that cabinet, went through his trash to verify he had no security material there, rearranged a few papers on his desk, put on his navy blue jacket and then left his inner office, saying goodbye to his secretary, who asked, "You have your umbrella, Mr. Coborn? It's raining pretty heavily." He said nothing, but raised the small folding black umbrella that he was carrying, indicating to her that he was prepared. Then he strode down the fourth floor corridor, took elevator to the lobby floor, and went out the front entrance.

Kingsley got out of the car, as did the two other men. They kept up with Coborn as he walked hurriedly, his umbrella steady over him as he made his way from the embassy to a pub located a few blocks away. When he arrived at the pub, he carefully placed his umbrella in one of several brass umbrella stands against the wall adjacent to the entrance and headed toward the bar to sit at the sole stool at the bar's end.

Kingsley followed him in, taking a table along the back end, but with a good view of Coborn. The men who had been in the car with him, both tall and heavily built, joined him shortly. Both were dressed well; one had on a dark gray suit with gray tie on a light gray shirt, the other a dark blue suit with matching shirt and tie. All had placed their umbrellas alongside the wall next to the table at which they were seated. The pub was crowded, and although Kingsley ordered beer for all three, no one touched their glasses. After about an hour, Coborn slid off his barstool, walking slowly to the exit, reached for his umbrella, and left.

The heavy rain had stopped, leaving only a slight drizzle in its wake. Coborn unfolded his umbrella and continued walking down the street, crossing it and heading toward a row of small shops. Kingsley stayed behind in the pub while the two men who were with him left immediately after Coborn exited.

One of the men walked a few feet behind Coborn, the other followed several feet in the back. Despite the rain, the sidewalks were crowded with departing workers headed home. When the two men following Coborn saw him go into a flower shop, the man in the blue suit walked past Coborn, stopping a few feet beyond the shop. Coborn soon came out of the shop, clutching his flowers, and headed toward the taxi stand. The gray-suited man hurried up behind him, calling out, "Mr. Coborn, Mr. Coborn...wait up, wait up."

Coborn turned to see a tall black man reaching him.

"How are you? It's been several months since we met at the embassy. Don't you remember me? Rene Etienne Lebre, Ambassade Cote d'Ivoire." He spoke with a slight French accent.

Coborn looked askance. He had never seen the man before—at least he didn't think he did. But then, maybe....

"No, I don't recall that I have met you. Perhaps I have. What was the occasion?"

"Your embassy July 4th celebration. How can you forget? There were not many black faces at the function." He laughed. Coborn was now embarrassed. Maybe he did see this man. And he was right; there were black faces at the party, but not that many. He should have remembered.

"I'm sorry. Of course. I've had so much on my mind, so it took a few minutes for me to recollect. How have you been?"

"Actually, very good. I left my government's service just a few months ago, and am now working for a trading company here in London. I like it a great deal. And you? You're still with the embassy?"

"Yes. I hope to be there for a little while longer, then I think it will be time to retire."

As they spoke, the blue-suited man approached, not paying attention to either one of them. Suddenly, he collapsed, falling on Coborn and taking him down with him.

"Dear me, Mr. Coborn, look...are you okay?" Coborn tried to get up, but as he did, the gray-suited man leaned over and reached for his head, turning it slightly to expose his ear, and pressed a small pen into the ear. Coborn immediately collapsed, the nerve agent would keep him unconscious for up to three hours. The blue-suited man rose quickly and he and his colleague helped to lift Coborn into a car that had driven up. A small crowd gathered.

"Not to worry, our friend has had a bit too much this early in the evening. He'll be fine." They gently placed him in the car and got in themselves, closing the doors behind them. The car carefully left the curb, the crowd watching as it gathered speed and made its way in the rush hour traffic. The only evidence they left were three black umbrellas resting haphazardly on the sidewalk. One by one, they were picked up by strangers, who, seeing that they were in good working order, took them and proceeded on their way. One muttered out loud, "Tipsy man. He wouldn't remember if he had an umbrella or not."

Coborn didn't show up at work the next morning, which itself was unusual. Calls to his apartment went unanswered. Even Alleana was worried when he didn't show up the night before as he had promised. He had never done that before. She didn't know where he lived, only that he worked at the embassy. She didn't even know his real name. She only called him 'Coby.' That is what he asked her to call him. Maybe, she told herself, he had to go away on embassy business, hoping she was right. She really loved 'Coby.' He made life happy for her, and she hoped he was happy with her. She would wait. He will come, she told herself, Coby, you can't leave me without seeing me. You can't. I love you, Coby.

After a few hours and many unreturned calls, the ambassador asked the embassy's security officer and Arnold Baldwin, his counselor, to go to Coborn's apartment to see what had happened to him. As the apartment was rented by the embassy for Coborn, the security office would have a key, provided that Coborn had not changed the locks, which he was under instructions not to do without notifying the embassy security officer. The very first thing Coborn did upon arrival at the apartment was to have the lock changed—several times. He gave the Security office the key for the first change, thereafter he ignored the instruction. It was none of their business how I live, he always told himself.

It was another hour before the security officer and Baldwin were able to get into the apartment. Even the apartment manager's master key didn't fit the lock Coborn had installed. A locksmith had to be called who proceeded to use a variety of keys until he found one that would open the door.

Coborn was laying on his bed, nude, his thin body showing the results of age, his stomach protruding from his otherwise slim stature. A bottle of prescription tranquilizer pills lay by his bed, a plastic bag over his head, its loose ends tied tightly around his throat by a heavy piece of sisal packing twine. His clothes had been placed carefully on a wooden valet next to the bedroom's large picture window. Nothing was touched in the neatly kept apartment. He left no note. The medical examiner later said that he had committed suicide, sometime between 7:00 and 8:00 the evening before he was discovered.

According to his personnel file, Coburn had no heirs, other than the wife he had divorced some time ago. On the beneficiary page indicating where he would want his final pay, any retirement benefits, and payment for unused sick leave, he had indicated that those funds be sent to the Pastor of First Presbyterian Church, Clayton, Missouri, the church where he had worshiped with his mother's family when he was a boy growing up in this St. Louis suburb. As he had direct deposit of his payroll check to Citibank, Washington, the bank manager would have to look at the account to see if there were any instructions left upon his death. Regardless, Coborn had only about $1,600 in that bank account. A review of all records available to the embassy, the Department of State, and a search of his apartment didn't reveal any other bank records. Coborn's wallet was untouched, money still in the appropriate section, and his key ring next to his embassy identification card, the ribbon on which it hung neatly folded around the card and on the night stand next to his bed.

Upon his death, all the security combinations at the embassy were changed, even though it was unlikely that anyone learned of those codes from Coborn. As part of the review of Coborn's activities, the security officer interviewed his secretary and learned of the annual physical he had with a London physician. When the physician was interviewed, the security officer was told of the doctor's recommendation to Coborn that he have a psychiatric evaluation. To the security officer, it was clear that the evidence clearly supporting the medical examiner's diagnosis that Coborn had committed suicide

Ambassador Roger Davidson asked Baldwin and the security officer to take an inventory of the apartment contents, making sure that there were no files or computer material belonging to the embassy. This was done quickly. After Coborn's body was removed and the police gave their concurrence, two security officers spent an entire evening carefully itemizing the contents of the apartment, including listing three keys on a small steel key ring. One key was identified as the apartment key, one fit the ignition of Coborn's Honda Accord, the other was unidentified. One of the officers thought it could be a health club locker key, but after checking Coborn's bank checking statements and canceled checks for the last year, the only payment to a health facility had been for the Royal Automobile Club, whose manager could not identify the key. However, the statements did reveal a debit for a payment for a security deposit box at the Citibank's Kensington branch. It took the embassy attorney a few days to get authorization from the Kensington Borough Civil Court for permission to test the key on the safety deposit box. When finally opened, there was found in Coborn's box, No. A-459, several documents and bank statements for a company called Crandex, Ltd. The total deposits in the three accounts at Barclays Bank, Guernsey, totaled one and half million pounds.

Baldwin was worried when he was given the information by the security officer.

"What in God's name was Coborn doing with corporate documents in his rental bank box, and where did all the money come from?" Baldwin shook his head in disbelief. He rushed to the office of the ambassador, his mind maddened with worry that Coborn may have been a spy. "Where else would he get that money? Inheritance? No. No record of that in his file. Good investments? No record of that either. This is hell, pure hell."

"Mr. Ambassador, a couple of things. The first, nothing of importance in the way of any embassy documents or material on Coborn's computer was found. But, the inventory did turn up a bank safety deposit key. We opened the box and found several documents about a corporation in which Coborn was apparently involved. In itself that is not a problem, but the bank documents indicate that the corporation had one and half million pounds in three accounts."

There was stunned silence as the ambassador closed his eyes for a moment. After a few minutes, he spoke, his voice barely above a whisper. "I hope he wasn't a spy, Arnold. I just hope he wasn't. Dig into this quietly. I know you'll have to involve embassy security, as well as the station chief. Draft a short memo for me to send to Washington. I have to alert them about the possibility that Coborn may have sold unknown information to people unknown. I never thought this would happen here. Never. Coborn was checked and double-checked, as we all were before coming here. Too much information flows through here. And he was in charge of its distribution—including the security material. Check everything, Arnold, everything. I want to meet the station chief, the head of security, and you this afternoon at 3:00. We have to find out what this man did." He paused for a few seconds then added, "Arnold, do you really think he committed suicide? Do people commit suicide leaving a million and half pounds unclaimed? Do they?"

"Hard to believe, isn't it? But the medical examiner said it was suicide."

"Maybe, maybe. I just don't know. Okay. See you this afternoon."

British Air Flight 310 for Lagos departed at 10:30 p.m. Kingsley sat alone in the first row. He savored the glass of champagne the stewardess had given him. Leaning over, he raised his glass, to the two men sitting across from him.

"Thank you, boys. Good job. The drinks are on me." There was laughter as they began their four-hour flight to Nigeria.

Twenty-Three

Keiran wasn't content to be driven by Jennifer late Saturday afternoon in heavy rain. Even in a cab, he was anxious. He like to be in control; he felt more secure driving himself; he didn't enjoy seeing her weave in and out of the traffic at high speed, seemingly impervious to safety. Keiran shifted occasionally in his seat, straining against his seatbelt, finally loosening it a bit, staring steadily straight ahead, asking, "Jennifer, why don't you stay in one lane?"

"You mean you're not comfortable? I don't believe that." She turned her head for a moment to see an obviously unsettled Keiran.

"No, I'm not," Keiran mumbled. "Definitely not. I will tell you this, though, tomorrow, I'll drive you back to London."

Jennifer began to turn into another lane when Keiran cautioned, "Please, Jennifer, keep your eyes on the road!" His voice was now a trifle higher pitched than usual.

"My God! I feel like I'm back at the studio. I also have a director in the car. Do I continue in this lane or do you want me to pass the car ahead of us—which is going too slow. What is your opinion? And before you answer that, I'm happy that you agreed to let me drive out of love. It would have been a surprise if you agreed to my driving on the basis of an unemotional clinical analysis of the merits of my understanding of the English system, compared to your clear inexperience."

"Yeah, sure. Don't take my agreement this time as a permanent contract between us when you and I are together in a car. You are definitely not driving when we are in Venice." Keiran put his hand on Jennifer's left thigh, thinly covered by the black slacks she was wearing, squeezing it gently. "Your Uncle's home…how far is it?"

"Keiran, don't distract me. Move the hand or we'll get into an accident. Venice? You're going to drive in Venice? That'll be a scene, driving on the canals." They both laughed.

"My Uncle's home is about an hour, or an hour and fifteen minutes, given the weekend traffic."

"You know, this is my first time outside of London other than flying out of Heathrow or Gatwick. Getting away from the office, Farris, Zoran and all that craziness, and of course, Leyden's death on Guernsey, and now Sir Robert's death. Too much is happening. Can there be such a thing as too much coincidence?" Keiran turned toward Jennifer, his voice much softer and lower.

"Does seem a bit strange, Keiran. Can't doubt that. The only connection to all these persons is the fact they all knew each other in some fashion. Runnard because of the report on investigating Farris and Hemmrich; Mr. Leyden was your client's rep on Guernsey. A connection yes; coincidental deaths? I just don't know Keiran. Really bizarre happenings. Sir Robert's memorial service was at noon today. You didn't go?"

"I got there too late. The church was packed. I did get into the vestibule and that was about it. For someone who, according to his own view, had angered the establishment, there were plenty paying homage…including the Prime Minister. Maybe they came to make sure he was really dead. He was a decent man. You could tell that by his moral approach to the practice of law. I only wish he had lived longer so I could have learned from him. Didn't think much of Farris or, for that matter, Hemmrich."

"I gather neither do you? Enough business talk, though. We're here to enjoy an overnight stay with my uncle. Try to discuss with him anything but your office situation, okay? I've already told him a great deal about you. He'll probably ask a whole slew of questions anyway. He's pretty inquisitive, especially about anyone in whom I've taken an interest."

Keiran leaned over and kissed Jennifer on her cheek, chuckling, "You're interested in me? How would I ever know that?"

"You're awful and I've told him that along with the fact that you're gentle, brilliant, strong, wise, and at times arrogant, sort of in that order, and that I've fallen in love with you."

"Good," Keiran replied in a tone of self-satisfaction. "You have all the right adjectives. You should immediately take the next exit, park the car, and we can make passionate love one more time."

"I just said you're awful, Keiran Hogan. Absolutely incorrigible."

"I see nothing wrong with a brief interlude of sex. Besides, I'm willing to bet that we have separate bedrooms at your uncle's house."

"My, my, my. You're pretty demanding. Anyway, you don't have to be concerned. The bedrooms we will be using are adjoining, in between is a bathroom. I'll leave my door open or you can leave yours open."

"I'm making a command decision now. You'll come to my room."

"Spoken like the sexist person which you are. I just may come to your bed. If my feminist friends found about that decision, they would feel that I've abandoned the cause. Maybe you should come to mine? I bet you do." She turned and her smile was wide.

He loosened his seatbelt again, leaning over to kiss her, his hand rubbing her thigh and reaching toward the soft center between her legs.

"Stop! What am I going to do with you? And you're worried about my driving? I'm worried about your self control!"

Keiran laughed.

There was a pause, then Keiran, frowning, asked in an earnest and soft voice, "What happened at your meeting with Medill? You haven't said a word about that. If you don't want to tell me, that's fine. I just want to know if…."

"Would I ask you to meet my Uncle if I was still involved with Craig? I told him I liked him a great deal, but loved another—you. The reason that I had never accepted his offer for marriage is that I was always unsure whether I wanted to be with him forever." Her voice was soft and serious. "He did ask me to attend some award function at the bank in a few weeks. He felt I owed him that at least."

"What did you say?"

"I told him I'd think about it, but that it would be difficult for me to be there. I'll see. You would understand if I went, Keiran?"

"I wouldn't like it, obviously. I can't stop you from going. It's up to you. What I'm interested in though is, are you sure about me?"

"Yes. Very sure."

"Then that should answer your question about going. Maybe, now I just…I guess I better get some shut-eye for a few moments. Rest my weary eyes. Do you mind if...?"

"No, go right ahead. Just don't snore or talk in your sleep. Sometimes you do." Her laugh was delicate.

"I do?"

"Sometimes…and only for a few moments, until I touch you. Then you stop."

"Good. You can touch me anytime…all the time. You know, Jennifer, I never…I can't get you out of my thoughts. Not at all…not at all." He slid down in the seat slightly, resting his head against the side of the headrest jutting up from his seat. In a short moment, he was sound asleep.

She worried about him so much now. She had never had this feeling about a man. Her intimacy with Keiran was total. She reflected how entirely different from Medill he was. He had such a kindness and selflessness about him. He was so gentle with her, yet their passion was total. Maybe she shouldn't have told him about Medill's request to have her at the awards function. She was deeply in love with Keiran, and never wanted to lose this remarkably happy feeling she now had.

The miles sped by quickly. At exit 23 off the M1, she turned gently off the motorway onto a two-lane country road and slowed her speed. It was about 6:00, the summer sun was trying to peek through the thinning rain clouds. There were now few cars on the road. Altogether, it was a peaceful day.

With the exception of the very few years she had lived in Lebanon with her parents, the only home she knew was the one she was going to now—her uncle's country home in West Clandon, Surrey. She knew the house so well. The name her uncle and aunt had given it was 'Greenways'—the view from the home was of an uninterrupted meadow, thus its designation. It was about ten kilometers beyond the center of the town, where a small combination pub and inn was located. Guilford's House, named after its owner, catered not only to the village patrons, but also to the occasional passing tourist seeking some solitude in the countryside. She drove past the inn and the scattering of village homes, slowing down as her uncle's home came into view.

Greenways House, a moderate sized yet stately, red brick, three-story home of Queen Anne design, was set away from the main road by a narrow paved driveway, lined by towering fir trees standing in solemn rows that led to a circular drive in front of the house, its facade nearly covered by ivy. Two large pots graced the ten-foot oak double doorway, the lavender and white impatiens overflowing their sides and giving the entrance a romantic feeling. The lawn was luxuriant and closely clipped, making it appear like a carpet. As Jennifer parked the car, she noted a magnificent evergreen oak placed to the left of the house, the old swing still hanging by a darkened thick rope from the largest branch—how many days she had spent on that swing, the happy memories, always the happy memories at this, her real home.

"Keiran, we're here. Wake up." She unbuckled her own seatbelt, leaned over and, taking his head in her hands, kissed him on the forehead. She began stroking his hair with one hand, "Keiran, we're here."

His eyes began to open. She drew his face to hers and kissed him on his lips, pushing his hair away from his forehead, gently repeating, "Wake up, Keiran. We're here."

He spoke slowly. "Man, I need a lot of sleep, Jennifer. The worst thing in the world is to wake up from a nap that is only half a nap." He stirred, mumbling his words as he unbuckled his seat belt, rubbed his eyes vigorously, then opened the car door and slowly got out.

"You have to stay awake." She left the car, walking around to take his hand as they walked to the front entrance.

"Okay, okay, but stretching out on a bed with you is what I need."

"You'd be too tired."

"Try me." He snickered as he grabbed her around her waist.

"What about our bags?" she inquired.

"Our bags?"

"Yeah, sleepy man. Our bags."

Keiran hurried back and grabbed the two bags that were in the back seat, as well as his briefcase. "Do you have to bring the briefcase, Keiran?" she asked, a scowl crossing her brow.

"I promise I won't open it. But I'd like it with me, just in case." He pressed her hand.

"Just in case?" Jennifer looked at him. "You must promise me you won't open it. Period."

"I promise." He carried one bag by its straps on his shoulder and held his briefcase and Jennifer's folding suitcase in one hand, allowing him to grasp her hand.

"See that swing hanging from the oak tree?" He looked over and saw a slowly moving flat board swing, pushed gently by the slow wind. "You don't know how many hours I spent there when I was young, my favorite pastime. My aunt would bring a book, sit on the lawn and read while I took to the heavens on the swing. Actually, if you swing high enough you can see the village below. I tried not to do that when my aunt was there with me. She always worried that I would fall off. She was the best of women, Keiran. How I miss her so very much."

"Happier times now though, Jennifer?" Keiran asked, a concerned smile crossing his face.

"Much happier, Keiran. Much happier."

Jennifer lifted a large brass knocker, tapping it forcefully against the oblong brass plate with the scrolled letter 'B' engraved on it. The knocker hit the space just below the cross line, and the years of tapping had left a discernible circle in the plate. "Don't you have a key to the house?" Keiran asked.

"Yes, I do. When I come with a guest, I don't use it. My, you're impatient, Keiran. Someone will be here soon." There was no answer, so she lifted the knocker and tapped it against the plate for several more moments.

"Coming, coming...."

A bellowing voice came from inside. In a moment, the door swung opened and a short, rotund woman, dressed in a dark gray dress with a starched white collar and apron stood there, her grimace more menacing than her voice. "Miss Jennifer. Come in. I'm sorry it took me a few minutes. I was in the garden room serving Mr. Berley, and Ms. Sorenson. I thought Marisa would answer. You know Ms. Sorenson. She bothers him so much, and he can't say no to her." She whispered her last sentence.

"How have you been, Grace?"

"Fine. Mr. Berley is always in better spirits when he knows you're coming. He just got back from a trip to America, and for a few days he wasn't in good humor. But he seems fine now."

"I meant to call him while he was overseas, but forgot. I'm sure he is upset about that. Grace, meet my friend, Keiran Hogan."

Keiran extended his hand, which Grace took, shaking it swiftly.

"Mr. Hogan, welcome. We haven't had such good weather today—rain, and a great deal of it. Tomorrow is supposed to be better. Good omen. To me weather is always an omen of the future. Wouldn't you agree, Miss Jennifer?"

"I think so. Yes, definitely," Jennifer smiled as she looked at Keiran.

"And Marisa? Where is she?"

"Probably in the kitchen. She is the best cook around, but she claims she can't hear too well—or maybe she doesn't want to walk the distance to the front door. She hears Mr. Berley very well, though. It's me that she says she doesn't understand." Grace laughed at her own comment. "Mr. Berley likes her. She's been with him for such a long time...."

"As have you," Jennifer interrupted.

"Yes, we have, haven't we?" There was silence for a moment. "Well now, your bags? Can I take them upstairs for you?"

Keiran smiled, looking at Grace's small frame. "No. Thank you, though."

"We're going to settle ourselves upstairs. Then we'll be right down."

"Okay, Miss Jennifer. If you need anything, just ask. Mr. Hogan, same with you. Well let me see if Ms. Sorenson needs any more tea. She's a theater star, you know." Grace snickered and hurried down the hallway.

Keiran and Jennifer went up a grand, curved, oriental-carpeted staircase leading to the second floor. Along the walls on that floor were uniformly framed old black and white photos of family groups as well as some individual photos and scenes of what appeared to be orchards and one photo of a large stone house with a small pond in front.

"What are these?" Keiran asked.

"My aunt and uncle's parents home in Lebanon. A long time ago, Keiran." Jennifer passed two doors, then came to a third, opened it. "Your room, Keiran." She walked into a large, off-white room, a large brass bed in its center, the bedspread a vibrant green and white, assorted bed side tables and one big easy chair near a large open window, the sheer drapes billowing slightly from the mild wind. Identical vases of summer flowers sat on the dresser, framing the small gilt framed mirror hanging above. Keiran placed his briefcase on a nearby desk. He placed his bag on the bed.

"And your room, Miss Jennifer?"

"Yes, Mr. Keiran. This way. She opened a door to reveal a large bathroom with an oversized tub and separate shower. Moving over to a partially opened door, she revealed another bedroom. "Actually, when I was a child, my aunt lived in the room that you will be in. Of course, it's been redecorated since her death, and this was my room. It's been changed as well."

Jennifer's room was painted a mild yellow, the bed a simple wooden frame, the bedspread a pale yellow with white with yellow roses embroidered throughout, a small desk and chair faced the opened shear curtained window, small kidney-shaped marble top tables separated three easy chairs opposite the bed. Flowers in a crystal vase were also on her dresser.

"My aunt loved flowers around the house. Grace carries on that tradition and keeps the garden herself, although my uncle has Nathan, his workman, come every day to do any heavy gardening or other work around the house. He lives in the village, as do Grace and Marisa, but they all stay in the house when my uncle comes here. They have rooms on the top floor. You can see for miles from up there…another favorite place of mine when I was young."

"This Nathan certainly keeps the lawn and hedges trimmed," Keiran noted. "One thing I really never minded when I was a kid was mowing the lawn. I really found that, like swimming, pretty restful for the mind.

Crazy now, isn't that? Well, my sisters would never do it anyway. So that just left me."

"The smart ways of women! I know I'm going to like your sisters. Now do you want to wash your face and wake up?" Jennifer asked. "Or are you now wide awake?"

"Shall we shower first?" Keiran took her in his arms, hugged her, and kissed her passionately while exploring her body. She pushed him gently away.

"Keiran, wash your face. We've got to go downstairs. My uncle will be waiting for us."

"Later then?"

"Much later." She smiled.

Keiran held Jennifer's hand as they walked into the garden room, where her uncle, Paul Berley, sat with Rose Sorenson. Filtered light came into the room from three walls of glass, lace-draped windows rising from a chair rail to the top of the ten-foot ceiling. French doors led onto a large patio that surrounded a swimming pool. White cane furniture covered with green and yellow pillows was arranged so that the pool and patio were visible. On the patio itself were several pots of geraniums and daisies.

"This is handsome, Jennifer, truly beautiful." Keiran whispered.

Jennifer held his hand tightly as she approached her uncle, dropping it as she reached him, leaning over to kiss her uncle, then turning to kiss Ms. Sorenson.

"Uncle Paul, Rose, meet Keiran Hogan."

"Welcome, Keiran Hogan." Berley extended his hand, which Keiran shook vigorously.

Sorenson didn't rise, but held out her hand, which Keiran gently shook.

Jennifer's uncle was a large man, as tall as Keiran. An impressive man, thought Keiran, broad shoulders, clear gray eyes, thick black hair with many streaks of gray. He wore an open-collar gray shirt with black slacks, his black-stockinged feet in black leather loafers. Sorenson, although seated, appeared to Keiran to be tall and slender, her blond-white hair drawn back, her eyes were small and blue, her face flawless white, her mouth, somewhat full, was colored with a pale beige gloss. She wore a long flowered dress buttoned down the front with several buttons left undone near its bottom, so that her legs were free. Around her neck was a large oblong silver-bordered necklace studded with lavender and white stones, the colors matching the colors of her dress.

"Good to meet you both," Keiran said.

"Now Jennifer, I want to know why you didn't call me while I was in New York. Not one call, Rose. Not one. What do you suppose the reason is for such a lack of respect?" Berley had a big smile on his face as he spoke.

Jennifer laughed. "Oh, Uncle Paul, I knew you would be busy! Seriously though, we've been so involved in the Mayfair bombing incident and I was working on several stories about that continuing plot. I guess I just got so involved that I totally forgot, which I shouldn't have. I'm sorry." She moved over and sat in the empty chair next to him. Keiran moved over to the settee and sat next to Sorenson.

"Likely story. You've forgotten this old man. That's what you've done!" Berley smiled as he looked at Keiran, then Jennifer. "And am I to understand that Mr. Hogan has kept you busy?"

Everyone laughed. Keiran lowered his head for a moment, not knowing what to say.

"Come now, Paul, that can't be the sole reason. Can't you see that Jennifer has been busy with her professional duties?" Sorenson's eyes twinkled as she looked at Jennifer and then Keiran. "And, certainly you have been as occupied." Without waiting for a reply from Berley, she turned to Keiran and asked, "Keiran, that is such a unique name. I haven't heard that name since I played at the Trinity Players Theater in Dublin —I don't want to remember how many years ago it was. I always thought the name so melodious. A family name, of course?"

"Yes. Actually, my Grandfather's first name—my mother's father."

"Don't let Rose fool you," Berley interrupted. "She is still one of Britain's greatest actresses, if not the greatest. She will be honored by the Queen later this year for her work in drama and now, of course, her two best-selling novels." Berley spoke with evident pleasure. "But, before any more talk, please, Keiran, help yourself to a drink. Jennifer?" He pointed to a green marble-topped side table where various bottles and decanters sat, alongside a large silver-plated ice bucket and assorted glasses.

"Jennifer, what would you like?" Keiran asked.

"Mineral water, please," she replied.

Keiran rose. "Anyone else want their drinks refreshed?"

"No thank you, Keiran. I'm fine," Sorenson replied, as she turned to Paul Berley. "You are my best promoter. You know I haven't been on the stage for the last three years. So I still can't believe that I will be honored in this fashion. You must come, Paul. You must be with me. I won't have it any other way. Of course, you must too," she turned to Jennifer, "and bring your friend Keiran. Your uncle has promised to host a dinner for a few of my old drama friends. You still are doing that, Paul?" She winked at Berley.

"Of course, Rose, if only you limit it to your one hundred closest friends. I must say, they're a crazy lot at times."

"Not any crazier than your financial colleagues. All they discuss is the latest exchange rate and which government is doing what to make the money go up or down. Absolutely dull, Paul. You must admit that my friends are more interesting than your moneyed comrades."

"I certainly would admit that, Rose," Berley replied.

"We can soon call you Dame Rose Sorenson. Congratulations, Rose." Jennifer rose and greeted Rose with another kiss on both her cheeks. "This is exciting, very exciting news."

"My congratulations as well," Keiran added. "Mr. Berley, your drink?"

"Yes. I'll have a bit more scotch, a splash of water, one ice cube." He handed the half-empty glass to Keiran.

Keiran didn't take long to make the drinks. Etched in the silver sign hanging around the necks of the decanters were the initials "PB" in bold script. He placed the three drinks—Jennifer's water, his own plain tonic, and Mr. Berley's scotch—on a tray and walked back. He served Jennifer first, then Berley, and placed the tray with his glass down on the small table in front of where he and Sorenson were seated.

"Welcome, Keiran. Cheers to you, Rose, Jennifer. Thank you all for being here." Berley raised his glass toward Keiran.

"Cheers to you, Mr. Berley and again congratulations to Ms. Sorenson," Keiran responded.

"Here! Here!" Everyone raised their glasses in salute.

"Well, Keiran, I believe we are off to a good start. The scotch you poured me from the decanter is twenty-five-year-old Johnny Walker Black Label. You should try some. What did you pour yourself?"

"Tonic water. If I had a drink now, I'd fall asleep. It's been a different kind of week, and a pretty long day."

"No doubt. Jennifer tells me you were on Guernsey, then up to Dublin, and tomorrow you're going to Venice. A great deal of traveling for you."

"Yes, it's. Some of the travel is probably unnecessary. But then, when you're with a law firm, you sort of do what your partner wants you to do."

"Of course. Your firm is...?"

"Kenton & Ward. We also have offices in New York, where I started, and in Washington, D. C., where I worked for about three years before coming to the firm's London office."

"Kenton & Ward. At certain social and financial gatherings, I believe that I've met one of your partners…Farris. Yes, Duane Farris."

"You know Mr. Farris?"

"No, not at all. Just had the occasion to meet him from time to time. Actually, I believe that he came to our London office with some of your New York partners to discuss the firm's abilities and so forth. Obviously a marketing trip. Seems like a reasonably knowledgeable man."

"Keiran, Uncle Paul….you promised no shoptalk. Keiran, he'll have you describing your office furniture soon."

"Well, that will be simple. I have very little."

Everyone laughed soundly.

"So, you travel a great deal?" Sorenson asked.

"Yes. A bit too much right now, though. I'm sure it'll slow down soon."

"When we were on the road in America and even here in England, it was fun when I was young. But as I got older, well, I won't admit that I am older, the travel became sort of a bore. Thank God I don't have to do so much of that anymore. The best part of not being sought after!"

"Now don't say that, Rose. You are sought after. You just refused to star in a West End play," Berley said.

"You're too kind, Paul. It wasn't my kind of play. Besides, I think it's better to fade away when you're on top than to wait until you're pushed. I like my writing now. It's enough." Sorenson then turned to Keiran, remarking, "You'll like Venice, Keiran. A city of unlimited possibilities. And don't forget a gondola ride. Timeless—a ride on those magnificent, silent watercraft is memorable."

"You've been to Venice, then?" Keiran remarked.

"Yes, a few times. Paul also. You were there just a few months ago, Paul?" Sorenson looked at him inquiring. "And without me, no less," she smiled coyly at him.

"Venice. Great city. Unique. You'll have a great time there. And Rose, I invited you, but you wanted to work with your editor on your third novel. So I took second place to your writing. Is that fair, Keiran?"

Keiran looked at both of them then smiled. "Should I answer that question and get in trouble?"

"You'll get in trouble if you don't," Paul Berley responded, laughing warmly.

"Okay, Ms. Sorenson, I was told that Venice is not a place to be without a woman by your side. So…." Keiran answered.

"You're absolutely right, Keiran," Sorenson replied, "but I had a deadline, and Paul has a difficult time understanding that. He likes me to write but prefers that it not interfere with his own schedule. Besides, he came back to London before I could even get organized to meet him in Venice. Now Keiran, what will you be doing in Venice?"

"I'll be joining a client of the firm who is completing a business deal with his customer there. He said that I could bring Jennifer with me, if I wish. Would you two like to join us?" Keiran, in his generosity, looked at Jennifer to see any sign of agreement. She smiled, but the smile told him that she wanted them to have a few days to themselves.

"That's very kind of you, Keiran. Why don't you see what your own program is and then let us know? It would be good to join you, perhaps for a day or two. Interested, Rose?"

"Venice? Of course. And I promise I won't back out."

"Enough of travel talk. Now, Keiran, Jennifer tells me you're an international business lawyer. What does that mean?" Everyone chuckled.

"Uncle Paul!" Jennifer, her eyes wide, exclaimed, "No more business talk!"

"Now, Jennifer…just a few modest inquiries. I think I should know what this young man really does at Kenton & Ward. I may want to give him some of my business, although I've been with my own firm for many years."

Keiran, now a bit embarrassed, smiled at Jennifer, then responded, "It's no secret what I do. Mr. Berley, I've only been here about ten weeks and have been working on several projects for a major client of the firm, a Zoran Hemmrich. He has several companies that are involved in commodity sales. I've been looking at the contracts and I suspect I'll join him in Venice to actually sit in on his negotiations. Being part of business negotiations will be more interesting that drafting a contract. That, in a nutshell, is what I do."

"Well, good. You are enjoying the work?"

"Yes, to a certain extent, I am."

"Ah! Enjoying work. We all seek that. Now, my niece is thoroughly enamored with her work. Jennifer, tell us the real story behind the bombing at Mayfair. Rose taped all your programs while I was gone, and your special. Is it true that a gas leak was the source?"

"That is what the police continue to say. Of course, there are doubters, but it appears to be what happened. There will be a follow-up report tomorrow. One of our investigative reporters has spent the past week digging around and trying to check out what rumors are true. As far as I know, he's found nothing new. He did find a list of those in attendance, so we have all the names. Interesting lot at the place, including a client of Keiran's law firm."

"Really! Such a strange event," Rose added.

"A client of your firm?" Burley inquired.

"Yes, he was lucky, though. He left just before the explosion. A very, very fortunate man." Jennifer replied.

"I would say so. So, my niece, the police want us to believe that the explosion was caused by leaking gas?" Berley asked, putting his glass to his lips taking a sip. "Just seems improbable that a gas leak would occur in central London. Those mains are checked all the time—especially with that area being so close to Buckingham. Strange event, no doubt about it."

"The police are still maintaining that a gas leak is the explanation. Many rumors, of course, as to what really happened, but not one has checked out. Some say the American and the British governments are happy because, in one fell swoop, many of the financial supporters of the Serbian cause have been taken out. I think it's horrible though, killing all those innocent people," Jennifer said, adding, "I'm happy, though, that you had the time to watch the broadcasts—all of them." She rose and kissed Berley. "Now what criticism do you have of the broadcasts? I know you'll have something. I have that feeling."

"I never miss Jennifer," Berley commented, turning to Keiran, "and you shouldn't either. I turn it on in the office, no matter what I am doing or who is visiting me."

"Well, now…I try, but it's hard." Keiran smiled as he looked at Jennifer, his eyes saying, Please help me. I'm in trouble.

"His hours are awful, Uncle Paul. So I forgive him."

"Spoken like a loyal friend," Sorenson commented. "I don't understand, though, Jennifer, why would we and Americans want to undertake such a risk? Just imagine if it was found out that they were both behind the killing of so many—what was the number, about 40 or 50?—to accomplish what? Awful thought, really, isn't it, Paul?"

"Probably not. But then, memories linger a long time. Hate is hard to overlook. I know from personal experience. It is a difficult emotion to disregard. Certainly, if all the people at the restaurant were Serbs or Serb supporters, then logic would dictate that whoever committed this act, if indeed it were not an accident, would be someone who had a grudge against those in the room, or perhaps only a handful in the room. Your client who left early…again, give us his name?" Burley asked.

"Zoran Hemmrich. Have you ever dealt with him?"

"I believe he did try to get us to take him on as a client for his currency trading. But we try to stay with large corporations, banks, and a few individuals that meet our criteria for private currency trading accounts. I can't say that I remember him directly, but the name does sound familiar. So, he is the lucky client?"

"Yes. He's a pretty substantial one for our London office."

"A client that, I am sure, your partners would be reluctant to lose."

"Very reluctant." Keiran commented.

"Uncle Paul. No more shoptalk with Keiran. You promised."

"You are constantly giving me directives, Jennifer. Does she do that to you, Keiran?"

Keiran looked longingly at Jennifer, then said, with a wide smile, "Yeah, actually I don't mind it."

"Rose, I now leave it to you to change the subject. I shall remain mute." Everyone chuckled.

"Jennifer," Sorenson asked, "I've always been interested on how you obtain your stories. On the way over here, I heard on the car radio that a U. S. Embassy official had committed suicide—at least that is what was being reported. I assume you'll have a report on that on the late evening news. How do you put a story like that together?"

"Well, the director on duty will assign the story to a reporter and camera crew, who will probably go to the American Embassy for any comments, try to get an interview with the police, or with any neighbors who will speak on camera. Archives will be searched for anything on the person and we'll wake up our correspondent in Washington to see what he can dig up. It'll all come together in about an hour, sometimes less, and be written for the reader. A little chaotic at times, but by airtime, everything settles down. Certainly, they'll have a report on the 10 o'clock news. As it was a U. S. Embassy official, we'll probably spend more than a passing minute or two on it."

Keiran turned to Jennifer asking, "Do you remember the name of this person?"

"I'm sorry, I don't Keiran. I was rushing out to be on time for you."

"Well spoken," Berley responded.

"I believe his name was Jefferson Coborn. It was a name I would remember because my co-lead in the last play that I was in, oh, about three years ago, was Jefferson Corton, a great star—still is—and very active in film now. The names were so similar, I could not forget." Rose Sorenson added.

"Mr. Berley," Grace walked in, calling at him, "Marisa says that dinner is ready."

"We should go. She is not the kind of cook that likes to be kept waiting." Berley explained, rising from his chair and taking Sorenson by her arm.

The name was familiar to Keiran. It was the same person he had run into when he left the ambassador's meeting as well as when he went to Farris' home for the meeting before he had left for Guernsey.

"Did you know him, Keiran?" Jennifer asked.

"I think so, I think so."

He took Jennifer's hand and followed Berley and Sorenson into the dining room. It'll be interesting to know the rest of the story, he thought to himself. And Farris? What is he thinking now about the suicide of someone at the embassy? Nothing is simple in this town.

Twenty-Four

It was the urge not to accept the fact that Runnard had died of a heart attack that pulled Keiran to drive back from Jennifer's uncle's home directly to the club rather than to Heathrow for his flight to Venice.

"Aren't you supposed to be going to Venice?" she asked, looking at him quizzically.

"Yeah, I'll take a later flight. I have to check on something first. Jennifer, this Runnard heart attack doesn't make any sense."

"Keiran, don't make his death into something that it isn't. He was an old man with a serious drinking problem, or at least he had had a serious drinking problem in the past. That kind of behavior generally doesn't help your heart. Besides, don't you have more important things to do?"

"Maybe. Anyway, we're here. Your uncle and Ms. Sorenson are great and I enjoyed meeting them. I'd like to do it again soon. Maybe they'll come into London and we can treat them." Keiran winked at Jennifer, leaning over to kiss her as he turned off the engine. "Now, you have to admit I know how to drive."

"Keiran, you're a sexist. And I thought I'd never fall in love with one. No matter. You will call me before you leave?"

"No doubt to that." He went around the car to open the door for her, took her to the driver's side, giving her one last kiss and handing her the car keys saying, "drive carefully."

"You're awful, Keiran Hogan. Keiran—your bags. They're in the back seat. Must be Freudian, you keep forgetting your bags."

"Freud? Who's he? Take care, Jennifer." He reached in and grabbed his overnight bag and his briefcase.

"He was the world's most famous...."

"I know, horse trainer." Keiran laughed, waved, and hurried up the stairs, turning one more time to see Jennifer drive the car into the afternoon traffic.

He headed straight to the turkish bath center. Maybe that is what brought on his heart attack. Too much steam. But he knew that the attendants regularly looked after the older members in order to assure that they were okay. It was known that a couple of members had, over the years, passed away while swimming in the pool, even though the attendant on duty was careful to watch the seniors during their swim practice and monitored them carefully. Everyone had to sign in and out at the bath's reception area, and again when they entered the steam rooms. They also had to sign out as they left the steam room, and of course, when they exited the bath reception area. The double sign in and sign out assured that no one would be unaccounted for at the end of the day.

"Swimming today, Mr. Hogan?" asked senior attendant Jeffrey Harrington as he rose from his seat behind a long, mahogany counter at the bath's entrance. He turned the revolving book stand holding the sign in book so that it faced Keiran, allowing him to print and then sign his name and club number.

"I don't know if I'll have the time. Just checking on a matter before I head out for another trip," Keiran replied. He paused for a moment, flipping the pages of the book back to the last day he saw Sir Robert in the steam room—the day he died.

"Busy day for you, Jeffrey?" Keiran inquired as he scanned the pages looking for Sir Robert's signature.

"Not so bad...steady. It's Sunday its a slower day. Find what you want? Can I be of any help?"

"Not really. Just making sure that I've not missed too many days of my swimming routine." Keiran saw that Sir Robert had signed in at

4:00 p.m. Wednesday, but there was no sign out. He noted that Jefferson Coborn had signed in a few minutes later.

"Times indicated in these sheets generally accurate?" Keiran inquired.

"Pretty accurate. I check and actually remind the member of the time as he signs in. The police asked me the same question, Mr. Hogan. You're not working for them now, are you?"

Keiran smiled as he turned the stand around so that it now faced Harrington.

"No, not this week at least. Keep my bags; I'll pick them in a few minutes. I want to check the steam area for a moment. See you later."

Walking briskly, he headed toward the corridor that led to the steam room lounge area. The attendant was folding towels behind a large, gray marble-top table. A similar sign-in-book was in the center of the table.

"Good afternoon, Hector. Crowded back there?"

"Moderately," Hector Fernandez, a stocky, barrel-chested man with a soft smile and dark eyes, replied. "Not like the week. Sundays should be a day of rest." He laughed slightly. "I guess the members enjoy resting on the chairs in the hot rooms. You going for a steam first, not swimming?"

Keiran marveled at how the staff knew the habits of the club's regular members. "No, I just wanted to look at the sign-in book to see if a friend of mine came in the other day."

"Isn't it awful about Sir Robert, Mr. Hogan, sir? He was so nice to all of us on staff. God only knows why he takes us when he does."

"Yes, only God knows. I shall miss him too. Too quick. I had just seen him a short time before he had his attack." Keiran spoke as he flipped through the pages. He reached Wednesday's page, again seeing Sir Robert's name. He skimmed down and came across the printed name and signature of Jefferson Coborn. He had registered only a few minutes after Runnard.

"Is this Jefferson Coborn a regular member?"

"Intermittent, Mr. Hogan. He is not regular at all. He works at the U. S. Embassy. He told me that. Not a happy man. He started to come more frequently, though, just these past several weeks. Yes, I know what you're thinking. I saw the report on the news. He's been taken by his own hand, God be with him and forgive him. Actually, sir, he asked about you a few times." Hector had a gold cross on a gold chain hanging from his neck, which he touched a few times as he spoke of the deaths of Sir Robert and Coborn. "No one knows the ways of God. No one."

"He did? I've never met him," said Keiran with surprise.

"Perhaps he heard about you from other members. You know, sir, everyone believes we have an Olympic swimming champion here. That may have been the reason."

"But I'm not. Anyway, thank you Hector. I hope to see you later."

"You take care of yourself, Mr. Hogan, sir. Don't get overtired. Even as young as you are, rest is necessary."

"You're right. Rest is important."

Keiran thought there was something about him that prompted everyone at the club to give him guidance. Not a day went by when Vanessa Anderson, would not have some advice, and it was all health related, including giving him a sample packet of vitamin pills she received from an order she had placed with her favorite Doctor Nigel of TV fame. Someday, he told himself, he would try to analyze what made him look or seem so vulnerable. Keiran was on his way back to the front desk when Jeffrey appeared.

"There's a Mr. Farris waiting on the line, Mr. Hogan. I told him you'd be back as you left your bags here. He said he would wait, and asked me to try and find you. Urgent, he said, Do you want to take the call, or should I say that I looked but could not find you?"

"I'd better take it, Jeffrey. Thanks for finding me. Next time though…." Keiran's grin was wide.

"I know sir…I won't be able to." He laughed quietly as he saluted Keiran and handed him the portable phone.

"Mr. Farris, I'm just finishing up here and getting ready to go to the airport and take the plane to Venice. The attendant said the call is urgent. What can I do for you?"

"Did he say that? I hope I didn't give him that impression. Perhaps I did. I probably told him it was important that I speak to you. And it is."

"Yes, sir. What is it you need?"

"Just a reminder to remember to accede to whatever our client asks you to do. As he told you, he expects to conclude some business while you're with him, but it's primarily a social visit in order for you to meet some of his business associates and his family. This is a unique opportunity for you. He obviously believes that you're an extremely capable attorney, as do I. I know you won't let him down. I would also ask you call me periodically to advise me how things are going and what you and Zoran are discussing—discussion of a business nature of course, nothing further than that. Understood?"

"Yes, Mr. Farris. I'll be in touch. I appreciate the opportunity to take the trip. You need not worry, I know how to behave," Keiran said with an edge in his voice.

"Keiran, you know I wasn't implying that you aren't able to conduct yourself in the highest tradition of the firm. It was simply a reminder that I would give any associate who would be accompanying a client. My comments shouldn't be taken beyond that."

"Yes, I understand. Is there anything else? I have to get ready, sir, and get to the airport if I'm to catch the plane to Venice. I have to ring off, sir."

"Yes. Have a safe flight and let me hear from you."

"Certainly. I'll fax the office to let you know I've arrived."

"Again, have a nice flight." Farris hung up.

Keiran pressed the power switch off the portable phone and returned it to Harrington.

"Everything okay, Mr. Hogan?"

"Yes. Nothing important. Enjoy the rest of your day, Jeffrey."

"Don't forget to take it easy, Mr. Hogan. Rest."

Keiran smiled, but didn't respond.

He stayed in his room briefly. As he rapidly packed his small case with some clean clothes, he reminded himself that the club staff must now wonder why his bed had not been slept in recently. He'd have to figure out an excuse, but he doubted they would inquire. He knew that there would be some gossip and Vanessa Anderson would ask at some point—in her own way she would ask somehow. He grabbed his passport, wallet, and glasses, lifted his bag on his shoulder, and took the elevator to the reception floor. He looked at his watch and saw that time was running very short. There was one last thing he wanted to examine before he left.

He went directly to the reception desk where Vanessa Anderson was still on duty.

"Another trip, Mr. Hogan?"

"Yes, to Venice. Will you keep my mail?" He smiled.

"Don't we always? At this club, we pride ourselves in taking care of our members. By the way, Mr. Hogan, will you be needing your room cleaned every day? It seems that…." She snickered as she said the last few words.

"Yes, I do. I have been traveling, as you know, and staying with some friends when I work late."

"Of course. Important to have the room tidied up just in case you need it. You'll be gone for how many days?"

"About four or five. Before I leave though, there is one thing that I'm wondering if you can help me with. Sir Robert, did he have a regular doctor?"

"Yes, Doctor Gregory Schultz. He would come to club and see Sir Robert often. Like Sir Robert, Dr. Schultz is also has been retired for about five or six years. Still, he tended to Sir Robert, even though he rarely listened to any doctor, I suppose. Maybe he listened to Dr. Schultz—I doubt it though."

"Is Dr. Schultz a member of the club?"

"Yes, he is. He's usually here on Sundays. Actually today he should be arriving in a few minutes. He usually gets here around 5:00 o'clock. He goes to the library, I believe, or perhaps to the bar downstairs. I know he doesn't go to the athletic area. Of that I am sure. Perhaps he meets others here or plays cards in the card room, or billiards. Why do you ask, Mr. Hogan? If you need a doctor, the club has a list of eminent physicians who are presently practicing. Are you feeling ill? Dr. Schultz is a very nice man. I would recommend, however, that you see a doctor who is in active practice. That's just the proper way to do it, now isn't it? Dr. Nigel always reminds people to go to a doctor who has kept up with medical advances. You know these advances happen so rapidly. Best to…."

"Well, you have a good suggestion. Still I'd like to visit with Dr. Schultz…something personal, you understand."

She lowered her eyes, and replied, "Certainly…personal."

"Now, do you think that Dr. Schultz will come in this evening?"

"Yes."

"How do I find him? Will you be so kind as to give me his phone number?"

"That won't be necessary, Mr. Hogan, as I see him coming in right now. Right on time. Weren't you listening to me? I said he comes every Sunday at 5:00 o'clock. I don't as a habit give out incorrect or incomplete information to our members. You needn't worry about whether what I say is accurate. It always is," she responded with a sense of smugness in her voice.

"Yes. Sorry, Ms. Anderson. I'll listen more carefully next time."

Her eyes rounded and her pout disappeared. "I don't think you ever will, Mr. Hogan. Regardless, if you turn around, you'll see a gentleman in a dark brown suit, as tall as you and slim. That's him. He'll come here first for his mail. He'll be here in a few moments. What about your flight, Mr. Hogan? Won't you be late?"

"Yeah, I know I won't make the flight. Would you do me a favor? Can you get me on a later one—about nine o'clock or so?"

"Mr. Hogan, you can go to the travel desk at the club for those arrangements. You do know that we have a travel desk for club members?"

"Of course, but in the interest of time…and it's Sunday. I suspect the travel desk is closed. It would be helpful, and I would be grateful if you could get me on the later flight to Venice."

"All right. But just this one time. I'll let you know if I'm successful. I seem to remember, though, that the last BA flight to Venice is around ten, maybe later." As she spoke to him, she began typing on her computer keyboard. "If you're interested, I'm also going to send a message to our travel desk, which, for future information, is located on the lower level, room L-100. And they're open Monday through Saturday from seven to seven. You should try to plan ahead, Mr. Hogan. It really is important to plan ahead."

"Certainly. The lower level, room L-100. Certainly, I won't forget. Perhaps you can also cancel my six o'clock flight. I won't be needing that seat." Vanessa Anderson looked up from her keyboard.

"Mr. Hogan, did you think I would not cancel your earlier flight?"

"Right. Yes. And thanks. You're a super person. You truly are."

Anderson now lowered her head, saying softly, "You should know, I don't do this for everyone…and won't do this again for you. Familiarize yourself with the travel office. It will save us all time and effort," she cautioned.

"I won't forget your advice. Not at all," Keiran countered.

"Dr. Schultz. Good evening." Anderson greeted the man standing behind Keiran, who stepped aside.

"I'm sorry. Taking too much of Ms. Anderson's time," Keiran remarked, as he looked at Dr. Schultz, a man with a full head of white hair, clear brown eyes, walking with the aid of a cane. He disregarded Keiran's comment and looked straight past him to Anderson.

"Vanessa, my dear, do I have any mail?" he asked gruffly in about the same tone, Keiran mused, as Sir Robert.

"Yes. The usual from the club, Doctor. And how have you been?"

"I don't want to see any bills. Send them to my office. I've told you that many times."

"We follow your orders assiduously. You'll not find a bill in the packet." She handed the small stack to him. "Dr. Schultz, this is Mr. Hogan, a friend of Sir Robert. He has been waiting for you." Keiran turned slightly and smiled.

"Dr. Schultz, how are you?"

"Fine. Now, what do you want?" he asked brusquely. Before Keiran could answer, Schultz turned to Anderson, flipping through his mail. "I don't want any of these. Discard them."

"But you haven't opened any of them…" she protested.

"So? I don't want to. Get rid of this rubbish. Pure rubbish. Now, young man. Your name again, and tell me why I should talk to you. I am not in the active practice of medicine. Use the club's register of doctors for any ailments that you may have. Looking at you, though, I can't imagine that you have any."

"Hogan, Keiran Hogan. I'd like to talk to you for a few minutes, if I may."

"About what?"

"It's personal. I wouldn't feel comfortable discussing it in front of…"

"Why not? She knows everything anyway." He laughed loudly. "Are you a member of the club? If not, go away."

"He's a member, doctor. A very active member," Anderson chimed in.

"Good. Okay, follow me. I'm going down to the bar for a drink—mineral water, mind you. Then off to the billiards. Do you play billiards?" He now extended his hand to Keiran's and shook it firmly.

"Yes, I do. Not good at it."

"Everyone says that all the time, thinking that this old man must be a whiz. Well, in truth I was a whiz when I was younger. Anyway, come. I've seen you around here, at the pool, swimming as if you hadn't a care in the world. Ah! Young minds. Peace and tranquility. Not like we old folks, wondering how we are going to leave this planet and meet our maker, not that it matters. So, you knew Sir Robert. How did you come to meet him?" They walked slowly down the five steps from the reception platform to the main floor and across to the stairs that led to the bar and billiard rooms.

"By pure accident, sir. It was late, well, really early one Sunday morning, around 1:00 a.m. or so. I had come from a dinner party, went to the library, and there was Sir Robert. I thought he was sound asleep, until he came over and spoke to me. We had a good conversation for over an hour."

"He was never a great sleeper. Never. All the years I've known him, if he had three or four hours solid sleep, I'd be surprised. Healthy as a horse though…despite the drink, which he would swear off periodically."

They walked down the wide marble steps past several meeting rooms and into the large oak-paneled bar, beyond which were the billiard rooms.

"Would you like to sit at the bar, or at a table?" Keiran asked.

"Table. Especially if you're going to talk to me about something personal. It's probably about sex and whatever disease that you have. I hope not."

"No. No, not at all. I want to talk about Sir Robert."

"Oh! Well, then, let's sit down. I have a feeling this may be a very short conversation, if I don't like the direction that you take."

Keiran followed Dr. Schultz as he weaved his way toward an empty table by the back wall. For a Sunday, it was crowded. Most eyes were glued to the football match that was on each of the three televisions sets that hung from the ceiling over the bar. The noise level was high given the multiple conversations being conducted in the room, every so often punctuated by a shout signifying a score or at least a correct move by those who supported one team or the other.

"Psychologically, sports are a good outlet for male aggression. Without sports, we'd probably have more domestic civil wars than we have now. Now, your concern about Sir Robert...?"

Before Keiran could speak, a waiter came over with a bottle of mineral water for Schultz with a glass fill of ice.

"Your usual, sir. Will you require something else?"

"No, but this young man will want something...."

"I'll have the same," Keiran replied. The waiter nodded and left.

"I've only met Sir Robert twice. The first, as I told you, was in the library. About a week later, I met him in the steam area. In fact, it was the day he died, we had made plans to meet for dinner. He appeared in good health to me. I'm just surprised to hear that he had heart trouble. Did he?"

"No, not at all. He was in generally good health, despite his drinking habits. He didn't, unlike some of our fellow members, have a colossal appetite for alcohol. He certainly liked to drink his port and of course, his scotch. If you're asking whether I believe he died of a heart attack, I would question that. The club called me, of course, when they found him slumped in his chair. There were several doctors in the club at the time who went over to see him before I arrived. But there was nothing they could do. He had been dead about an hour or so before I had arrived. I called his sister. She lives in Knightsbridge and it wasn't long before she was here. As you may know, his wife passed on several years ago. He had no children, but his younger sister took charge of all the arrangements. She was as surprised as I was. He had some medical problems, but his heart wasn't one of them. At least I never saw heart problems, and I saw him, as I said, quite frequently."

The waiter arrived with Keiran's drink.

"Your water, sir. Anything else, Dr. Schultz?" the waiter asked as he poured some mineral water from the bottle into a glass and placed it in front of Keiran.

"Keiran?"

"No, this is fine. Thank you." Keiran raised his glass, "Cheers, Dr. Schultz. To the memory of Sir Robert."

"Cheers," Schultz replied, his voice uncertain and unsteady.

There was silence for a moment before Keiran continued.

"Could it have been the heat in the rooms?" Keiran asked.

"No, I don't think so. He never really went into the third room, the hottest, and as you may know, the first room, the mildest, is about 30 degrees Celsius, perhaps more, but not much more. Usually he stayed in the first room. I've met him there many, many times."

"What is strange is that I left him in good spirits that afternoon. No symptoms of any problem."

"Well, Keiran, sometimes an impending heart attack will give warning signals, but not always. So it's possible that he died of a heart attack."

"Could the cause have been something else that was made to look like a heart attack?"

"Are you suggesting that foul play was involved?" Dr. Schultz raised his glass and drank the rest of the water, and then poured the little that remained in the bottle into the glass. "Water is the best medicine. So, you're suggesting someone did something to Runnard?" Schultz paused and added, "Deliberately?"

"I just don't know. I'm just questioning. You probably saw in the paper yesterday and today about the American Embassy Administrator, Jefferson Coborn, who committed suicide."

"I glanced at it. Not of much interest to me. Americans always do stupid things—forgive me for saying that."

"Well, sir, he was in the steam room area at the same time as Sir Robert, and he left about fifteen minutes after I did, around five thirty."

"What are you implying, Keiran?"

"Nothing, yet…and what I am thinking may be an intellectual stretch. I just find it strange that Sir Runnard died of a heart attack when he didn't have any heart problems and then the man who was there the same time commits suicide. Strange occurrences, wouldn't you agree?"

"Oh, I don't know about that. The world is full of spiders that look as if they must be tangled in each other's webs. In any event, there were others in the room, as well as the attendants. So, what could have gone wrong without someone seeing something?"

"Sure, in the bath's reception area—where I last saw him and you found him—there were three other men in addition to myself and Sir Robert. Jefferson Coborn may have been one of the three. I don't remember seeing any of the faces of those three, as they were pretty much covered with towels."

"Robert was taken out by someone? Highly unlikely at this stage of his life. I know he was disliked because of the study—an investigation he conducted a few years back that showed some complicity between certain government officials and some private entrepreneurs to sell arms to those who should not receive them. Maybe you're aware of the study…?"

"Yes, I am. He spoke to me about it at our first meeting, partly because his investigation involved a partner of my law firm, as well as one of the firm's biggest clients."

"Well, then, you probably know that the report was filed with the Prime Minister and others. Nothing was ever done concerning his recommendations. It was a sad thing in his mind. He had spent so much time and effort coming up with the real truth of what had taken place. Tomorrows became difficult for him after that, but eventually he snapped back and shut out whatever unpleasantries remained. His old eyes didn't only look at memories, Keiran. My God, though, it's been some five years, maybe longer, since that report was issued. I don't suspect that a grudge would be carried on for that long. If someone wanted to get rid of him, there was plenty of opportunity to do it years back."

"Yeah, you're making sense. I only knew him for such a short time, and I wanted to get to know him more. Maybe I'm in denial about his death and its cause. Maybe I'm looking for a reason to make his death seem more understandable, at least to me"

"There was one thing that bothered me, however," Schultz added. "He didn't have a towel wrapped around his head, as is usually the case in the bath area. He only had a towel around his middle. This is, in itself, not much, except that when I was with him, he also had a towel draped over his shoulder and back, leaving his chest free—something I had never seen him do before. He always wrapped himself fully. Those two differences stand in my mind, but I didn't think they were significant and I didn't tell the police in my brief interview with them. I don't know. Perhaps someone found him, tried to help him by removing the towels but got frightened and left. I doubt we have someone like that in the club, but one never knows. We could always make a mistake in the club interview process. Then we also have people like you—reciprocal members, a concept that I oppose and voted against because of that very reason. You want to know who the members are and now all sorts of strangers come into the building. Well, I don't want to digress. Those are the two matters that aren't consistent with the way he usually towel-wrapped himself to go into the hot rooms. Not consistent at all. You have the names of the others in the bath reception room?"

"Well, I did go through the list and found Mr. Coborn's name, which, of course, stood out because of the news reports about his death. I could contact the others and see what they know."

"Why on earth would anyone want to murder Sir Robert? It makes absolutely no sense. He was in his early eighties, not practicing law, slowly fading away, not bothering anyone. There doesn't appear to be any logic to your theory. But then, who knows, perhaps...?"

"I suppose that if I hadn't seen the article about Coborn having taken his life, I would not be thinking in this manner. It just seems to be a troubling accident of fate, that's all. I hope that you haven't minded discussing this with me."

"No, not at all. Not at all. Made me think about the towels, and now that I think of it, his mouth. Usually in heart attacks, it's open—you know, trying to grab some air. But his mouth was closed. Even at my age, I'm getting slow at observations. Still, I'd be very, very suspicious that his death was murder. Where is the motivation, Hogan? Where?"

"I don't have an answer to that. Not at all. Can one die by foul means and then the perpetrator make it look like a heart attack?"

"Only a skilled person. If you smother a person, he'll die of suffocation and an autopsy will show that the lungs would have collapsed for lack of air, the heart would not be as damaged as it would normally be in a natural heart attack. There are other indices, but no autopsy was performed here, so I just don't know. Although he was a Catholic, I believe that his sister had the remains cremated and is to have them scattered at his country place in Wales. Maybe she had an autopsy performed, but I doubt it. I would have known. She would have told me. I was at the Memorial Service, along with hundreds of others. It was an outpouring he would not have understood, given the treatment he was subjected to several years ago. The passage of time makes some feel guilty, I suppose. Were you there?"

"I got there a minute or two after the service started. I could only get into the vestibule, no seats in the main church. Well, maybe I'm just mistaken. Maybe I'm trying to connect the dots when there are no dots to connect," Keiran replied.

"Maybe, but I agree with you. If you look at the two events, they appear to be strangely connected, although I just don't know why or how. Keiran, you'll just have to figure out what the motive would be. That, to me, is the key to finding out if poor old Robert was murdered or died quietly without pain. I pray it was the latter. You make me worry now that it may be the former." Schultz said wearily. "This conversation, however, makes me less sure of the cause of his death."

"I hope it was the latter too, Dr. Schultz. I hope so very much."

"Were you interviewed by the police?"

"Yes, but very briefly, as I had left before his death. I believe they interviewed the others in the room as well."

"Strange, Keiran Hogan. We shall meet again, Keiran, upon you return from...?"

"Venice. I leave for Venice this evening."

"I'm sure you'll find that city beyond a dream. You'll have a most memorable visit."

"I hope so, Dr. Schultz, I sincerely hope so."

Twenty-Five

It was almost midnight when Keiran arrived at Venice's Marco Polo International Airport. The terminal building was fairly devoid of people at this late hour, as the flight from London was the last to arrive for the day. He walked the short distance from the airplane arrivals gate down a short, wide corridor to the only open passport control booth. There were about 60 passengers on the BA flight and the officer in the booth waved them through quickly, pausing only to give cursory glances at their passports before bringing his rubber stamp forcefully down on the documents, making the only noise in the otherwise still place. Keiran would not have noticed the last passenger off the plane, if it were not for the momentary commotion caused by a woman with a large pack on her back. As she turned suddenly, her pack hit the man, causing his eyeglasses to fall to the floor. Keiran was in line several paces ahead of them and, like others, turned for a moment to observe the scene. The woman, obviously embarrassed, apologized repeatedly. The man just smiled, picked up his glasses and placed them in his pocket. Tall, slim, and with an angular face, he was soon joined by another man. They stood together for a moment without conversing and then proceeded to the control booth. By the time they reached the booth, Keiran had left the passport control area.

He thought he had seen the man before, but maybe not. The lighting in the area wasn't bright and besides, did it make any difference whether he was familiar with the man or not? He had an eye for remembering faces and thought of it as one of those things that clutters the mind for no apparent reason.

Keiran followed the signs for the water taxi, joining several others in sharing the *vaparetto* to Venice proper. He stayed on deck all through the forty-five minute journey, watching the passing marking posts that lined the channel. The shining lights of the city appeared through the darkness, the dome of the Basilica of San Marco, itself lit up like a harvest moon against the night sky, provided the landmark toward which the boat sped through the darkness, curving one way and then the other across the lagoon. Keiran's thoughts remained on Jennifer. If only she could be here with him to see this sight. Earlier he had asked her to join him and she said she would later in the week, but "only, Keiran, if your business is concluded so that we can spend time together. I don't want to spend time alone, wandering the city, while you're with your client." She was right, of course. He kept thinking of her last glance at him and he felt terribly alive with love. How he missed her.

The *vaparetto* docked at the Gritti Palace, the hotel overlooking the Grand Canal, its splendid Gothic facade bathed in soft floodlights. The warm wind had been blowing steadily and the Italian national and European Community flags hanging from wall poles above the second floor of the hotel were fluttering. As Keiran stepped off the boat, a porter in a green waistcoat hastily came up the dock, and picked up his overnight bag.

"*Prego*, please, this way."

Keiran glanced over to the outdoor terrace cafe adjacent to the dock where several tables were occupied with late-night patrons. The clatter of their conversations was absorbed into the sound of the mild waves of the Grand Canal lapping against the hotel's foundation wall. Soft piano music played in the background. A serene setting, Keiran told himself, as he followed the porter, walking quickly past the scene into the sedate, plant-filled lobby to the highly polished mahogany wood registration desk.

"Good evening, I'm Keiran Hogan," he announced to the reception clerk.

At a private dock across the canal and partially facing the Gritti Palace Hotel, a dark brown speedboat reduced its speed, muffling the sound of its engines as it approached its docking point. The boat's captain tied a line to the dock, steadying it while two men hurried off and headed towards the darkened villa. The boat slid away at low speed until it was some distance from the Gritti Palace Hotel; increasing its speed, it disappeared into the night.

"Yes, *Buona sera Senor.* Good evening, Mr. Hogan, we've been expecting you. A guest of *Senor* Hemmrich, eh," remarked the reception clerk, a modest-looking man dressed in an evening suit with black tie, his eyes somewhat magnified by thick rimless glasses. When he smiled, his eyes narrowed as if he were trying to analyze the new guest of the hotel. He had the lilting accent of an Italian who had either learned english from a teacher from England or had been educated in England.

"*Prego*...Please sign at the 'x' on the registration card. I'll need your passport for a moment...I'll make a copy of your passport identity page. *Grazie,* also fill in the remainder of the card." Keiran fished into his side jacket pocket for his passport, turning it over to the clerk, who kept looking over Keiran's shoulder and never steadily at Keiran, as if there was someone behind him waiting to register.

"*Molte grazie, Senor Hogan.* I'll leave the passport in your box, okay?"

"Yes, that'll be fine," Keiran replied as the reception clerk bowed slightly and disappeared through the door a short distance from the reception counter, marked '*privato.*' Keiran reached for the desk pen provided by the clerk and began filling out the form when he felt a tap on his shoulder.

"Mr. Hogan."

Keiran turned and recognized one of Zoran's assistants, a thin smile crossing his lips.

"Mr. Hogan, Mr. Hemmrich is on the terrace and would like you to join him after you've finished here. I'll wait for you and take you to him."

"Sure, okay." There was no joyous anticipation in Keiran's response. This client is like a shadow gliding over every move I make, Keiran thought to himself as he returned to his task of completing the form. Just as he was finishing, the clerk returned, handing him back his passport.

"We still have to notify the police of all guests who come to Italy. A relic of the old days. We still have to be tolerant of the old rules until, hopefully, Italy enters into the European Union, and this formality will vanish. Your room is 520 and you have a good view of the Grand Canal. Will you need a wake-up call tomorrow morning?"

"Perhaps. I'll let you know later. Would you have the porter take my bag to my room? That would be helpful."

"Your briefcase as well?"

"No, I'll take that with me. Just the one bag."

"Certainly, would you like your key now?"

"Yes, thank you."

"I know you will have a nice stay," the clerk said as he handed Keiran the room key, which was attached to a large brass handle on which was written, 'Gritti Palace.'

"I certainly can't lose this." Keiran smiled.

"Unlikely," the clerk responded cheerfully.

Holding his key by its long narrow handle, Keiran turned to Zoran's assistant, "Lead the way, Mr…?"

"Alan…Alan Simpson. Did you have a nice flight Mr. Hogan?"

"Yes. Uneventful."

They walked at a brisk pace to the terrace. Keiran had remembered seeing Simpson with Zoran, but they had never been formally introduced. He figured that the names of bodyguards, or 'assistants' as Zoran liked to call them, were only important to the person they were guarding, not to anyone else. Probably made sense if one was in that line of business.

The tables on the terrace were lit primarily by candlelight. Several side sconces on the building facade provided more illumination, as did the light emanating from the lanterns around the perimeter of the terrace.

In such subdued light, Keiran had failed to notice Zoran and his bodyguards when he arrived. Obviously, though, they had seen him.

Zoran rose from the table, as did his other assistant, who quietly retreated to an adjacent table.

"Keiran. It is good to welcome you to Venice, a city, I am convinced that has the power to enchant." Zoran, dressed in a dark blue open-collar silk shirt and dark gray slacks, extended his hand, shaking Keiran's warmly, smiling in what Keiran thought was a wearily indulgent manner. "Most serene, Venice is. You must have your lady friend join you. Venice needs to be shared with someone you love. Will she be coming?" Zoran sat down, his hands pointing to the chair where he wanted Keiran to sit. Simpson said nothing and joined his colleague at the next table.

"I've asked her to join me later in the week. By then, I am hopeful we will have concluded our business. I didn't want her to come when I'm not able to spend time with her," Keiran said confidently, his eyes fixed upon his host.

"Wise decision, Keiran, very wise. I'd like to meet her when she does come. It would be my honor to have dinner with you both." Zoran cleared his throat as he continued, "And Duane…did you see or talk to him before you left London?"

"Yes, he called me at the club. I told him I would fax the office upon my arrival. As soon as I get upstairs, I'll send off the note," Keiran added simply.

"Let me not be so rude as to immediately begin a conversation about work. No, not yet. We must first drink to your arrival with some good Italian red wine, perhaps even a little antipasto. Hungry?"

"A bit. I only had a snack on the plane. Actually, I wouldn't mind more of a meal."

"Good." Zoran raised his hand slightly. The waiter hurried over as if on cue.

"Yes, Mr. Hemmrich?"

"We're ready. Please bring the order now, together with the wine I have selected."

"Certainly, sir. Right away." Keiran noted that Zoran appeared anxious to make a good impression. His smile seemed to be forced and the softer notes of his voice seemed, to Keiran, to be put on for the occasion. Zoran seemed distracted. Perhaps he was holding back something that he wanted to tell Keiran, but was unsure of when to speak about the hidden topic he had in mind. Keiran noted Zoran's constant, uncertain tapping on the table with the fingers of his right hand. Little noise was made, as the table was covered with a heavy green and white cloth.

"You were detained in London by office work? Sunday is a day I would hope Duane didn't have you working."

"No, no, certainly he didn't have me at the office. As you may know, I was away for the weekend and simply could not get back to London in time for the earlier plane. Overstayed my time at the club as well. I must apologize. I hope you got the message that I would be delayed."

"Yes, I appreciated you giving me notice. I should have remembered. Must be old age." Zoran smiled as he raised his right hand and tapped his forehead. "Ah!" he continued, "the lack of discipline in youth! How well I remember! Your swimming routine. Duane has told me about your daily practice, although, I suspect you have had to suspend your systematic exercise at times. Is that true?"

"At times. There are times I can't adhere to my routine, but I try to as often as I can. I swim about five or six days a week, depending upon where I am and what I'm doing. I suspect there's no swimming pool here, though."

"No, not at this hotel. They do have guest privileges at the Sports Club on the Lido, the beach area for Venice, just across the lagoon. Check with the concierge. It's about a twenty or thirty minute boat ride—not far at all. The hotel's own boat will take you there and bring you back, no problem."

The waiter rolled a stainless steel cart, its glass top covered with a dark green cloth, over to their table. Taking plates and wine glasses from the cart, he quietly placed them before Zoran and Keiran, filling each plate with an assortment of grilled vegetables, calamari, black and green olives, scallops and shrimp, all lightly covered with olive oil, oregano, and basil. A basket of bread accompanied the meal. After serving

Zoran and Keiran, the waiter went over to offer the same selection of food to Zoran's assistants.

"Wine, Keiran, one can't be in Italy and eat without wine. To do so would be sacrilege."

"Sure, and wine will help me sleep...not that I have trouble sleeping!" They both laughed.

Slipping out the side door of the villa directly opposite the Gritti Palace, two men dressed in dark suits, both carrying briefcases about the size of those that hold laptop computers, silently got into a gondola, it sole dim light shining against the darkened water. The two men sat across from one another. Under the night sky, and with no bright moon, a third man, dressed as a gondolier, slowly directed the gondola across the canal to a small dock adjacent to the main public dock where the water taxis and larger public boats were docked for the night. The two passengers left the boat and hurried along the side street facing the back of the Gritti Palace, entering the hotel by a side door which led directly to the reception area. They then headed into the small indoor, wood-paneled lounge directly adjacent to the outdoor cafe. There, they sat down separately. One picked up a German newspaper from the reading table, the other an Italian paper. A waiter hurried over to take their drink orders. Both asked for mineral water. Each placed his briefcase on the floor next to their chair's side table.

After a few minutes, one of them got up, took his briefcase and walked back toward the reception desk, turning briskly down the corridor that led off the reception area to the right. At the end of the short corridor, he paused before a room marked: '*Privado. Bagaglio. Entrata Restringere.*' Taking out a plastic key card, he slid it into the lock. Within seconds, the lock's green light came on. Quickly, he entered the deserted room and walked to the door directly facing the dock. A row of palm plants in cisterns hid the docking area from the outdoor cafe. Only the last section of the dock would be visible from the cafe. It was there that the boats docked for those coming or leaving the hotel. He walked the dock briskly, stopping for a moment and glancing at the cafe before striding out to a bench where he sat down as if waiting for a water taxi. He placed his briefcase under the bench and slid it back as far as it would go—the back of the case touched one of the pier's support columns. He looked at his watch and then looked out at the lagoon to see a gondola docking. He got in and, with a smile, greeted the gondolier, who then maneuvered the boat into the Grand Canal, hugging the embankment while disappearing around one of the canal's many curves.

"So, Keiran, is Duane still as anxious as ever? I like him a great deal and he has been a stalwart partner of mine, but at times he reminds me of a man of parts and no passion, or perhaps a misplaced passion. Does he seem to you that way as well?" Zoran made a distressed grimace as he spoke, as if he were displeased with Farris' anxieties. "Sometime those moments cloud Duane's otherwise brilliant mind."

Keiran paused for a moment, feeling uneasy in responding to the question. He could not talk about Farris to Farris' own client. That would be stupid of him. Keiran tried to guess from the expression on Zoran's face whether he was serious. Certainly Zoran must have known that Keiran, an associate of the firm, could not agree with him in his judgment about Farris.

"Well, you know, Mr. Hemmrich…"

"Please, please, Keiran, call me Zoran. We need not be this formal now," Zoran said, his eyes glued to Keiran.

"Okay. Well, Zoran, lawyers are paid to worry for their clients," Keiran replied flatly.

"True enough, but anxiety is the one characteristic about Duane that I least admire. When a lawyer is anxious, it makes his client anxious, would you not agree, Keiran? A vulgar habit, anxiety." Zoran spoke with the intensity of someone who was angry.

"Perhaps. Frankly, sir, do you remember the meeting last week in Dublin? With all due respect, you were anxious that the phone in the conference room wasn't working and you then adjourned the meeting. I don't know whether you or Mr. Farris was more anxious about that. So, I guess it depends upon the situation."

"True enough." Zoran paused for a moment, cutting a few grilled peppers in half, piercing them with his fork, then carefully raising them to his mouth, chewing slowly. "These are the best. You should try some, Keiran. Now, a toast. Raise your glass, Keiran. We will drink to Venice, a city of dreams and love."

Keiran brought his glass to Zoran's, clicking it gently. "To Venice, a city I am anxious to discover." Zoran laughed.

"So you're anxious as well!" They both took long swallows, before placing their glasses on the table.

"Maybe sometimes," Keiran smiled broadly, "but rarely."

"I have certain instincts, Keiran," Zoran replied, his voice turning serious, "many times I do change my routine, primarily because I believe that if someone knows your routine, then that someone can do harm to you, if he so chooses. I have no doubt whatsoever that there are people out there who wish to do me harm. After all, they're my competitors, and many of them will use sharp practices against me, so small is the scale upon which we all arrange our values in this business. This business is not one where competitors play by any set of fair rules. On the contrary, it's the reverse. I am not an old woman in trousers, Keiran. One can't be in this business and be successful unless one is tough—and careful, one must be very careful. Any other thought is just an unworthy sentimental notion," Zoran said with a grim smile. He paused in the full flow of his talk, then continued, "I've learned from hard experience that as nice as it would be to have the comfort of one day being exactly like the previous one, one day for me is never exactly like another. This is the only pattern of my life."

There was a momentary awkward pause as both Keiran and Zoran ate a few more items from their plates of antipasto, the pleasant sounds of forks and knives cutting into the vegetables supplanting conversation. Keiran choose grilled tomatoes; Zoran stuck to his grilled peppers. Keiran looked at Zoran with scrutinizing eyes, trying to understand whether he was a man who knew himself or simply had been so buffeted by the business that he had chosen that he no longer distinguished between reality and fantasy. Or, maybe in his business, Keiran surmised, those two merge.

"Now, about Farris. He is thinking, as you may know, of slowing down a bit, taking more time off, and perhaps in a year or two, even retiring. In the short time that you have been with us, we both believe that you have the wherewithal to take over, to help me in all my legal dealings—and as you know there are many. Although my products may not be what everyone wants, they're products that someone always wants at a given time. And each time a product is sold, we need all the legal documents to ensure that the sale is genuine and that we get paid. What do you think? Do you like the kind of legal work you're doing for me so far? I need not mention that it would be lucrative for you."

"The work has been interesting, Zoran, no doubt about that. Candidly, it doesn't even appear to be complicated. No, I don't mind continuing for a while, and although Mr. Farris is a master of his own life, it's my belief that he won't retire or slow down anytime soon. He doesn't give me that impression, not at all. Just the opposite, actually. One thing though, he is a hard worker. And, certainly, a call from you is taken as a command. You are a good client of the firm, after all."

"So loyal you are, Keiran! Loyalty is important. Absolutely important." Zoran looked at Keiran, feigning frank astonishment. "You wear your loyalty, Keiran, as if it were a soldier's faith."

"I'm not telling you anything that is not true. He does work very hard…and for you particularly, I suspect."

"Well, I would hope so…at the prices your firm charges me, I would expect that he be a perfectionist. Naturally, I would also expect you to continue to work very, very hard on my behalf." He laughed loudly and Keiran smiled broadly. "So you have no objection to working with me full time? You would be part of the firm, of course, but most of your time—probably all of it—would be devoted to my work."

"I'd have to talk to Mr. Farris and see what he thinks. Whatever he says is fine with me, although, I really, in all honesty, Zoran, have to know about the amount of time and travel I would be asked to perform on your behalf," Keiran added.

"You're worried yourself. A man in love, I suspect. Yes, that's it, no doubt. When someone is in love, travel and work are secondary—as they should be."

"As a matter of fact, it has nothing to do with that, Zoran, nothing at all. I just want to know what time and travel commitment is required of me." Keiran now had a slight edge to his voice, which Zoran didn't fail to notice. Zoran nodded, then smiled.

"You're correct of course. You need to know the time commitments and so forth. We'll sort that out later. That's it. Period. End. Any other questions?"

"I really don't have any, Zoran, other than what I just asked you. You're Mr. Farris' client, I work at the firm, I've been assigned to you by Mr. Farris. I'll do all I can to help. That is how I view my assignment." Keiran spoke matter-of-factly, but with no warmth or joy in his voice.

"Fine. Now, I understand that you're familiar with the Runnard report." Zoran said simply and calmly. "If you're going to be my counsel, you have to understand one basic matter of principle with me. I am convinced that the report was and remains nothing but a treacherous hatchet job by the disgraced old fool who headed the commission. The government investigated my businesses with the expectation that I was dealing in goods and with countries that should not have received such goods. The whole affair turned out to be silly; a report was issued and it was a slipshod job. Nothing accurate about it." Zoran paused, appearing to make an effort to continue to speak quietly and without rancor. He continued with a certain quietness and ease while maintaining a dominating force. "You know, quite frankly, Keiran, we all live in a whispering gallery. No secret can be breathed without an instant reverberation of rumor from unexpected quarters. Being active in my business generates all kinds of hearsay—hearsay is a legal term of which I am sure you're familiar, an echo that distorts the truth and of course alters the character of the person against whom the hearsay is being directed. That ugly report—the so-called Runnard Report—maligned my name totally. Until then, the general public didn't even know about me. I am happy to say that I believe that my name probably means no more to them after that malicious report than it before. You should cast your eye over the report, if you haven't already. Perhaps you can pick out its heart and agree with me that it's full of weaknesses insofar as it states as fact, innuendo, hearsay, and downright falsehoods. In reality, it would never have survived full sunlight, which is why the government never considered the report's recommendations worthwhile. I don't seek publicity. I like a quiet life with my family and friends. Isn't that what you want as well?" He moved uneasily in his chair, staring with a look of sadness that Keiran couldn't understand. Keiran was again silent, wondering if Zoran's last words really governed his life.

"No, sir, I haven't had the chance to read the report. Mr. Farris, I am confident, represented your side well."

"Of course he did. I'm proud of how he handled the entire matter. He was superb!"

Keiran took another sip from his wine glass as Zoran continued, "It is true that it has been a struggle. Nothing was ever given to me. I have had much success and some failures. Certainly I have had to use methods that aren't necessarily humanitarian. It is a mistake to think that capitalist businessmen are humanitarians. That shirt you're wearing was probably made in China for less than one pound, yet you likely paid more than 30 pounds for it. So much for business idealism. Certainly, my trade has put me in close touch with some of the most despised, yet prominent, men in the world. I don't apologize for this. I have always met them and done business with them in complete privacy. They expected that, as did I. And Duane did his best to protect me…until that renegade Runnard decided to take after me. It didn't work, and was never designed to work. What is the saying in the States…? 'What goes around comes around.' You may know that this Runnard died a few days ago in London, at your club, a heart attack I believe. I am not unhappy about that passing. Not at all." His voice had dropped to almost to a murmur.

Keiran tried to sort out the monologue and was silent again for several moments. He noticed for the first time that the piano music had stopped and that only a few tables were now occupied. The only sound now was the slap of the waves of the canal against the hotel's retaining wall and the soft lilting calls of the few gondoliers still plying the waters.

"You shouldn't worry about the clamor from a long-ago report, Zoran. Besides, you seem to me to be a man of wills, not really influenced by past memories or shadows of things past. Did you ever find out the real reason you were investigated in the first place? Was there a reason beyond what has been made public?" Keiran asked in a low voice.

"I have always felt that someone in the U. K. government believed that my business dealings were with people the government believed to be bad. Over the years, I had signed several contracts for cement with certain overseas government companies. The U. K. thought these were cover deals for arms. They were proven wrong. Duane brilliantly worked hard on my behalf and managed to rebut the charges in the report. I think this Runnard chap read into my heart his own misery and I'll never forgive him, even in death I won't forgive him."

"No truth to any charges then?"

"No. They tried. Toying with my bank accounts and having the Inland Revenue audit the accounts, but nothing ever came of that. All our corporate records were clearly organized and, despite Runnard's chase, they found nothing untoward. That is why, Keiran, it's so important to have all our corporate documents and records precise."

"We're pretty careful at the firm. You needn't worry about the accuracy of corporate records if we are in charge."

"I like your confidence, Keiran. It shows in your face, the way you carry yourself, and the way you respond to Duane and to me. You have an almost merciless concentration, which I admire. Now, to be sure, Keiran, everything we discuss is 'attorney-client' privilege, isn't it?"

"Yes, it is." Keiran didn't reply to what he believed to be patronizing comments by Zoran, and he didn't want to spend any emotion on disagreeing with Zoran's concept of giving him direction. As Keiran looked at Zoran, he knew that he would be uneasy working with him. Zoran was the kind of client who dominated his lawyer, an arrangement that would not be at all splendid and in all likelihood would be terrible.

"Enough of the heavy conversation." Zoran abruptly changed his tone, his voice louder and now friendly and eager. "I want to get more acquainted with you. So, young man, how has life been treating you in London? Enjoying the old city, I should think."

"I have no complaints. I like the club; the folks at the firm are generous. No, I don't have any complaints. Have you lived in London for long?"

"I have a home there and, as you know, I am a British subject, but my main home is in Cairo, and I have a few other homes in other locations, including one here in Venice. Although I was born in Lebanon, my father moved the family to Cairo after the founding of Israel. He knew that area of the world would be a difficult place to raise a family. We lived in Cairo until I was about twelve, then we moved to London." Zoran lowered his head for a moment, toying with the remaining food on his plate with his fork. He paused and then announced, "More wine. We need more wine." He motioned to the waiter who rushed over.

"Yes, Mr. Hemmrich?"

"Pour us more wine, please." The waiter filled Zoran's empty glass and topped off Keiran's, which was still half-full.

"The past. Shadows of the past never leave, now do they Keiran?"

"Perhaps not," Keiran replied quietly, looking steadily at Zoran. There was a long silence now, during which Keiran thought, for a moment, he saw a mist come to Zoran's eyes. "Sir, yes, we are products of our past. One of my teachers in high school said it best: 'Human life passes away from this world. It is a shadow in a world of shadows. Every day we should remember that it's a day that we should, we must make worthwhile.' At least that's what he said. Rings true...yeah, I think it does."

"Ah, Keiran. Rugged honesty you have, you're a philosopher as well as a counsel. Enough of this serious talk. I'm repeating myself on that admonition and yet we continue. Enough of that! The theater. Have you seen any theater in the time you've been in London?"

Despite Zoran's radical departure in conversation topic, Keiran could tell by the concentrated expression in his eyes that Zoran was doing some pretty hard thinking—and it wasn't about theater.

In the inside lounge adjacent to the cafe, the sole patron placed his paper down on the side table, took a drink of his mineral water, placed four 500-lira notes next to the glass, and left. He retraced his steps past the reception desk and out the side door, walking briskly along the street until he got to the public dock, which was now filled with several water taxis and private boats, all tethered to the dock for the night. The ticket booth was closed and there was no one in sight. He strode to the dock, positioning himself for a clear view of the Gritti Palace's private dock. Leaning against the dock's rail, he stood as if enjoying the evening breeze, his briefcase still in his left hand.

Abruptly, Zoran looked at his watch and announced swiftly, "I'm afraid, Keiran, it's 1:30—time for me to take leave. We both need some sleep. I'll see you here at the hotel tomorrow at 8:00 for breakfast. We'll proceed from there."

"You're not staying here?"

"No, not tonight. I have a suite here, but I'll stay elsewhere tonight. I'll see you in the morning. Have a good night's sleep. We have much work to do tomorrow."

Zoran turned for a moment to the table where his assistants were sitting. They rose just as he did. "Good night Keiran. Have a good rest."

Zoran strode toward the dock where his personal cruiser had just arrived and was docking, its engines idling. Just as he and his assistants stepped onto his boat, an explosion, muffled in part by the large girth of the dock's piers, blew apart one of the support columns holding up the hotel pier, sending wood fragments into the canal and onto parts of the cafe, as well as onto the deck of Zoran's boat. A portion of the deck began to sway, until it finally slid into the water. Zoran's boat immediately revved its engines, speeding away into the canal at high speed.

Keiran jumped from his seat, as did the few others in the café, all running into the hotel proper. Within minutes, the sirens of police boats could be heard in the distance. Keiran and the other patrons milled around the empty bar. The reception clerk and three other hotel personnel all appeared stunned as they gathered in a group, staring at the damaged pier. They were all speaking excitedly, and to Keiran it seemed as if they all spoke at the same time.

He stood for a while, surveying the confused scene, and then headed toward the elevator. Sure, he was worried about what had just happened.

But the explosion was small, dismantling only one of the piers that held up the end of the dock. It had to be an accident, he told himself as he pressed the 'up' button on the elevator, trying to put behind him the confused ending to his first night in Venice. His second thoughts about Zoran were now resurfacing. Keiran had the feeling that Zoran probably bullied the people with whom he did business, but beneath all that bluster was a very lonely, strange, and bitter man. Just as he was about to board the elevator, he remembered that he had left his briefcase in the cafe. Walking back, he looked again at the damaged deck. An accident? Yeah, has to be. He thought he now was sounding as suspicious as Zoran. He picked up his case and decided to walk the three flights to his room. Good exercise for me. Yeah, I need exercise. This is crazy, just crazy.

Twenty-Six

A groggy low voice whispered into the phone, "Hello?"

"Diana? This is Keiran."

There was a stony silence and then a click on the other end. "Damn," he muttered as he redialed Diana's London apartment.

"Diana I need your help," Keiran pleaded, seated on the edge of his bed, his eyes shut tight.

"You need my help? You, the disciplined, focused, in-love with a 'news reader', arrogant flake, need my help?"

There was silence.

"Keiran, I don't want to be unbearably rude, but you have some nerve to call me when you stood me up for dinner, again. I no longer indulge in the hope that you'll keep your promises. Your offers are now as common as dishes and they're as frequently broken."

"Diana...please...."

"I sent you an e-mail about my change in plans," Keiran's voice was now weary. "I really did. Diana, listen, I'm in Italy with our client Zoran. Come on now, give me a break, Diana. I can't be everywhere. Don't you read your e-mail?" Keiran implored, his voice soft and gentle.

"Yes...and no. I deleted yours before I read it, knowing it probably detailed one of your many excuses, which I would have refused to accept anyhow."

"Come now, Diana. What is this? I did let you know. This trip to Italy was a quick decision by Farris. Give me a break."

"You need my help. Really, now, a madman needs my assistance. How generous of you to call and seek my aid," she giggled.

He was getting angrier with her, but he needed her help and she was right. He had made several promises to her—all broken for one reason or another, and he realized he should not have been so loose with his commitments to her.

"Okay, I promise."

"I must be crazy to believe you, Keiran, but what is it that you want so urgently that you woke me up?"

"Diana, you must listen to me, please. You know last week Farris spoke of the billing increases and that we had to bill all our time to a client—no more unbilled time?"

"Yeah, I remember. You're calling me at this hour to discuss that issue? Get real, Keiran."

"No, no…Listen Diana. This is no joke. I'd like to know what Farris is doing to my time sheets. How much is he jacking them up? I need to get into the billing system of the firm to find out."

"Keiran, you know that your computer passcode only allows you to get into the time you've billed and the firm's research database, nothing more. You know that. Why are you asking me? I'm no different than you."

"Yes, you are, Diana. I need Farris' passcode, and I know you know how to get it."

"You need Farris' passcode!? You need a partner's confidential passcode that will allow you to access not only to your client's information, but also to all the others as well as the information about associate ratings? So what planet have you just come from? No, don't answer that. I'm feeling my amber crystal and I know from the tension in my hand that you're just crazy. I should be calm and treat you as if you've simply gone nuts and hang up on you. You have gone nuts, Keiran. Certifiably off."

"Listen, Diana. I don't give a crap about associate ratings. I just want to know what billable time he has attributed to me. Come on, I know you know his passcode."

"Keiran. Listen carefully and put your brain back into some traction. He randomly changes the passcode every day. Because of his paranoia—you know, like your paranoia now—he doesn't keep the same passcode. When he comes into the office in the morning, the first thing he does is change his passcode. He even changes the passcode using his laptop. The only person who knows all the passcodes is the network administrator, who is in New York. Why don't you call her up and ask? Her name is—let me see if I can remember it—Penny Vaughn…right, Penny Vaughn."

"Diana, you're pulling my leg. Penny is the copy room girl. Why are you doing this to me?"

"Oh! I'm sorry; I must have misspoken. Well, let me call you back with her name, okay? And, you bastard, you can call her as early as you're calling me."

"Don't hang up, Diana. Give me the passcode. Please."

"Keiran, did you understand what I just said? Even if I knew Farris' passcode for yesterday, I wouldn't know tomorrow's…I mean today's. It is tomorrow now. Besides, do you really have to know what he is doing to your time? You keep track of your own time, don't you?"

"Yes, I do. But come on now, I know you're a computer hacker in real life, Diana. Don't jerk me around on that. How else would you know what is going on in the firm all the time? You have a talent I wish I had. Give me today's passcode. I need it."

"Now you're ordering me around. Do you order your 'news reader' around, Keiran? Does she obey you like a—well, how do I say this delicately—like a pet?"

"Cut it out Diana. Just cut that crap out. If you don't want to help me, fine. Forget it. I've had enough. I just thought you'd want to help, that's all. Obviously I have gotten it all wrong. Do you want to help me or not?"

"You're crazy, Keiran. Firm security will trace the entry passcode back to your computer no matter where you are. The log on signs you in and identifies you immediately through the phone connection you're using, just like caller ID. No difference."

"I've rented a computer and I'm accessing it via wireless."

"Firm security will still find out. You're delusional, Keiran."

"Why haven't they caught you?"

"Well, brilliant Keiran, I know how to do it. You don't. Anyhow, you jerk, it's your life. Okay, Farris' passcode for yesterday was 6789F. I figured out the random nature of the computer code and each day the numbers are sequentially used, the day before it was 6788, but the letters are randomly selected, so all you have to do is have the correct number and just try your luck on the letter. There are only 26 letters to the alphabet, so it doesn't take that long to get the right combination. Simple and not very secure, obviously. But then, of course, he could've change it again to another random system. I don't think he's done that. He is a man of supreme order and routine. Bear in mind, love, that after three false tries, the computer security program automatically shuts down access, so you have to get it right quickly. And if you get it right the first time, security won't even be warned of an impermissible penetration."

"What will the code be today? You know what it will be."

"I don't know why I help you, Keiran. It should be 6790T…but don't hold me to that. Try it once. If it doesn't work, call me back. By the way where are you?"

"Venice. Thanks, Diana. Despite some of your comments, I really appreciate what you're doing for me. Beneath all your language is a gentle and super person. I'll never forget you on this one. I promise." Keiran spoke gently and softly.

"Sure. Gentle? Super? Try beautiful, sensuous, desirable. Yeah? Promises. Promises from Hogan are as worthless as a summer sandstorm in the Sahara."

She hung up.

Diana wasn't so much a computer geek as she was an intrusive person, maybe being insecure in other ways made her want to know as much about the office personalities as possible. How she was able to get away with her computer hacking is something Keiran just didn't understand. She had probably even tapped into his e-mail data bank, but he didn't care. He was careful and never sent a personal e-mail from his office computer. He had his own personal laptop computer and a separate e-mail account for his family and friends. This time, however, he had rented a wireless laptop, not knowing what the Internet connections would be, as Zoran had said they would be leaving Italy later in the week, although he hadn't indicated where they would be going. So a laptop with wireless ability made sense. Italy might be just the first stop, and he wanted to be sure that he had the ability to use his computer wherever he was.

It was close to 3:30 a.m. when he turned on his laptop. The glow of the screen was especially warm and pleasant as he worked the keyboard, bringing up the Internet. He typed in the Kenton & Ward direct access Internet address, watching the screen for the firm's main page welcoming message. A smiled flickered over his lips as the connection was made. 'Welcome to Kenton & Ward.' He scrolled down to the Administrative Office link, then scrolled down to the client listing. When the client welcome page appeared, centered on the screen were the words, in bold, large letters: 'Access limited. Submit your passcode.'

"Here goes," he said aloud. He typed in the passcode that Diana had given him—6790T.

Restricted Client Billing Information. Access to this information is by proper identification of the client name and/or number. Remember the client name must be exact. For example, The Alpha Company has to be entered in as The Alpha Company, not Alpha Company. If the latter is entered, the computer will advise that there is no such client. Assigned client numbers cannot be accessed at this page. Please enter only the client name.

Keiran slowly typed in 'Benton Industries.' The screen immediately filled up with the billing summary for the current month: $2.0 million fees, $250,000 expenses for a total of $2.25 million. Good God! That much in one month!

Uncollected fees and expenses after the present month: 0
Client credit analysis: Excellent
Payments: within 30 days
Account: Current Summary to date: $18 million fees; $5 million expenses
Address: P. O. Box 232400, St. Peter Port, Guernsey C.I.
Phone: 734-7954
Contact: David Leyden.

Keiran linked to the breakdown of attorneys and time billed per attorney. Listed there were Farris, Hogan, two attorneys whose names he didn't recognize from the NY office, and one that he knew from the Washington office who had left the firm several months ago. All were billing the current month. Keiran's billing averaged 80 hours a week, which was ludicrous. He worked hard, but nowhere near the 80 hours indicated, and certainly not for the 30-day period of the month indicated.

Just as he scrolled down to get a detailed breakdown of the previous month's fees, as well as the other corporations he knew to be Hemmrich's shell companies, the phone rang.

"Mr. Hogan, you have a call from London. Do you wish to take the call?"

"Yes, yes, I'll take the call."

"Keiran, this is Diana." She sounded quiet and her voice was serious and calm. "After we talked, I was thinking about the security features of the firm's computer system. Maybe you should log off right now. Security will notice that Farris' passcode was used at a strange hour and the computer is programmed to alert the user of any time anomalies regarding log on and log off. Using his passcode at this early hour will automatically send Farris an e-mail with this information. Log off now; don't stay on any longer. Maybe he'll think it was just a fluke. Keiran, log off, okay? I don't want you to get into any trouble. In the meantime, I'll try to get more information on Zoran's companies. Protect yourself, Keiran. I have a funny feeling that things aren't right. Did you know that Farris is being asked to answer some questions from the London police regarding the suicide of some functionary at the American Embassy? Doesn't that seem strange? I understand the police have traced some of the dead man's calls to our office here—and all were to Farris. Maybe it's nothing. I don't want to sound suspicious," she whispered, but he could tell she was concerned.

"Thanks for the warning. I'll see you when I get back. Promise I will."

"Log off now, and forget the promise." She spoke firmly.

"Okay, I'm doing that right now. Bye."

He immediately exited the page, turned off the computer, knowing that the billing moneys were ballooned, as were the expenses. They were probably kick-backed to some of Zoran's own companies as 'consultants.' But where was all this money going? And did Farris own some of the companies that some of the expense money went too? A convoluted way to make and launder money, Keiran decided. One thing he knew, he had no intention of being part of Farris' scheme. Why would Farris take this chance? Who else in the firm was involved? And Zoran, Keiran thought, was certainly not a man lost in his surroundings. What crap. How in the hell did I get into this crap? He had the feeling that he had sped down a long road, an unthinkably long road with no exits.

He took off his glasses, a baffled look on his face, bewildered at what was happening…shit! This was just plain crap. He slipped out of his shoes, turned off the lights and flopped on the bed, tired, still wearing his shirt and slacks. Sleep was what he needed. He'd clean up in the morning. What should he do with this information? Should he even care? Over and over again he had asked that question as the events unfolded. He now knew the scam—or part of the scam—and he wanted out. He could always quit and go back to Washington or New York or even join another firm. Yet London is where Jennifer was and he had to be near her. No more leaving someone he didn't want to lose. No, he'd stay in London. Maybe call Grayson. After all, he had suggested that his firm might be interested in Keiran.

I'll do that. Yeah, I'll give him a call when I get back to London. We'll have a drink or something. Keiran closed his eyes, these thoughts still weaving through his mind as he quickly fell asleep, the desk lamp still on, his suitcase unpacked, his shoes tossed beside the bed.

"I'm not joking Duane, a pier holding up part of the hotel deck blew up just as I was leaving. No, don't think that I'm dreaming. It happened. Luckily, I had just stepped on the boat or I would have been hurt…seriously hurt." Zoran spoke in an agitated voice at high pitch like someone who had just stepped back on a sidewalk curb, narrowly avoiding a speeding car.

"I'll call Keiran and find out what happened. Was it a small explosion?" Farris asked, his own voice low and soothing.

"To be perfectly honest, we sped away quickly. What I did see, though, was the end of the pier fall into the canal."

"This time, Zoran, it may really have been a gas explosion."

There was a snicker over the line and then laughter.

"Oh, you're a clever one, Duane, a very clever one. Let's hope this time it was a gas explosion and not something more sinister."

"I'm sure it's just that. Anyhow, Keiran will find out and let us know. Now, about Keiran. What's your view at this stage? Can you work with him?"

"I like him. Keiran is silent and strong, somewhat arrogant, but that may be a sign of insecurity. He will do. I can work with him and he'll turn in due time. We all know the power of money. In truth, the best way to destroy a man's morality is by money. Do you agree, Duane?"

There was silence that prompted Zoran to inquire softly, "Duane. Are you still there? This cell phone sometimes breaks up. Are you there?"

In one swipe, Zoran had described Duane Farris when he was young. He knew his own greed for money had destroyed him. It may have made him a powerful partner in the firm, one that others noticed, but at the same time, he had tampered with his soul, and now his soul was a barbarous relic. He and Zoran both knew he no longer had any morality. Yet, to be confronted directly by Zoran—himself a believer in the god of money—maybe the loyalty between them was slipping away. Was it young Keiran? Was Zoran now enamored with him? Would he turn to him, use him and discard Farris? Farris was silent, thinking he should protest Zoran's view, but he also knew he was a coward; his voice would not be raised. He believed he was wronged, but that nothing could be done. He was under a guillotine and Zoran could release the blade at any time. It was that simple.

"Agreed, Zoran. Absolutely.

"Now what about that crazy embassy suicidal mole of yours? Where does that stand now that he's dead?" Zoran asked.

"Well, frankly, I don't really know…."

"Duane, I've always been worried about the money you paid him. I hope that the procedures you used for those payments were indeed untraceable."

"I don't see how any tracing could be done. I just don't see that happening."

"Okay. Will you be joining us tomorrow or perhaps later this week?"

"Probably not. I think it best to stay close to the office as these things sort themselves out. Perhaps I'll come down on Thursday or Friday, I'll let you know. In the meantime, you should know that I'm testing Keiran on this trip. I've asked him to call me with briefings on your meetings. Let's see whether he will do that or not. That is always the first step, as you know, following instructions."

"Of course. Well, anything else, Duane?"

"One thing, and it may be nothing more than an innocent event. As you know we have a computer security program that alerts us as to any unauthorized use of our systems. As I'm talking to you, I've received an alert on my screen that my passcode has been used to get into the firm's billing data."

"Duane. Come now. Do I need to know this? Probably another firm trying to find out what your profits are. Really, I've got to go. You figure that out yourself."

"Perhaps. But the person who broke into the system has an Italian country code. It could be Keiran Hogan."

"Duane, this is something that I don't care to hear. You handle this. Italy is a big place with lots of computers and lots of hackers. Besides, do you care if Hogan knows how much profit the firm is making?"

"Perhaps not. Well, I'll just keep an eye out and see where all this leads. Thought you'd be interested."

"I'm not. I like the kid. Goodbye." Zoran curtly hung up.

Zoran replaced his cell phone in his side pocket, pondering Farris' attempt to sully his own associate's character. Is he jealous? Zoran reflected. This stupidity with the mole…and Duane's confidence that money tracing would not reveal who was paying him. Well, Duane better be right. I never thought that was a good idea anyway. What information did he ever provide? That the U. S. government was undertaking an arms dealing interdiction program through the CIA. It's stupid, and Farris probably made a mistake here. Stupid Farris. I've been mistaken in thinking he was a marionette. This obsession with the so-called mole in the embassy was moronic. We'll just have to see how all of this will play out. It may be necessary for Duane to meet his maker. After all, he could have done this on his own for some unknown reason. And, of course, like everyone, he could have an accident that would result in his death. I knew all along that he was utterly dispensable. If something is traced to me, I can always say I trusted Duane and never looked at his bills. I had no idea what he was doing with the expense money. No idea whatsoever. Besides, I can help this young Keiran move up the ladder in the firm. Money is the defining item in that firm. That is the one certainty in all of this. Besides, I like this new man, I like him a lot.

Zoran's cruiser drew alongside his villa's dock. Villa Giovanni—named for his son—was a meticulously restored three-storied home, its soft pink and white facade glowing from spotlights carefully positioned to highlight its magnificent, almost confectionary, look. He spent so little time here—maybe two or three months a year, in spurts, his wife and family joining him from time to time. Yet, when he could, he came and used it for business. He found that Venice was relaxing to those who came to see him, and he enjoyed dealing with a relaxed customer.

He could not go to sleep right away. The explosion bothered him. Accident? Maybe. Too small to be a real threat to him. Even if he were on the deck when the explosion occurred, the most that would have happened is that he would have fallen into the canal. And I know how to swim, he laughingly and proudly told himself. There were now calls to make and business to which he must attend.

Twenty-Seven

Bob Grayson'a phone was ringing. Rubbing his eyes, he was trying to read the time on his bedside clock while fumbling for his glasses. "Keiran! Well, I'll be. Where are you and what time is it? Ah! Now my eyes are focused. Let's see, it's only 5:00 in the morning. Good. I normally get up at this time, so I'm delighted that you called. Actually, it's a surprise wake-up call. What's up…? What makes my friend call at this unusual hour? Don't you sleep?"

"Well, my sleep has been fitful the last few hours. I'm in Venice," Keiran answered, propping himself against the headboard, the pillows providing his back with support. He kept his eyes partially closed against the early sunlight streaming in from the open window that, happily, also allowed warm breezes to come in, bringing fresh life to the room. Disturbing this somewhat tranquil scene were the intermittent noises of the *vaparetti* now beginning to ply the Grand Canal, making sleep difficult even if he wanted to go back to bed. "I have to learn to close the window, or better still ask for a room on the other side of this hotel." Keiran said aloud. "The noises are too much and to early."

"What did you say, Keiran? You have to learn to close the window? You're in Venice? Boats are bothering you…the price of a view in that city is also enjoying the clamor." Grayson laughed.

"Sorry to call you so early. I should realize that I'm an hour later than you. Gosh, it's 6 o'clock here, but then…." Keiran's voice trailed off.

"No matter. What gives?" Grayson asked, knowing that Keiran wasn't the kind of man to call at such an hour unless the matter was compelling. "Don't concern yourself about the time. What is going on?"

"Well, I was thinking…do you recall your comment that if ever I wanted to work at another firm in London, I should consider your firm? So my question is, do you have a job opening at your office, and what kind of legal work would it entail?"

"Why do you ask? Farris working you to death? We're not any easier at my place."

"No, it's not that. Upon reflection, I just would feel more comfortable in a different work setting. We can talk more when I get back to London. I just wanted to know if you were serious about the job offer. If not, that's okay; if there is an opening, I'd like to inquire and if I like it, I may pursue the opportunity with you."

"Spoken like a confident person—'If I like it....' Why not? You have to like a job or your life becomes unbearable, which is what I gather is happening to you now. Sure, there is an opening…always an opening for a bright young man like yourself. When will you get back?"

"In about a week or so. Perhaps at the end of this week. So, you have an opening?"

"Yes, I do. Let's meet when you get back from Italy. I assume Venice is treating you well…?"

"That may not be true. Early this morning as my client was getting on his launch, the end of the pier he had just stepped from fell into the canal. A bit of an explosion tore one of the piers causing the dock to collapse. He's lucky he didn't fall into the water. Other than that, yeah, it's a beautiful city, Venice. I only wish that…."

"…Jennifer was there, right?"

"How do you know?"

"My wife knows everything and she in turn passes it on to me. Give me a call when you get back and we'll talk. Now that you've awakened me, I'll get up and read the morning rags and see what turmoil the world is presently in. In the meantime, you lucky man, relax. Sit on that magnificent hotel terrace and sip a cappuccino as only the Venetians know how to prepare—makes your blood circulate more efficiently.

And stay away from that pier. Doesn't that fancy hotel you're at conduct maintenance on its docking pier?" Grayson laughed as he continued, "The Italians...well you know wine, women, song, and then maintenance. You're supposed to be laughing now, Keiran, are you?"

"Yeah, sure. Thanks, Bob. Thanks a lot."

"No trouble." Grayson hung up.

Keiran held the phone for a few moments, wondering strangely if he had done the right thing, questioning if he had been too anxious and hadn't thought through this whole matter of money laundering via jacking up the fees for the client with whom he was now working. And how did he know it was money laundering? He didn't really. It was just a supposition. Surely, the firm's auditors would find out about the elevated expenses that were being tacked on to the high monthly fees and the exorbitant reimbursements of consultants and accountants located on Guernsey. Somebody must have been alerted by such numbers.

Keiran needed to find out more...or better still, be prudent and just leave. He felt sick to his stomach, and he didn't like that feeling. It reminded him of the time he was driving back from his home in Quincy, Massachusetts to Princeton with his then-girlfriend. She barely spoke to him, and it was obvious that she had not liked his family and, by affiliation, him. That feeling infuriated him. Being so angry at her attitude brought on the nausea that was so bad that he had to stop the car a few times to use the restroom, where he lost some of his breakfast that miserable morning. He felt the same way now.

Maybe he was too inquisitive, but he had stumbled onto something and he didn't want to be part of this program. If he started down that road of deception, then he would have to be blind not to realize that he would be part of the game. No, he had to leave Kenton & Ward. Grayson gave him the impression of being someone who would not deceive him. He would at least talk to him and he felt comfortable in doing so. Maybe he would even leave the field of law. Maybe he should have trained for the Olympics years ago. Maybe...a host of things. He knew he should call Jennifer, but the time, and the fatigue.... Finally real sleep was so overwhelming that the sounds of the *vaparettos* outside on the Canal became meaningless. He was now too exhausted to hear anything. He knew he had done the right thing. After all, he could always turn down Grayson's job if he didn't like what was being offered.

Grayson was unsure whether he wanted to hear the request he had just received from Keiran. The law firm of which he was the Senior Partner, Williams & Stevens, wasn't really a law firm. He was part of the Central Intelligence Agency's scheme of select proprietary companies, an anonymous group whose very existence would never be acknowledged by the agency. For the past five years, he had headed the 'firm' in London, with the prime mission of tracking and eliminating those involved in major arms deals, and the subsequent money laundering that went in tandem with armament sales. Heading the list was the now worrisome attempts to sell missile technology to the unfriendlies. His operation was small. The three 'lawyers' in his office, together with two 'administrative' staff were specially drawn from the agency because of their skill in several languages and ability to operate in multiple disguises. Although he was a lawyer by education, he had spent most of his career in the agency. What his 'law office' generally did was, through techniques of harassment and 'accident', disrupt arms sales that were destined for unfriendlies. Many times the harassment was sufficient to drive the dealer to other avenues of business. If the 'hints' were not taken seriously and the dealers refused to bend, then a more permanent solution was found.

From the beginning of his posting in London, his suspicions of Farris were bolstered by details in the Runnard report and other sources, mostly competitors of Farris' client, Zoran Hemmrich, who would always claim that arms were being sold by him illegally. Virtually all those leads turned out to be worthless, driven only by the competitive pressures against Hemmrich. The report recommendations went nowhere because of Farris' friends in the U. K. government, one of whom he had already identified as Lord Kilborn Foster, a member of the House of Lords, and well-connected to the arms industry in England. During the public airing of the Runnard report, Foster had continually and persistently attacked Runnard as being "in a permanent alcoholic stupor."

The transfers of money that Farris made to his own account were in line with his salary and bonuses from the firm and in line with the astonishing fees paid by the client Zoran Hemmrich. To date, Grayson was unable to trace Farris' other accounts—probably concealed through a string of offshore companies that would be impossible to find without some inside help.

Despite his efforts and successes in driving many of the arms merchants out of the business of dealing with 'unfriendlies', one big merchant remained and that was Hemmrich. Grayson knew that driving out arms dealers was like getting rid of drug lords—you have to hit them and hit them and hit them, over and over again. Getting a big one, though, made everyone else pause. People still had the desire to live and live well off their riches. What good is gaining all that money if one ended up dead?

There was only one proven way to stop these merchants…and that was to start what he called, the 'chicken shit' scenario. Slowly, very slowly, over a period of time, there would be minor accidents—perhaps an automobile 'fender bender', small fires at the dealer's home or office—then the bribery of bank personnel for account information and generating false withdrawals that took time to correct. These were all annoyances progressively getting more serious. He only wanted to be efficient and not take any lives. But when hints were ignored and more serious hints were scoffed at, then the ultimate solution became the only solution.

The problem with businessmen like Zoran was always that the profits were so high and the risk of being caught so low, that the 'why not?' attitude prevailed. Naturally, they were helped by lawyers and bankers, all taking a slice of the pie. And Grayson now had received scattered information, which he was desperately trying to verify, that Farris and Zoran were now trying to sell missile guidance systems to North Korea. Do they really need more money? Greed, pure and simple. And they were secure in the knowledge that, after all these years, they hadn't been caught. As important, both Farris and Hemmrich, having avoided disaster because the U. K. government had not acted upon the Runnard report, probably believed they were immune forever. Thus, all Grayson's 'chicken shit' annoyances had been ignored.

Now Grayson was faced with the prospect of obtaining, by the luck of the draw, someone from Farris' London law firm—Farris, and perhaps a few others in his firm, he surmised, being the center of the technology transfer to North Korea of missile guidance systems, parts of which had been bought or stolen. His instincts told him they were involved, but the information he had from CIA headquarters wasn't certain. The agency's own account called into question the public reports indicating that the North Koreans were buying their guidance equipment from China. That may have been, but guidance instrumentation from United States was of the highest quality and it would be well worth the attempt by the North Koreans to purchase the engineering blueprints of that technology. That was certain. When and where and by whom the transfer of this technology was going to take place had, up to now, eluded Grayson and his group.

The unusual nature of his cover was such that not even successive American ambassadors knew of his law firm's affiliation with the agency. That in itself was against the regulations of the agency, which held that the ambassador had to know of any undercover operations occurring in the country of his posting. An old hand at the agency, who had trained Grayson before he went undercover in London, had described the ideal covert operation as one that remained secret from inception to eternity. Grayson's operation followed that rule. In the agency, the director held 'Crescent Eagle' tightly. Neither individual agent names nor the geographic location of the operation was ever disclosed. If, by some fluke, the operation was compromised, it was so designed to be shut down immediately and its existence denied.

The goal of 'Crescent Eagle' was to terminate operations like Zoran's that had been heavy in selling technologically advanced weapons—or parts of those weapons systems, or even mechanical and engineering drawings of those systems—to those unfriendly to the United States. Zoran's role in supplying the North Koreans with missile technology was different from his past arms transfers and was out of character for him. In fact, he had slowed down his deliveries of arms to his regular customers. The only reason that Grayson could give for this change in behavior was simple...the money was too good to avoid doing the deal. The North Korean test of an intercontinental missile over Japan had convinced the director that Korea had help in assembling the guidance needed for an accurate missile launch. Grayson knew that in carrying out his mission, there would be no middle ground with regard to those dealing with North Korea. Those involved had to be eliminated.

He knew all too well that success in covert operations has to do with an enormous amount of luck. Sure, planning and rehearsals were important, but just as important were patience and luck and the patience to wait until one is lucky. Here was a lucky break. The only problem was that Keiran was sincere about practicing law and Grayson didn't have a law firm that could take on such legal talent. Somehow he had to get Hogan to help him. Yet he knew that it wasn't going to be an easy task and he'd have to seriously think about it before involving him.

And, in the back of his mind, he still was trying to sort out who had implemented the plot that blew up the Parrot Restaurant. His experience told him it was surely no accident—not with the guest of honor being a heavy purchaser from Zoran. Besides, it would not serve any purpose for the west to get rid of him and the others, as the hostility in the former Yugoslavia wasn't going to go away simply because their supporters in London were blown away. On the contrary, it would make their surviving supporters, of which there were many, more determined to continue the ethnic battle. In that particular case, assassination would not be an option, as it would not accomplish anything of value. There were still millions of Serbs in the old Yugoslavia who thought the same way about their neighbors—they hated them and in turn were hated. No, the hit at the Parrot made no sense. The police didn't, as yet, think it was anything but a gas explosion. Certainly, though, that didn't make sense, either. Gas explosions were so rare in London—this appeared to be the first in several years. No, there was more to that event than met the eye.

Right now, though, he had to figure out what to say to Keiran when he would meet him in a few days to discuss a job with his 'law firm.'

Keiran lay back on the bed. His sleep had been deep until the ring of the phone woke him. His head pounded with a headache. He needed a long swim, which he knew this morning would be impossible, a long shower, two aspirin, and a good breakfast. Then maybe, he pondered, he might feel normal. When did Zoran say we would meet? he asked himself. Nine, it was nine, wasn't it? He answered the phone

"Yes?"

"Mr. Hogan, your wake-up call. It's 8:00 and the weather today is blue sky, the temperature is now 28 degrees Celsius."

"Thank you, thanks...." Keiran hung up the phone. He walked over to the large casement window, closing it to muffle the sound of boats plying the waters of the Grand Canal. He took off his clothes, threw them on the floor, crawled under the covers, and was back to sleep. I only need an hour or so, he said to himself, just an hour.

His peace was short lived. The burst of rings on the telephone went on for a minute or two as Keiran struggled to wake, mumbling as he pick up the receiver, "Keiran Hogan."

"Keiran, my friend, this is Zoran, my assistants are on their way to pick you up. We'll have breakfast on the terrace of my villa. No hotel food, an excellent Italian breakfast by my chef. Did you have a good sleep?"

"Well, it was sort of short for some reason. Can you give me an hour or so? Sorry I'm a bit late."

"An hour? Sure. Why not? No problem. They will pick you up around 10:00, okay?"

"Yeah. Thanks, Zoran. 10:00 will be fine. I'll be downstairs by the hotel pier around then."

"One last thing, Keiran. Dress informally. You need not wear a tie...and please don't bring your briefcase. We'll have a casual morning of discussion. Later on, we'll attend to business."

"Okay. See you later." Keiran hung up.

Keiran liked to take a long, hot shower, but with time fleeting, he settled for a short tepid one, hoping that the cool water would wake him up and get him moving quicker. He knew that Zoran's assistants were probably downstairs now waiting for him at the hotel quay. Zoran's constant change of arrangements underscored the different nature of this client. What was supposed to be business meetings and discussions about new corporations now turns out to be a social occasion. Having made up his mind to leave the firm, Keiran toyed with the idea of departing now. Hell, I'm not happy. Why prologue this agony? But he knew that would not be professional. He would give his notice when he went back to London—with or without another job. He had enough money so he could live for a while looking for something more suitable. He'd have to talk to Jennifer first, though, and see what she thought. As he was toweling himself, he believed all these thoughts were a bit juvenile. What mattered was that he didn't want to lose control over his own life and, from the beginning, he believed that working with Farris would lead to just that, something that his whole psyche would not accept. Beginnings are always indicative of endings, he had learned. Sure, his high school swimming coach was speaking about training for swim meets—coming on time and training hard was the beginning and the end would be victory. Still, the beginnings in London, although personally rewarding because he met Jennifer, were less than acceptable professionally, unless he had totally misunderstood what was going on with Farris and Zoran.

He reached for his brief case and then, remembering that Zoran said not to take it, replaced in on the desk chair, making sure it was locked—not that it contained anything of interest to anyone but himself, and possibly Farris and Zoran.

As he suspected, one of Zoran's bodyguards was in the lobby waiting for him, standing directly in front of the elevator.

"Good morning, Mr. Hogan. Did you sleep well?"

"Good morning to you, Mr. Simpson. Did I sleep well? No, as a matter of fact. What woke me up were the motorboats—what do they call them here, the *vaparetti*? The noise of their morning runs is hard to miss."

Simpson merely nodded. "We are just few minutes away from Mr. Hemmrich's villa. This way please. You know the hotel dock has been damaged, so we'll walk to the public dock. Not too far. Okay with you?"

"Sure. The walk will help me wake up."

They walked briskly the few blocks to the public dock, where the highly polished dark brown, low slung cabin cruiser was waiting. Simpson stood aside as Keiran got into the cabin, taking the seat nearest to the front.

"Make yourself comfortable, Mr. Hogan. We'll be at the villa in about ten minutes or so." Simpson then left and joined one of the boat crew who was piloting the cruiser. Another crewmember came forward and asked Keiran if he wanted coffee or orange juice.

"Nothing, thank you. Appreciate your asking though."

The boat cruised at moderate speed past weathered, but obviously luxurious *palazzi*, their side walls slapped by the waves from the many boats plying the Grand Canal. It passed gondolas whose lone oarsmen gently rowed their shining, black, slim vessels, hugging the sides of the canal away from the motor launches. The sun was golden, the sky a spectacular blue; it was a day to enjoy, and perhaps, in a burst of optimism, Keiran reflected, today might be just that kind of day.

Twenty-Eight

Zoran stood, his right hand shaking Keiran's strongly. "Keiran, I have the pleasure of introducing you to Sir Kilborn Foster, member of the British Parliament, and Rene Orizal, my financial consultant, who lives in that other beauty of a city, Paris. Gentlemen, the new man at Farris' firm, Mr. Keiran Hogan." Two men were standing by a bank of floor-to-ceiling windows overlooking the Grand Canal, the glow of the morning sun brightly washing the book-lined anteroom. The breeze was soft and warm. In the center of the modestly sized room, four oxblood leather wingchairs were placed around an oval table set with a coffee service, and decorated with a flower arrangement in a trumpet shaped wine colored crystal vase.

Keiran, quickly noting that they all looked at him like appraisers determining a price, extended his hand to each and smiled, repeating "Nice to meet you."

"A fine night of sleep, I assume?" Zoran asked as he lightly put his arm around Keiran's waist, motioning him to one of the chairs, where he sat down.

"A little restless," Keiran said, as he reached to pour himself a cup of coffee. "I didn't realize the *vaporetti* started out so early. After what happened early this morning to the hotel dock…made sleep a bit difficult."

"Not two worry about the dock. That hotel management got a bit of advice from me this morning. I'll cancel my permanent suite unless they maintain their dock. I may even authorize you, Keiran, and your partner Duane to sue. Having splinters fly at me as I was getting on my boat is not something I would recommend to anyone. Enough. End."

Zoran looked at the group in self-satisfaction as if he were a priest who had just given absolution for a ponderable sin.

"Yes, how can we speak of such things in this beautiful city? Venice is beautiful, *vaporetti* or not!" interjected Foster, who sat on the edge of his seat, twirling his spoon, occasionally putting it in his cup, finally setting it down on the saucer, lifting the cup gently, barely taking a sip before replacing the cup on it saucer, so gently, that it scarcely made any noise. He did this several times as if nervously trying to decide whether the coffee was too hot for him. Dark suited, with a vibrant blue tie against a dark blue shirt, Foster appeared to Keiran to be pleasant man, with an altogether fluent manner of speaking and the general demeanor of one who demanded respect. His face was small, dominated by sharp, piercing eyes and a slightly upturned nose with nostrils that quivered as though always on alert for some scent. Sitting opposite Zoran, his gaze on Keiran was direct, as he continued, "A scar on an otherwise flawless city face. Yet, so necessary. Without this means of transport, it would be impossible to function in a city with a crazy network of canals. Keiran, I don't believe that, once you know Venice, your appreciation for it will never be dulled."

"This city, to me, is like a beautiful and warm woman who chatters on too much," spoke Orizal, a man with loose fat jowls, little pale eyes behind rimless glasses, his voice trailing off in a muddle of words. His hair seemed tinted a light red, the color was spread unevenly, no doubt it had been dyed an even darker shade at some point. His voice, unlike Foster's, was by no means pleasant; its raspiness grated on one's ear. He seemed to have discovered the art of using teeth for something besides eating. His smile was constant, wide against a heavily tanned face, although Keiran noted, it had less geniality than most frowns.

"Spoken like someone with such experience," laughed Foster.

"Certainly a sage remark," Zoran joined, his head nodding in agreement.

"I can ignore a verbose woman," Orizal interrupted, "so long as she has the beauty of a Cleopatra. And Venice, despite the clutter of noise and at times the confused tourist, is as beautiful as that ancient queen."

"Only you, my friend Rene, being of an historical bent...only you could describe Venice in such graceful terms, but that is what you would expect from someone with a Ph.D. in ancient history from the American University in Beirut," Zoran remarked.

"Received, I might add, before the current turmoil drove away the better professors. Now, that disheartened learning center, so great in the past, is returning to its normal functions, thanks in part to the Syrians, who finally are holding the country together and, in the process, keeping Israel a bit off balanc," Orizal added.

"Yes, along with others struggling over a piece of real estate that, were it not for religion, not one person on this planet would truly care about," Foster said, unsmiling now as he continued, "So goes the vagaries of existence. Life's luck to you, Keiran Hogan, to be born and live in the United States, where the last war fought on your soil, was your Civil War. No more bloodshed between your own peoples on your favored land—at least anything on the scale of a real war."

"No doubt about that, sir. America is certainly a rising sun for many of us. My ancestors, coming from Ireland, believed in that wholeheartedly."

"And, in you, they have a success story, I'm sure." Zoran commented.

Keiran hesitated for a moment, and then smiled at Zoran's comment, softly saying, "I hope so sir. I hope I'm trying at least. I'm trying very hard."

"America, where every man gets his chance, regardless of his birth, gets a golden opportunity to shine, to work, to be himself and become whatever he wants to. Unfortunately the rest of the world, or at least many parts of the world, aren't as blessed," Foster declared. "Unfortunate, that to achieve what America now has still pits people against one another in conflict—sometimes sensible, often senseless, but conflict nevertheless."

"Dear Kilborn, you're sounding like a man of moral principles and that I know you aren't!" Orizal rejoined.

Everyone laughed. Keiran smile awkwardly, not yet understanding whether Orizal was being critical or being funny, or both.

"Yet without conflict, what clients would we have?" Zoran now spoke in low, pensive tones, as if wondering aloud what business he would be in but for conflict.

"Correct. Our clients come as a result of the greatest of the four horsemen of the apocalypse—war!" Foster emphasized the last word with a shout, then dropped his voice to a murmur, "Suppliers like us have been around since the first millennium. Sad, but…wars, conflict, once blood is shed in quarrel, reason and right are swept away by the rage of anger and calls for revenge."

"And the phones in your office ring incessantly, Zoran. Incessantly," Orizal mentioned sharply. Calls to us for the weapons with which to fight these wars, semi-wars, make-believe wars…all needing arms and all thinking they will win."

Keiran said nothing as he listened to the conversation, reaching for the first time for his coffee, its first swallow bringing him a certain refreshment.

"Heavy discussion this morning, gentlemen. Not such a charming manner to meet our guest on his first trip to Venice. I apologize to you for such rudeness!" Zoran laughed as he emphasized his last phrase. "No matter though. Our normal procedure, Keiran, when we do meet is to review any outstanding business contracts or arrangements. Usually Duane is with us giving us his legal take on our most recent activity. We have in you a worthy alternative to Duane. Worthy indeed. Now gentlemen, however, we shall defer our business session. It is too beautiful a day not to enjoy a lovely breakfast on the terrace." After a slight pause, Zoran turned to Keiran, "We should be conversing with Keiran about our magnificent location rather than detailing the intricacies of our business, which we will return to later."

"I'm here to learn as much as I can about your business. I'm completely in your hands, sir. Whenever you're ready to engage in those conversations, I am as well," Keiran answered politely.

"Spoken like the good counsel you are. Anyway, later this morning, we will meet with our contracting partners in this deal, one of whom I believe you met in Dublin a short while ago. We're going to finalize certain details of our arrangement and I want you to be with me when we meet with them. So it's wise that Farris sent you here to be part of this matter. After that meeting, I would hope that we could discuss some other subjects that need my attention and your input. I would think that we'll be finished by tonight, no later than tomorrow. Within that time frame, please feel free to ask your lady friend to join you—all expenses on me, of course. You need to take a few days off and relax and enjoy this remarkable city. You would agree to that, Keiran?"

"I've got to call her and see whether she can come. I know she would enjoy this city. I'll let you know later this afternoon. That is a very generous of you, Zoran. Very generous. Thank you," Keiran remarked gently, "I appreciate your offer."

"Zoran is an exceedingly generous person. I keep telling him to scale back on his largesse," Orizal quipped.

"I look forward to an increase in Zoran's beneficence!" Foster interrupted, his voice now bellowing in a loud chuckle.

"Spoken like a truly greedy politician!" Orizal commented.

"And man in general is not greedy? Come down from that high perch, Rene," Foster gently admonished Orizal. "Greed—and I dare say everyone in this room has that element in his makeup—greed, one the seven deadly sins of man, is in the eyes of the beholder. That is the query that has to be answered. We have free will and what is greed to one person may not be to another. True, greed is one of the basest qualities in human nature and no one can disagree with that. But, again, it's how one defines 'greed.' Hogan, at your young age, I'm sure that you have experienced your own concept of greed?" Foster asked, inviting Keiran to reply, looking directly at him, his thin smile now widening. "How do you define greed?"

Zoran looked at Keiran, carefully analyzing how he would respond, what words he would use, what attitude he would take. Keiran looked back at him, his eyes not displaying any emotion, then spoke directly to Foster, "I suppose it's like the definition of pornography. A Justice of our Supreme Court said, 'you know it when you see it.' With greed, it would probably be the same. What is a rational, reasonable commission or compensation for a deal, for example, would be greedy if not rational or reasonable given the contract amount. If the commission is half of the contract amount, for example, that would probably not pass the test and be considered greedy and out of line with normal business practices. So, one has to look at the facts to make that determination. I do know, from my experience in Washington, that some of the partners of my firm believe that business deals often collapse because of the greed factor—one side wanting too much and the other unwilling to compromise. Yes, I agree, it's how one defines greed and who is doing the definition. One should, of course, always be sensitive to another's interpretation, even when one doesn't agree with that interpretation."

"The serious wisdom of youth!" Zoran loudly proclaimed, apparently satisfied with Keiran's response. "We must honor the wise among us. Keiran's statement is astute. We are all greedy by choice, my friend Kilborn Foster. By choice and nothing is wrong with that. Nothing. Capitalism is greed hidden behind an economic theory of choice. Business corrupts everything it touches." Zoran paused for a moment before continuing, surveying the group, paying especial attention to Keiran's reaction to what he was saying. He noted that Keiran's expression was one of serious interest, and that Foster and Orizal where gently nodding their heads in agreement. "It corrupts politics, sports, literature, art, labor unions, corporations, and so on. There is nothing wrong with that, so long as we recognize what business does. It also provides the wherewithal for this great civilization that we call the 21st century—all these technological advances—nothing comes for free and everyone wants to get paid. We all vote for gold in the long run, now don't we?" Zoran closed his monologue, folding his arms across his chest in a gesture clearly indicating how splendid he considered his statement.

"Zoran, your philosophical approach is admirable," Foster countered. "I think George Bernard Shaw predated you in expressing similar thoughts, though".

"Then I am in good company…very good company!" Zoran exclaimed.

"I agree with our young counselor," Orizal continued, looking directly at Keiran, his smile now a bit tired. "Keiran, you have a considerable point. Greed is defined by the facts of the situation. Free will allows us to decide whether or when we will partake of this most deadly sin. Again, what is a sin to one person may not be sinful to another. We all have free will. Nevertheless, there are circumstances that impact on that free will. Is that correct, Keiran?" Orizal questioned, his voice, now a trifle nervous.

"Naturally," Keiran acknowledged, "you have to rationally analyze the circumstances that impact free will and find out where that analysis leads you. Sometimes getting at all the facts can be a bit difficult, and certainly people look at the same facts differently."

"Again, the insight of youth? Excellent!" Zoran interrupted. Gentlemen, it's certainly not my intention to continue this heavy, intellectual discourse this morning. Before we adjourn for breakfast, I want to make one simple, additional point to our dialogue. One thing upon which we can all agree, I am sure, is that all our customers believe they're on the right side of a conflict. Our commissions and fees are set as a percentage of the contract, and to a certain extent dependent upon delivery schedules and difficulty in obtaining the necessary merchandise which the customer wants. As you know, with the exception of Keiran, who has yet to be involved with me in negotiations with our customers, I am always open as to how I arrive at our commission. If the customer balks at our recommendation, then we must, as a matter of principle, listen to his reasons. We certainly don't have to agree and we don't argue about what I believe is fair, given the circumstances surrounding the contract. The more difficult the contract, the higher the commission and fees. A product less complicated to deliver should not have to carry the same burden of a commission as a contract requiring a more complex delivery arrangement and complex product for such delivery. All of you here realize—again, except perhaps for Keiran—that many of our customers are governments who wish to support this group or that group with arms and wish to do it in a fashion that hides their true involvement. Our customers are those that need arms to settle conflicts and we provide those arms. We don't get involved in the political machinations of either side of the conflict. Yet, it's understood that once we sell to one side, we don't sell to the other. To violate that unwritten rule would be suicidal.

And we never promise anything more than we are able to perform. Some find it immoral to deal in arms. I don't. But we cannot deal with both sides in a conflict. Absolutely, this is not my way."

"Well said, Zoran. An honest portrayal of what we do. And, frankly, at times, I believe we are doing a patriotic thing in helping some groups overcome pretty ugly government leaders. Yet, in the final analysis," Orizal observed, turning first to Foster and then to Zoran, "we don't take sides."

"You're losing me here, gentlemen," Keiran remarked, lowering his voice. "I understand the philosophical background everyone here is positing, but I thought that your businesses were basically the sales of commodities. Is it commodities or is it something else?" Keiran looked directly at Zoran, his eyes now cold behind the wire rim glasses he was wearing. Keiran's words seemingly silenced the group. No one spoke for several moments.

"Enough! End! Period! This serious talk must stop. To me it appears that it's time to eat," Zoran laughed. "Let's adjourn to the dining terrace and have Anna serve us. We need to fill our stomachs with a solid Italian breakfast. An empty stomach at times makes for an angry, perhaps distressed mind. I don't think I'll get any disagreement about that view. Now let's proceed." He rose from his chair; his extended hand pointed Keiran the others to the adjacent dining room.

A trim, middle-age woman, in a gray and white uniform, who had been standing by the double doors during the conversation, moved swiftly to lead the group through the dining room and directly to the small terrace overlooking the Grand Canal. There, she stood behind the buffet table, covered with a lime green tablecloth, set with several highly polished copper chafing dishes and platters of fruit and breads carefully arranged on large china plates. Zoran motioned to Keiran to go first.

"*Buongioro, Signor. Per piacere,*" Anna spoke quietly as she handed him a china plate, its border matching that of the serving plates, a crest in its center with the letter 'H' in its center. Swiftly, she opened the tops of the chafing dishes, revealing scrambled eggs with mushrooms, warm

Italian sausages cut up in bite-size pieces, and a mixture of fried potatoes, peppers, onions, and tomatoes.

"Please take a bit of everything," Zoran suggested, as he followed Keiran.

"I can't avoid doing just that," Keiran replied. "Everything looks so attractive and I am hungry."

"Good, Anna is the best cook around and her breakfasts are notable. Don't forget the fruit and hot bread," he said to Keiran. Then turning to Anna, he directed, "When we are seated, please bring us some coffee and orange juice. The table looks admirable, Anna. Thank you for doing, as usual, such an elegant job."

"*Grazie, Senor Hemmrich, grazie.*" She smiled at him.

"Ah! Breakfast in Venice overlooking the Grand Canal with its parade of colorful boats, those gondolas—you must take your lady friend on one of those, definitely, Keiran, you must." Zoran moved to a large wrought-iron table covered with a tablecloth similar to that of the buffet table; a large green and white umbrella over the table provided some shade from the morning sun. When all were seated, he raised his hand slightly toward Anna, who came over with a silver coffee pot, pouring its liquid first into Zoran's cup.

"Strong Italian espresso, and of course, with a bit of grappa liquor in it. This combination, Keiran, will warm the body and soften the heart." Zoran smiled slightly, his voice now betraying, Keiran concluded, a bit of annoyance at Keiran's last comment about commodities and arms dealing.

He realized that they were taken aback by his talk of 'commodities.' He is, after all, Zoran's lawyer, or at least one of them, shouldn't he know what is going on? The forced stillness at the table angered him even more. He didn't want to be taken as a fool who was now in fear for having said something that called into question his client's words. Fear he didn't have. So he continued his questioning. At this point he wanted to know what his client did or didn't sell. To hell with how anyone felt. What is he, Keiran reflected, a lackey or a lawyer?

"If your companies are dealing in arms, Zoran, why do your contracts always specify cement, fertilizer, or in a few cases, as I recall, steel scrap?"

Keiran firmly asked, softening his comments by adding, "Or, perhaps I misunderstood the totality of what your companies do," giving Zoran some wiggle room if he wished to correct himself or correct Keiran.

"Young counselor. I announced we were finished with heavy discussion. End. However, you're new here and have asked a reasonably good question that needs to be answered. By your question, I have the impression that you may believe that my companies hide the true nature of the shipments. Well, we don't do that. That is the truthful answer. Many times, we combine the products for shipping, and what you have been working on is the commodities portion of the shipments. Farris handles the arms portions. I had thought by now he would have briefed you on the division of the shipments, but perhaps not, or perhaps he was going to wait until you got back to London to give you that information. No matter. We don't try to hide anything or do anything impermissible, Keiran. I don't believe your comment suggested that we are doing anything as such. Am I correct?"

"No, I'm not suggesting that at all. Not at all. I admire your business sense, and from what I know, you don't do stupid things." Again silence fell on the group for several moments. Keiran surveyed the scene as all, save Keiran, continued to eat without saying a word.

"Thank you for your kind words about my business sense. Certainly, I try not to engage in imprudent business deals. That is why we have your firm as our counsel—to prevent us from doing any thing improper. We expect you to continue in that tradition, Keiran. With no exceptions." Zoran looked at Keiran, who had placed his fork down on his plate, listening intently to Zoran. Zoran's argument to Keiran seemed far too detailed to be true. Keiran didn't reply, believing that his silence was a sufficient answer.

"These eggs are delicious, I'm going to have more." Foster, speaking randomly, rose from the table and went to the buffet, where Anna stood and swiftly opened the top of the chafing dish that held the eggs.

"Yes, I'll have more myself," chimed in Orizal, exchanging glances with Foster.

Keiran wasn't immune to what he saw happening at the table. He had, in his direct comments, obviously hit an exposed nerve and both

Foster and Orizal knew what had happened and were trying to avoid any further discussion by seeking more food. When they came back to the table, Keiran observed that the amount of additional food on their plates was minimal. Zoran kept eating slowly, finally commenting, "I admire your forcefulness—your frankness—in advancing your opinions, Keiran. I have confidence you will do so on my behalf many, many times. You have a calm intelligence and a serene urbanity that I admire. Candidly, it's an honorable man who tells it likes he sees it—is that the phrase that Americans use? And as I've said before, to you and perhaps others who are concerned with our business, what we do doesn't in any respect provide us, in our old age, with a vivid imagination or memory of a more romantic career. The business in which we are now engaged is honorable, acceptable, and makes us a great deal of money." Zoran concluded, his smile now completely vanished, as he looked to Keiran for response.

"As a lawyer, I have faith that everything comes out right, if the facts are truthful," Keiran was speaking slowly and firmly, like a man who had heard too much mush and had had his fill of it. His eyes again fixed firmly on Zoran, he continued, "I have no doubt, from what I have seen, and from what Farris has said, that you, Zoran, have the ability, facility, and temperament for the business you're in. The law demands clean hands and my understanding is that I'm here to make sure this is the case with all your companies with which I am involved. Directly, I have to know everything, Zoran if I'm to be an effective counsel to you. You understand, I am sure, that no matter how lucky one thinks he is, at some point, luck runs out. That is why I believe it's important to construct the legal papers based on true facts and not on falsities. Who knows when those true facts might come out and cause a great deal of difficulty for the person who based his legal documents on falsehoods? I just don't believe that a system based on falsehoods ever succeeds."

"So young! And yet you speak like one who has had the experience of many years. Of course, Keiran, I agree with what you're saying. I guess I'm a bit confused. Do you think that Farris has developed for me, over these years, and with my concurrence, an inappropriate legal strategy for all my companies and their business dealings? Come now. As you stated earlier, I'm not that ignorant. It was a struggle to build my business; it was never easy. I don't intend to do anything that would jeopardize what I have accomplished."

"No, I am not saying that at all. It is the documents that I have drafted for the companies on Guernsey, and for our meetings in Dublin that specified 'commodities'—in one case, many metric tons of cement. Today, I hear that some of those 'commodities' are actually arms. Nothing wrong with that if the exporting and importing countries allow such arms sales and purchases, but why hide the facts, unless of course there is something that has to be hidden…? That's all I am saying, nothing more."

There was silence as Zoran glanced around the table, measuring the impact of Keiran's questions on his colleagues, who continued to eat, not showing any interest in this conversation.

"Yes, of course," Zoran continued. "You did a very good job with those documents. Farris has the others, those regarding the sales of armaments. During the course of our meetings today, you will hear of other arrangements. You must know everything if you're to be our counsel. I will hide nothing from you. In due course, you will take over for Farris, so you must know everything of importance. But first we must work with one another and get to know one another more completely. I'm sure you will acknowledge what I am saying. Not to prolong what now appears to be a lecture from me to you. Yet as we speak, you should be aware that it's not a pleasant atmosphere—not pleasant at all—in my kind of business. Companies, countries, and even individuals all tap each other's telephones; plans for the newest military technology are always for sale, if not at major arms shows supported by national governments, then surreptitiously to whoever is the highest bidder; formulae for the newest biological weapons are being offered, and the highest bidder always that wins. Loyalty is a figment of the imagination. Loyalty remains elusive in the modern business world. What did I say earlier? We all vote for gold in the long run. It is a concept that will never vanish. It will always be with us. Of that I have no doubt."

Keiran had indeed heard a lecture and a threat. He would either go along with what Zoran told him was the true nature of the business and his customers, or he would not be the beneficiary of Zoran's generosity. He understood the game, and he knew he would never be the player that Zoran needed.

The water glass fell from Kilborn Foster's hand first, followed by a sharp scream from him, as he fell from his chair, one hand clinging to the his arm, from which blood began to trickle.

"Help me! Help me!" he mumbled as he fell to the ground, fear and anger in his eyes. Zoran instinctively hit the floor, reaching for Keiran, pushing him down as well. Orizal, who had been sitting next to Foster, froze for an instant, his face taking on the look of horror and dread.

"Down, Rene, down!" Zoran yelled. "Keiran...!"

Keiran crawled over to Orizal, grabbing one leg of the chair and pushing it so that Orizal would fall. That was sufficient to shake Orizal out of his paralysis, and he dropped to the floor quickly.

"Keiran, keep down yourself!" Zoran said, his face showing a fear that Keiran had never seen before, as he pushed a button on his cell phone to alert his security detail on the first floor. No one dared look up as several more bullets shattered glass on the buffet table, tipping over the chaffing dishes, spilling the sterno cooking fuel and setting fire to the tablecloth. Anna, who had fallen to the terrace floor near the buffet table, now crawled over to the dining room door, and collapsed with fright. In a matter of seconds, three security officers arrived, their guns drawn. Simpson, who had escorted Keiran yesterday and today, quickly observed the scene.

"Stay down! Down on the floor!"

One bodyguard quickly put out the flames by grabbing a pitcher of water and throwing it on the cloth, and continued by flinging pitchers of various kinds of juice on the smoldering table cover. Simpson and another bodyguard crawled along the floor of the terrace. Reaching the balustrade, they peered through its ornate carved openings, looking at a villa directly across the canal. All was now silent. Whoever sent the bullets across the canal was now gone.

"Get Kilborn to a hospital," Zoran rose, calmly instructing Simpson, who was removing Foster's jacket, grabbing a napkin, and tying it tightly around the wound

"It's not serious, Mr. Hemmrich, not at all. He'll be fine," Simpson replied.

"I'm leaving for the airport with Orizal. Join us there, Alan, when you have taken care of Kilborn." Slowly bending down over Foster, he whispered, "Don't worry, my friend, we'll take good care of you. Just relax." Foster didn't hear anything. He was still unconscious.

Zoran went over to Anna, helping to steady her as she began to get up. "Of no concern, Anna. Just an accident. Everything is fine. Must be a mistake, some crazy person, just someone crazy."

Zoran held her as she stood up, mumbling, "*M'aiuti, per favore, Senor Hemmrich, M'aiuti, prego, prego.*" Standing in the terrace doorway, a worried look on their faces, a man and woman in service uniforms similar to Anna's stared at Zoran, who motioned the man to take Anna.

"Not to worry, my friends, not to worry. Clean up here. Arrange everything nicely. All is well. Don't concern yourself with this," Zoran said softly, his eyes betraying a certain sadness as surveyed the scene.

"Shouldn't I call the police?" Keiran inquired.

"No, Keiran. It's not necessary. I'll find out who did this soon enough and take the appropriate action.

"But won't they want to know at the hospital how Foster got his bullet wound?"

"Yes, Simpson will go with him and tell them it was an accident. He is registered to carry a gun in Italy, so there will be no problem. It is a slight wound from what I can see, a shock to Foster, but nothing serious, I don't believe. I'll drop you back at your hotel. Take the rest of the day off. I'll give you a call late afternoon. I'm sorry this has happened. I truly am."

Keiran looked at Zoran, his face drawn, masking anxiety and fear. Following him off the damaged terrace, Keiran now felt like a wrecked sailor in the lull between two storms.

Twenty-Nine

As Zoran's cabin cruiser sped along the Canal towards the Gritti Palace, weaving around the late morning *vaporetti* and other boat traffic, Zoran sat in the semi-darkened cabin, the window shades drawn, his arms clutching the arms of the small, leather-backed captain's chair. His earlier fear having totally vanished, his face now took on a defiant look. A flaming distrust in his black eyes darted from Orizal to Keiran and back, his words came out sarcastically and with an edge of furor, his lips were compressed and his whole body spoke of hostility and fearlessness.

"An anonymous group whose existence they believe will never be identified. If that group thinks my silence will remain, they're in supreme denial. They will soon have a nightmare from which they will never recover. If they wanted to kill me, they should not have wasted any time. It was their mistake to threaten me. I don't threaten easily. I'll hunt them down. Enough is enough. Keiran, I am sorry that you were here when something this venal happened and I apologize that my courtesies as host were not full and complete. I shall make this ugly morning event up to you. I understand now that the explosion at the hotel pier was probably meant for me."

Suddenly changing his tone and manner, he added, "The only good thing is that my wife and my daughter were not with us. They are elsewhere. For that I am thankful to God."

Gazing at Zoran, Keiran remained standing, his right hand gripping the cabin side bar. Orizal had placed himself on the cabin's bench facing

Zoran and remained mute. Keiran tried to understand the bitterness in Zoran's voice. For a moment, he felt sorry—not for himself, but for Zoran, whose wealth and status had not brought him any security. Just the opposite, Keiran silently told himself. If he didn't understand it earlier, Zoran now knew the limits of existence and one's ability to control life. He looked to Keiran as if he were now a trapped animal full of fury and uneasiness, not knowing how to escape.

"Zoran," Keiran quietly said, his voice soft and reassuring, "it has been an interesting morning. That's for sure. My advice sir, though, is that we notify the police. It just appears to me that they may help to find out who fired those shots. The shots could have been random…and maybe others along the Canal have suffered in the same way this morning. Who knows? We should call the police."

"Those shots were not random. They were directed at me. And Keiran, there will be no police involvement. No one was seriously injured; Foster will be fine. His arm was barely grazed. The marksmen knew what they were doing. I'm sure that if whoever did this intended to kill me—and perhaps all of us—they would have done so. No, it was harassment. I understand what is happening. I had taken some precautions and believed those to be satisfactory. Obviously, they were not. So, it appears to me that this group wants to wage war against me. So be it. I don't mind…and I intend to win. Police—no, absolutely not. The minute I call them, they will want to interview me, you, and everyone at the villa. It would make the press, and that is exactly what I don't want. No publicity. None. Let the other side guess as to what happened. Let them wonder what my next move will be."

"I understand your concern," Keiran said, his hands tightening on the rail, "but I still believe that the police should be notified. It's serious stuff when someone shoots at you, Zoran. And how will you find out who the others are? Do you think that it's the work of competitors to the present contract we are working on now? Or to some other contract that you have executed? How will you know who is after you without some police involvement? Besides, even if you suspected a competitor, wouldn't you have to have unmistakable proof of which one…of which competitor would actually do something like this?"

"Be assured, Keiran, I won't leap into the dark. I have some idea of who is responsible for this morning's interruption of our breakfast. Regardless, not to worry Keiran." Changing completely his manner, becoming serene, he continued, "Did I mention to you that I was pleased with how you handled the police interview on Guernsey? I still haven't been called; I assume that you haven't either."

"No, not a word. I suppose they feel there is nothing to be gained by talking to you. Apparently, Leyden had a heart attack. I'll just wait until they call me. I told them to advise me first if they wanted to talk to you, not that I objected to them calling you directly, but I wanted to know when or if they were inclined to interview you, so I could be present."

"Well, regardless, I am pleased with how you conducted yourself. Farris was as well. Now, as important as all of this is, we must not forget my earlier suggestion. I would invite you, Keiran, to ask your lady friend to visit Venice. After today, you deserve the time to yourself. Do some shopping, visit some of the museums, enjoy yourself—again, all at my expense. In fact I'll send over some funds to the hotel for you and her so that you won't have to wait to submit an expense account and so forth. I won't take no for an answer. Absolutely not. Good."

Zoran looked at Keiran and waited a moment for a response. Keiran just nodded his head slightly and said nothing.

"But there is a matter we must attend to first and that is to meet with our customer who has come to Venice to conclude our arrangement. I'll let you know where and when the meeting will occur. The sale to this customer is crucial, Keiran. I cannot lose this very lucrative business under any circumstances." Zoran sounded an emphatic note, his voice now rising, his hand jutting out toward Keiran in emphasis.

"Well, I'm prepared to meet with them. I'm familiar with all the documents; Farris went over everything with me. He said that you would have additional information to share with me when we met. So, I'm ready whenever you're. As for my friend coming over, I'll call her and see what her schedule is. I appreciate your offer, but it isn't necessary to send money to the hotel. I can handle her visit on my own. I'd feel more comfortable that way."

"No, I won't have you reject my hospitality. That is not proper!" Zoran now laughed loudly. "The funds will be made available. What you do with them is your own concern. It shall not be any other way. Period! End. Right, Rene?"

Orizal, sitting quite still and obviously frightened, made no effort to join the conversation…if, in fact, he was listening to it at all. His eyes seem to have changed from blue to gray and his thin, sun-browned hands, folded in a manner that suggested prayer, continued to tremble slightly. His shoulders now sagged; he sat as if he were a prisoner waiting to be executed.

"Rene, are you awake?" Zoran asked.

"Yes…sorry. Zoran, I was just thinking of what happened this morning." He spoke in a quick, jerky manner, glancing at Keiran and then fixing his gaze at Zoran. "Of course," he continued, nodding in agreement, "I agree with you about the police. Most definitely."

"Good," replied Zoran, turning his eyes on Orizal like a professor appraising a student who gave a good performance on an oral exam. "Then it's decided, Keiran Hogan. You will accept my hospitality. No other discussion. I shall call you later about the customer."

Keiran smiled. "We'll see…we'll see. Before I plan anything, I think it prudent that I wait to hear from you about the time of our meeting with the customer."

"Yes, of course. You'll get word later this afternoon."

Zoran's cruiser slid into the public dock just beyond the Gritti Hotel whose own boat dock looked as if some giant saw had sliced its end off. The explosion had done its work well, Keiran noted to himself. A line was passed to him to steady the boat as he leapt the short distance from the boat to the pier. As soon as Keiran was on the dock, he turned to watch the cruiser glide away into the boat traffic—heading back, it appeared to Keiran, in the direction of the villa they had just left.

Keiran walked the short distance to the hotel and went directly to the outdoor cafe, sitting down at an empty table along the side of terrace overlooking the canal, any discernible expression gone from his face. Workmen were feverishly working on the damaged pier. As hard as he tried, he could not shake the awful feeling that the end wasn't going to be predictable or pretty. In the distance he could still make out Zoran's cruiser as it disappeared around a slight curve where Zoran's villa stood with a commanding view of the Grand Canal in either direction. Ordering a beer, Keiran wanted desperately to wind down and have some quiet time to himself. He didn't know whether those bullets were intended to kill or to warn Zoran. Maybe Zoran was correct in his assessment that it was only a warning. A warning about what? What was there about Zoran's activities that obviously roused feelings in others to the point where they wanted to eliminate him?

Taking long swallows of his drink, Keiran understood that, only by chance, he was now assigned a complicated, probably dangerous client by a partner who was probably corrupt, and in all likelihood, deeply corrupt.

This is crazy, he told himself. Just nuts. A veritable black hole. For the first time since he left Washington, he wanted to get drunk, to forget what he had gotten himself into. Well, the luck of the draw brought me to this office. If I was still in Washington…shit. Okay, Keiran, I'd be unhappy as well. That was different. This is different. I know who I am. I'm better off because of Jennifer, but worse off in my practice. Okay. In Washington, I wasn't better off. I disliked my practice and well…had a screwy love life. So, here I am. Okay—yes, I am better off. I've found the woman that I want to spend the rest of my life with. And that is something easier to accept than worrying about my practice with this nutty firm.

Nothing is easier than self-deceit. I just can't smile away the client, the partner, and the firm by saying that everything will work out in the end. Tomorrow will be the same with Farris and Zoran—probably worse and certainly not better. Oh shit…! Stop it! How long do you want to argue with yourself? Naturally I know what I want and it's not this.

He now knew he had obstacles around which he probably couldn't negotiate. One thing was very evident…the experiment with Kenton & Ward was over.

"Mr. Hogan, you have a phone call. Do you wish to take it?" Keiran looked up, a pained expression on his face. He really didn't want to hear from anybody.

"Sir," the hotel attendant inquired, "shall I ask the gentleman to call back?" He held the portable phone out for Keiran to take.

Keiran hesitated. It was probably Zoran already, he thought. And he just dropped me off.

"Well, perhaps I should. Yes, Thanks."

"Keiran Hogan here."

"Hello Keiran. Do you understand that I had the compulsion to call you right back after you called me earlier this morning? But then, I knew you probably went right back to sleep after you had awakened me. You'll notice that I've waited for a reasonable hour," Grayson laughed.

"Oh…Bob. Hey listen, I'm sorry I disturbed you. It's just that…."

"Why not? When you think of something, call the person regardless of the time. Try that on some of your clients and see what happens. Either they will like you for being so diligent or they'll fire you for waking them up!"

Keiran chuckled. "Precisely the point. What can I do for you this more acceptable hour?"

"Well now. Repeat what you said to me this morning. I want to make sure that I understand what you were saying…something about leaving Farris' firm? Correct? Or did I imagine the call and the conversation?"

Keiran laughed again, reaching for his glass and taking a long swallow.

"It sounds if you're drinking…water?"

"No, beer. I needed it. You would never understand what I just went through."

"Your client driving you mad?"

"Let just say, Bob, the client and I had a unique breakfast meeting that was interrupted by something totally unexpected. This was, of course, after one of the hotel pier supports exploded early this morning."

"Are you telling me that you want to lead a boring life? Anyway, young man, the way I figure it's about 11:30 in Venice and so you should be drinking wine. The waiter must think you're an American…an ugly one at that!"

"Right now, I feel ugly, but not like an ugly American. Almost everything happening to me right now is grotesque." Keiran paused for a moment, then continued, "Now that you mentioned it though, as I look around now, I see you're right—everyone seems to be sipping from wine glasses. Well, no matter. It's beer time for me. As for my earlier thoughts this morning, yeah, I meant what I said. I'd like to know what you do at your firm, what I would do if you have an opening, how much you pay—you know all the things a talented lawyer like myself would ask of a prospective employer. Understand?"

"We do have an opening. Corporate work—similar to what you're doing now, I think. Best we talk when you return to London. Or perhaps I may be coming to Venice. I'll let you know if my business will take me there. How long will you stay?"

"Unsure as yet. I have to do a great deal of thinking and get some more facts. I want to stand right when I make the decision. But I am interested, Bob. Thanks for considering me."

"Okay. Stay in touch. Call me when you leave Venice."

"Can't promise that with what's going on here. If I can't call you, I'll see you in London. Thanks much, Bob. Thanks."

"Take care of yourself, Keiran. Remember, the only thing necessary for the triumph of evil is for a good man to do nothing."

"There you go again with another one of your throw out phrases. That one I know. It's from Edmund Burke."

"How did you know that?"

"I wrote a paper on him in college."

"I better get off the line before I prove myself ignorant…." Grayson laughed. "Goodbye, Keiran."

"Goodbye, Bob."

Keiran picked up his glass of beer and took a long swallow, thinking of Grayson's last statement and the other enigmatic expressions he would toss about from time to time. Not-so-subtle advice from Grayson, but why? Did Grayson know something about Farris and Zoran that he wasn't going to divulge to Keiran?

The scene on the Grand Canal now thronged with people riding in a myriad of boats—mostly gondolas and the noisy *vaporetti.* The damaged pier didn't prevent the many patrons who were coming in for lunch. This graceful spot overlooking the Canal on this most sunny day was cheerful and bustling. They all gawked for a while at the workmen hustling about, and then went back to their lunch and wine. The Italians. Nothing seems to bother them. Amazing. A great attitude to have. It's not a time to be alone, though. Not really that kind of moment. Keiran quietly told himself. He finished his beer, rose from the table, and walked back into the lounge, heading toward the elevator.

Jennifer would like this…Yeah, I should be sharing all this with her. Well not all of what is happening. He laughed aloud to himself, remembering that he had been shot at earlier that morning. The dangers of practicing law, he smiled, as he pressed the elevator up button. Turning his head for moment, he saw two men seated in the lounge, both in dark suits, one of whom he thought he recognized as the telephone man who was in the restaurant at St. Peter Port, Guernsey. No, come on, Keiran, he chastised himself. You're acting like a blockhead. You need some uninterrupted sleep. This vision is coming from exhaustion. Get a grip of yourself.

As he boarded the elevator, he looked again at the man in the lounge. The man looked up for moment, giving Keiran a full but fleeting view of his face.

Yeah. That's got to be the guy. But why is he here in Venice? On vacation?

He sat on the bed, taking out his cell phone, pressing his preprogrammed number for Jennifer's studio. It was almost 1:00 in Venice, and about noon in London. After a few rings, she came on the line.

"Jennifer Berley."

"Jennifer. Keiran. How have you been?"

"Keiran, where have you been? I thought you'd call me when you got to Venice last night—but there was no call. So I just suspected that you were either tired—I can't believe that—or you went off with your client. Which was it?" She laughed as she continued, "And to think, I thought you were so courteous!" Her laughter filled the line.

"Wow…!" Keiran uttered a low exclamation that sounded like the beginning of a protest hastily checked. "Already asking for a report. The good news is that I'd like you to come and join me here in Venice. How about tomorrow? I think that I'll finish all the business that needs finishing this afternoon. Zoran said I could have the rest of the week off. We can tour Venice together. Venice is not a nice place without a woman at your side…."

"You mean a woman that you love at your side…." Jennifer interjected.

"Yeah, especially on my birthday. I almost forgot, today's my birthday. I'm 31 years old. Have to call my Mom and Dad. They'll be wondering where I am today."

"Your birthday! Congratulations. Why didn't you tell me your birth date? I need to know that fact. I do bake cakes, among other things."

"I like the other things and then the birthday cake."

"Keiran, you're terrible, just terrible."

"Listen, I'm having a miserable time here without you. Strange things are happening—like bullets flying around during breakfast."

"What? Are you joking? Bullets? What are you saying?"

"Just kidding. Wanted to make sure that you were alert. You know how these television personalities are—sometimes asleep!"

"Don't kid like that, Keiran. I worry about you now, so you shouldn't joke about things like that. One bit of news, though, that may interest you. The police are going to interview your partner, Duane Farris. Apparently, the American Embassy man that committed suicide, Jefferson Coborn, received substantial payments from someone—he had some offshore accounts. The telephone records indicate that he had several calls over the last several months from Mr. Farris. Sort of an interesting interlude, wouldn't you say? One has to wonder what the man at the embassy was doing for Farris. I suppose that he could have worked for him on the side. British Foreign Officers are prohibited from other employment while they're members of the Foreign Office.

I suspect it would be the same with U. S. Foreign Service personnel, although I am not sure. Hasn't made the press yet, but our sources at police headquarters have told us that the detective in charge is trying to arrange a meeting with Farris in the next few days. Should be interesting."

"Farris involved with the guy at the embassy who committed suicide? Are you sure?" Keiran sounded incredulous.

"Absolutely. As I've said, they traced some of the money that went into the man's bank accounts from wire transfers from companies. They are trying to find out if Farris or your firm represents those companies. Strange, isn't it?"

"Very. Why in the hell would Farris be dealing with this Coborn when he knew the ambassador? Makes no sense, none at all."

"Well, I can think of one reason—inside business information of whatever nature that would interest Farris, and perhaps his clients, especially Zoran."

"Hemmrich."

"Maybe. Yeah, could be."

"And, Keiran, did you read the morning *Financial Times*?"

"No, not yet. Haven't really had the time."

"Well, they're reporting that the police are trying to interview everyone on the list that was discovered in the debris at the Parrot Restaurant. You know that Hemmrich's name was on that list, right? So I suspect they will be interviewing him as well. I suppose you're going to be pretty busy with that one as well—or will Farris handle that himself?"

"I don't know, Jennifer. Just don't have a clue. Makes sense for Farris to take that interview with Zoran, not me. I have some idea of what the two of them do, but it's not a complete picture yet. More important, though, will I see you tomorrow?"

"You will. I'll take the late afternoon BA flight to Venice. I'll leave you a voice mail at the hotel and also call you on your cellular. Can't wait until I see you, Keiran. I really love you. I do."

"It's crazy being without you. See you tomorrow. I'll be waiting. Bye for now, I love you."

"Love you. Bye Keiran. Be careful."

"I will, don't worry, Jennifer. Please don't worry."

He pressed the receiver once to disengage, then dialed the front desk.

"This is Keiran Hogan. When does the launch leave for the Lido Sports Club?"

"In about ten minutes, *Signor Hogan*. Come by the desk for your pass. You will use the pool at the Sports Club?"

"Yes, thanks. Be there shortly."

Thirty

The fever of the day's events dropping completely from his mind, Keiran moved through the water for his hour-long swim. The pool at the Lido Sports Club, its water a teary blue, was sparsely attended—most everyone on this sun-drenched day being at the Lido beach, directly fronting the club. There were two other men in the pool staying faithfully in their channels; the pool was veined into specific lap areas by vibrant yellow, bobbing, plastic marking buoys. Soft symphonic music played over the loudspeakers that were centered along the gray-blue marble pool walls. Palm trees in square gray-blue ceramic containers were positioned around a small seating area at the shallow end of the pool. The seven wood-slatted lounge chairs, arranged in a single row, with cushions tightly covered with light gray towels, were unoccupied.

Swimming always made him think more clearly, without confusion, and allowed him to be honest to himself, "to make his record true", as his teachers back at St. Francis school used to advise as part of the morning prayer ritual. The teaching monks were deadly earnest about their code of conduct, and whenever he had to break away from those rules, he worried.

Was he now being too hasty? So what if your client is crazy and paranoid? And your partner is less than honest? Should he be less sensitive? Weren't all law firms the same? Isn't that what he and his former girlfriend would talk about all the time…the business of law rather than the law of business? The corruption of law partners and clients was unpleasant to contemplate.

Come on, Keiran, he thought to himself. The people who choose to practice law are no different than the others who populate the planet. So the bills to clients are enhanced. Who cares? Wouldn't the client complain if he cared? No, in this case, Zoran isn't fussing because he is an integral part of the program. Why worry, Keiran? Why? After all, you don't send out the bills to the client. Your only job, Keiran, repeat, Keiran, your only job is to do the grunt work—draft the documents, make sure that the paperwork is all in order, correct, and ready to be signed. Yeah, correct to accomplish what the client wants, which in this case is to hide the true nature of the deal. Cement? Sure. Cement that masks the rest of the cargo, which is armaments—illegal to sell to the intended party, who is also masked by a false name. But do I really know that? When these fellows sit down and sign these documents, the customer and the client, they know the documents are false, but what do I really know? Nothing. Have I seen the cargo? No. And do I really want to know? Farris has been with this guy for years. If I hadn't run into Runnard, I'd never know, now would I? But then, what about this morning...? Bullets aimed at Zoran, and yes, even the minor explosion on the hotel pier, just seconds after Zoran stepped onto his boat. What has Zoran done to so upset people? And who has he upset? It's best to get away and move on, Keiran. Yeah, move on. The indiscriminate twisting nature of life, Keiran thought. Grow up!

Remember Aaron Hubbard, your buddy at the New York office of Kenton & Ward, the guy who always made you feel even more insecure when he bragged of hitting on every girl in the office?

"Keiran, only the pretty ones who have big bazookas and long legs. I'll get them all, every single one. You're too serious about all this law shit, Keiran. You have to get with the program. Come on now. You have to get real." My buddy who 'lost' certain documents needed to comply with a court order to turn them over to the opposing side in a contract dispute involving multi-millions of dollars. Remember over several beers, and in between telling you that you have to get laid more often, Aaron announced how he was going to make partner sooner than most?

"It pays to lose certain things in life—you know, your virginity, and then documents that would bust your own case wide open."

"You mean you destroyed the documents?" Keiran asked, hoping that Aaron was just showing off. "You have to be kidding, Aaron. That's a joke, right?"

"No joke, my buddy. When the partner came in and asked if I had found the documents, I knew what he meant. So I never found them. I'm still looking for them. You see, my Irish pal, if you got laid more, you wouldn't think so much of nonessential things like documents. A woman is more important. You have to admit that, my Irish pal. How in the hell do you think I'm going to be a partner before you?"

"Aaron, don't fool like this. Even if it's true, you shouldn't be mouthing off. There are ethics...."

"Ethics...?" Aaron interrupted. "You believed what we were taught in old man Peterson's ethics class at Columbia. I slept through the class and still got an A. It's all bullshit and when you know it's then you know how to handle the law. Look around you, my Irish pal. Have another beer. You're going soft on me. This is the modern life of the law, Keiran. If you believe otherwise, say goodbye to a career in our law firm. There's not a thing in hell you can do about it...not one friggin' thing. Ah! You need to get laid. Come on, we're wasting valuable time. I get the blonde tonight."

Keiran knew that Aaron was probably right. Here was Keiran, close to the end of his fourth year of being an associate, and Aaron was expecting to make partner next year, his fifth. Farris had simply told Keiran that he was on partnership track. Yeah, sure. The track is what Farris wanted him to take and any deviations from what Farris wanted would certainly extend his time there. No, Keiran thought. No, I'm not going to burn out in a brilliant blaze set by Farris. No, I'm not wasting my days trying to ride in a direction that he, or anyone else for that matter, wants me to go. Farris and his kind are dry rot. I'm not going to join them. I don't give a shit about a partnership at Kenton & Ward, early or ever.

As he lifted himself from the pool, he grabbed his bath towel, which was hanging loosely on a chair beside the pool. Wiping himself briskly, he turned to walk the short distance to the dressing area. As he turned, he saw another of Zoran's bodyguards waiting alongside one of two corpulent, bronze, nude statues that framed the tiled, arched dressing room entrance, the surface of each nude figure oozing droplets of moisture glistening wetly like a dog's nose.

"And what brings you to this part of Venice?" Keiran smiled, "An afternoon swim?"

His face was sweating from the pool's moisture, and there were deep creases in his swarthy brown suit. Tall, heavily tanned, with a nose jutting out of his face like a beak, his eyes, the dull light of the color of glue, were fixed on Keiran. He spoke softly and haltingly.

"Mr. Hogan, I'm Peter Morris of Mr. Hemmrich's staff. I don't believe that we've been introduced, but, of course, you know I'm with him and my colleague all the time. Unfortunately, Alan is still at the hospital with Sir Kilborn Foster, so I've been sent here to escort you to Mr. Hemmrich, who said that it's urgent you come with me to see him. He said that you would understand. I'll wait while you change. I didn't want to disturb you, however, while you were in the pool. Mr. Hemmrich indicated that I not do that."

"That was thoughtful of him," Keiran sighed, then said with irritation, "He wants to see me now? Is that what you're telling me? Does he realize that I just left him a few hours ago? I mean…I only hope this is really an emergency. Is it an emergency?"

"I can't answer your question, Mr. Hogan. All I know is that he tried to call you at the hotel, and they said you were here. He also attempted to call your cell phone, but it must have been turned off. Perhaps you were already in the pool," Morris replied, his eyes now downcast.

"The hotel told you where I was? I thought the hotel staff were forbidden to tell anyone where the guests go unless they were specifically directed to do so?"

Morris, now wary, noted Keiran's obvious anger, and didn't respond.

"Yeah, sure. Why am I so stupid to believe that hotel personnel would honor their word to just an ordinary guest like me?" Keiran hesitated, "I suppose you passed a few lira for that information. Anyway, Mr. Morris, wait for me in the reception lounge. Your suit will wilt even more if you remain here. I'll be out in ten or fifteen minutes. Don't panic if I take a few minutes longer."

"I'll be waiting," Morris answered.

"I'm sure you will…yeah, you'll wait."

For a minute, Keiran watched Morris exit toward the reception lounge, seeing him reach into his pocket for his cell phone to report to Zoran that he had found Keiran. Angrily, Keiran pushed the swinging doors into the dressing room, throwing his towels into the soiled linen bin, heading toward his locker. The caprice of this client, he thought angrily. So unsteady. So much for an afternoon of peace and quiet. I'm getting pissed at this guy. He doesn't do anything on a schedule that he will keep. Ah, what insecurity does to one's psyche. Yet, maybe, with what happened earlier in the day, the noisy confusion in his mind was understandable. What am I thinking? He's a jerk. Pure and simple.

Removing his swimsuit, he reached for some clean towels and headed toward the shower stalls. Turning the shower on full blast, he wanted badly to stay awhile under the swirling hot water, to take a steam, and to relax fully before venturing out. Time was all compressed now and, despite his fatigue at Zoran's rapid changes in plans, perhaps out of Zoran's desperation, fear, or anxiety, or all three, plans had changed, Keiran knew he had to comply.

Okay, Keiran Hogan, consider this a great adventure into a hell that is an interesting place to visit. He was smiling at his own thoughts. Yeah, sure. Pure crap. He finished dressing, placed his wet suit into his gym bag's internal plastic pouch, checking to make sure everything was in its place, then strode out to meet Morris, thinking that the motor on that cruiser had probably been running the entire time.

The quay at Lido Beach, nine miles long and about a half mile wide, is generally filled with private boats and some grand yachts, all entertaining their passengers and owners for a day in the sun on Venice's most notable and spectacular beach. No one noticed a small rowboat making its way effortlessly about a quarter of a kilometer from the beach, rowing past the docked boats, past the furthest slip where a sleek cabin cruiser was anchored, its small Italian flag fluttering in the mild breeze. The two men on deck were dressed in white uniforms, and one, with a cloth in his hand, was wiping the inner brass railing that circled the modest cabin that jutted softly above the boat deck. Several radio masts—unusual for such a vessel—hugged the cabin top. The other man in white was wiping clean the glass portholes on what appeared to be a perfectly maintained vessel.

The rowboat passed the cruiser slowly, the oarsman straining against the waves made livelier from the approach of a *vaporetti* that was headed towards the quay. It kept going several meters, before turning and heading toward a small sandy beach at the end of a rocky promontory. Jumping out of the boat, a man pushed it toward the deserted beach. Making sure the boat was secure, he took out a large canvas bag. Quickly, he set up a telescope, adjusting its tubes and pointing it toward the dock he had just passed. If one looked closely, one would have noticed that the telescope had no lens, but in fact had an opening about 7 millimeters wide and a scope positioned on top, three-quarters of the way down the tube. The tube itself was encircled by another layer of metal and at its front were several exhaust holes. Working quickly, the oarsman steadied the instrument on its tripod, moving it slightly so that he could see the lower side of cabin cruiser he had earlier passed. Satisfied that he had calibrated correctly, taking into account the mild waves rocking the cruiser, he gently took a small square black container—about six by eight millimeters—and inserted it into a square opening at the bottom of the tube. Keeping two bullets in reserve, he would fire three shots toward the boat's exterior, the bullets were specially designed titanium-tipped, high velocity, and capable of penetrating up to a foot of steel. They would hit the cruiser and puncture its fuel tanks, making only the sound of a hammer hitting a nail…a sound, in any event, that would be lost among the noise of many boats coming and going along the quay. Those noises were certain to mask any that he would make as he pressed the trigger, sending the first bullet on its way. It was followed in quick succession by two others. When they hit the boat, the openings they would create in the boat's stern would be too small—only about 3 millimeters in size—to be immediately noticed.

All three shots hit their mark perfectly. In about five minutes, the boat would be leaking its fuel. As a good fisherman, he would have to call the Venice Harbor Police and notify them of this 'stupid' boat polluting beautiful *Venezia*. Packing his equipment with ease, he loaded it onto his boat. Replacing his sun hat, he pushed the small boat out, climbed in, and adjusted himself and his oars. He would now leisurely row back to the beach, return the boat to the rental, and remove his gear, telling the attendant that he had obtained great photos for his magazine.

Sure enough the engines were running, Keiran laughed as he walked with Morris along the walkway from the Sports Club to the quay and then onto Zoran's cabin cruiser. The first thing he notice when he boarded was his black leather suitcase and his laptop computer case together in a corner in the passenger cabin.

"Peter, what the hell have you done? Packed my bags?"

"Yes, Mr. Hogan, Mr. Hemmrich felt it would be a waste of your time to go back to the Gritti and do the packing yourself. Time is so short; he thought you would understand why this was necessary. Besides, we will make our way to the airport, which is much closer from the Sports Club than from the Gritti. We did check the room carefully to make sure that we included everything," Simpson said, somewhat satisfied with his last comment.

"Okay, that's it." Keiran reached into his jacket, took out his cell phone, punching in the numbers of Zoran's private line. After two rings, Zoran answered softly.

"Yes, Keiran?"

"Yeah. It's me. Nice to know you have caller ID. Listen, Mr. Hemmrich...."

"Please call me Zoran, Keiran. I don't like this formality between my counsel and me," Zoran interrupted.

"Okay, Zoran. What I don't like is for your functionaries go into my hotel room and pack my bags without my permission. I want to know how you got the hotel personnel to let you into my room. This is not the kind of behavior I expect and I will find it hard to work with you under these circumstances. I make my own decisions." Keiran spoke with deadly earnestness. One thing Keiran believed was that he never wanted to be seen as if he had the helplessness of a weakened chick.

There was a long silence. Morris, who had been watching Keiran, turned the other way, mouthing silently, Don't shout at Mr. Hemmrich. You'll regret it.

"Time is of the essence, Keiran. I thought that you would appreciate our taking care of these simple administrative matters." Zoran responded rather defensively, his voice now agitated.

"Sir, it's very simple. If you want me to come to meet you, you call me. I'll decide how to get there, and how long I'll stay. I don't mean to show any disrespect, but you must appreciate this is how I prefer to operate."

"Certainly, I understand your view. The situation is now critical."

"Critical. Must be beyond that if you have Morris check me out of the hotel after packing my bags and bringing them onto your boat, so that I can meet you at the airport. Wouldn't it have been simpler just to call me, leave a voice message, and tell me when you wanted to see me?"

Again, there was an uneasy silence. Keiran knew that Zoran was probably thinking of how to respond. Keiran himself didn't care. He simply didn't appreciate what Zoran had done. He didn't cross the line in decorum, although his voice was more direct and louder than normal. Forget Thomas Jefferson, who said to count to a hundred before speaking if you're really angry. Keiran was beyond outrage.

Finally, Zoran spoke, his voice just above a murmur.

"Our customer had a problem getting to Venice. They are now in Florence, where we shall have our meeting. I thought by taking care of simple things, like packing your bags and so forth, I would be assisting you…with the time short…."

"Florence! Zoran," Keiran now interrupted, "You want me to believe that? You told me earlier that your customer was already in Venice. What is the truth?"

"Circumstances have changed, Keiran. They are now at my villa outside Florence. We shall meet them there."

"Mr. Hemmrich, I'm not one to lose my balance. All you had to do was tell me to be in Florence at such and such a time and place and I'd be there. I don't like being in a cage, sir, when you control the key. Where in the hell do you think I would have gone? Back to London?"

"You must understand that events have taken a turn that I had not expected. Farris is on his way from London to join us in Florence. The situation is serious. Perhaps you're right. I should have simply left you a voice message. I was only thinking of your own comfort and convenience by having Morris get your bags."

"Thank you for thinking of my comfort and convenience," Keiran replied, his voice now tinged with a sarcastic edge.

"Now then, Keiran, what do you intend to do?" Zoran inquired stiffly.

Keiran was silent. What could he do? First Zoran drove him down a blind alley by saying the customer was in Venice, now he says things have changed and we have to be in another city. Like a malicious chess player, Zoran now asked him what he intended to do.

"I don't think you handled this well, Mr. Hemmrich. Not well at all. Where do you want me to meet you?"

"At the airport. My boat will take you there. I'll be in the restaurant. You'll be met at the airport dock."

In the middle of what was a pleasant afternoon, Venice Harbor Patrol Captain Giuseppe Sylvester was thinking only of going home when his shift ended at 4:00. It was his wife's birthday and he had promised to take her out with their two sons, ages 9 and 11, to *Taverna La Marchini*. There, he could have his favorite meal of roasted chicken with black olives, some pasta, and good Chianti—even though his wife would argue with him about spending too much money. *Giuseppe, piacere...piacere, troppo costoso.*

He had lived in Venice all his life; he knew the lagoon and the canals that crisscrossed the city like the marks of his hand. He wasn't a reluctant cop—one who gave a warning and let an errant boatman off with a warning. No, he took them in, always gave a ticket if they were speeding and hauled them into the police dock if they were polluting. Why his toughness? He was known as *il Martello*—the hammer. He loved Venice, as all true Venetians do. The city was slowly sinking—by perhaps a few meters a year—and he blamed the influx of tourists, and the increased boat traffic they brought, for the damage. He believed that Venice was a city for the few who appreciated its fragile and beautiful nature, rather than for the many who came and barely understood the city.

When he saw the low, highly polished, dark brown cabin cruiser speed from the Sports Club heading toward the marked buoy route to the airport, he noticed the oil slick that followed it and was getting larger as the boat picked up speed. He hated it when those who didn't care mistreated his Venice.

"*Avanti, Paulo, avanti,*" Sylvester said to his helmsman, snapping his jaws shut, his cheeks sinking into his rugged face. "*Prego, seguire le battello...stupid turista...Avanit Paulo...prima che contaminmare tutto Venezia.* You see the boat, *numbero 56890*, 'Golden Arms'? Look on the left...look at the oil...! Stupid...*absolutamente stupid.*"

Sylvester's patrol boat veered sharply and headed toward Zoran's boat. Picking up speed, it zigzagging, swaying from side to side, its horn making a loud, piecing noise, the flashing blue lights on the patrol boat's cabin ceiling sweeping the way ahead. Closing in on Zoran's cruiser, Sylvester took out his hand-held loud speaker.

"Slow down, you have a fuel leak. Follow me to the Santa Margarita police dock."

Sylvester repeated his warning twice.

"Franchesco, call the station, tell them we are intercepting a polluting cruiser and taking it in," he said to his other assistant who was surveying the increasingly larger oil slick through his binoculars.

"Do they mean us?" an incredulous Morris, his face knotted, asked his deckhand, who was now slowing down the boat.

"Yes, Peter, it's our boat."

"Are we leaking something? Fuel? How? How could that be? This boat is checked all the time. Nothing can be wrong…but where is the leak coming from?"

Morris ran back to the stern, shouting as he passed Keiran, "We have a fuel leak…a fuel leak." Keiran rose from the side bench, following Morris. There was no need to go to end of the stern. As soon as he left the cabin, he could see the slick increasing in size. Morris stared at the growing sheen of fuel on the water's surface, reflecting a rainbow of colors from the sun's rays.

Morris glared at Keiran as he went back to the front of the cabin, his eyes suggesting that Keiran was at fault.

"Peter, the fuel gage is going down rapidly. Something must have punctured the fuel tanks."

"But what could it be? I haven't hit anything."

At first, Keiran was perplexed by the frantic conversation between Morris and his two-man crew. He surveyed the interior of the boat—every piece of wood trim highly polished, the small table and chairs immaculate, the hardwood floors buffed spotless, the interior brass trim on the widows gleaming. Like them, he couldn't believe that the boat had sprung a leak. It didn't seem reasonable.

"Mr. Hogan, can you come here, for a moment, please?" Morris's voice rose as he looked back to get Keiran's attention. Keiran hurried to the forward cabin. "Zoran wants to talk to you again."

From the police loudspeaker, Sylvester's voice boomed, "*Sostare! Sostare! Poliza*. You are leaking fuel. Follow me."

"Yes, Zoran?"

"Appears you've come up with a problem. I won't be able to meet you at the airport. However, handle the matter with police with care. Explain that you're a guest on your way to the airport and that you represent the owner. The registration of the boat is in the name of one of our companies, *Companie Delora*. Tell them you're the attorney for the company and so forth. I'll see you in Florence. Please take the evening train. Call me with your arrival time. I'll have someone meet you at the train station. You see, Keiran, how the unexpected happens. One never knows, does one? Thank you, and see you this evening." Zoran hung up, not waiting for any reply from Keiran.

"What did he say to do?" Morris asked, his attempt to hide his anxiety failing, as he took out a cigarette. Lighting it, his hands were shaking visibly.

"You're not taking me to the airport. I am the lawyer for the company that owns the boat. You are the owner's assistant and the two crewmen are also employed by the owner. Anything strange in telling the truth?"

"No, I guess not. It's just that I don't understand this leak. Look at it! It's coming from underneath the tanks. How could there be damage to our tanks? They're double hulled, made of aluminum and reinforced with steel on the outside. They're almost bullet proof," Simpson said, his eyes darting from Keiran to the police boat, now almost appearing shamed by what was now happening.

"Well apparently, they're not that secure. Not at all, not at all," Keiran replied, wondering himself now about the various events that were plaguing Zoran's schedule.

"Follow the patrol boat, Morris; don't screw that up." Keiran said, the displeasure on his face now sunk into weariness. "You're in enough trouble already."

Shaking his head back and forth in despair, Morris replied, "Hard for me to believe this can happen and to this boat. Leaking fuel? It's hard for me to understand…."

Thirty-One

Farris said, his voice sullen, "Yes, Zoran. I'll be at the meeting. You know I wouldn't forget something as important as that. I've had to wait an extra day, as the London police want to see me concerning Coborn's death. I understand they're talking to everyone who appeared on his computerized phone list…at least those of us from the past several months. Nothing to be distressed about, though. I'll see the police tomorrow around ten o'clock and then be on the one o'clock plane for Florence."

"Can't you postpone the meeting with the police? What we are doing here in Florence is much more important," Zoran asked, his tone clearly indicating that he was disturbed by being advised of yet another problem. "We need the material in your possession to conclude with our customer."

"No, I can't postpone. Besides, I simply want to get this irritant over with. Yes, yes, I know you need the material. I won't let you down and you should not think in that manner. I've sent a sealed set to Hogan and I've kept one here. He'll get what you need on time. Along with what you've experienced in Italy, I would advise that we now shut down our systems for a while. We'll wind up this contract and take a long sabbatical. We need a long vacation. You agree?" Farris concluded quietly.

"Yes," Zoran answered curtly. "Someone is closing in on us…I feel it. Ever since Dublin, there have been crazy happenings targeting me—and now your involvement in London with the Coborn mess…One wonders what will come next. We must now stay on course, Duane.

Your delay will place me in an embarrassing position. I'm upset beyond words, Duane. You are letting me down at this critical time."

"I'm not doing this intentionally. The situation here prevents me from coming. I'll be there tomorrow. Besides, perhaps the Mayfair incident…." Farris added.

"Perhaps what?" Zoran interrupted, his voice now as cold as ice. "That, Duane, is something that needs no further discussion. End. Period." A sort of strain now settled over them. Farris felt it painfully. He continued, his voice now reluctant and slow.

"There is nothing that I can tell the police other than my requests from time to time to verify information normally given to us at the ambassador's monthly meetings."

"Well, Duane, it's a regrettable matter," Zoran responded with an edge in his voice. Farris knew from history that Zoran was exasperated beyond reason that so much had gone wrong and so quickly. Yet Farris also was aware that Zoran would never admit to a mistake, and what he did at Mayfair, to Farris, was a mistake beyond all reason. All those people dead, awful, he silently told himself as he listened to Zoran's irate voice.

"I'll be in Florence tomorrow, Zoran. Keiran can attend to you in the meantime."

"Hogan is doing just that now. He left Venice by train and is on his way to meet me here."

"Is he behaving…satisfactorily?" Farris inquired, pausing between his words.

"He's been a calming influence, actually. Direct and forceful, he is. Arrogant yet studied in his manner of approach. Keiran took quick control of the situation at my villa and subsequently when the police stopped my boat in Venice harbor. From what I've seen so far, I've great confidence in him. I do."

There was now silence that seemed unnaturally intense.

"The boat problem? What boat problem? I wasn't made aware of any boat problem. Hogan hasn't briefed me on that," Farris spoke with annoyance. "You may now understand my problem with him…he doesn't inform me when he should."

"Calm down, Duane. My, my, your anxiety is worse than mine. Nothing serious. The boat sprung a leak and the harbor police took it in for violation of the pollution control laws. It's okay, Duane. Right this instant, we have more important things to worry about. Yes, Hogan is doing a very dependable job. I suspect that he was waiting for an opportunity to call you. He's been pretty busy."

"That's good," Farris responded, his voice now sounding distant and aloof. "He certainly is complicated for a young man. I still believe, though, he may be too upright for us. In my zeal, I may have been too hasty in judging that he was like us, only younger. We shall see. We shall soon see."

"You know, Duane," Zoran continued, his coldness not having faded away, "sometimes I listen to you and worry that your thoughts are, of late, somewhat scattered, and formless. I know, Duane, that you've been under a great deal of strain. So have I. Surely, Duane you still understand, that we live in a society of greedy people. I don't suspect you have forgotten that rule of life. Hogan is no different and understands this simple element of logic. After all, why is he a lawyer? To do good? Come now. I've yet to meet a lawyer who is not on the take. The pursuit of truth is not part of the game. The pursuit of victory is the only game. And, may I add, the pursuit of money. I certainly don't have to remind you, my friend, that money is the foundation of our…" Zoran paused for several moments, "…our friendship."

Farris hesitated. The frankness of Zoran's comments made Farris grave, uncertain, and perhaps even sad. He always knew there was something horrible about Zoran, and now it was being directed at him. Now, though, something like a twinge of fear, both mental and physical, went through Farris. Finally, he responded by simply saying, "I agree, Zoran. Totally agree."

"And I can assure you that after this trip, Keiran Hogan's blind lust for money will be evident. Very evident. Frankly, without that trait, he is no help to us, regardless of how bright he is," Zoran said stiffly.

"Agreed. You are correct."

There was again silence.

"Now, Duane, you do have the originals of the special materials for the customer? You must bring them with you, together with the computer discs."

"Yes, I have them. I would not have trusted them with anyone, even Hogan. No, I have them. You should not concern yourself with that issue."

"I concern myself with every issue, Duane. Goodbye. See you tomorrow."

Farris held the phone for a while, turning it to fully face him as he gazed at its mouthpiece, his lips forming words that came out as a whisper.

"There was a time, Zoran, when you would jump at my word; now you don't care for me; you don't care if I get caught…just so long as you aren't compromised." His eyes became misty, and finally he let forth a long, low guttural sound.

"You know, you never really were as loyal to me as I was to you. You're a betrayer of trust, that's all. It was me, my brainpower, that saved you over and over again…me who formed the companies that fronted from your arms deals. You're just a stupid shit head…you're brain dead without me. Goodbye, Zoran, goodbye." He spoke into the dead phone before replacing it in its cradle.

Farris sat alone in his drawing room, the chandeliers dimmed. The drapes were drawn across the windows, shutting out the late afternoon sun, and the only illumination was now coming from the lights over the oil paintings hanging in the room. In this dim light, he stared at the portrait of Sir Christopher Cradock, which hung in its place of honor over the mantle.

Oh! Did you make a mistake, you silly ass. Pretending to be strong when in fact you were weak. Believing time was on your side to stave off a blow you knew to be coming. I won't make the same mistake. No, I won't. I know clearly time is not now on my side. That luxury is something that I don't have. Not at all.

He gazed at his half-full glass of wine, slowly twisting it, watching the deep red liquid slosh around. The insulin he had taken from his wife's supply had been injected into his thigh earlier in the afternoon. It would take effect within the next hour. He had chosen insulin because he could get rid of the syringe and it would be impossible for anyone to attribute his death to anything other than a heart attack. As death would come soon, he was worried that the glass would drop from his hands, spilling liquid on the Iranian silk rug. No sense in ruining a perfectly good carpet. Gloria would not take kindly to that.

He laughed slightly, making the kind of sound that is caused by pressure rather than by ecstasy—high, detached, and discordant. A surly smile crossed his thin lips as he remembered the genesis of the carpet, which was given to him several years ago as a gift from an Iranian customer of Zoran's. The carpet had been taken from one of the palaces of the Shah, who had been deposed by Iran's new leader, the employer of Zoran's customer.

My, you're beautiful. Look at the soft green and gold threads, the vibrant leaf designs, the scrolls along the border. He held his glass tightly as he rose slowly; his eyes were fixed on the carpet as he walked across it in short steps, like a priest might pace around an altar, his face serene as if in deep prayer. How many have walked on this carpet? How many? The appraiser said this gem is over a hundred years old—older than the Shah, older than his father, from a century when others ruled. Look at this color…still intense after more than a hundred years, but for one particular section where the color was slightly diffused.

"It was caused by blood…" the customer had said, "blood from the body of one of the Shah's closest aides. Shot during the uprising…most unfortunate. Yet we cleaned it very well, very well indeed," he had advised Farris. Blood. Always blood and death. Arms of death, victorious death, always victorious. He carefully sat down on the discolored spot, holding his wine goblet securely.

It was a mistake to put Coborn on the payroll. I should have realized he was unstable. He was to eager to help me—asked few questions, did whatever I asked him to do. Yeah, his information made me richer; I sold most of what he gave me to others. Even Zoran doesn't know that

I made side deals for the intelligence Coborn gave me. Stupid Coborn. Getting himself in an ego-building posture, killing that derelict Runnard to blackmail me. I should have seen it coming. Coborn was too weak, far too weak, decrepit…feeble. Coborn, you deserved to die and I'm happy I decided to have it done. You silly ass, you stupid silly ass. You imbecile.

He was getting delirious now and, grasping for breath, his mind hurried as he stared down at the carpet. There was the faintest tremor in his face. He placed his glass down on the carpet. Freed from holding the liquid, he took one hand, and, leaning over, began to trace the intricate scrolls that ran into one another with no end and no beginning.

Alpha. Omega. Eternity. Beginning. End. The gold must be paradise; the green, earth; the red, life; black, death. Eternity. I sit on an allegory of life…my life. How I wanted to be more than I was born to be…I sold myself…oh! It was good when I had power in the firm, all those deals, those successes, the things we did together, Zoran and I. We were powerful, we were, we decided…didn't we? All things fell in order for us, Zoran—yes, even the stars, men, the silent growing things, the seas, the mountains, the plains fell in order for us to obey our command. Everyone was obedient, Zoran…obedient to us. You're right, not the obedience of love, fulfilling a lasting desire. No, the obedience was to the passion we had for money. Now, the lasting desire, it's…the gold isn't it? Paradise is gold…. Paradise is my last desire…. It will be better than here….You, who created all things, you promised paradise, didn't you? It will be a greater peace with me winging upward toward you, God.

Farris squirmed slightly, alternately staring at the glass of wine then at the scroll, continuously tracing its pattern with his index finger. So beautifully curved…endless. No end and no beginning. Perfect, isn't it? How I'll miss this place. Gloria…if only she knew how I did this for her and the family. Can't embarrass them, my two daughters…. No, can't do that, cowardly to do that. Face this like a man…face this like a man. No other way.

Stupid Zoran blowing up all those people because he was owed some money. And he didn't even ask my advice. Did it on his own. How much more has he done on his own? And now he wants these discs and engineering drawings…Hah! Hah! Shit, missile components and all that crap about guidance systems so he can sell them to the North Koreans who will then blow up even more people. What idiocy…and I'm part of it. No, I'm all of it. Without my brains and the documents I've created, nothing would ever be done. I'm the brains. That shit Zoran is nothing without me. He's dead, just like I will be. No matter, he'll never get what he wants. I lost them like all the other documents I've lost for him. You suffer now, you dumb bastard. Without those two things, the Koreans won't only fail to pay you, hopefully they'll eliminate you.

From behind him, Farris heard groaning, the faint sounds of voices calling him, voices borne on the gusts of high winds. Farris could not make them out.

"What are you saying? I can't understand." He wondered where he was, in what part of the world, whether he had begun the great route he had chosen to take—the road to his final goal, paradise. But the voices told him nothing.

"What are you saying to me?" His mind was now confused and the sound of the wind seemed more like the fury of a hurricane. He finally heard his own triumphant cry, collapsing on the carpet, the glass of wine knocked over by his hand, its liquid rapidly soaking into the fine silk. His body quivered for several moments. He tried to utter some words, and managed only a faint cry before his breathing finally stopped.

The housekeeper knocked twice on the door to the drawing room before slowly opening it.

"Mr. Farris, sir, there's an urgent call from the American Ambassador's assistant, Mr. Baldwin. He said it's important that he speak to you…." For a moment, the low light in the room prevented her from seeing his crumpled body lying of the floor.

"Mr. Farris? Mr. Farris, are you here?" She edge quietly into the room. "Mr. Farris? Mr. Farris...?" Her words stopped as her steps brought her a few meters from Farris' body, his eyes open and staring at the portrait of Sir Christopher Craddock.

“Dear, dear…Oh dear,” her voice was trembling she ran from the room, shouting, “Mrs. Farris! Mrs. Farris! You must come quickly…you must come quickly!”

Thirty-Two

Speaking cheerfully, Grayson said, "Keiran, Bob Grayson here. Hope you don't mind my giving you a ring on your cell phone. What did we do before we had these handy little gadgets? Can't escape pesky calls now, can you? Where are you now?"

"On an express train from Venice to Florence," Keiran replied, gazing out at the passing countryside, a light drizzle hitting the train window.

"Florence—as great a city as the one you're leaving. You didn't have much time, though, in Venice. Perhaps not so bad after all. You would only want to spend a long time there with someone other than a client."

"Bob," Hogan laughed, "you know how to hurt a guy. What can I do for you?"

"Just a friendly call to let you know that my own client now has me coming to Italy sometime tomorrow, and as luck would have it, I'll be in Florence myself. I had planned to head for Venice after a few days in Florence to visit you and discuss our firm's opportunities. Now that you will be in *bella Firenze*, this makes our meeting easier to arrange. How does this sound to you? We'll have dinner and discuss the plans that you suggested the other day—unless of course you have changed your mind. Have you changed your mind?"

"Didn't know you spoke Italian." There was laughter over the phone line.

"Like a native, *molte grazie*."

"*Prego*, how's that, Bob? My accent as good as yours? Don't answer that question. As for my career plans, have they changed? No. Haven't at all. Sure, let's meet. It'll be a good time for you to tell me how your firm works and what I would do if I were to join your operation. I don't think, though, that I can meet you for a few days because I'll be pretty busy with Zoran. I have no idea how long our meetings will take, but I would think not any more time than that will be needed. Where will you be staying in Florence?"

"Unclear. My secretary is making the arrangements and I'll let you know after I arrive. I assume it's okay to call you again on your cell phone. Do you know where you will be staying yourself?"

"Just as uncertain about where I'll drop my bags as you are. One thing is positive, though. I'll be picked up at the train station by Zoran's security staff. Then, and then only, will I know where I'll be staying. I can call you if you give me your cell phone number. Come to think of it, I only have your office and home phones…not your secret cell phone number."

"That number I keep for very special people. You're almost in that class…but not quite."

"Am I hearing what you just said correctly?" Keiran sounded stricken…then he laughed loudly.

"I'm so on the move and I turned this damn thing off often, otherwise, I'd be bothered all the time by the infernal beep. So I really use it for outgoing calls, not so much for incoming. Giving you the number is probably a waste of time as I wouldn't answer the phone anyway."

"Not a bad idea keeping the phone turned off; I'd like to do it myself. The only problem I have is that one of Kenton & Ward's office rules is to keep the office-assigned cell phone on all the time, even when you're plugging it in for a battery recharge. Instant communication is what is desired by Mr. Farris. If you've got a different rule on that score, probably one of the best reasons to talk to you. On that basis alone, seems like a sensible place to work."

"You're gathering the right impressions about my place, Keiran. What have you been doing to keep yourself busy and out of trouble?"

"Today was a regular day. Bullets interrupted my breakfast at Zoran's villa, followed this afternoon by a few hours spent with the Venice Harbor police. All in all, the wish for a peaceful, slow day went by the boards. Zoran believes that a competitor is after him and is trying to scare him away from doing some deals. I don't believe that he scares easily, though. Then, on top of the bullet scare, his cruiser, which was taking me to the airport, sprung a fuel leak. A big 'no-no' in Venice. We were stopped by the Harbor police for a pollution violation. Zoran wasn't on the boat. He had already left earlier in the day. Long story, but after paying the fine of lira equivalent of $1,500, the police insisted that the cruiser be towed to a repair shop. I didn't stay around to find out the cause of the leak. Zoran's staff assistant will take care of that. Besides, Zoran wanted me to catch this Eurostar speed train to Florence. Right now, I've just finished a beer and was settling down for a couple hours sleep until you called. So nothing much eventful happened today."

"Bullets? Fuel leaks? Have you had too much beer? No, can't be that. You don't drink that much. You must be dazed."

"Dazed? No, being shot at is something that I accept. It's the leaking boat that irritated me." Keiran laughed, but it was the now the laughter of disillusionment, hard and bitter.

"You hang around some strange clients," Grayson replied, speaking slowly. "Dangerous stuff you're in, young man, huh?"

"Come on now, Bob," Keiran answered, dismissing Grayson's comment. "Law firms live on a system of attachment to clients, maybe even to flawed ones. Not such a terribly new approach…even for you. Anyway, Zoran told me he is pretty confident of his pursuer—if one really exists or if it's just his paranoid habits. Who knows? Maybe it's another competitor. His kind of business certainly doesn't attract angels. What more can I say? Your place a bit more peaceful? Better behaved clients, I assume?"

"Perfect clients. Perfectly suited clients, I must admit. Absolutely perfect, just like *Mary Poppins*." Grayson laughed slightly.

"The privileged life of a lawyer who has perfect clients. You are so fortunate Bob, so very fortunate," Keiran replied, his voice having the edge of sarcasm.

"Hey, don't get so nasty! I'm your friend, remember? Anyhow, I'll see you later. Will give you a jingle—that's if you haven't turned your phone off."

"Are you listening Bob? I can't. Firm rules. I'm a slave to this piece of equipment. See you when I see you."

"It won't be long, Keiran. Not at all. Try to remain sunny, joyful, and of course, sweet dreams."

"Yeah, sure."

Keiran flipped the cover of his phone closed, placing it in his side pocket. The ring, set on loud, would not be muffled enough so that he would not be able to hear it. Strange though, he silently told himself, when he answered the phone, his caller ID indicated that Grayson's call originated in Italy…in Florence. He's already there? He can't be; I'll have to have this phone checked out. Right now, I'm beat. I need some shut-eye.

He arranged the pillow the attendant had brought him, moved his chair leg rest as he reclined his seat, placing the dark green flannel blanket over his legs. The sound of the train moving at high speed lulled him to sleep quickly. It had been a very long day—one he would always remember whole and in detail. Reaching up, he turned off the reading light and quickly dropped into a deep rest.

Zoran was displeased. He had left the meeting with his Asian customers to take a telephone call from Farris. Without the material Farris held, the deal could not be concluded. He glanced at his watch, noting it was 7:00, an hour past the time Farris would have arrived if he hadn't changed his plans.

I'll take care of him later. Preoccupied with that damn stupid mole. I told him that that guy would eventually cause us trouble. But, no, he didn't listen to me. Then he had to call on my people to arrange the 'suicide.' To me, Duane, your usefulness is approaching its end. I don't like messy surprises like what you're doing to me tonight. No, Duane, not tonight. Of all times, not now.

As Zoran hurried back into the dining room of his villa in Fiesole, he frowned and stopped for a moment, thinking that he had heard someone behind him. Turning quickly, he noted only his own bodyguard trailing him by a few steps. Strangely, he had forgotten that bodyguards always accompanied him. Shaking his head slightly, he muttered quietly, "I have to control myself. I must have the forbearance of a stone. Don't show otherwise."

His assistant moved quickly in front of him to open the dining room door, holding it open. Zoran strode into the room, which was brightly lit by two chandeliers centered on the dining room ceiling, their brilliance directed on the table and casting shadows on the cream-colored walls, carefully decorated with oil landscapes of the Tuscan region. Seated at the oblong mahogany table were Ho-Lee, the procurement advisor to the North Korean Prime Minister, Sun Chung Han, the head of the North Korean Missile Program, and four bodyguards who had accompanied them—at least that is who Zoran assumed they were. Perhaps they were members of the North Korean intelligence services. It didn't matter. They never spoke. Zoran sat down at the head of the table, alone but for his own two assistants and without his counsel, whom he knew he would miss. Regardless of Hogan's smarts, he could not really replace Farris. I'll have to wing it for a while. No other alternative. Zoran's thoughts were silent. The steady and increasingly heavy rain, forcefully hitting the room's tightly drawn, lace-curtained windows, didn't make the atmosphere in room any more pleasant.

Weather delay. Yeah, weather delay. I'll say Farris was delayed by the bad weather. But the plane he was supposed to be on has landed…and landed safely. Concentrate now, Zoran. Don't be a fool. It'll all work out, he reassured himself as he surveyed the faces of his guests, who were now all looking at him, believing that something was wrong because of Farris' absence.

"Gentlemen, the weather has delayed my advisor's attendance. He is on a plane from London, but as you can see," Zoran glanced toward the dining room windows, "the rain is quite heavy. June is an unsettled month in this part of Italy…inclement weather today, sun tomorrow." Zoran forced a smile. "Nevertheless, Mr. Farris' own assistant, Keiran Hogan, whom I believe you, Mr. Ho-Lee, met in Dublin, will be joining us in about thirty minutes. He is on the express train from Venice. Regardless, I believe that all the papers are in order. If there are any last-minute changes, we can make them when Mr. Hogan arrives, but I don't think there will be anything significant. We agreed to everything in Dublin, despite the interruption at that time."

The North Koreans looked at Zoran, their faces not indicating in any fashion what they were thinking. In point of fact, Zoran told himself, there certainly wasn't any shining radiance as he looked at the two officials, their faces complete masks, eyes hidden behind gray-tinted black horn rimmed glasses. They were never friendly, only respectful. Of all the customers he had over the years, these men, dressed in identical, semi-Nehru styled dark blue suits, he found to be the least friendly. Even at the few social occasions, such as dinner or lunch, they were silent, not engaging in conversation unless he or Farris had commenced speaking. Although their English was excellent when they did speak, their responses to questions were always taut, without elaboration. It appeared to Zoran that they didn't enjoy speaking at all, at least not in English. The officials would speak to him in English and then to each other in Korean. Yet he had never hired his own translator to be at these meetings—he was beginning to think this had been a mistake on his part. Zoran had agreed with Farris that the absolute confidentiality of these meetings took precedence over having a translator who could not be trusted. Besides, what he was doing—selling guidance missile technology and the related computer programs—wasn't clean legally, regardless of how Farris had structured this deal. Yet, Zoran admitted, Farris was normally cleverer than he was in terms of hiding the true character of this particular deal. Damn, damn, Duane is clever, but where in the hell is he now? Zoran silently contemplated, momentarily toying with the pencil in front of him, trying to appear calm and without worry.

The missile guidance system diagrams were stolen by the U. S. Air Force Missile Command's Deputy Chief of Staff. At the age of 48, he was passed over for promotion to Brigadier General because of a sexual harassment charge against him, later proven to be baseless. Nevertheless, that event had effectively ended his career. Colonel William Meade wasn't so much bitter as he was determined to make sure that whatever loss of revenue he would have to absorb as a result of the non-promotion and subsequent forced retirement would not be permanently lost. Downloading the missile system guidance program from his computer was a fairly simple job. He had security clearance that allowed him access to all such data. Hard copies of the schematic diagrams of the guidance system itself proved a bit more troublesome. The sheets were large, about three feet by three feet, and ran some twenty-five pages. Reviewing them in the secure document room at the Pentagon, he decided to put in a request for a new set, telling his enlisted airman assistant that the present set appeared to be a bit worn. Normally, the original from which the copy is made is destroyed when the new copy is made. This time, he asked that both be given to him.

"I'll take care of the destruction of the original," he had told the enlisted man who was handling the document room document requests. He folded the old copy as best he could and forced the large bundle into his briefcase. He had simply cut out the small bar code from each page, thus removing the only security device that would have alerted the guards as he left the Pentagon through the electronic screening doors.

Although much guidance data was on the copied computer disc, Colonel Meade believed the material would have more worth if he had actual hard copies from the manufacturer of the system that guided the medium range missile, Alpha-5, toward its target some 5,000 kilometers distance. His instincts were right.

To avoid suspicion, Meade waited several months after his departure from the Air Force before he attempted to peddle the material. He was ready to sell the diagrams and computer disc for two million dollars, the amount he had calculated he had lost due to the early discharge and non-promotion. He told himself that he just wanted to be fair. That he was selling out his country never crossed his mind. A government that worries whether and with whom I screw is not really interested in defense, he had rationalized. They're worried about insignificant things.

Shortly after he left the Air Force, he signed on as a consultant to a company specializing in the export and import of airplane parts and materials. Through a network of retired Air Force friends and associates, he heard of a company located in Singapore that was hoping to open a representative office in the United States. Meade had contacted them to tell them that he was now available for employment. He signed on because they granted his wish to open the office in San Diego and would basically leave him alone, without any real supervision. It wasn't long before he discovered that the company's clients included countries with which the United States had embargoed trade. On a trip to Singapore, he was involved in a discussion centered on missile parts for a 'special client.' He said that he had access to some material, but that the cost would be high…some two million dollars.

"Show me a sample," was the reply of the company owner, Peter Yew. When Yew arrived in San Diego a month later, Meade showed him not only the sample, but also the complete set.

"Two million."

"Okay, I'll take it."

"Once I have the money, I'm quitting. Understood?"

"Understood. We close the office. Not of any concern, not at all," Yew had responded. "You Americans. I'll never understand you. Such a beautiful country, so much freedom."

"Please, Peter, no moralizing. It's not becoming for either of us, especially you, who helps arm all those drug lords in Asia. Do you want the information or not?"

"Certainly. It's just that when I first met you, I had the feeling that, how shall I say this, you were one of us. How fortunate to have met you, William. How very fortunate."

"I'm not one of you, Peter. Not at all." Meade spoke emphatically, appearing like an indigent man caught in the act of shoplifting claiming he was about to pay for the goods when caught.

"Of course. I misspoke, William, just misspoke. That's all."

Yew had asked for and obtained a substantial discount on arms he was buying from Zoran when he turned over the missile documents and computer disc to him.

"This will make up the difference in the cash I don't have right now," is what Yew had told him. Zoran didn't believe Yew, who lived like a modern-day millionaire. "The Koreans are looking for this. I'll see what I can arrange."

"Why don't you sell it to them yourself?"

"Ah! Zoran, my friend. Even I know when I shouldn't sell something."

"It's stolen?"

"Yes," Yew replied. "I only deal in legitimate arms sales." They both laughed. "No, Zoran, I really need the arms. I've promised them to the guys, you know, next door. Very long story, but I need the discount. You take these papers. I don't need them. I need the discount." Zoran gave him the discount, knowing full well that Yew was either in trouble with his own customers, having perhaps reneged on promises, or had borrowed funds that he had to repay quickly. Zoran accommodated him not only because he was a good customer, but also because he knew the data provided by Yew was worth much more than the discount he was giving him.

It was a few months later that Zoran and Farris met the people now watching him in his dining room. The negotiations with the North Koreans began with their immediate distrust of what Zoran promised he had. To convince them, he took a calculated risk of showing them one sheet and asking them to take it back to their own labs for study. It was three months before Zoran heard from them again.

Their meeting started out strangely. Mr. Ho-Lee showed up in Geneva, called him and asked him to come to meet with them quickly.

"We will be here for only a couple of days. Can you come on such short notice?" It was a respectful request, always quietly respectful, Zoran thought. Yet when Mr. Ho-Lee called, his tone was direct. He expected Zoran to say yes, and Zoran complied.

He and Farris left immediately on Zoran's private plane. It was at that meeting that a solid commitment to engage him was made by Mr. Ho-Lee.

"We need the rest of the material that you have for sale. Shall we discuss the amount necessary for that to happen?" Thereafter, it was a speedy discussion of the amount of money and how that money would be transferred. Zoran was surprised at how quickly Ho-Lee agreed to the $50 million price tag.

"They probably would have given me more," he had told Farris during a break between meeting sessions. To hide such a transfer, the Koreans would also buy 300,000 metric tons of cement, shipping it via Singapore. The bill of landing would indicate Singapore and it would be sold to one of Yew's companies, which in turn would break up the shipment and send a very small part of it on to the North Koreans and keep the rest for resale.

"Better for me this way," Yew had told Zoran. The Koreans understood the scheme and had no objections. "Whatever you wish, Mr. Hemmrich. We have no objection to this method. We understand how difficult it would be for you and your company otherwise," Ho-Lee had said at their Geneva meeting.

The $50 million price tag included the transportation and insurance charges for the cement. All in all, a solid review-proof deal. The cement was to be shipped over a period of six months, but the complete set of drawings and related computer data would be handed over to the Koreans at the time the first shipment was arriving in Singapore. That arrival date was set for the day after the meeting in Florence.

One-half of the funds had already been placed in one of Benton Industries' Channel Islands bank accounts. Now, Zoran had to turn over the rest of the documents to the Korean customers. The fact was that Farris had the set of drawings with him, and if he didn't arrive, or have an explanation for his absence, then the deal would be off. The funds on deposit would have to be returned, and Zoran was afraid that the Koreans would seek revenge, believing that advantage had been taken of them somehow. His anxiety increasing, Zoran now felt afraid. His main bodyguard assistant, Alan Simpson, was tied up in Venice trying to get the cruiser repaired after discovering that bullet holes had caused the fuel leak. And of course, the bullets earlier in the morning at his villa didn'thing to diminish his fright. Still, he could not show this emotion.

He spoke haltingly now, "Shall we have some light refreshments while we wait for Mr. Hogan to arrive?"

"Mr. Hemmrich, do you have the material that we came to get?" Mr. Ho-Lee asked.

"Yes, of course."

"Well, then, why can't we proceed right now? We can have refreshments later. Yes, later would be better. My preference would be that we conduct our business first. Wouldn't you agree, Mr. Hemmrich?" Ho-Lee said, looking steadily at Zoran with unblinking eyes.

"Naturally. I have to inform you, though, that the material is with Mr. Farris and that Mr. Hogan also has a set. So, whoever arrives first will have the material you want. I'm sorry that there has been a slight delay. Not to worry though. All will be finalized shortly. But we have to wait until one arrives."

"We are a very patient people, Mr. Hemmrich. Very patient." Mr. Ho-Lee turned to his colleagues addressing them in Korean for a few moments. Then he turned, "You do expect your aides to arrive tonight?"

Several moments passed in silence. Zoran, his hands clasped together and motionless on the table, finally spoke, saying softly, "Yes, I do."

"If they don't," Ho-Lee continued, almost in a murmur, "I would request that the contract be canceled and that you return our funds immediately via the usual channels. Of course, we would want to cancel the remaining shipments of cement. However, once the special material is available again, you may contact us at that time. We have a great deal of respect for you, Mr. Hemmrich. Yet it's hard for us to understand why you don't have the material here. You knew we were coming some time ago. First Venice and then you urged us to come to Florence and to your villa here. Surely you have made arrangements to conclude our contract. Otherwise, why did you invite us to come?"

"As I explained to you, Mr. Farris, my counsel has all the documents with him. He had them in a secure place in London and it was his task to bring them here for you. Mr. Hogan has a second set, which he will bring. This was a backup copy made just in case the originals were delayed for some reason…as is the case now. We do our planning correctly and thus have the backup plan I have just described." In a studied show of anger and frustration, Zoran continued, "Frankly, and with all respect, I'm taken aback by the admonition that I didn't plan the conclusion of this deal properly. That just isn't the case. There's no reason for us not to complete this deal. None whatsoever."

Mr. Ho-Lee smiled, his lips barely parting. "Naturally. Certainly, we mean nothing untoward. As you say, it's your staff that has been delayed. So we shall wait. Thirty minutes is not too precious a time period to wait for the material. But you can understand our own anxiety. We have waited so very long for these matters to be concluded. Our comments aren't personal in any fashion. We do owe you a debt of gratitude. So we shall wait. Perhaps now we shall have some refreshments."

Zoran knew Ho-Lee was lying. And Ho-Lee, he suspected, knew that he was stalling. Hogan didn't have a second set of the diagrams, nor did he have a copy of the computer disc. Neither Zoran nor Farris would have trusted Hogan or anyone else with this interaction. They had been with Farris in his personal office safe for over a year—the time needed to conclude the deal—sealed in several large envelopes and untouched, or so Farris had assured him.

"Let me call Mr. Hogan and see if I can reach him on the train. Will that make you feel more comfortable that we are indeed not asking for more unnecessary time?"

"Whatever is your will, Mr. Hemmrich. We have confidence in you. However, it's up to you to call your own staff and verify whatever concerns you. We will excuse you if you wish to make the call outside."

"No, no, no. I'll make it right here so that you will be assured we are doing all we can to conclude this matter." Zoran took out his cell phone and pressed in Keiran's number, hoping that he could reach him on the train. The short repetitive burst went on for several moments, until Keiran answered, his voice groggy as if he had been sleeping.

"I hope this isn't you again, Bob." His voice was barely above a whisper.

"No, it's not Bob. It's Zoran, Keiran. Did I wake you from a nap?" There was a long pause of silence.

"Zoran. I'm sorry; I must have dozed a bit. Yes. I'm almost to Florence, I think. Let's see, my watch says a quarter to seven and we are scheduled to arrive at…."

"Seven-ten, I know. One of my assistants will be there to pick you up. He'll identify himself, but I believe you've seen him before. His name is Armand, Armand Roubier. He'll take you to our villa in Fiesole, a small town about 20 minutes away, perhaps thirty minutes in this rain. We are waiting for you to arrive. I assume that you have brought the material with you."

Material…? Hogan thought for a moment. What is he talking about?

"I have copies of the same contractual documents and financial sheets that you have, nothing in addition. Mr. Farris did tell me that he was bringing some additional material for you, though. Is he on his way?"

"Yes. He's been delayed by the weather. Should expect him later this evening. Are you having a pleasant train trip?"

"Yeah. This is a beautiful train. Can't beat the ride, actually."

"Well, that's good. We'll see you shortly. Don't forget the material. We'll need it directly upon your arrival here at the villa. See you then, Keiran."

'Okay. Goodbye Zoran. See you in due course."

As Zoran pressed the close button on his phone, he knew that to extricate himself from what now was appearing to be a failed deal, he would make a spectacle of Keiran in front of the customers. He had to. There was no alternative. First and foremost, he had to save himself. Before that, though, he'd meet with Keiran alone and explain what had happened and that it would be necessary for him to take the fall. Isn't that what a client's lawyer is supposed to do? Hadn't Farris taken the fall so many times before for him? There will be no change in the method. Farris had better have those documents and disc. God, he'd better have them.

Keiran tried to sort out the brief conversation with Zoran. Maybe, still half asleep, he was hearing things that were not really spoken. But that wasn't usually a problem for him. He understood perfectly well exactly what Zoran was saying—was he bringing the material?

What the hell is he talking about? Keiran asked himself. This is all crazy. Keiran reached under his seat for his briefcase, pressing the arm button to raise the back of his seat and lower his leg rest. Opening it, he quickly read through all his files. All he had were the contracts and other papers relating to the contract. Zoran had the originals and like Farris, he had copies. Crazy, just crazy, he thought as he fished in his case for his toiletries kit and left his seat to go to the restroom and clean up before his arrival. Some cold water on his face and brushing his teeth would help his psyche.

Thirty-Three

As he stepped out of the car that Zoran had sent to bring him from the Florence railway station, Keiran knew this meeting would not be a merry one. Uncharacteristically, Zoran was standing inside the open villa doorway, waiting for him, flanked as usual by two assistants. The bright light coming from the foyer where Zoran stood bounced off the heavy rain, giving the appearance of heavy meteor shower in the sky. Keiran hurried in, exclaiming as he ducked into the entryway, "Not a good night, sir. Not at all." Keiran extended his hand.

"Not at all," Zoran repeated caustically, his smile tired and fixed, his right hand jutting forward to shake Keiran's, who noted that it was sweaty and shaking. "Please come in. There are some preliminary matters that I want to go over with you before we go into the dining room where my customer is waiting." Zoran walked briskly into an anteroom just off the front entrance. A glass-topped coffee table was in the center, surrounded by several red and gray striped damask upholstered chairs. The room's walls were a very dull gray, the floor covered with an Oriental carpet in shades of gray and red.

"Here, we can have some privacy," Zoran muttered anxiously as he sat down, waving aside his assistants, who immediately left the room, closing the double door quietly behind them.

Keiran sat next to him, placing his briefcase gently on the table. He had left his suitcase in the car, hoping that one of the assistants would bring it in—if, in fact, he was going to stay the night at this villa, which was more garishly furnished that the one in Venice.

"Why the tension in your voice, Zoran? Is something wrong with the contract and the customer?" Keiran was solicitous in his manner, noting that Zoran was obviously distressed and jittery.

"Well, perhaps yes, perhaps no," he answered, his dark eyes fixed on Keiran. His host was clearly pensive, unhappy, and worried. He sat on the edge of his chair, ready to leap, it seemed to Keiran, at any given moment, probably hearing his own heart pounding.

"First, Keiran, I appreciate again how well you handled the situation in Venice, especially helping Simpson when my boat was stopped by the police." He was now looking up at Keiran gently. "However, I have some very disturbing news regarding that incident. Simpson called me to tell me that the leak was caused by three bullet holes in the fuel tanks."

"Bullet holes? How? When? I heard nothing that sounded at all like the bullets that hit your villa's terrace. Nothing at all," Keiran replied, shaking his head, his eyebrows not knotted in surprise.

"That is what Simpson told me. He is fairly accurate in his information and I have no reason to doubt what he has relayed."

"What are the police doing with the boat now?" Keiran asked.

"They've impounded it, trying to figure out what happened. They've asked Simpson and the crew to stay a day or so to answer any questions. True, it could have been one of these environmental groups trying to stir up trouble by causing even more pollution, maybe to test out the police reaction and so forth. I don't know. But Simpson said the questions have not been probing. You may have to go back to Venice and attend to that matter. I'd like to keep all of this out of the press, obviously. I can't concern myself about that right now. A much more serious matter now confronts us. Farris will be late to our meeting. He was unable to leave London this evening and won't be with us until tomorrow morning, noon at the earliest. He is bringing the additional and most crucial contractual material with him. It is needed for the completion of the sale. I need your help in this."

"Sir…?"

"Please, Keiran, I've asked you to call me Zoran."

"Sorry. Zoran, the only documents I have are those that you and he both have—the contract for the cement you're selling."

"Of course. Absolutely," Zoran exclaimed, his voice becoming unsteady. He seemed at times to be stuttering from pure fright. Was a guy like this really scared? No way, Keiran thought.

"Nevertheless, Keiran, you must do what I am going to ask of you. I am not in the mood to argue with my lawyer. Especially not at this moment."

"Well, first, let's see what it's that is bothering you, and what needs to be done," Keiran asked, patiently. He reached over to open his briefcase to get out his writing pad.

" No, no. No notes. You can easily remember what I am about to tell you. My customer is waiting for the material that we contracted to sell him," Zoran said, now nervously eying Keiran.

"What material? As I understand the contract, a portion of the cement is due tomorrow in Singapore. What has gone wrong? Is that delivery not to be made? Start from the beginning, Zoran. I have to know everything."

"There's nothing wrong with the cement shipments, neither the one scheduled for tomorrow nor the subsequent ones."

"Well then," Keiran asked frankly, "what could be wrong?"

"There is an additional element to this shipment that I was under the impression Duane had discussed with you."

"Zoran, let's stop this vagueness. What element? Aside from the cement deal, Farris discussed nothing additional with me. Nothing else. He didn't share with me any dark secrets about this business deal."

"You're absolutely certain?"

"Zoran," Keiran interrupted angrily, "this conversation, sir, with all due respect, is beginning to irritate me. Listen to me. Why would I tell you any different? Maybe Farris told you one thing and forgot—deliberately or otherwise—to tell me."

"Well, that is hard to believe. Don't the two of you talk to one another? This is ridiculous. I'll see that it doesn't happen again. You don't know about an integral part of the deal. Truly amazing. I'm shocked that Duane didn't tell you," Zoran was now pounding out his words with his fist. "See, even my number one lawyer is letting me down. I'll tend to him later. Regardless, Keiran, let me tell you the problem." Suddenly, he became humble, almost anxious to please, a change that, for Keiran, made an erratic situation even more confusing.

"Be specific, Zoran. No crap."

Zoran smiled nervously.

"Come on now. Relate the story."

"Well, when we go into the meeting room, and after pleasantries, I will ask you if you have the special material. You'll have to say no, of course. I will berate you, and it may be harsh. This will all be an act, as I have no right to be upset with you; only Farris will feel the real brunt of my anger. He has let me down and I'll never let him forget what he has done. Never!" Zoran shouted, now rising from this chair and pacing the room, his head down, repeating again, "Never!"

Looking down at Keiran, who was still seated, he explained, "That, Keiran, my counsel, is the only way we will save this contract. Farris is delayed and, unless I can keep the customer here overnight, we won't have a contract and I'll have to return the advance that they have deposited in our bank account for this deal…a deal that I don't want to lose. Do you understand?" Zoran returned to his seat, now visibly sweating, drops of moisture appearing on his forehead.

"You want me to take the fall for something that I know nothing about, right? A bit nutty, if you ask me, Zoran."

"Right. Attorneys do that for clients, don't they? Listen carefully, Keiran. This deal will be my last. Both Farris and I want to retire from the stress of these kinds of highly competitive business contracts. The last few weeks have enforced my view on that." Zoran spoke softly, like a man who had seen the future and accepted it. "I need your help in getting to that point. As my attorney, I must ask you to understand what it's we are trying to accomplish. A great deal of money is at stake here. Without your cooperation, I'm finished. I'll make it worth your while, over and above what the firm pays you, if you'll help me out right now. You can't abandon me right now, when I need you the most."

Keiran made no reply, but looked directly at Zoran for several moments, the uncomfortable silence broken only by the incessant ring of his cell phone. He frankly didn't know if Zoran was faking his anguish or was genuinely concerned. How can a client as skilled as this one is say with a straight face that he's finished if an associate doesn't cooperate? It was crazy, just crazy, Keiran thought to himself silently.

"I'm sorry, Zoran. I have to take this. It may be from my office. I'd like to turn it off, but rules are that we have to keep it on."

"Okay. Be brief, though. We have to get back to our customer. But," Zoran hesitated, "Understand that I don't want you to do something that you wish not to do."

Keiran remained silent as he took out the phone from his side pocket, flipping open the top.

"Keiran Hogan."

"Keiran, this is Diana, I don't know where you're exactly, but don't let on about what I am telling you, especially if you're with your client."

"Hi, Mom. Fancy you reaching me in Italy. I'm having trouble hearing you, though. Speak a bit louder. How are things going? You and Dad, are you on your way to visit me?"

"Listen, Farris is dead," Diana's voice hushed and distressed. "Yeah, I know you probably think this is joke, but it isn't. He was found late this afternoon in his house. They think it was a heart attack. I don't think your client knows yet. He probably won't know until the morning when someone from the firm will start notifying clients. I think there is something fishy here, though. He watched his health so carefully, his weight, saw the doctor every six months.... I just don't believe it."

"Oh? No, I didn't know that. So you'll be coming later than planned?"

"Keiran, what's even stranger is that the police have a list of the phone calls that Farris made to the embassy guy who killed himself, Coborn. Know the name? Get this; they think Coborn and Farris had something going. What, we don't yet know. Maybe you should be careful. HenHen said the police want to interview all of us at the firm. Especially those who worked closely with him—that's you, love. I'm worried about you, Keiran. Are you in a safe place? Can you get away? Your client may be a bit creepy, if you know what I mean."

"Certainly, Mom. When I get back to London, I'll check on the hotel and other reservations. Don't worry, Mom. I'm fine."

"Call me later when you can. I'll have more info. Again, be careful. I don't want you to get hurt."

"Okay, Mom. I love you too." Keiran returned the phone to his side pocket, trying hard to maintain his composure and trying to sort out what Diana had told him. Farris dead? Impossible. What in the hell is going on? Am I sitting across a guy that emanates bad karma? And he wants me to take a fall for something about which I know nothing.

"Everything fine with your family?" Zoran inquired.

"Yes. Thanks for letting me take the call. My mother is such a worrier."

"Mothers generally are. Well now, we must go in. I ask you to help me in this matter, Keiran. I'll reward you handsomely. I certainly will."

Keiran made no reply as he rose from his chair, following Zoran, who opened the anteroom door and held it for Keiran. Together, they went down the corridor, followed by the two assistants who had been waiting outside the room.

They strode silently, side-by-side down the short, burnt colored, ceramic tiled floor to its end, which opened into a large room that was brightly lit by a crystal chandelier. Everyone rose as Zoran walked in. He spoke quickly.

"Please gentlemen, be seated. Well, now...." His voice was businesslike and low as he returned to the head of the oval mahogany table, sitting down and gesturing to Keiran to sit at his left. "This young man is Keiran Hogan, Duane Farris's key associate in developing our contract. Keiran, you already know Mr. Ho-Lee, the procurement advisor to the North Korean Prime Minister." Keiran stood and reached over the table to shake his hand.

"Nice to see you again, sir."

Silently, Keiran's concern for what was going on heightened as he focused on what he had just heard, "procurement advisor to the North Korean Prime Minister."

"Mr. Sun Chung-Han, scientific advisor to the Prime Minister."

"My pleasure to meet you, Mr. Chung-Han." Scientific advisor? What the hell is Zoran selling to these guys besides cement? Keiran wondered. This wasn't good, not good at all.

"Dreadful weather, gentlemen. Untimely rainstorm has prevented Farris from arriving tonight. He is to be with us no later than noon tomorrow. I just spoke to him and he has assured me of that. Regardless, Mr. Hogan is here, so we can now proceed. Keiran do you have all the documents?" Zoran asked softly, his expression solicitous as if he were asking his staff for another cup of coffee.

The beginning of the game. Keiran looked at Zoran, whose lips were tight as he asked Keiran the question. He could not help but feel the stare of three sets of eyes on him as he opened his briefcase, bringing out several folders, placing them in front of him but not opening any.

"Where would you gentlemen like to start? The main contract or the appendices regarding the delivery timetable and financial schedules?" Keiran asked, ignoring Zoran's question about additional documents.

"Well, we're very familiar with the material in your folders, Mr. Hogan. What we are waiting for is the schematic diagrams and computer discs of the special equipment that we ordered along with the cement. Do you have those items?" Mr. Ho-Lee asked, his voice soft and serene.

"Of course," Zoran interjected, "you do have those, Keiran, don't you?"

With that statement, Keiran knew the act had begun. There was no sense in embarrassing the client in front of his customer, but there was also no sense in demeaning himself. Requesting him to lie would, in effect, end his career with this client. And Farris was now dead. He had no idea what this meant at the firm, for him, or for the client.

"The schematic diagrams and computer discs. Certainly. The only problem is, I don't have them," Keiran responded softly, his tone businesslike and even. "There must be a misunderstanding. Mr. Farris insisted on handling these highly important matters himself. Before I left London, I asked him if there was anything further I should bring with me on this trip and he said he would take along whatever else would be needed. I'm sorry, but I don't have the additional material you want at this time. I'm sure, though, that Mr. Farris will have those items tomorrow when he arrives."

He heard Zoran's sigh as he finished talking.

"Mr. Hogan, Mr. Hemmrich," Chung-Han spoke now, his voice barely above a whisper, "we are most disappointed that the material is not here. As you know, upon your advice we went to Venice to meet you, then you hurriedly change the site of the meeting to Florence. We accommodated you in this change of venue. Now, you tell us the material we came for is not available. This is unpleasant news, Mr. Hogan, Mr. Hemmrich. Most disagreeable. We are losing confidence that you indeed have the items we have bought."

Zoran looked again to Keiran, his eyes pleading for help. But what could Keiran say beyond what he already had said? The material these guys wanted no one had. And what is the material, anyway?

Keiran turned to Mr. Ho-Lee, "You are missing...?"

"Schematic diagrams of an advance missile guidance systems, one that provides accurate altitude and heading, stabilization, vertical reference, direction and so forth, as well as the computer discs that have all the details for the system we have purchased," Ho-Lee finished, his voice betraying no emotion. Keiran was silent as he surveyed the group. That was the sale, something that could not be put on the manifesto of the cement shipment. A hidden purchase of a product prohibited for sale to North Koreans. He knew this was illegal trade from his time in Washington working on trade issues.

"Well, Keiran, I am disappointed in both you and Duane. It appears to me that you have not organized yourself for this meeting. It is embarrassing to me to be this unprepared. Our customer must believe that, despite four meetings with them and the many phone conversations leading to this final session, the material that is part of the agreement is not here. Most unsettling. Most frustrating," Zoran said with a forced smile, revealing now a less than enthusiastic reception for Keiran.

Keiran, trying to control his anger and disgust, reached over and took his files, replacing them in his briefcase, not responding to Zoran's comment. He had no sympathy for Zoran. He knew he didn't belong either with the client or with the firm. This experiment in London was over for him.

"Mr. Hemmrich. There is no need to continue at this point. We can wait until Mr. Farris arrives. This is an understandable delay. We continue to be surprised that you waited until the last moment to arrange for the additional material to be delivered to us. Reason would dictate, would it not, that you have the material a few days ahead of our arrival," Mr. Sun Chung-Han spoke in a hushed tone, his hands steady on the note pad in front of him. "I believe there is no alternative other than to wait. Perhaps you could give Mr. Farris another call to make sure he will be on his way tomorrow?"

"Of course. I just spoke to him earlier but, certainly." He glanced at Keiran with no expression in his eyes, bearing his disappointment stoically. "Keiran, see to it. Call Duane and ask about his latest itinerary. We want to be certain he is on his way."

The most direct route from Florence to Fiesole is a narrow, winding road that makes its way to the hills, where the town sits overlooking its larger neighbor to the northeast. On this road, which straightens out just before entering the town, are large ornate villas hidden from view by imposing walls and gates, all with commanding views of Florence and the surrounding countryside. Also on this road is the electric substation that supports Fiesole. A large metal sign in bold black letters against a white background attached to the substation's chain link fence warns any wanderer to stay away. '*Pericolo. E vietato entrare.*' The substation's two electric generators are housed in a small brick building, ivy covering one side of the windowless structure. One generator was always running and a backup spare, most often silent, comes on whenever the power is interrupted by an overload, which is most often caused by lightening strikes on the adjacent tower.

Outside the building, wires from the pylon brought electricity into the station where it was transformed by the generators into a level safe for distribution to the town. From the substation, supply cables were split into a number of feeders, and then taken overhead into the town's many homes and businesses. A feeder line ran into a small, gray transformer that was attached to the top of a pole about 15 meters from Zoran's villa. Lines from this transformer further reduced voltage before it was fed into the villas occupying the street.

Flood lights illuminated the facade of Zoran's three-storied, pale yellow, classic, tailored home, mostly hidden behind a similarly colored four-meter-high wall, its entrance way barred by a closed wrought iron gate. Clearly visible through the gate were three black sedans—two Mercedes and one Volvo. Lights shone through the sheer drapes in all the rooms facing the villa's front, giving it a festive look, as if a party was going on inside.

The rain pelted the white paneled van, printed across both sides, the logo of Monte Edison Italiana. Two men, dressed in heavy black ponchos, exited the side door. Working quickly at the base of the pole that held the transformer, they attached a circular plastic package, about six inches in diameter, around the base of the pole. The men molded the material, pressing it tightly against the wood, and then closed the circle by inserting a miniature electronic ignition cap. After checking to see if the material would hold, the men disappeared into the van, which drove slowly down the street, stopping at the cross street farthest away from the pole, still in a position to observe it and Zoran's villa.

"Ready?" Grayson asked.

"Everything's set," one of the men replied.

The second man held a small radio transmitter in his hand. Looking at Grayson again, he pressed down on the button that sent a low-wattage radio signal to the miniature receiver at the base of the pole, causing an intense, brief flash. In split seconds, the base of the pole exploded, sending the pole across the road, its transformer crashing down on the street, wires pulling away and scattering, sparks coming out in all directions. All the streetlights went out and were followed immediately by all the lights in the homes. Grayson observed the scene.

"Okay, put on the goggles."

The rain was now coming down in sheets; the wind was making movement difficult. The group made its way slowly to Zoran's villa, which was still dark, aside from a few flickering lights—probably flashlights, Grayson guessed.

They peered though the gates.

"John, ready? Bill?" Grayson said.

"Ready." From under their ponchos, both men swiftly drew out silence-suppressed sniper rifles with night scopes. They aimed at the front tires of the first Mercedes, hitting both the front and back right tires, and followed quickly by repeating the process on the second Mercedes, then the Volvo.

"Windows now?"

"Yes," Grayson replied.

The first shots targeted all the windows on the right side of the house, followed quickly by all the windows on the left. Finally, bullets flew into the front door, piercing its 5-inch oak door effortlessly.

The group hurried back to the van. Climbing in, Grayson took the wheel. He quickly proceeded to cross the street, stopping briefly.

"Any lights on yet? He's got to have a generator in that place."

"Nothing yet," came the reply.

"Okay, let's go." He wondered where Keiran was in the mess he had just left. He's resilient. He's okay, he thought to himself.

Thirty-Four

Hemmrich shouted, "Roubier, the lights! What's wrong with the lights?"

"The storm must have taken down some poles. The backup generator should come on in a minute or so, sir," Roubier explained calmly.

"A minute? Why not automatically when the power is down?" Zoran exclaimed, confused.

"It will. It just takes a short while for the system to recognize that the power from the outside lines is no longer...."

The first volley of shots sprayed across the room, ricocheting in all directions, piercing the sheer drapes, shattering the windows into jagged pieces of glass. Zoran screamed.

"I'm hit! Keiran, Roubier, I'm hit!"

"Get down, Mr. Hemmrich. Down," Roubier shouted. Keiran dropped from his chair, hitting the floor, his hands cushioning the fall. He heard shouts and cries of pain from the North Koreans who were screaming in their own language. An instant later, a second volley hit, this time aimed lower, violently hitting the table and chairs with such force that it sent splinters of wood flying everywhere as the table collapsed into two discordant pieces. Keiran, now on the floor, felt bullets seemingly inches from his head. Every instinct told him to yell, but his throat was now too tight to offer more than short gasps of air. The final wave of bullets sent scattered shots into a now silent room. Oh shit,

Keiran cried silently as he lay still on the floor, waiting for the madness to stop, hearing only the pounding of his heart.

The chandelier lights flickered for a moment, then came on in full force. Keiran remained motionless, trying to collect himself before rising. He began to blink, almost like a dog, trying to adjust to the change to intense light from the darkness and chaos. Finally, he rose slowly, looking at the damage—the table shattered, chairs torn up, glass pieces and wood splinters everywhere, rain hurling into the room from the damaged windows, water dripping down onto the windowsills and finding its way onto the carpeted floor, the drapes billowing uncontrollably as the wind whistled through the room, its sound mixing with the groaning from the men huddled on the floor.

Zoran lay prone, his hands up to his face as if he was trying to push out the sound of the bullets from his mind, moaning, "Oh, God. Oh my God." He didn't move until Roubier and the other assistant came over to help him up, each hanging on to an arm, straightening him slowly. As he rose, they carefully tried to brush off the glass chips and wood splinters that covered his back. To his right were the prostrate bodies of Ho-Lee and Chung-Han, both hiding behind a cover of their own bodyguards, who had leapt to shield them when the shooting started. As Keiran surveyed the scene, incredulity surged in him. He scarcely dared even to try to realize what had just happened, only understanding that today there were no golden hours, just a whirlpool of horror and darkness.

"Keiran, are you okay?" Zoran called, still flanked by both his assistants, his voice childlike and hushed, his head slowly turning from side to side in a serpentine movement, his eyes wide and frightened.

"Sure," Keiran replied, steadying himself against a wall, staring at the scene. "Who in the hell is after you, Zoran? My God…the second, or is it the third time in one day? Someone is after you."

"Be sure, I know who it's, Keiran. I know who it's. Now it's I who must take revenge." To Keiran, his expression didn't indicate confidence in his statement. As Zoran moved over to Keiran, he cried out, his voice cracked, "Roubier, Chavez…go to our guests. Help them…. "

The Korean bodyguards rose quietly, not speaking, shaking off debris from their bodies. Two, with drawn side arms, went to the shattered windows, forcefully tearing down the loose drapes, tossing the white fabric to the floor, and peered out into the darkness, the rain blowing onto their faces. The street was dark, no lights shone. Thunder rolled in the background and lightening pierced the sky. They turned and spoke to their counterparts—Kerian didn't need to know their language to understand that they were telling their principals that they couldn't see anything outside.

Mr. Ho-Lee rose first, a bodyguard brushing him off as he was helped up. His face was slightly scratched from the flying glass; his glasses were smashed and lay among the wreckage on the floor. Mr. Sun Chung-Han followed, his nose bleeding slightly, probably from hitting the floor too abruptly. His own glasses were gone as well. A bodyguard handed him a handkerchief, which he held against his injury. The room was silent. With each moment, the silence grew more intense, as everyone, their faces shocked in fear, surveyed the rubble around them.

Finally Zoran spoke in a whisper, his head lowered, eyes shifting to the floor and then to his guests. "I'm sorry, gentlemen. I'm sorry," he repeated. "Tonight I can't think of anything further to say that would express my disgust at what has happened. Please, let us go to the drawing room. We should be able to find some peace there. There is a private bathroom adjacent, or any of our upstairs bedrooms can be used to refresh yourselves. My assistants are now checking out the villa and its grounds. I believe that whoever did this is gone. If they wanted to harm us further, they would have been here by now. Please, this way.... "

"No, no, no, Mr. Hemmrich. Thank you for your offer," Ho-Lee responded with a slight smile that didn't suggest happiness, adding, "I don't believe that we need to do anymore talking. What happened this evening is most troubling. We don't wish to stay here any longer." He then turned to Chung-Han and the guards, instructing them to gather their briefcases from the debris.

Zoran was silent again. He simply stared at Ho-Lee. By his looks—his brow furled, his eyes now blankly staring ahead at nothing in particular—Keiran knew that Zoran longed to be able to explain what happened, to be able to assert that it was linked to something other than his own business and life. But he could do was to repeat his expression of sorrow.

"I'm sorry that this has occurred...."

"So are we, Mr. Hemmrich. This has been a strange episode for us and we won't proceed with you until you provide us with what we ordered and for which we have paid you well. We'll give you until noon tomorrow to provide us with that special material. If you have it, please come by the hotel. Otherwise, we leave for Geneva. Do not contact us unless you have the material. Do you understand, Mr. Hemmrich? We aren't interested in any more meetings without the provision of the material."

"Agreed," Zoran replied, his tone now revealing resignation. "There is nothing further I can say. I'll see you in the morning. Just as our meeting was interrupted, I received word from Mr. Farris that he has sent the material by special courier to Florence, as insurance, should he not be able to get here tomorrow. I have no doubt that I will make your noon deadline."

"We shall see, Mr. Hemmrich, we shall indeed see." He paused and looked at Zoran, a cold hatred in his eyes. "Now, however, we need one of your assistants to lead us to the hotel from here. Are you able to spare someone?"

"Roubier, show the gentlemen to their cars. Lead them back to Florence."

The anger in Ho-Lee's eyes could not be avoided as he passed Hemmrich and refused to extend his hand. Zoran was left with his hand hanging in space for several moments before he put it back to his side. Keiran saw a look of keen regret come to Zoran's face. It wasn't a pleasant sight to see the procession of six men treading carefully, each trying to avoid the glass and wood fragments littering the floor. The Korean guards hovered closely to each of their principals as they left through the bullet-marked double drawing room doors.

Zoran made no move to follow them, his head down, his own anger exhausted from the chaos of the events in one day. Keiran now viewed him as a man who knew he had lost. He remembered that look from his swimming days when he would be on the podium to receive an award, looking around to see those who were not as successful, each with a sort of a vacant stare of resignation. Keiran scanned the floor, looking for his own briefcase, which he had opened just before the attack. Now, its contents were scattered across the side of the floor near where he had been seated, the case itself resting upside down, covered with glass remnants and pieces of wood. Zoran remained speechless as Keiran carefully picked up his case, brushing off the rubble. He picked up the papers, brushing them off and placing them in the case.

"Do you have everything, Keiran?" Zoran asked.

Keiran noted the obvious agony in Zoran's voice.

"Yeah, I believe I do. I think I should be going as well. Will I be staying at the same hotel as your customer?"

"Yes, you are."

"Will you be at the hotel as well?" Keiran inquired, as he closed his briefcase.

"No, no. Not at all. I'll call you if I need your help. In the meantime, call Farris again. He told me that he has sent you the material for tomorrow's meeting, by express courier, on the off chance that he may not be here. So at least we'll have what these bastards came for. Why I deal with them, I'll never understand. I don't need this shit." Now Zoran's voice took on a more defiant tone, almost as if on cue—once the Koreans left, his former persona surfaced, if for no other purpose than to convince Keiran of his toughness.

"Do you know that before this deal, I had very little happen to me? I mean such as what happened this morning, tonight. No, this deal is the cause. I think I know which one of my competitors wants me out, but that bastard can also go to hell."

"Who is the competitor?"

"You don't want to know, counselor. But he'll be history when I get going. Pure history. Let's go. I'll drop you off at the hotel. Nothing we can do here. I'll have a few of my assistants stay here until we can get some repair people on board. Nothing can be done tonight. Yes, the police will want to know what has happened. I believe it was an attempted robbery, don't you think so as well? What else is there to say? Maybe the police won't even come out on such a horrid night."

"Zoran, why would you have the material sent to me rather than to wherever you're staying?"

"No one is to know where I am staying, not even Duane. You have my cell phone number. That's how you can reach me."

Keiran and Zoran strode out into the hallway only to find Roubier rushing down the corridor, carrying Keiran's overnight case.

"Now what?" Zoran said aloud.

"The tires on the two Mercs have been damaged by the bullets. The Volvo wagon seems to be okay; a bullet grazed two of its tires, but I think I can make it to the hotel."

"Well, then, pile the bastards in that and take them away. I have my own car in the garage and Chavez can take me. Get those creeps out of here. I'm sick of their smiles and their faces. In fact, I don't like yellow people. Just get rid of them. They're untrustworthy anyway. Right, Keiran?"

Keiran didn't answer Zoran, but turned to Roubier to say, "Thanks for remembering my case." Roubier handed the black leather case to Keiran, saluted Zoran, and turning around, rushed back along the corridor.

"Now, Keiran, I want to show you my gratitude by giving you a handsome bonus for taking care of me during this time of turmoil. I'll make sure of that, Keiran. You'll not have to wait for a check from your firm; I'll do it directly. This is from me to you. How's does $25,000 sound? Okay for your troubles in the last 24 hours?"

Zoran's comments stirred a sense of uneasiness in Keiran.

"You know that I can't accept your generous offer. Firm rules, you know. Besides, I was sent here to help you and that's what I'm trying to do. Right now, I want to get to the hotel, clean up, make some calls, have a drink, maybe two, then hit the sack. Would you care to join me at the hotel for a drink?"

"Not tonight. No, another time. Chavez," Zoran called out to the assistant who had been standing by him throughout the conversation with Keiran, "are you ready?"

Chavez nodded, then led the way down the hall, away from the front of the house and toward the kitchen. Keiran noted that several more assistants had arrived and were milling around in the kitchen, where the kitchen staff of three, seated at the large worktable, were sobbing and shaking. Zoran ignored everyone and proceeded to walk out the back door, turning a slow left until he came to the opening to a covered walkway that led to the three-car garage. Chavez pressed a button on his handheld remote control, causing the door to lift.

"We won't have any trouble in this car, Keiran. It's got more armor than a tank."

"That's reassuring," Keiran replied.

The drive to Florence was in silence. What more could be said, anyway? Both Keiran and Zoran were lost in their thoughts. Keiran didn't want to make small talk; he only wanted to call Jennifer, his parents, and then sleep. Zoran kept tapping his fingers on both knees, stopping every once in the while and mouthing words silently with his lips. Finally, he turned to Keiran, saying faintly, "Why don't you call Farris now? I want to talk to him, tell him what has happened."

"Do you think it's a good idea?" Keiran asked, "Maybe we should wait a few hours until things settle and then give him a call. Frankly, I have to organize my thoughts. It's been that kind of night. But if you wish...."

"Maybe," Zoran slowly replied, "you're correct. I could tell him we were shot at again, but frankly, Keiran, in my last conversation with him, he seemed distant and uninterested. Why don't you call him after we've received the material? He said that he'd sent the material to your Hotel, the Villa Medici. That is where we're putting you up for the evening. You'll enjoy the hotel—it has an indoor pool."

"That's good news." Keiran continued to stare out the darkened window; the rain seemed to be falling more gently, the wind seemed to have calmed down.

"This has been a different kind of introduction to London practice, hasn't it, Keiran?'

"Can't argue with that." Keiran turned to him, fixing his eyes on Zoran, asking, "Frankly, should you be going through with this deal? It doesn't take much analysis to see that one of your competitors doesn't want you to complete it. It's quite obvious."

"Keiran, if I fled from every deal because of a worrisome event, there never would have been deals. I think I've told you that before. No, I just haven't been as forceful in warning my competitors as they're now warning me."

"I know that it's not legal to sell what you're selling to the North Koreans…and I don't mean cement."

"On that you'd better talk to Duane. I had the same problem, but he said that all the documents are legal. In fact, we aren't selling the special equipment directly to them. It is being sold through an intermediary….Why am I telling you? You already know how it's being done."

"No, I don't, Zoran. I didn't even know about the special equipment. And I don't understand why, if you knew the special material was on its way to me at the Hotel here in Florence, you created that charade at the meeting with the Koreans. What was the purpose of that? Is it true? Is the material coming?"

"Talk to Duane. I have no idea why he kept this information to himself. Did he think you wouldn't find out?'

"I may not know everything, Zoran, but what I do know is that you've been shot at least twice and your boat has been targeted. How much more warning do you need to call it quits…at least on this deal?"

"I thought I told you after this morning's incident: I don't quit. Understand? I don't quit. Period. End. They'll have to kill me before I run away with my tail between my legs. I told you, I'm not an old woman in man's clothes. Soon, my actions will speak and you will see. Well, here we are."

"Thanks for the lift, Zoran. Take care of yourself."

"Oh, I will, Keiran. Not to worry. Now, have a good night. Chavez?" Chavez jumped out of the car to open the back door for Keiran, who slipped out into the light rain, not looking back at Zoran as he walked into the hotel.

Thirty-Five

He was tired, angry, and sickened by the day's happenings. Keiran knew he wasn't the right man for this client. My whole nature revolts against the idea of working with Zoran, he thought. Once I head down that road with him, it will be only the beginning and his requests will be his never-ending. The knowledge of Farris' private history of slavishly being Zoran's acolyte persisted like static from an improperly tuned radio. Okay. That's Farris. I'm certain of who I am, certain of who Zoran is, and certain of Farris. We don't mix well together. Their's may be a ruthless world, but I don't want to share it.

His drapes had been closed and his bedcovers turned down by the hotel maid prior to his arrival. A soft light came from the lamp on a side bed table, the shadow of its cone-shaped shade casting a circle on the darkened ceiling. The atmosphere was peaceful. The fierceness and fire of the day was gone. A sensation of calm washed over him. He dropped his bags, took off his clothes, discarding them on the floor, and then lay on the bed, bringing his forearm over his closed eyes. Lying in bed in the subdued light, he heard a church clock chime. It was 9:00 p.m.

Not right now. Give me a few minutes, just a few, he thought silently. He tried to sleep, but it didn't come. He thought of going swimming, but even that wasn't possible, as the pool had already closed. He should call his parents and Jennifer, but passed over that as well. Later, a few minutes, I need just a few minutes alone. He wanted to suppress the odd fear of flight that he now had. It was his nature to face things, never to turn his back. Every time he prepared for swim meets, his coach, Brother Joshua, would remind him that courage is a virtue and that those extra laps of workout might make the difference between victory and defeat. Easy to give up, courageous not to.

Fuck it. Get off this shit. You're not 16, Keiran. You're 31. Act it.

He'd shower, go down to the bar, and grab some food and drink. The room telephone rang as he closed the bathroom door behind him. Take a message, he thought as he smiled to himself and turned on the shower, stepped in, and let the hot water bring him some relief.

Two floors below, Diana Peters was on the phone speaking with the reception clerk on duty who had notified her of Keiran's arrival.

"Are you sure you gave Mr. Hogan the message?" she asked.

"*Si, Signorina.* I personally gave him the envelope."

"He's in his room now?"

"*Si, Signorina.* Yes, he should be in his room."

"That's fine. Thank you for your help."

"*Grazie et buona notte, Signorina.*"

"Good night to you."

Diana hung up.

That miserable creature. I come all this way through a rainstorm to deliver his material, and what does he do? Refuses to return my calls. What else could I have expected? You should have expected this, Diana answered her own question, then, laughing, she grabbed her purse and room key, flipped off the room lights, deciding that a personal visit from her would be more worthwhile. Dressed in an austere, form-fitting, dark blue suit with a skirt slightly above her knees, her blond hair brushing her shoulders, a solid gold chain around her neck, she quickly strode down the hall to the elevator.

"He'll be devastated when he sees me," she smiled.

Despite the 'Do Not Disturb' sign now hanging from the door, she rang the doorbell button several times, hearing it buzz loudly. There was no answer. Brutally, she then kept her finger on the button, creating an uninterrupted buzz. That should wake him up. It did, and the voice coming from inside wasn't pleasant.

"I hope whatever you want is important," Keiran shouted. "Can't you read the sign? 'Do Not Disturb'!"

"It is important, open the door. It's Diana."

"Oh, no," Keiran sighed as he opened the door, standing there in his bathrobe.

"My, my, my, Keiran don't you look sexy. Just out of the shower? Yum, delicious."

Keiran looked at her with a blank stare. "What's going on, Diana?"

"Keiran, hello there. Let me in." Diana stepped inside the threshold, brushing Keiran aside.

"Yeah, sure. Come in," he said in a tone of bemused resignation, closing the door behind him.

"Grab a chair." Keiran switched on the overhead light, then went over and opened the drapes. "Want a drink?"

"Mineral water only. Well, ducky, I'm here to save your career."

Keiran strode over to the mini-bar, bending over to collect two bottles of mineral water. Diana's eyes were watching his every move.

"You have a great derriere—the outline in your robe...."

Keiran turned abruptly, shooting a sideward glance at Diana, as he opened the two bottles of water. "Diana, don't get wise now. I'm not in any mood. Now, what did you say about saving my career...?"

"When you get so stern, you're actually more handsome, but since you're really being mean—and I presume you do know the difference between stern and mean—I'm going to leave and not tell you why I am here. To hell with you, Keiran Hogan." She rose, heading toward the door.

"Wait up, Diana. Slow down. I'm tired and need some rest and relaxation. I was going to dress and go downstairs for a drink and some food. Come with me. Don't get so silly on me. Let's have a calm time."

Diana paused for a moment in front of the door, her eyes fixed on Keiran. Silent, she returned her eyes to the deep gold fabric that covered chair she had occupied a moment ago, saying, "I still think you're a real creep. However, given that you've semi-apologized, I accept." Diana's voice was now soft, “but I’m not leaving your room because I don’t trust you’ll meet me downstairs and I’ll embarrass myself by sitting alone at the bar waiting for someone who will never show up.”

“You? Alone?” He laughed. “Here’s your water.” He handled her the bottle of mineral water, adding, “You don’t need a glass, do you?”

“It would be nice. Since you asked in the negative, I’ll say no.” She took the bottle, and took a short swallow.

“Ah, perfect. I’m still staying here, in your room, until you're ready. And, Keiran Hogan, if you’re worried about dressing in front of me, I’ve seen naked men before. You’re not the first.”

“I’m sure of that, but you know, we American men are shy, so turn around and look out the window. Florence at night is pretty.” Keiran chuckled, taking off his bathrobe, discarding it on the bed.

Diana did as he asked, rising from her chair, bottle of water in hand, commenting as she got to the window, “I like it when the rain stops, gives everything a fresh look. You know, everything smells clean.” She then turned and to see Keiran, in his shorts, putting on his shirt. “You know, clean like you're now, clean and neat. You realize that you haven’t kissed me—not in the passionate way that I know you kiss your news reader friend; but just a friendly, European, ‘glad you're here’ type of kiss.”

She walked over and planted a kiss on Keiran’s cheek as he continued to button his shirt.

He put on dark gray slacks, tucked in gray shirt, and, sitting on the bed, slid into his loafer shoes.

“Don’t forget a tie.” She could not take her eyes of his shape, thinking silently, Why don’t I have him? She knew her face was now scarlet.

“Well that’s interesting, Diana. Are you blushing or is it some new makeup?”

“Keiran Hogan, go to hell. Where’s your tie?”

“I’m not wearing one tonight. Not necessary. We’re in Italy, you know.” He put on his dark blue jacket, saying, “Let’s go, Diana. You’d better have something worthwhile to say to me, for I’m not in the mood for any jokes.”

He opened the door, motioning Diana to go first. She moved closer to Keiran as he was locking the door.

"Not even a real, deep kiss. This will remind me how truly awful you're, Keiran Hogan. Don't forget your key."

Keiran nodded then shut the door behind him.

"Now what is it, Diana. Why are you really here?' he asked as they strode together down the hallway to the elevator.

"I wonder, Keiran, if you're always this curt or is it only when you need sleep, sex, or both."

Keiran laughed as he replied, "Diana, I'm tired. I've been shot at twice today, and I can't think of sex when that happens to me."

"Shot at? Come on now, Keiran. You do need a drink. You're hallucinating. Must be the Italian wine, too much or too little—which is it?"

"Neither. Apparently, someone is after Zoran. First in Venice this morning, then we abandoned that city for here. Then this evening, another shoot-out. Diana, someone is after that guy. And, he won't call the police. It's nuts."

"Bullets? Are you serious?"

"Yes, Diana. Real bullets."

"Did you tell Zoran about Farris' death?"

"No. When you called earlier, you told me that someone from the firm would be calling him. Even if I wanted to, it wasn't the proper time. We were about to go into a meeting with Zoran's customer. For all I know he may be trying right now to reach Farris.

"It'll probably be morning when he's notified. I think it may even be the managing partner from New York who'll call him. HenHen was trying to work all of it out amidst her tears. It was something to see, HenHen crying. You know, Keiran, I believe they were genuine tears."

As the elevator door opened, Keiran let Diana go in ahead of him. As he entered, he noted that the man Diana stood beside looked strangely familiar. It was the man he had seen on Guernsey—the telephone repairman who had called the ambulance when Leyden keeled over. He had seen him in the lobby of the hotel in Venice, and now here in Florence. He didn't acknowledge Keiran, but looked straight ahead.

Three others were in the elevator, two men and one woman. They all rode in silence to the lobby floor. Diana, closest to the elevator door, left first while Keiran remained, pressing the 'Door Open' button. His eyes followed the familiar man as he hurried down the corridor, heading in the same direction that Keiran and Diana were about to take.

"Lounge or restaurant?" Keiran asked, loosely taking Diana's hand.

"The lounge. Your talk about hailing bullets gives me the shivers and I need to steady myself. Yes, I need a drink"

"Good. That's my thinking, too."

"You were pretty lucky when you were transferred to our office. I was thinking on the plane that Zoran was one of the few clients that Farris kept to himself—until you came. I'm still trying to figure out why you were assigned to Zoran. He did use some of the other associates in the office, including me, on small matters, but never let anyone travel with the client as you did. I calculated that he finally decided he needed more regular help. You know, I don't think he spent time on anyone other than Zoran."

"Well, Diana, I wish he had kept the client to himself totally. This kind of initiation I could really do without."

The walk was brief as the lounge was off the corridor facing the elevator bank. Walking slowly, Diana, her hand tightening now around Keiran's, observed, "Do you realize that everything, including the walls of this corridor, is done in Tuscan gold? And the carpet is a deep shade of burgundy."

"Diana, we're in Tuscany. What do you expect? White walls and gray carpets?"

"Well, maybe." She laughed.

While they stood at the lounge door, surveying the crowd in the long, narrow, dark wood paneled room, Keiran was trying to locate the man he had just seen on the elevator.

"Doesn't seem to be an open table, Keiran. Shall we go to the bar? Or we can go up to my room and have room service," Diana teased.

"We could, but we won't," Keiran replied as he took Diana to the bar, dropping his hand and placing it gently now around her waist.

"Oh, I like this," she smiled.

"I'm being polite," Keiran replied as he led her through the crowd, finding two seats at the end of the row facing the white-specked black marble bar top. He pulled out one of the black leather covered stools for Diana, who slid onto it.

"This is fine, Keiran. I like your gracious persona, not your other one, that treated me so horridly while I was in your room."

"As usual, you exaggerate. I try to be generous at times. Now what is it that brought you here to Florence?"

"The special material you needed. According to HenHen, Farris wrapped the package himself, pretty securely—you'll know what I mean by securely when you see the package. He called me and asked me to standby just in case his interview with the police on the Coborn mess would go longer than he anticipated. When he had his attack, HenHen called me and, well, here I am. I have no idea what's in the package, but I've got it in my room. Must be very important or it could have come by commercial messenger. You know, Keiran, the conversation with Farris was strange—asking me to standby to take a package to you. I couldn't believe that he wouldn't come to a meeting with his own client."

"Did he sound bitter when he spoke to you?" Keiran inquired.

"No. Actually more calm than usual. A bit tired, yet soft and direct. No extra words, though. Just take the stuff to you should that become necessary."

"This is a very confusing situation. Farris dead. Material here. Zoran probably more interested in the material than in knowing that Farris is dead. Anyway…what will you have to drink?"

"Gin and tonic," Diana said with a catch in her voice. Looking at Keiran, she continued, "We can have such fun together, Keiran. Such great fun."

Keiran laughed under his breath, "I bet we can. I bet we can…. Giving up on mineral water?"

"No. If you're going to drink, so am I."

"Make that two gin and tonics," Keiran told the bartender, who was busy wiping the front of the counter and placing cocktail napkins in front of them.

"I didn't know you drank gin."

"I didn't know you did, either."

Drawing her face closer to Keiran's, Diana lowered her voice as she asked, "Keiran, what is this material and why is so important?"

"Diana, I don't believe you don't know. I know that you've broken into the firm's data banks and know the full story."

"I have, Keiran, but nothing about Benton Industries could be retrieved, aside from the draft corporate documents. That's the company, isn't it?"

"Yeah, that's the company. I'll tell, you Diana, this project is messy. I think that Zoran is selling something he shouldn't; what he's selling is probably hot, and Farris was in on the deal."

Diana fixed her eyes on Keiran. "I know you're not drunk. You've haven't begun to drink yet. And being tired and without sex wouldn't provoke you to make such a statement unless it was…."

"True," Keiran interrupted. "In my mind, Diana, I've been trying to compile some sort of balance sheet as to why Farris is in on these deals. What they're doing on this one—and probably on a lot of others—isn't legal."

"Keiran, you've got to know that Farris is a master of camouflage. He's never wrong and he does everything so that it's airtight, legally. He's just not that stupid. You must know that."

"That may be," Keiran countered. "Sort of strange, though, that before he dies, he has the most important part of this deal sealed in some package and sent here by you. It's almost as if he knew his life would be cut short."

"Keiran, when did you get paranoid?"

"Since coming to Kenton & Ward. London."

They laughed together.

"Your drinks," the bartender interrupted, placing two tall glasses in front of them.

Keiran nodded, then lifted his drink to clink Diana's.

"Cheers, Diana."

"Cheers to you." Keiran took a short swallow. Diana, kept the glass longer, drinking about a third of it.

"Diana, I guess you needed the drink."

"This gin and tonic is mostly tonic. Only in England do they know how to mix this drink, but that is another story. Anyway, Keiran, you know that when you asked me to help you break into the firm's computer billing system, I thought you were crazy. Then I remembered the only time Farris really jacked up my fees, you know more than the normal amount, was when I did a small memo for one of Zoran's companies—long before you came. I spent about 10 hours on the contract, when I saw the billing report for my time, it had 80 hours attributed to me for that one client. I work hard, but not that hard. I never thought anything about it, until you called. Appears to me, based on what you've found and what little I did, Farris only increases the time spent on Zoran's account."

"Why the hell would Zoran want to make the firm richer than it already is?"

"Keiran, don't be naive. Farris' power in the firm comes not because he is a brilliant lawyer, which he probably is, but because he brings in gobs of money. You know, the stuff that's in our paychecks and allows us to live nicely."

"Did you look at the expense reimbursements?"

"Yeah, I did. Farris uses a lot of consultants."

"I've never met any of them. None. I'll bet it's just a way of getting money into Farris' own pocket."

"Keiran, nasty talk," Diana said, taking a another long swallow. Placing her glass down, she continued, "Very nasty talk. Can get you into trouble. Better to let it alone. Farris is dead, anyhow. Why bother even thinking about such things? When he's buried, that little sideline of his will go. It's pointless to think otherwise."

"Maybe, Diana, maybe. I can't hand over that package you brought to Zoran. I can't."

There was a sort of tender toughness in Keiran's eyes, and Diana knew he meant what he said.

"Don't be temperamental, Keiran," she spoke softly. "What I brought doesn't belong to you. It belongs to Zoran. You have no ownership rights. God. I'm really sounding like a lawyer. 'Ownership Rights.' You understand what I'm saying." She laughed lightly.

"Yeah, you want me to pass on what I know to be illegal to Zoran, and guess what, Diana, that gets me, and possibly you, involved. Farris wasn't stupid. He wants me included. He wants me stuck in his web…and you know what? He would have succeeded if Zoran's customer hadn't slipped up and spilled what he was buying at our confab earlier this evening, before the bullets starting flying."

"What the hell is he selling?"

"Mechanisms that go on top of rockets to direct them over oceans to their targets."

Diana stared at Keiran, then took another swallow of her drink to finish it.

"I'd like another one."

Keiran motioned to the bartender to bring two more drinks.

"Not a good thing, Diana. Not good at all. Now you know why I can't deliver the material to him, and neither can you. We just can't." Keiran's voice was serious and firm.

"Well, well. I knew I'd find you at the bar with a beautiful lady," exclaimed Bob Grayson, who put his arm over Keiran's shoulder.

"What the hell...? Bob, so you really are in Florence!"

"I told you I was coming," said Grayson, who was dressed in an open collar, off-white shirt, navy blue blazer, gray slacks, and highly polished black loafers. He added, "Now who is this beautiful lady?"

"My colleague from the firm, Diana Peters. This is Bob Grayson, another American lawyer in London. I think he has been following me these past several days." Grayson laughed as he extended his hand to shake Diana's.

"Is he treating you well, Diana?"

"So-so. Nice to meet you, Mr. Grayson."

"Staying at this hotel?" Keiran inquired.

"As a matter of fact, yes. We can meet tomorrow morning for an early breakfast."

Grayson then looked at Diana, and back to Keiran. "Let me correct myself, a late breakfast."

Diana giggled, looking at Keiran, who smiled. "Early breakfast is fine. Seven?"

"Sure, seven. See you then. Take care of this young man, Ms. Peters."

"I will. Definitely, I will."

"Bob," Keiran laughingly said, "I think you're following me. Everywhere I go, you're there. And what is worrisome is that everywhere you are, something bad happens to me."

"Keiran, have you had too much to drink? And, what's happened to you now?"

"No, answering your first question. Second, another hail of bullets flew by me this evening."

"Diana, does he always joke this way?"

"Always. Absolutely and undeniably always."

"The pattern is getting too familiar Bob, so, like a good lawyer looking at the facts, I don't know if I should be around you. I suspect that in a few minutes, we'll see another problem hit me."

"I usually bring good luck," Grayson countered, patting Keiran on the back. "See you in the morning. Bring a hearty appetite." Looking again at Diana, Grayson added, "I think you will. Definitely. Well, just wanted to say hello."

"Get out of here Bob, you're trouble." Keiran laughingly raised his hand to shoo him away as he if were swatting a pesky fly. His eyes followed Grayson, who moved through the crowd to a far table, joining two other men, whose backs were to Keiran.

Is one of them…? Keiran asked himself silently. Yeah, the profile…. It's the man who was in Guernsey, in Venice, and now Florence. With Grayson. No, it couldn't be. No, no, no…!

"Let's get back to the more immediate issue. The material you brought—we just can't give it to Zoran. It would be wrong."

"You know what that would mean for you and me?" Diana's voice was now worried. "Immediate dismissal from the firm. These documents belong to the client. Not to you, not to me. Understood?"

"I understand that they're being sold to a country our client is not supposed to be dealing with—North Korea. These are schematic diagrams about missile guidance systems as well as the computer program telling the thing to go from here to there. All illegal. All wrong."

"So, who will believe you? I didn't know what was in the sealed documents until you just told me. For all I know they're legitimate corporate material. Zoran can always deny what you say and the North Koreans are never going to say 'Yeah, it's us.' Drop it, Keiran. Give the documents to Zoran and then make an excuse to go. Don't you know you have to be flexible?"

"Like Farris, like Coborn, like Zoran. No, that's not my idea of flexibility. That's dishonorable and dishonest."

"Coborn—there is more to the story with him and Farris. The police sent over a list of corporations to which Coborn had funds wired. I saw the letter. The letter asked if Farris had any knowledge of these companies."

"I'm not going to ask how you got the letter."

"Don't. The police must suspect Farris. Something must have been in Coborn's apartment and something led them to Farris," Diana replied. "They must know more than they're letting on."

"All these consultants, Diana," Keiran added, "were simply ways of getting more money from Zoran via the firm to whomever they wanted to have the funds. Look. Farris hired a consultant for one of Zoran's firms to do 'x'—whatever 'x' is—then billed the firm; the firm passed on the bill to Zoran, who reimbursed the firm. Nice way to launder money. And why not? Farris and Zoran had many people to pay off probably in this business—which isn't cement, Diana. No way."

"So, maybe Coborn was a hidden 'consultant'?"

"Who knows? You said the police traced phone calls. What were they all about? The next ambassador's session with U. S. lawyers?"

"It's crazy, Keiran. Just crazy," Diana said, shaking her head.

"Want to hear something crazier? The day Sir Robert died, Coborn was in the steam room at the RAC. I think he had something to do with it."

"Paranoid plus, Keiran. That's where you've now descended. We definitely need another drink. You have really lost it, Keiran. Totally. Runnard died of a heart attack. End of story."

"Yeah, yeah, yeah. And all those calls from Coborn were for lunch. Get real, Diana. Can you imagine that ego having lunch with a functionary at the embassy? Only the ambassador would be graced by Farris' presence on such an occasion. And Farris dies before being interviewed by the police about who? Coborn. Another heart attack. Coborn, suicide; Runnard, heart attack; Farris, heart attack. I mean, Diana, are we dense or what?"

"Maybe you should have been a detective. Actually, I know a lawyer in my past who is a London detective now. I should call him...."

"You'll call no one, Diana. No one. This whole seamy scene of Zoran and his dealings with Farris and the firm makes me wonder...whether I fit in."

"Just do your work, Keiran. And get your pay. Leave the honor or dishonor to the partner in charge. When we're in charge, we'll change things. The practice of law can be a painful business."

"Yeah, at times very painful. Change it? I don't know about that, Diana. Farris started out as an associate. What is there about the business of law that corrupts us? Is it the money? The desire to win at any cost? Both? Or does the practice of law lead to the corruption? Maybe we'll be the same. Who knows."

"No, Keiran. You won't be corrupted. And neither will I. I guess I should tell you, I'm leaving the firm at the end of next month."

Keiran looked at her, his face steady as he fixed his stare on her. "Don't kid now, Diana. It's not nice."

"No, I'm not kidding. I need to do something different. I've been at the firm five years now. Sure, I'd be made a partner, but I just want to get into a different environment. I don't know yet what I'm going to do. Take some time off. Visit my sister in Perth, Australia. See some friends in the United States and Canada. Then I'll decide. When I told Farris last week, he didn't seem surprised and made no effort to keep me at the firm. His mind was so distracted that I wonder if he even heard what I was saying. Anyway, I sent in my letter that same day. I should have called you and told you, but you seemed busy yourself. There, that's over with."

Again silence. Keiran looked at his drink, now just ice cubes.

"Another drink?"

"I don't think so, Keiran. What are you going to do with this package that I have to give to you?"

"I just don't know, I just don't know."

"I'll miss you Keiran, I really will. You're the only great thing in our office."

Keiran leaned over and kissed her quietly.

"I'll stay in touch with you," she continued, "I mean, I have to get you into my bed!"

They both laughed.

"Well, what do I say now?"

"Nothing. Listen, Keiran. There's not much I can do here. The package is in my room. You can come with me to get it or not. I only had to deliver it to you. That's my job. Now, if you want me to take it back, saying I couldn't find you…well, I'll try that, if you want."

"No, I'll come up and get it."

"Keiran, quit. Please quit this mess. It may be arms, missile components, and sales to the wrong people, but don't cause a fuss. Just leave the firm. I don't want anything to happen to you."

"Yes. Shall we go?"

"Once I give the package to you, I'm no longer involved. I'm leaving first thing in the morning. The way you're describing things, it's messy. But I think you should give everything to Zoran. After all, the markings on the sealed package say: 'Zoran Hemmrich. Hand Delivery.'" Diana moved her full lips nervously as she repeated, "The material doesn't belong to you, Keiran. Understand?"

"I understand, Diana. I understand fully."

Keiran glided off the bar stool, taking Diana by the hand again. As they meandered through the crowd, he eyed Grayson, who was sitting in deep conversation with two men. One was certainly the telephone man from Guernsey. A few coincidences are understandable, but this was too many—and they all involved Grayson.

Thirty-Six

Zoran Hemmrich had asked for an explanation as to why the missile guidance data disc and schematic drawings were missing and he was acutely aware he had been told a hundred lies. He sighed profoundly. Even Farris had now failed him. He was unable to reach him by phone; there was no answer either at his home, his cell phone, or at the office. And Hogan, despite his honest look, was also lying. He had no proof, but his instincts told him that the phone call Hogan had received earlier wasn't really from his mother. To think I had welcomed this young man, despite Farris' sometimes uncomfortable feelings about him. An honest look hid the blackness of deceit.

Farris had been supremely organized in all our dealings these past several years, Zoran thought. Now, his discipline has collapsed. He wants me to believe that an interview with the police is more important that this meeting This Hogan, his flunky, comes unprepared.

"No, there is more here," he murmured to himself. "There has to be more. A disappearing partner means a betraying partner. No doubt, Farris has turned."

Again and again, he nervously tapped his fingers on his knees, haunted now by the thoughts of betrayal by the one person whom he had trusted the most. With these worries of treachery came a sense of loneliness. Perhaps it was actually fear that came across Zoran; fear that enfolded him like black shadows on a foam-covered sea. This shifting and unsettled feeling was hateful to his strong and frank nature; he felt suffocated by the mystery of events that had now surrounded him.

What should have been a triumph in a business deal was now beginning to be, for him, in clear sight of disaster. He now had a strange sensation of what he felt to be the hidden hand of Draculic, that deadbeat shithead who, from death, was dealing him a final, perhaps fatal, blow. It has to be his group, Zoran thought. They're after me. They've found out. Somehow they found out. Farris? Could it be Farris? Is he cooperating with the police because of his own shit with Coborn? Yeah, that has to be it. These last two days…nothing like this has ever happened to me before. It has to be Farris. Farris has spilled the beans. That weak shit.

By the time he arrived at his destination, a darkened villa on the Arno River, the rain had stopped. The street was dim; the sole street lamp casting the only light, its rays dancing about the fine mist that was all that remained of the earlier rainstorm. He was accompanied by two of his assistants, one of who was hurriedly getting out and opening the car door for him. He sat for a few moments, absorbed in his thoughts.

"Mr. Hemmrich, sir, we are here."

"Stay here. Wait for me. I'll be several hours. One of you must always be awake. Stay in touch with Deiter. He should meet us here about four this morning. By then he should have finished what I wanted him to do." His voice was stern, concealing his nervousness and anxiety. Soon, though, he knew he would gain the release he so urgently needed. The mental pain gnawing at him like an uncontrolled fungus would soon vanish. "Thank you boys. Stay awake now. Important. Can't miss Deiter's call."

He entered the villa, an unimposing red brick three-storied building under a small stone archway jutting from the first floor. No light filtered through the villa's tightly closed, gray, shuttered windows. Two faintly lit wrought iron coach lamps framed the heavy wooden door, '17 Via Cardinale,' etched in its tarnished brass plate. The door was divided into four intricately carved panels—the two upper panels depicted nude women riding unsaddled horses, their long hair flowing behind them as if they were riding into a strong wind; the lower panels contained nude women in various stages of embrace, their horses tethered nearby. He pressed the doorbell, looking straight into the small peephole set in the door, which he knew to be the lens of a security camera. After a brief moment, a low buzz sounded, indicating the lock was disengaged. Zoran swiftly opened the door and entered a dimly lit foyer, its floor black marble, the walls a cardinal red, the hall's wood trim a burnt gold. Waiting for him was a tall, slim woman, her head piled high with black hair, her eyebrows no more than thin black lines above iridescent blue eye shadow, her high-boned cheeks on a powdered white face rouged red like a fiery sunset, her bare, cup-like breasts held in place by leather straps—the only other clothing she wore were knee-length black leather boots and she held in her left hand a silver-tipped riding crop.

"*Senore Hemmrich. Buona sera. Ah! Bene, splendido, m' uomo*." She reached over and kissed him, her hands reaching for his face, then falling down across his chest and resting on his crotch, gently squeezing his hardened penis. "*Ah! Molto indurire. Bene.*" Zoran was silent. Taking him by the hand, she led him down the short, darkened corridor, which was lit by the stream of light coming through a hall door.

He had now come into an airless underworld, peopled with invisible violence. And he was happy. His penis was straining against his pants. Soon, his worries would be forgotten and he would descend into a place that he called heaven. Others would call it hell. All tensions, real and imagined, would vanish and be replaced by the burning sense of complete release. To him, what he was about to endure was like a cloth of pure white; to others, it was a cloth stained with indelible filth. It didn't matter to him, for now his waters would be sweet, not acrid with salt. Soon, very soon, he would be entranced in an ecstasy of pain and worship. His orgasms would be complete and prolonged. When tomorrow came, he knew he could face life anew. He would be more farsighted and solutions would come to him easily. These thoughts made him smile as she undressed him, placing a silver-studded collar around his neck and attaching a long leather rope to it. Cracking her riding crop against his buttocks, she shouted, "*Avanti, mi schiavo!*" Zoran fell to his knees, now happy and content, a strong sense of excitement drawing in him.

"*Avanti, mi schiavo!*" The riding crop was again hitting his buttocks, thin wisps of scented incense floated in from an open door as he crawled toward the darkened room.

Deiter Engel had been an enforcer for the former East German *Statssicherheitsdienst* secret police. He knew little of the inner workings of the organization and was only used to work over suspects, convincing them to cooperate with the *Stasi*. He knew he was a thug, recruited from an East German prison where he was serving time for strangling to death, in an uncontrolled rage, a fellow army recruit. To become free, he had to accept the 'invitation' to join the *Stasi*. There, he quickly gained the reputation as one who had a spectator's enthusiasm for torturing people. 220 pounds, his face scarred and contorted by the beatings he himself had taken over the years, he had been a champion wrestler in school, and even made the 1980 East German Olympic team—only to be beaten in his class by a fellow Communist from the Soviet Union. He was expected to lose; his coach had warned him as much. Despite all the drugs he took to increase his strength, when told the fix was in, he didn't become demoralized. He knew his place in life.

As a special officer of the *Stasi*, he earned a reasonable salary and was given a small apartment where he lived alone. A few prostitutes came and went. When he was drunk, which was often, he became so violent that other residents in the building had to call the police, who then took him to jail so he could sleep off his binge. The officers with whom he worked used to laugh behind his back and call him stupid, slow, or even worse. But when they left him in the room alone with a prisoner from whom they wished to extract a confession, he was effective. Either the confession was obtained or he beat the men, and even a few women, to a bloody death. He remembered only one of these many deaths. A minister had allowed a small tunnel, no more than a crawlspace, to be built from his run-down parish church under the barbed-wire wall that separated the two Berlins. As the church was close to the wall, it was watched periodically and those who went to church were identified and fed into the *Stasi* files. It was when an alert *Stasi* officer noted the number of people entering the church was slightly different than the number who left it that the priest was arrested and brought to the *Stasi* prison in Berlin. That was the summer of 1989.

Deiter looked at the priest for some time, not saying a word. The room, as usual, had a bare light bulb hanging by a frayed cord from the ten-foot ceiling. A ten by ten foot wood table and two iron-framed chairs were the only furniture in the room. Once the two interrogating officers left, Deiter would enter, wearing shirtsleeves and a tie. He always thought it strange that the officers insisted that he wear a tie. Today, he wore a blue tie with a sailboat in the middle. Actually, he had taken it from a prisoner some time ago when that man didn't come clean and didn't survive.

"I know you, Minister Thomman. Now, where from?" Deiter sneered as he spoke, his voice marked with sarcasm.

Thomman, a slight man of about 140 pounds, his face pale but serene, his religious collar loose around his neck, remained silent as he slowly fingered his cross. Engel glanced at the silver cross, leaned over, and yanked it from his neck, its thin chain snapping quickly.

"You stupid man. You believe in this shit of a God. Let him come now. 'Here God,'" Deiter mocked, "'Come get your shit.'"

Thomman didn't move.

"So you like to dig tunnels. How many have gone through? What are their names?" He reached over and punched Thomman in the face, hurling him off his chair and to the floor. As Thomman's face turned, Deiter saw a small scar on his temple. Thomman didn't move. "Get up, you scum. How many have gone through? Give us the names," he shouted, then kicked Thomman in the face with his leather, hard-soled shoes. Screaming, Deiter then picked up the limp body and hurled it across the room against the wall.

"Talk! You talk to me you fuckin' shithead!" The body fell to the floor. There was no movement of any kind. "Your God took you away from me. Piss your fuckin' God. Fuck him too."

Deiter looked at the prone figure for a long time, wondering what to do. Usually, the prisoner yells for mercy and screams with pain, he thought silently. This one just went. He dropped to his knees and leaned over, picking up the man's arm, trying to feel for a pulse. There was none. Thomman was dead. "You cheated me, your fuckin' God cheated me." He kicked Thomman's face again and again in a fury, then stomping on it, yelling, "Fucker! Fucker! You cheated me, you fucker! You cheated me."

He walked out of the room into the central corridor that faced the seven interrogation rooms. The two officers who had been waiting outside rose from their seats.

"He's dead," Deiter said, and then strode off to the officer's lounge where he could grab a beer. Deiter knew the body would be delivered to the morgue and cremated. An autopsy would be out of the question—a waste of time and money. First, though, he'd wash his hands. He liked to look at blood, but not on his hands.

A few weeks later, the divide between East and West Germany, a wall built of a mix of cement blocks, barbed wire, electric fences, and free-fire zones, fell. Deiter panicked and stayed in his apartment, afraid to venture out, fearing he would be the target of the vigilante groups now seeking revenge against people like him. His supervising officers told him to stay put and that they'd be in touch. "Good will come out of this mess," he had been told. His officer was right. Soon, he became a security guard in a new security company organized by former *Stasi* officers. Over the years, he would travel as a hired bodyguard. He never understood what the men he protected did, but he did know they must have been rich, as the fee his company charged was $2,000 per day, plus expenses.

A few days ago, he rushed to Italy, hired for a few weeks by one of Zoran Hemmrich's companies. He thought the man nice and the job easy—all he had to do was to stay in a five-star hotel, follow a tall young man, rifle through his room and remove any documents, especially any packages from a specific London address.

"You understand, Deiter? It's important you understand."

"Yes," he replied. He had brains, why did people always treat him as if he didn't? It must be his size, he told himself. Deiter didn't worry though. He'd prove himself on this job, as he had on others.

He also had to find out about any women, or, as Mr. Hemmrich suggested, "Find out if he likes men as well, although I think that is not the case. But one never knows, so make sure." Same stuff he did in the old days...only now he didn't brutalize and kill people.

In fact, he liked this kind of work better. He saw a great many strange things. It was generally beautiful women and old men; he smiled to himself as he looked past the empty stool that separated him from Hogan and Diana. Different now—a young man and a young woman. Checking his watch, he noted that the time was almost 11:00. He had given the housekeeping supervisor 500,000 lira to send a maid to Hogan's room as well as to his lady friend's room to get anything there. A few more lira to a bellhop had bought the information that the lady friend was from the same company as Hogan, so why not look in her room as well? There, I am smart. I figured all that out myself. Herr Hemmrich will be proud of me. Very proud of me.

Deiter's English was good. Nevertheless, he had trouble making out all of the conversation he overheard between Hogan and Diana. He had placed a wallet in front of him. In his ear, he had a small receiver that allowed him to overhear a close conversation. The microphone was buried in what appeared to be a zipper around the wallet. What he did overhear through the din of the bar helped him understand what Hemmrich was after. Hogan and his friend had talked about materials that belonged to Hemmrich that were in a sealed package. Once he heard that, he went directly to the housekeeping office where, after flashing a 500,000-lira note, the housekeeper said she would give him the trash from the room.

"No, you must also look for a package—a sealed package. Bring it back with the trash. Look in both rooms. When you give me the trash, there will be another 500,000 lira." She simply nodded. So often in this hotel, she had made extra money because everyone wanted to look at the trash from rooms. "*Stupido*," she would think, shaking her head. Yet the money was good. This time, though, she actually had to look for something. No difference in her mind.

As he walked back into the bar, Deiter saw Hogan and the lady leave. Looking at his watch, then looking at the couple hurrying out of the room, he worried that the housekeeper would not be able to get in and out before the two had reached their rooms.

"I think you should give the stuff to Zoran and call it quits. Those things belong to him, not you or me," Diana repeated herself as they stepped off the elevator and walked slowly down the corridor to her room.

"Yeah, I know," was Keiran's only response. Keiran looked ahead and saw that a housekeeper's cart was parked adjacent to Diana's room. "Did you call for maid service at this hour?"

"No, must be putting down my bed and leaving me a mint. Why? Do you want me to ask for two mints and another set of towels? Are you staying with me tonight and sampling my charms?"

"Diana, stop. I told you I'm not in the mood. Strange time to turn down a bed," Keiran noted, looking at his watch. "It's eleven o'clock."

"So they do things differently here in Italy. Eleven may seem late, but here it's only the beginning of the evening." They stopped in front of Diana's room door.

"Well, that may be. But when does a maid close the door behind her? Don't they leave it open when all they're doing is pulling the bed covers down and leaving you a mint?" He spoke suspiciously.

"Keiran, you have now become so paranoid that I really worry about your stability. Here is my key card, be a gentleman and open my door."

"I won't need it. I bet it's open."

He tried the doorknob, and just as he was turning it, he felt a tug from the inside. He let his hands drop.

"*Prego. Scusa,*" the startled maid smiled nervously, one hand holding a brown plastic trash bag by its neck, which she dropped swiftly into the trash bin attached to her cart. She then quickly rolled the cart down the hall, stopping at the end room. Keiran's eyes followed her and noted that she didn't knock on the end room door, but entered it with key card.

"Diana, did you have that much trash in your room?"

"Of course not. I just registered earlier today. I did have some newspapers…maybe she took them. What does it matter anyhow?"

They both entered the room. Keiran noted that all the lights had been left on. Another strange characteristic of this maid.

"Where is the package you have for me?"

Diana went over to the desk where her briefcase lay. Opening it, she ruffled through its contents for a moment. Then, her soft voice shaking, her face stricken with fear, she turned to Keiran announcing, "Keiran, it's gone. The package is gone. It was right on top of my papers in the case when I left to see you. I don't understand…."

"Gone?"

"Yes! I placed everything in this case when I left London and I carried it on the plane. No one…."

"Oh, no!" Keiran rushed to the door, flung it open and ran down the corridor to the maid's cart. She was just coming out when he reached the cart.

"I'm sorry to bother you," Keiran smiled, "but I believe you accidentally took something that belongs to us."

"*Non parle inglese*," she responded while walking around to where Keiran was grabbing hold of the cart's handles, preventing her from pushing it forward. Keiran smiled back, looked into the trash bin attached to her cart, and pulled out the plastic bag that he recognized as the one that came from Diana's room. There was no other trash in the cart's bin and he noted that the room where she had parked the cart was marked '*Albergo Personale-Privato*.'

"Sorry, but this belongs to us. *Capisce*?" Panic gripped the maid's eyes. "I don't know how much they gave you to get this from our room, but here's something that will help you overcome your loss." Keiran reached into his wallet and pulled out a 100,000-lira note. "Now go."

Diana didn't leave her room, but stood in its doorway, watching what was happening down the hall. Keiran followed the maid down the corridor as she passed Diana's room, glancing quickly at Diana who stood still in the doorway.

"Keiran, what is going on? Why the trash?"

"Well, here is the bag of goodies, Diana. I'll bet that the package is in this bag." He walked into the room, placing the bag on the bed. Diana closed the door behind her.

"This is dangerous, Keiran. You should not have stopped her. It would have been a simple loss, and the client would have understood."

"Are you kidding?" Keiran looked at her in amazement. "You came this whole way to lose this? You want me to believe that? Besides, I know that this maid didn't just come up to the room and put your bed down at this hour. Zoran has spent a lot of time and money trying to get this stuff to his customer. And he's going to believe that it was stolen from this room? He'd have this hotel torn apart, this city torn apart to find it."

"Well until you interrupted the matter, it would have been incinerated with the rest of the trash. Besides, why not? People do steal things. Who knows? It could have been another client. All these bullets you say are flying around him—they're not from some stranger's gun, Keiran. Someone is after him, and maybe you know who it's. Zoran would have believed that it was another client. Want a drink? I need one."

"No, I don't need one and neither do you. I'll take this with me." Keiran held on to the plastic bag.

"You look sort of odd carrying a brown trash bag down the hall, but then I'm convinced you're odd. What will you do now, Keiran? If someone is after the material and bribed the maid to take my trash then maybe...Keiran, I'm scared. Really scared. Why don't you just say I lost the damn stuff? Wouldn't that be easier?"

"Come now. This is important. I...."

"If we lose it," Diana interrupted, "or maybe even destroy it, what harm will come? The Americans won't care unless it gets into the wrong hands. If it's destroyed, well...."

"That's too simplistic. The U. S. government would want to know how it got here. Besides, you just said that maybe somebody or someone is after this."

"Why drag yourself and the firm into this? Be sensible. You'd be involved. Being involved in this mess could ruin your career. Not good for anyone, Keiran. Please lose it. A lot of innocent people in the firm will be hurt if you don't."

Keiran looked at her, seeing a side that he never believed she had. She was crying, her face lowered, the sobs coming out softly.

"Diana, I'll go back to London with you in the morning. We'll take this with us. I'll call Zoran early tomorrow morning, tell him that Farris is dead, and that I've got to get back. I'll say you brought the wrong stuff. Come on, come to my room. We'll stay up there. The couch is bigger and I'll sleep on it tonight. I can't leave you here alone. No, I can't do that."

"Grab your bags and let's go.

He reached into the plastic bag and retrieved the sealed package, still untouched, its front a bit soiled from the remains of a coke can that had been in the trash. The package's tape was unbroken. He retied the trash bag and placed it by the trash bin by the desk.

Diana quickly folded her overnight bag.

"Here, give me the bag," Keiran said, grabbing it with one hand, holding the package under his other arm. "What do you have in this thing? You were only going to be here one day, maybe two."

Diana picked up her briefcase, now smiling, "Keiran, you never know what'll happen on these trips." She closed the door behind her, proud that she would at least be in the same room with him for several hours. How she loved his quiet and gentle man. By the flush in his cheeks, she hoped he was excited about her and not the events that now swirled around them both.

Thirty-Seven

At midnight, to promote energy conservation, every other ceiling light in the Hotel Villa Medici's corridors was turned off, tempering the glare of the yellow-gold hall walls. For those wandering along the halls at that hour, deep shadows made it difficult to admire the many scenes of renaissance Florence depicted in the oil paintings that hung on the now-dim walls. Regardless, Deiter wasn't interested in viewing the magnificence of the oils; he was concerned that he had picked the wrong room to start his search, reminding himself that the prostitutes he had used back in the old East German days would come to his apartment. Certainly, it was never the other way around. Now, he was having unexpected insecurities.

As he climbed the four flights to Keiran's floor, his breathing becoming more labored, he fingered the hotel master key pass card that would allow him to enter any room. On reflection, he thought his instructions were pretty vague—a package addressed to Zoran from the law firm of Kenton & Ward. The housekeeper had told him that the trash the evening maid had taken from Diana's room did indeed contain a small package, but the package was actually thrown into the room's trash basket; the maid didn't have to look elsewhere. Yet, as she left the room, Hogan had followed her and retrieved the trash bag.

So the girl wants to throw it out and the guy wants to keep it, Deiter thought. Why would she want to get rid of it? And why does he want it? Makes no sense. Whatever, it's got to be the stuff that Zoran wants. He stopped in front of Room 420, gently and deliberately inserted the card into the door handle slot, waiting for the sound of a click and the illumination of the green pinhole light on the brass door plate to go. He paused, waiting. Nothing happened. Was he inserting the card correctly? He flipped the card around, and inserted it into the door slot again. No click and no entry light. The card wasn't connecting properly. The housekeeper had given him a dead card. He now knew he should have beaten her up rather than give her more money.

"That bitch," he muttered under his breath.

Keiran had taken off his jacket, shoes, and tie and had loosened his belt, then laid down on the couch and had swiftly fallen fast asleep.

"Keiran, brush your teeth," Diana had admonished. But her words fell on deaf ears; he had already fallen fast asleep. She went over, kneeling down and placing her head lightly on his chest, listening to his breathing, wanting so badly to have him; to have him touch her deeply; to love her intensely.

"Oh, Keiran, you're such a fink, really you're. Not even a good night kiss from you." She rose, looked at him again, and went over to the closet, where she took out a blanket. Placing it over his stretched frame, she wondered what it would be like if they both were together and naked. Looking back at him, she quietly said, "Good Night, Keiran." She took off her suit, carefully hanging it in the hall closet, then disappeared into the bathroom, its solid wood door, two inches thick, would mask any noise and keep her from disturbing Keiran in the adjacent bedroom. She had decided to take a hot bath before going to bed, pondering that maybe, just maybe, Keiran would wake up and be in her bed when she finished. Dreaming of course, you fool, she shook her head, dropping her underwear to the tiled floor, and turning on the bath faucet. I'll never understand you, Keiran Hogan. Never.

Deiter tried unsuccessfully several more times—inserting the card, frustrated by the green entry light that would not illuminate.

"Having trouble, *Seniore*? *Prego*, let me try for you. You have your room folder with you, *Senore*?" Deiter turned to see a uniformed hotel security guard next to him.

"Room folder?"

"*Si*. Are you at the right room? These doors all look alike, you know."

"Of course," Deiter said, quickly placing the master key card in his pocket, reaching into his side pocket, and taking out his wallet where he had placed his own room card. "I have room 445," he said, looking at the room number. "Crazy. I've had too much to drink. I'm at the wrong room. Thank you for helping me."

"Your room is down the hall, this way, *Senore*. This way." The officer walked alongside Deiter until they got to Room 445. "Now try your card, *Prego*. Try your card." Deiter inserted his own room card into the slot and hastily let himself in. A close call, he silently told himself, and I accomplished nothing. Zoran won't be happy. No, not at all.

Diana dried herself slowly, looking at her slim body in the mirror, wondering what was wrong with her that Keiran didn't leap to make passionate love with her. She put on her evening perfume, arranged her nightgown so that the top revealed much cleavage, and quietly opened the door to the bedroom. She walked over to Keiran, leaned over, and kissed him lightly on the lips. He didn't move.

"Keiran Hogan," she softly said, "how can you be sleeping so soundly when I'm here?" Shaking her head slightly, she then walked over to the bed, slipping under its covers. She was soon also fast asleep.

Promptly at 4:00 a.m., Zoran stepped out into the darkened street, his energy sapped. The welts on his buttocks and back from the beatings he took from his 'slave master' still smarted. He was happy, though—a happiness that only came to him in this strange manner. His multiple orgasms had made, he believed, his mind clear of its prior confusion. This hidden place of his had brought him relief. He now knew what he had to do. If Hogan didn't have the material, then he knew that Farris had betrayed him and was cooperating with the police—probably telling them about his involvement with the Parrot matter and with everything else.

"Roubier," he asked his assistant, "did you hear from Deiter?"

"Yes. He said that he wasn't able to get what you wanted. He said that the trash was taken from the room with what you wanted, but that, somehow, a young man stopped the maid and took the trash back. He believes that the trash bag contained what you wanted."

Dumb jerk, Zoran thought. No matter, at least I know the stuff is here. Worthless hire. Absolutely worthless. If Simpson were here, I wouldn't need those idiots. Well, he's taking care of the mess in Venice. So I'm left with these dumb bastards. They take my money and never accomplish a thing.

Looking at his watch, he knew it was 3:00 a.m. in London. Farris had to be at home at this early hour. I don't care. I'll get the bastard out of bed. I need to talk to him now. He spoke silently to himself, taking the car phone from its cradle, pressing the button for the preset number for Farris. There were many rings before a sleepy voice answered.

"The Farris residence."

"This is Zoran Hemmrich. It is imperative that I speak to Mr. Farris. I would ask that you wake him. A very important matter."

There was silence at the other end.

"Did you hear me? This is Zoran Hemmrich. I need to speak to Mr. Farris." Zoran's voice was agitated and firm.

"Sir, I'm Matilda Beaverton, the housekeeper. Let me let you speak to Mrs. Farris. Just a moment please." Her voice was soft and sad.

"Mrs. Farris? Is that necessary? Isn't Mr. Farris there?"

"Just a moment, sir," Beaverton interrupted.

Strange, he thought. He'd never asked for Farris and got his wife. Something must be wrong....Something was terribly wrong. Perhaps Farris is in the hospital. Yes, that's it. That's why he's not here. He didn't want to tell me he's sick, he thought to himself.

It was several moments before he heard a soft voice come over the phone, a voice that was broken by sobbing.

"Zoran?"

"Gloria? Gloria Farris?"

"Yes, it's me, Zoran." she responded.

"I'm sorry to have to disturb you, but it's important that I reach Duane. Is he there?"

"Oh, Zoran. You don't know, do you?" The weeping became more pronounced.

"What's wrong, Gloria? What is wrong?"

"Duane is no longer with us. He died yesterday afternoon. We don't know how it happened. The doctor will let me know tomorrow, or I guess it's tomorrow now. So early in the morning. I'm sorry to have to tell you this, Zoran. He admired you so much."

"My God, this is a shock. Gloria, I'm so sorry. He was a true friend. I don't know what more to say now. Was he sick? What happened? I suspected that something was wrong when he canceled his trip to Italy."

"I really am not up to talking much more, Zoran. I hope you'll let me ring off. You understand, don't you?" She spoke softly, her voice was distant.

"Of course. I'll get to London tomorrow and come directly to your home. Will that be okay?"

"Yes, certainly. Please come by. Funeral arrangements are being made. I'll know more then. I must ring off, Zoran. Goodbye."

"Goodbye, Gloria."

Zoran replaced the phone to its cradle, stunned at the news. He had placed his trust and life with Farris, and now he was dead. Hogan knew, Zoran reflected. He had to know. That call Hogan received from his 'mother.' He knew Farris was dead at that time, and he didn't tell me. That young fucker. That son-of-a-bitch. I'm going to call him now. Wake that young fucker up.

"Roubier, take me to the Villa Medici and park across the street."

He grabbed the car phone, pushing in the number for the hotel. When the operator came on, he said curtly, "Mr. Keiran Hogan's room, please."

"*Prego.* One moment please."

The phone rang for some time. Finally a drowsy, girlish voice came on. "Yes? Who is this?"

"This is Mr. Zoran Hemmrich. Is this the room for Mr. Hogan, Keiran Hogan?"

There was silence on the line.

Keiran stirred on the couch, mumbling. Diana rose from the bed and hurried over to the couch where Keiran was slowly waking up.

"The phone, Diana. Who's on the phone?" He now sat up, rubbing his eyes, trying to get them into focus.

"It's Zoran Hemmrich, Keiran. Your client. Are you in?" she whispered.

"Yeah, why not?"

He rose and walked over to the desk and picked up the phone. "Pretty early in the morning, Zoran. What is it?" Keiran's voice was annoyed and sleepy.

"Well, it seems to me that you have good company with you. So, I can understand why you would not want to be disturbed." Zoran's voice was scornful. "Did you get the package from Farris? And did you know that Farris has died?"

There was silence again for a moment.

"Yes, I know he passed away. You sound angry—it must be because I didn't tell you. My office told me not to tell you, though. They advised that, because of your special relationship with Farris and your long history with the firm, the managing partner from our New York headquarters would be calling you directly to advise you of Farris' death. They felt that would be more appropriate than for an associate to advise you. I really don't know much more than that, Zoran. I would suspect that you would be getting a call from the partner soon. How did you find out?"

"You want me to believe your story? Is that what you want me to do? I've done business with your firm for many years, paid millions of dollars in fees, and you want me to believe that the call you got from your 'mother' was to advise you that the partner that I worked with and who knew all my business was dead, but that you were not to tell me? Do you think I'm fuckin' stupid?"

"Those were my instructions, sir. Plain and simple," Keiran answered.

"Plain and simple. I had to call his home trying to find out why he hadn't returned my calls. It was his wife who told me. This makes for a very unsettled moment for me. I don't understand why you didn't tell me."

"I was asked not to. Nothing nefarious about what I did, Zoran."

"You may not think so, but when your partner calls me—if he calls me—I intend to tell him that this was a very reckless decision on the firm's part. An associate knows that the partner with whom I have worked with for years has died, but he is told not to tell me. Dumb move, Keiran Hogan. I won't forget it. Enough. On to a more important matter. What about the material that Farris said that he sent you for me? Has it arrived?"

"I haven't seen it yet." Keiran knew he was shading the truth. He had seen the package, but not the material in the package.

"Well, I'm sure it will be on its way. I'd like to see you for breakfast at seven. I'll send a car to pick you up. In the meantime, go back to your lady friend. Enjoy yourself."

"Okay," was Keiran's only response.

"Goodbye, Keiran. You've been a complete disappointment to me. I will never understand why you did what you did. I'm not a stranger, you know." Zoran hung up.

Diana came over and sat next to Keiran, looking at him intently, her perfumed body making it difficult for Keiran to concentrate. She did look and smell beautiful. And she looked frightened, something he had never seen in her before. He thought her bright, yet brash, and supremely confident. She put her arm around his shoulder, tenderly asking, "Well, what do we do now?" her face furled into a frown.

"We get dressed, and take the next plane to London."

"You know he'll follow us."

"Maybe."

"So you talked to the maid. What did she tell you?" Zoran spoke angrily to Deiter. "Why would you wait downstairs for the trash bag?

Why weren't you waiting for her when she brought the bag out? That was a dumb move, Deiter, a really dumb move."

"She told me that as she came out of the lady's room with the trash, the lady and this Hogan kid came upon her. Hogan then went after her and took the trash bag out, saying that they needed whatever was in it. That's it. If I was up there with the maid, Hogan and the lady would have seen me and called the police. I did the right thing. I'm not dumb. I handled this the correct way."

"I don't think so. You were supposed to get the package. You were not able to do that. Don't expect any payment for a failed job. You understand, you dumb shit?" Zoran hung up the phone. He now knew for certain that Keiran had the package. And he had lied to him about it.

Deiter looked at the dead phone. Nothing had changed. He tried to do the job given him, and in the end, like always, he was called dumb. But he wasn't dumb, or stupid, or slow. It took planning to get the housekeeper to cooperate. It was only the luck of the draw that Hogan and his lady friend had arrived just when they did. A few minutes later and he would have had the trash, retrieved the package, and everything would be fine. He'd be a hero and smart. Now, he was called a dumb shit. He was tired of being called names—he was called names all the time, bad names. No one ever looked at him and thanked him for what he did. Many times, when he went on bodyguard trips, the clients he protected would not even look at him directly. Perhaps it was his size, his scarred face, his close-cropped hair, the eyes that never seemed fully open. Whatever it was, he never knew the real answer. And now, again, Zoran was calling him a name. He's the dumb shit, not me.

Grayson awoke from a short nap, concerned that events were moving to a climax and worried that Hogan would be harmed. His office in London had confirmed that Farris was now the real suspect in the Coborn mole case. The number of calls from Coborn to Farris and the depositing of funds into Coborn's overseas accounts that closely followed those calls were still just circumstantial facts, as the fund transfers could not, as yet, be traced to Farris. His death precluded any interviewing by the Metropolitan police. Coborn probably knew nothing about Grayson and 'Crescent Eagle,' but then, something could have slipped through. One had to assume the worse.

Then there was the Parrot Restaurant explosion, with Zoran being the only survivor. He left before the explosion. It was a mess made messier by what looked to Grayson to be a partnership gone haywire. Everyone was becoming an independent operator…but why? And Keiran Hogan, where was he in this matrix? He took out his cell phone and pressed in the number for Hogan.

It was answered quickly. "Yes?"

"Keiran. Grayson here. Breakfast later?"

"Bob, do you know what time it is?'

"Yeah, it's about five. Don't you go to the pool this early in the morning?"

"Sometimes, but not today. Listen, what is it? I'm leaving for London this morning, so I don't have much time."

"London?"

"Yeah. We can visit there. I'd like some more advice from you. By the way, Farris is dead. Died yesterday."

"I hadn't heard that. Sorry. He wasn't that old. What will you do?"

"I'm going back to London."

"Zoran Hemmrich, your client…I thought you had some meetings here and that after them, you'd be joined by Jennifer. Or at least I had planned to have dinner with you to talk about your future."

"Too much has changed now, Bob. I've got to get back. I won't be meeting with Zoran. He'll be pissed off, I'm sure, but he's into things with which I'm not comfortable. Well, you know the story."

"What flight are you taking?"

"The six thirty on BA."

"Do you need a lift? I've got a car'

"That would be fine, but I'm going to take the train to the airport. I think it's faster."

“No, it isn’t. At this time of the morning a car is more comfortable and more convenient. I won't take no for an answer. I’ll be downstairs with one of my colleagues to take you.”

“You win. Thanks. See you later. And, Bob…be on time.” He laughed and heard Grayson laugh as well.

“I’ll try,” Grayson replied. “I’ll really try.”

Thirty-Eight

Sitting in the back of his opaque-windowed Mercedes, parked in the dark shadows of a narrow side street, with a clear view of the classic, handsome front of the Hotel Villa Medici, Zoran knew his anxiety wasn't without cause. All the doors were shut now to his easily getting the documents and computer discs for which he had been partially paid by the North Koreans. Farris was dead; Deiter had failed in retrieving the package that was now in the hotel with Hogan…and his instincts told him Hogan would not turn over the material. Life, he pondered, was now bitter in his mouth.

"Hogan and that broad are now doubtless wrapped in sleep," he muttered. He needed the package. It was 5 o'clock and his meeting with the North Koreans would be in five hours. He could not show up empty-handed. He would have to produce what he promised them yesterday. Hogan would also produce; he would give the package to Zoran—willingly or not. One more dead man won't affect me one way or the other. He smiled as his thoughts focused on how he would take Hogan's life. That kid had so much promise…so much promise. An opportunity lost. It was foolish fancy, perhaps, but he wished that Hogan had turned. It's too bad. Most people his age have a passionate affection for money and power. This bastard ardently thinks otherwise. Well, he's about to learn that that kind of thinking brings unpleasant consequences.

"Roubier, Chavez," he called into the car intercom, "Too late to go to bed, gentlemen, not too early to continue our work. It's after five in the morning. Did you get some nap-time while I was busy earlier?"

"We took turns, Mr. Hemmrich. Not to worry, we're fine." Roubier responded calmly.

"Good. Drive to the front of the hotel. We'll leave the car in the driveway. I have a strong urge to see a guest of the hotel. Roubier, you'll go with me to his room. Hopefully, he'll give me what I want. If not, the hotel will have a guest check out sooner rather than later." His laugh was boisterous. "Chavez, you'll stay with the car. Any questions?"

Both Roubier and Chavez joined in the laughter.

Zoran kept a permanent suite at the Hotel to mask the real reason why, from time to time, he came to Florence. His family and any business calls would be directed to the hotel where he would collect messages when he finished with his personal activities at 17 Via Cardinale. Even his 'assistants' didn't really know what took place at that villa; they probably suspected he was seeing prostitutes—which was fine from Zoran's point of view. He believed, almost mystically, that secrets were best hidden by other secrets.

The doorman, resplendent in a dark gray uniform with gold trim and trying to shake off the fatigue of the late shift, was surprised to see the black four-door Mercedes draw up to the hotel entrance at this early morning hour. Quickly, one powerful man, well dressed in a dark blue suit and tie against a light blue shirt, a small gold circle in his lapel, jumped out, opening the passenger door to let out one of the hotel's favorite guests, Zoran Hemmrich. Although he rushed over to open the door himself, he was waved off. Upon recognizing Zoran, he had straightened himself, trying to make his fifty year old, five-foot-four frame taller, and brushing imaginary dust from his uniform. He knew that a brisk, '*Buon giorno, Senor Hemmrich*' to this guest would earn him a generous tip. Naturally, he would make a brief effort to decline the money before it was pushed into his hand, clearly indicating he was to take it. He would not be disappointed. In fact, he would be elated as Zoran gave him a 50,000 lira note. He opened the hotel's glass door, a wide smile on his dark, smooth face as Zoran and Roubier strode into the lobby.

Zoran and Roubier walked briskly on the inlaid marble lobby floor, nodding lightly to the clerk as they passed the reception desk and proceeded quickly to the bank of three elevators a short distance and to the left of the reception desk. The hotel security allowed anyone to push the elevator call button. However, for the elevator to ascend to a designated floor, a special security access card was needed. Zoran's permanent lease on a suite at the hotel allowed him his own card, which he inserted into the proper floor slot when the elevator arrived. The security officer seated at his desk facing the elevator also recognized Zoran and he said simply and softly, "*Buon giorno, Senor Hemmrich.*" Zoran smiled, and repeated the greeting. Then he and Roubier got on the elevator, followed by a tall young man who wore glasses and clutched a newspaper and a briefcase. He slid his card in for the fifth floor. He continued reading his paper and appeared not to notice Zoran and Roubier leave the elevator when it reached the fourth floor.

Grayson was alone in the lounge that was separated from the main reception area by a barrier of towering green palms and other foliage. The tables for coffee and light breakfast were set parallel to the bank of windows facing the front of the hotel. He was seated at the last table in the double row of several tables, and was able to see Zoran and Roubier enter the lobby and then the elevator. There were a few others in the section sipping their coffee and helping themselves to the small buffet of sweet rolls, juices, and fruit that had been set up for the early risers. Both of his men were seated in the main reception area—one facing the reception desk, the other facing the entrance. One rose, folding his paper, picking up his briefcase, and followed Zoran and Roubier onto the elevator.

"Diana, if I haven't told you, I appreciate your coming and helping me." Keiran looked at her, his eyes meeting hers. His were eyes that told the story of a man who was genuinely worried.

"No, I didn't help you. I should have lost this damn package back in London. Then life would be a great deal simpler for you and for me. You know, though, I haven't figured out why I came to Florence in the first place. It wasn't bright of me—not at all—and I'm supposed to be bright, brighter than you, probably."

"Diana, don't get carried away now!" Keiran's smile was broad. "Zoran wants the package Farris sent for him. You came as the courier. Not particularly intricate reasoning. I know Zoran didn't believe me the first time he asked for the data. And I don't think he trusted my response when he called just a few minutes ago. One thing I do know is that we've got to get out of here before he comes and breaks down the door to get the package of goodies. It's now a quarter past five. Are you all packed?"

"Oh, Keiran! Let's leave all our clothes here. I don't like them anyway, and I need some new things. It'll just burden us. I'll just take my briefcase with my laptop, and of course my makeup case!" They both laughed.

"You're impossible, Diana. There are priorities in life, I suppose. Your idea is good. I'll match you, but without the case."

"Do we take the package?" Diana asked.

"Yeah, we've got to get it to the American Embassy in London. They've got to know what it is and maybe can figure out who stole it. This is serious material."

The door buzzer was brief.

Keiran raised his hand, indicating to Diana that she be silent.

The second time, the buzzer was more intense.

"Just a moment We didn't leave any wake up call. Go away, whoever you're," Keiran concealed his voice, making it sound as if he were groggy from sleep.

"Keiran? This is Zoran. Open up. I need to see you." His voice was firm, but with a nervous shake to its tone.

"Zoran? You we're supposed to meet for breakfast at 7 o'clock. What are you doing here now?"

"It's serious. I need to talk with you right away. You know the reason."

"Well," Keiran replied, now annoyed, "I can't open the door. I'll see you downstairs. I'm in…well you know, I'm busy right now."

"Busy?"

"You know what I mean. I'll be down by 6 o'clock Now, please wait for me downstairs."

Zoran wasn't really perplexed, having just had his own sexual predilections satisfied. Yet he didn't trust Keiran.

"Okay, Keiran. I'll be downstairs in the lounge. Hurry. We've much to talk about."

"Thanks. I just can't get away now." Keiran answered.

Zoran said nothing further, but he certainly wasn't going to trust Hogan to meet him downstairs. No, he, along with Roubier, would sit down on the two baroque chairs opposite the elevators. Hogan would probably come out within half an hour, he surmised. Patience, stubborn patience, like steel. I'm going to win this one. Zoran folded his arms across his chest; Roubier picked up a magazine on the side table. He turned to Zoran and smiled, pointing to the headline on its cover, 'Florence, the City of Beauty and Calm.' Zoran laughed lightly, commenting, "Not this week."

Keiran motioned Diana into the bathroom, closing the door behind him.

"Now? You want to take a shower with me now?"

"No, Diana. This is the safest place to talk. Now listen. Zoran never travels alone. His bodyguards are always glued to him. And one or two are outside the door right now. They'll be waiting. We'll go out together, you with your bags. On second thought, take your entire luggage; I'll just take my briefcase. He doesn't know the size of the package; he'll think it's in my case. I'll leave the rest of my clothes in the room. I'll tell him that I'm going to check out later, not knowing how long he wants me to stay to wind up things after our meeting. I'll even introduce you…"

"I already know him," Diana interrupted, "I met him a few years ago. Maybe he forgot, though. It's been a while."

"Okay, fine. Bob Grayson offered to take us to the airport at around six, so you'll go with him. I'll call him and tell him about the change in plans. He'll help you."

Diana nodded her head, signifying she understood.

"Get on the very first plane to London, Diana. You have my cell phone number. Call me when you get to the airport. You promise?"

"Yes, Keiran. This is madness, but I'll do it. But what is going to happen to you? Oh, what the bloody hell. Maybe if we survive this nonsense, it will be as faint in my mind as a dream of a distant loving evening with you. Anyhow, sir, you don't have a pleasant body odor. You need a shower and a clean shirt. If we're to go on this caper—isn't that what you Americans call this kind of adventure, a 'caper'?—then we should look as if we had raunchy sex. You know, relieved and beautiful looking."

Keiran smiled, leaned over, and kissed her on the cheek.

"Is that all I get?"

"Timing, Diana. Everything is timing."

"Out, you creep. Get out now. I'll only be in here for a few minutes."

Diana was true to her word. In a few minutes she had showered, put on her makeup, and an alluring perfume. She wore only her panties and bra as she left the bathroom, leaving the door open for Keiran.

"You're next, smelly man."

"No one's ever called me that," Keiran said while looking at her.

"Maybe it's because no one has ever been with you while you slept on a couch, fully clothed, sweating throughout the night." She laughed at her own statement. "You're just plain dull. Ugh."

A scowl crossed Keiran's brow. He was thinking that maybe she was right. He had taken off his pants, shirt, and socks and was standing in front of her, bare-chested. She stared at him, and her stare aroused him.

"Me? Smell?"

"Yeah, you do. Remember, you didn't clean up last night."

"You are merciless. You should try to keep that quality in check." He smiled as Diana reached over, picked up a box of tissues on the bedside table, hurling it at his groin.

"Get in there before I attack you."

She realized that their desires, like their hearts would never be in accord. There wasn't much of a contest. Keiran was in love with someone else. His passion was for a simple TV reader. Her thoughts were still as she finished dressing. She hated and dreaded encountering a man who didn't succumb to her charms. Yet with Keiran she couldn't have those emotions. His manner was new and beautiful to her; she wanted to meet someone like him and she had a vivid sensation that she probably never would. Such was her fate.

She would never tell him that she had intercepted HenHen and asked to take the package rather than send it with a commercial courier. The rest of her story was false.

I tried. Maybe if I had gotten him in bed, it wouldn't have made any difference. She finished dressing, picking out a dark green suit, quickly putting it on while trying to forget Keiran's nude body in the shower. If one looked carefully, one would have noticed that her eyes welled up with moisture. Stop it, you jerk, she admonished herself. Get a hold of yourself. She put on a simple strand of pearls, her gold watch, and a small emerald ring her mother and father had given her upon her graduation from Cambridge—at the top of her class.

A shower is a reflective place for someone with a great deal on his mind. Under the steaming, streaming flow of fine warm water over one's body, the mind becomes composed; thoughts are clearer. What if the package didn't contain what Farris said it did? Keiran wondered. No, that wouldn't make any sense. Why would Farris not send his client of these many years the most important material for the most crucial contract of their relationship? But Farris was now dead. Another heart attack? And why did Farris have Diana carry the package from London? Understandable, certainly, to have it personally delivered. But he must have known he wasn't coming if he had arranged a back-up plan. Farris missing a meeting with Zoran on this most significant gathering? Did he know he was going to die? Get real, Keiran. This is getting more complex than it need be, and you're getting as paranoid as Zoran. He stepped out of the shower, grabbing a bath towel, and hastily drying himself. Winging it wasn't what he liked to do, but now that Zoran was probably outside waiting for him, improvisation was the only avenue to take.

Shaving wasn't a problem. He didn't have too. After brushing his teeth he put on some deodorant. I smell? She's got to be kidding. No one has ever told me that. He put on some clean shorts and opened the door from the bathroom to the bedroom to see Diana holding a shirt for him.

"I think this would go great with my suit—dull gray. I don't want you to outshine me when we leave. I want all eyes on me and not on you. I want to get out of here alive," she snickered while going over and kissing him on the cheek. "Now you do smell delicious."

" Thanks for the shirt. You know what you're to do now?" His tone turned serious.

"Yes, I do. I go outside with you, say hello to creepy Zoran, go down the elevator with you, hope Mr. Grayson, the man I met at the bar, is there, and hope that he'll take me to the airport where I wing my way back to London with the goodies. In the meantime, what are you going to do?"

"Create another package."

"With what, asshole? With what?"

"Watch the language, Diana. You're only beautiful when you don't use bad language."

"From what planet did you come? And why do I like you?"

"Well, let's think…." Keiran looked around the room, his gaze ending on Diana's makeup kit—a dark brown box-shaped case about fifteen by twelve inches with a depth of about ten inches.

"No. Absolutely not. I have all my makeup in here; it's all organized."

Keiran went over to the desk where Diana had placed her makeup case, commenting, "Ah, perfect size."

"It's not perfect size. What will I do for makeup if I meet the man of my dreams? Women always need makeup. It's as essential as orgasms—probably more so."

"Not today," Keiran laughed. "Take the makeup out of the case. I'm going to put the originals in it."

Diana emptied the case on to the bed.

"You, Keiran Hogan, are an absolute ass…."

"Don't finish that word! And I'm not. Now lets get the paper off the real item."

"Don't look at me. I am just an observer to this document robbery."

"When this is over, I'm going to take you to dinner. I promise."

"Sure, sure, sure."

Keiran looked at the sealed package. The two-inch wide brown adhesive tape encircled the brown wrapped package in the form of a cross; one segment across the width another across the length.

"Diana, do you have a safety razor? You know, something to shave your legs with?"

"No, I have them waxed, you idiot."

"You have to have a shaver. What about your underarms?"

"My, aren't we getting personal." Diana opened her makeup case and drew out a small plastic box. Opening, it she took out a small silver safety razor.

"Here—but I want it back."

Keiran looked at it a moment and then unscrewed the bottom of the razor's stem, which opened the top of the razor and allowed him to remove the blade from its position in the razor.

"Diana, come hold the package for me, please."

"I don't think this is going to work, Keiran," replied Diana, coming over to the side table where Keiran had placed the package. He carefully slit the tape at one end of the package, allowing him to open the flaps of the wrapping paper at that end.

"It looks too tight to slide out. And look, my case is slightly smaller than the package."

"Yeah. But let's try. Hold the other end, and let me see what I can do."

Whoever wrapped the package had wrapped the box with a plastic bubble wrap and then over-wrapped that with the brown mailing paper, making it impossible to slide out.

"We'll have to take all the paper off."

"The one thing you have to be careful about, is the facing paper—where the address label is. You can't disturb that."

"Yeah, I know." He began to cut the tape on the other three sides of the box. Now the paper was loose enough to slide off.

"We don't have to worry about this inner plastic wrap.

In a few moments, he had the box clear of the plastic wrap and the outer paper.

"Should we look in it?" Diana inquired.

"No. Besides, it's sealed tighter than the outside. You carry any scotch tape in that case of yours?"

"Of course. I'm always prepared. Don't you come prepared?"

"Here—and I want it back."

"Okay. Do you have the envelopes and paper?"

"Yeah. Here, you fink." She thrust over three envelopes filled with blank copy paper.

"Thanks."

Keiran carefully put the envelopes as well as a smaller one in which he had placed the computer disk with the contract data and blank paper in the package Diana had brought with her, sealing it carefully. Then he placed the original disks and drawings in the make-up case.

"Here, Diana. Does it work?"

"It's okay. Keiran, I'm worried about you. You'll be with Zoran and he'll hit the ceiling…or worse…when he opens this package."

"I'm just the messenger, Farris sent it. He'll be angry with a dead man. In his paranoid state, he'll attribute it to Farris. Being angry with me won't accomplish anything. If I were him, I'd worry about the North Koreans. They'll be pissed beyond reason. Ready?"

"Sure, why delay? The longer we wait, the wilder the impending disaster my imagination conjures up. Besides, I'm not good at waiting for anything."

"Are you always this pessimistic?"

"No, only when I'm afraid for my life."

Keiran went over and put his arms around her. "Diana, you'll be fine. I promise you."

"Yeah, like all those promised dinners."

Keiran smiled wryly and shrugged. He then leaned over and kissed her on the cheek.

Diana didn't react.

"I'm ready."

Zoran saw them first. Holding hands, they strode down the corridor.

"Look at them, Roubier. He's as satisfied as a rooster. Shit, he is a rooster. I wonder how many times she came? Some swing she has, eh? Some swing."

Keiran spoke to him first.

"Zoran, you're waiting for us up here? I thought we'd meet downstairs in the lounge. What gives? By the way, you remember Diana Peters of our firm?"

Zoran looked at Diana for several moments, finally smiling and saying, "Of course, of course. A few years ago. Duane had you working on some matters for me." He leaned over and kissed her on both cheeks.

"How are you Mr. Hemmrich? Enjoying Florence?" Diana said cheerfully, her flirtatious eyes fixed on Zoran.

"Yes, as a matter of fact, I am. And you?"

Diana turned to Keiran before responding. "Couldn't be having a better time, actually." Zoran didn't fail to notice the eye contact between the two. He silently told himself he was right, Hogan had been delayed because of his penchant for sex. Maybe he wasn't such a bad young man after all.

"Well, now, shall we go downstairs?"

"Certainly, Zoran. Diana is leaving for the airport. Her ride is downstairs. Then I can go with you. Oh, by the way, this is for you."

Keiran attempted to hand over the package to Zoran, who waved it off as if he were disinterested. "Roubier will take it, thank you. Thank you very much. My mind, though, Keiran, is on the death of Duane. I am finding it very difficult to understand how his life was snatched from us. You know we go back a long time. He was such a brilliant lawyer. More importantly, he was a good and loyal friend. We must conclude our business directly, Keiran, so we can get to London for Duane's memorial service. I should think we could be off no later than three this afternoon. Ms. Peters, would you like to join us on my plane? Can you stay a few more hours? I'm sure Keiran would enjoy your company on the flight back, as would I."

"Without doubt, I'm sure he would." She smiled broadly at Keiran. "But I have to get back much sooner. I have a crucial meeting with a client at noon today. I simply can't stay. I'm sorry. I'd enjoy being with Keiran for a few more hours." She leaned over and kissed Keiran on the cheek. He didn't move, but continued the charade.

"I'll miss her on the flight as well. Duty calls in our firm, and I'll have to remain here while she goes back. Life is so unfair, wouldn't you agree Zoran?"

"With that I do agree. Life is not fair. Well, shall we go downstairs? Will you join us for some breakfast, Diana?" Zoran asked softly.

"I'd like to, but I do have to get to the airport. The flight will have breakfast. I can't eat too much if I'm going to keep my girlish figure," Diana answered warmly and convincingly.

"Well, I can understand that." Zoran looked at her approvingly. Keiran said nothing; his expression revealed only polite interest.

Roubier pressed the elevator down button.

"A short stay in Florence for you, Diana. Have you been here before?' Zoran asked.

"Yes, several times actually. When I was a child, my father took us here for several summers—for vacation. He rented a villa not too far from here in the Chianti wine country. They were good days for my sister and me. We loved it."

"A favorite part of Italy for me as well."

Keiran remained silent, eyeing the elevator doors as they opened quickly when they arrived at the lobby floor. Walking briskly, hand in hand with Diana, he headed toward the hotel entrance looking for Grayson. He glanced at his watch. It was a few minutes after six.

"Keiran! Keiran Hogan!" The cry came from his left. Hogan turned to see Grayson and another man walking briskly toward them. The Grayson's colleague was the man he had seen in Guernsey and Venice. Another time he'd pursue this with Grayson. For now, he had to get Diana off and with the package to London.

"Bob, you're up. I thought you'd forgotten." Keiran held Diana's hand tightly. "Thanks for offering to take us to the airport."

"You mean Diana. You're staying, Keiran. We have much to do," Zoran interrupted, annoyed with Keiran's statement.

"Of course. What am I saying? By the way, Mr. Zoran Hemmrich, say hello to Bob Grayson, another lawyer from the United States who practices in London."

"Lawyers. Surrounded by lawyers. What more can I say? Good to meet you. Mr. Grayson." Zoran extended his hand to Grayson.

"Please call me Bob. When I'm called Mr. Grayson, I feel as if some judge is about to do nasty things to my client."

"Likewise, call me Zoran. When someone calls me Mr. Hemmrich, I think he's asking for a contribution." Everyone laughed.

"My associate, Nick Alderson. Nick, Keiran Hogan and Zoran Hemmrich."

Alderson was tall and trim, his face bronze with an aquiline nose, his mouth a bit large, his dark thick hair was tidy, and his hand, which was now extended to Keiran and Zoran, big and lean.

He smiled, said nothing, and shook their hands vigorously.

"Well, if you're going to stay longer in Florence, let's have dinner. Zoran, would you care to join us?"

"That's a kind invitation. Keiran and I hope to finish our meeting early this afternoon and will be heading to London by three o'clock. Perhaps another time."

"Certainly, in London. I'll give a call to Keiran and he'll pass it on to you. Diana, your car is ready."

Alderson reached for her bags. She held on to her laptop case and her briefcase. Leaning over, she kissed Keiran lightly on the lips, "Take good care of yourself and thanks for a lovely evening. See you in London." Zoran eyed everything silently, musing that Hogan must have had a great evening of sex. Grayson looked on a bit incredulous, knowing that Hogan was now expressing a serious interest in Jennifer. Yet he detected a light and uncomfortable response from Hogan; it wasn't a response that would encourage an onlooker to think that there was deep love between them. The theater was good, but he wondered about the reality. More important, why wasn't Hogan going back to London with her?

"Take care of yourself, Diana. See you later." He smiled broadly as she got into the dark gray BMW as Alderson held the door open for her. He placed her bags in the front passenger's seat, right next to him. Within moments, the car left the hotel driveway and disappeared around the block.

Thirty-nine

Zoran looked steadily at the car bearing Diana as it left the hotel driveway.

"Beautiful young lady, Keiran. You are a lucky man. I assume you had a worthwhile evening?" He turned to Keiran, his lips pursed, birdlike, raising his hand to his gray shirt collar and bringing both ends together briefly in an attempt to ward off an imaginary burst of cold wind.

Keiran nodded in a reserved but gentle way. "I have no complaints whatsoever, Zoran. None."

"Good. Now on this perfect day—look at the sky, a brilliant blue…not a cloud, not even a wisp of a cloud in the sky—we go to work. I'm anticipating we will conclude by early afternoon. Enough time to get back to London."

Zoran, emitting a cough, moved quickly toward the dark gray Mercedes where Chavez, who had seen him exit the front doors of the hotel, was standing stiffly with the rear car door opened wide. Keiran followed, but looked back briefly to wave at Grayson, who remained behind and observed the two through the lobby's floor-to-ceiling glass windows, his body partially obscured by several large ficus trees.

Grayson returned the wave then turned and walked away.

Zoran's Mercedes slowly made its way from the hotel driveway, disappearing around the corner into the light early morning Florence traffic. A small black Fiat van, the signs on its rear doors announcing a messenger service—'*Rapido Messaggero*'—turned down the same street, following Zoran's car. Grayson glanced at his watch, noting it was almost 6:30. He waited a few minutes, then quickly left the hotel, walking the half block from the hotel to a similarly colored Fiat van, this one without the messenger service sign. Settling behind the wheel, he took from his side pocket a five by five inch square flat screen monitor, which he placed on the dashboard, clamping it securely. Pressing a dark green button on the panel, the screen glowed with a view of the several blocks around his position. A red arrow on the screen displayed the location of his colleague in the van ahead of him.

As he settled back into his seat, Zoran turned to look at Keiran, his voice hesitant, his brow pinched into a frown.

"I'm still in shock, Keiran, absolute shock over Farris' death. Terrible. Tragic. A healthy man like Duane just dies." Zoran took a deep breath before continuing, "There must be more to it than that. His death troubles me strangely. Perhaps he never told me he was sick and didn't want me to know of any serious conditions he may have had. Were there any rumors in the firm about his health?'

"No, not that I know of. Actually, he used to pride himself in telling us how healthy he was. His death is a mystery to me as well."

"We were so close, so very close, linked together in so many ways. I just don't know what I'll do without him. I came to rely so heavily on him." Keiran could not fail to notice that Zoran's face turned sad, with small blue half circles shading his eyes, his hands trembling slightly, his voice lowered to a murmur. He obviously had not slept the night before.

"I owe an unending debt to him," Zoran continued. "He helped to make me as successful as I am today. I have to tell you that when he didn't send the package in time for yesterday's meeting, I was upset with him, momentarily believing that he had betrayed me. I should have known better. Both of us have gone through so much, for him to be disloyal is simply unthinkable. I made a mistake cluttering my mind with such a thought. There is no jackal in Duane Farris. None." There was a pause before he continued.

"Now as for you, Keiran, I have to be frank. At one time I had a good, solid impression of you. Now, it's only a mildly unpleasant one. Why? Well, I'm still smarting over the fact that—and it disturbs me gravely—that the moment you were aware Duane's death, you didn't tell me. Your excuse was rather flimsy. At this moment, you should understand that I still haven't heard from any partner of your firm. Perhaps the hour is too early for your partner to get up and give me that call. No matter. I'm not interested in talking to anyone from your office at this time. Well, then, as far as you knew, he had no heart problems?"

"I've told you all I know about his health," Keiran replied with a bit of impatience. "There is nothing further. As for my not advising you of his death, I was told not to, and I followed my firm's instructions. I'm surprised the managing partner in New York hasn't contacted you."

"No, there's been no contact whatsoever. No matter, the call will come when it comes. Regardless, with Duane gone, I'll have to think long and hard whether to continue with your firm. One other thing, Keiran—and perhaps your instincts detected the same strong feeling I had—but Duane was under some stress regarding the death of an official of the U. S. Embassy in London. A man by the name of Coborn," Zoran volunteered, his voice lowering into a murmur, speaking now like one who revered truth.

"No, I hadn't suspected anything," Keiran answered, his expression now revealing nothing but polite interest. "As for Coborn, yeah, I read about him in the *Times* before I left London. The police called it a suicide. In fact, I saw Mr. Coborn twice. Once at the embassy and the next time as I was arriving at Mr. Farris' house, he was leaving. It was the Saturday before I left for Guernsey. Mr. Farris must have had some involvement with Coborn for him to be visiting his home on a weekend."

There was silence for a moment as Zoran turned from Keiran and looked out the car window, appearing to be interested in the passing scenery. Without facing Keiran, he asked, "Did you mention to Duane that you saw Coborn leaving when you arrived at his home?"

"I'm sorry Zoran, I can't understand what you've said. You're speaking to the window and to not me. If you're asking me a question, you'll have to look at me. Words bouncing off a window don't reach me."

Zoran waited a few moments and then spoke, his eyes unsteady, darting from Keiran to Roubier then back to Keiran. Speaking in a tone with which Keiran was familiar, a manner of speech Zoran used when he wished to give a command couched as a request, he said, "Keiran Hogan, you never cease to amaze me. You have an arrogance that only comes from supreme confidence, or utmost stupidity. You do realize that I can get rid of you at any time and in any manner? Again, did you tell Duane you saw Coborn leaving his home? Please give me a straight answer."

"First, you can fire me any time you want and take any other lawyer in the firm. That's your prerogative. Second, I didn't think it necessary for me to advise Mr. Farris that I saw Coborn. I was called to Mr. Farris' home to discuss your new company, Benton Industries, and that was the focus of our meeting, not a discussion of who came and left his home. I assumed Coborn and Farris were friends, and it was none of my business Otherwise, what was he doing leaving Mr. Farris' home on a Saturday?"

Again, there was an awkward silence for a period with Zoran staring at Keiran and Keiran's eyes fixed on Zoran. It was as if there was a duel between them over who was going to turn away first.

Finally, Zoran looked ahead, reaching for the car intercom, taking it from its cradle in the service panel in front of him. "Roubier. How's the time?"

"Should be there between 9:15 and 9:30, sir. We'll make it. Traffic isn't a problem, sir."

"Good." He put the intercom back in its holder.

"What was Coborn doing at Duane's home? Interesting question, Keiran. I don't know for certain the connection between the two, but I believe that Coborn would deliver messages from the ambassador, perhaps, or bring documents. I just don't know. So I suspect that the police would want to interview Duane. Could that have provoked his health troubles? Perhaps he was on Coborn's phone list or his appointment calendar. I would think it was just routine, nothing over which Duane would get excited or anxious. Yet, who knows? Perhaps the stress of that possible involvement, along with his heavy work for me including this latest project caused him trouble. Maybe I helped bring about his heart attack with my constant requests for his aid." Zoran spoke now with a soft firmness, seemingly to convince himself that was those were the reasons for Farris' death.

To Keiran, the conversation was taking a puzzling turn. Did Zoran want sympathy? He responded gently. "Mr. Farris gave me the impression from the first time that I met him that he was used to pretty tough situations. An interview by the police shouldn't have upset him that much. After all, he's handled many investigations during the course of his legal career."

"You're right," Zoran answered. "All speculation. I'm sure when I get back to London Mrs. Farris will be able to update me on his last few days. It's very hard, though, especially now, for me to concentrate on our latest project, the most lucrative project we've had in a very long time. A lot is hinging on its successful outcome. You'll have to help me more than usual Keiran. Now the package, the material for our customers…you have it?"

"Roubier has it. Did you already forget that I gave it to him at the hotel? It's with him up front. You want it now? You wish to open it now…in the car?" Keiran inquired.

Zoran's whole attitude changed. Now he sounded more suspicious, cloudy, and fierce, his voice harsh. "No, no. No, I want to have it opened directly in front of those bastard Koreans who feel they can threaten me. I look forward to their apology. They will have to swallow their own words. Did I tell you I hate people with squinty eyes?" Lowering his voice as if to appear studious and serious, he continued, "You do know that Orientals spend a great deal of time trying to avoid embarrassment. This time they won't be able to avoid losing face. I'll make sure of that. In fact, I may ask for a premium payment on top of what I charged them. Don't I have a section in the contract that states that I can do that?" Zoran half shut his eyes, stretched his lips in a wintry smile, gently moving his head from side to side. "I want those bastards to pay me more for all the fuckin' grief that they have brought me. You understand, Keiran?"

Keiran was amazed, his brow furling. "Premium payment for something that's late? Maybe, but unlikely. There is a section in the contract stating that additional charges can be assessed due to port congestion, but no, there's nothing to cover when the lateness is our fault."

Zoran began tapping his fingers on his knees, appearing annoyed at Keiran's response.

"Listen, counselor, don't be so negative. I pay your firm a handsome fee for you to figure something out. I want to squeeze every penny I can from these bastards. They're trying to intimidate me with their silly threats, asking for money to be returned. What a fuckin' stupid request. Me, return money? Well, others have found out that I don't return money and if they insist they end up like that deadbeat rat and his buddies at the Parrot—dead. I don't like threats. During these past several days, my enemies were trying to intimidate me by sending bullets and bombs in my direction; well, counselor, if that doesn't stop me, you can be sure that crap from the Koreans is not going to scare me into returning any money. Understood, Counselor Hogan? Besides, my competitors, what few there are, are too fuckin' cowardly to confront me. They were and are simply jealous, envious shitheads. Duane didn't agree...he thought the hints of bullets, bombs, and strange happenings were from the U. S. government. So the U. S. government doesn't like what I'm doing. Fuck them too. Duane found out about some project called 'Crescent Eagle'—stupid name. A project to get rid of dealers like me, just me, probably. Well, they won't succeed either. Can you imagine? The U. S. government, which sells more arms to more people than I can even imagine, is upset because I sell to people they don't like. Fuck them. Fuck everyone." Zoran's voice now rose; his face became contorted with anger and he began to rub his hands together. "Grasp my concept, counselor? Get me more money. Period. End."

As quickly as his voice went from gentle to forceful, he reversed again and his voice now became a mumble. "Too much has gone on, even for me. I want to tell the bastards they owe me more money. Make something up, counselor, and don't fail me. You've failed me once by not telling me about Farris' death. And I have the feeling that you had that package yesterday, but for some reason chose not to give it to me."

Ignoring Zoran's outburst, Keiran asked about the government project, "'Crescent Eagle'—could Farris have heard about this information from Coborn?"

"I don't know. Maybe. Who knows, who cares? I feel that Duane was right, there's someone after me. Regardless, we're going on with this project."

Zoran paused, ignoring Keiran's suggestion, preferring to look out the darkened window. After several minutes, he turned to face Keiran, his face now drained of any anger. His eyes had lost the luster that comes from fury; his voice was barely above a whisper, "Do you like Chianti wine? We're going to a villa I own, Gaiole di Chianti…a perfect place to bring peace to the mind and body. Our customers have been there since yesterday."

"There aren't at the hotel?" Keiran inquired.

"No, I've registered them at the hotel, but they've been staying somewhere else. Isn't that clever?"

"Two things I've learned from you are that what seems to be reality is not and where we are supposed to be, we never are." There was slight laughter from both.

"You stay alive, Keiran, by doing the unanticipated. Regular habits make it easier, much easier, to be eliminated. You should remember this advice. Always remember." Zoran placed his hand on Keiran's forearm, "I have to tell you, my trust in you has faltered. I'm giving you a chance to make me believe in you again. Convince these bastards they owe me more money. You're clever. Farris thought you clever and bright. Persuade me you are by accomplishing this assignment for me."

"Just see how the meeting advances." Keiran's voice was low and steady, trying, by his tone, to calm Zoran's irrational and emotional behavior.

"Good advice. Despite your fuckin' arrogance, you do have good ideas. Stay with me, Keiran. Be loyal. No more shit like what you did with Farris death or with the package. I've been through so much in my life, this is just another line in my history book. Well, Keiran, your client needs some rest. We've talked enough. An hour's rest…that's what I need, an hour's rest. Need a breather yourself? Remember, too much sex makes men happy but sleepy. Something about our need to rest the most important muscle in our body—our cocks." Zoran laughed boisterously. "We've both had an exhausting evening." He smiled at Keiran, the kind of smile that shows envy and jealously. Zoran was silently thinking of what it would be to be young again and have the kind of real virility that only comes with the freshness of youth. Now it takes whips and subservience for him to have an ejaculation—and a weak one at that.

Keiran didn't respond, but slumped down slightly in his seat, his head resting on the small riser above the seat's back. He didn't fall asleep. He simply shut his eyes, trying to figure out how to get cover from the storm he knew was coming. The picture of Farris and Zoran was becoming clearer. With every review of events in his mind, early suspicions now became fact. Farris was dealing with Coborn who told him about an operation dubbed 'Crescent Eagle' that was meant to knock out Zoran. That had to be true. Embassy officials don't go to lawyers' homes just to tell them about the next embassy lawyers meeting. No, logic would dictate that the two had a closer relationship. And that relationship must have provided Farris with whatever information he wanted and paid for. Besides, Diana said the police wanted to question Farris about phone calls from Coborn to Farris. What kind of information could they have exchanged? How could it have helped Farris, and Zoran?

Don't be slow, Keiran thought. These guys are into arms dealing. The embassy has information on what the U. S. government is doing to stop these kinds of businessmen. So if two and two are still four, then Farris would have been able to get information regarding how close, if at all, 'Crescent Eagle' was to shutting down his and Zoran's operation. There would be no other reason for Farris and Coborn to be meeting at Farris' home. After all, the ambassador was a friend of Farris. Farris' ego would not allow him to seek out a mid-level employee, such as Coborn, when he could get information from the top. He knew the ambassador would never give him the information he needed, he's not treasonous.

So he goes to the guy who will—Coborn—with big bucks. This relationship wasn't accidental nor was it between strangers. Farris and Coborn needed each other. His death brought the police to Farris who would have had a hard time explaining away all the calls, meetings, and money. But then, Farris wasn't dumb; the money was probably as well hidden as the profits that Zoran made on all his arms sales. By dying, Farris protects his reputation; his family doesn't have to answer any questions and makes a graceful exit.

Where does Runnard fit in? Why did Coborn follow Runnard the day he had his heart attack? Farris hated him, but did he want to kill him? No, Farris wasn't that moronic. Let's assume Coborn, for some bizarre reason, ended Runnard's life, told Farris, and Farris was happy—or was he? Would he want to be dragged into that crime? Probably not. If he found out that Coborn did murder Runnard, how would he react? Would he try to dissolve his relationship with Coborn? Would Coborn then threaten to talk about their relationship? Would he demand more money from Farris? And would Farris in response think that Coborn was now unsuitable and expendable? Farris, being the type of man he was, would be worried if he could no longer control Coborn. Blackmail goes hand in hand with betrayal. Coborn could play both and Farris would find himself in a position in which he would not want to remain. That leaves.... Oh shit, Farris had him wiped out! But by whom? Of course, Zoran's buddies. Farris would not necessarily have the ability to hire hit men on his own. Only through Zoran would he have that capability. That being the case, Zoran must have known about the contact in the embassy, he would certainly have known about Runnard, and also of about Farris' decision to dispose of Coborn. With Farris' death all of this would become moot. No one would be left to talk about anything.

Until this package is opened, Zoran is protected. Who will he blame? Farris? Why would Farris want to...? Shit. He wants to get rid of Zoran as well. What is going on here? How many double crosses are there? To complete the circle, either they succeed together or fail together. Loyalty. Farris and Zoran loyal to one another? Forget it. Farris wants Zoran to fail as well; he wanted everyone to go down with him. Shit, maybe he even took his own life. Yeah, Farris is so duplicitous he'd even do that, and hide how he did it. What a fuckin' mess, Keiran Hogan, a genuine muddle of shit. It has been a wild journey, a fuckin' wild journey so far—the only triumph in all of this was meeting Jennifer. Now Zoran is telling me that everyone who crosses him will end up as dead as those poor people at the Parrot Restaurant. Zoran was the only one who left early. The guy for whom the party was given owed Zoran multi-millions and Zoran owed him an honest shipment of arms—sort of an oxymoron, given Zoran's view of business. Is Zoran responsible for killing all those people? No, he can't be that animalistic. Good God. If he would stop at nothing, then Farris would be the same—all under the cover of a law firm dating back to 1840. What could be a better cover for their business?

Well, Keiran thought, you may be smart, but you've just dreamed up a scenario that is either absolutely correct, or absolutely off the mark. Sure, but guess what, it's the only one that makes sense out of a string of 'coincidences.' Remember your criminal law prof, John Dugan? Dugan, the one who always came in with an Irish walking cap, explaining that his head was cold. He would laugh when you told him that a fact was based on a coincidence or two.

"They were planned," he would advise, "Try not to forget that, Mr. Hogan. Coincidences are rarely coincidences, and are most often planned." So what now? When the Korean customer opens the package, all hell will break loose. Betrayal. Judas. Zoran will think that Farris has betrayed him. The pieces of the puzzle may be coming together, but now what? When we arrive at the meeting with the Koreans, the package will be opened and nothing worthwhile will be in it. Zoran's reaction? He'll blame me. Koreans' reaction? They'll leave. What about the money they gave Zoran? No, if Zoran killed so many at the Parrot he won't mind getting rid of a few more for the same reason.

Okay, Keiran, buddy, knowing all this, what do you do? Yeah, what do you do?

"We're here, Keiran," Zoran hit him hard on the arm. "Get yourself together. We've got some serious business ahead of us. Roubier, call ahead to Simpson. Tell him to be at the front."

Keiran opened his eyes to see the Mercedes make its way along a short gravel road surrounded on both sides by vineyards. Ahead in a large clearing was a spacious two-story brick and stucco villa, planter boxes under each window holding a profusion of summer flowers. A sole plaque hung securely in the middle of the facade enclosed by the exterior of a small balcony jutting from the center of the second floor. The gravel road joined a large flagstone half-moon driveway where two cars were already parked.

"We're in Chianti country, Keiran," Zoran blurted out his words happily. Keiran could not help but notice Zoran's complete change of demeanor. He spoke now like a cheerful and ebullient man, free of the anger and darkness of just an hour ago. There seemed to be, for this moment at least, a calm in Zoran's face that Keiran had not observed before.

"All of these vineyards are mine. Some day soon, when I retire, I'll stay here for the season. This is a quiet place, not like Florence or Venice. Too hectic in those wonderful cities; here we can think; the silence is good for the mind. See that plaque over the entrance door?" Zoran lowered his car window to point out the black rooster painted onto a oblong shaped piece of weathered wood. "The symbol of the black rooster, the *gallo nero*, means that my vineyards belong to the wine consortium that produces Chianti Classico wine. Naturally, we'll have several bottles at lunch. Ah, Simpson is waiting for us. Good. He was finally able to conclude that ridiculous Venice matter. With your earlier help, of course."

Keiran marveled at the scene. The rolling hills in the background, olive groves on the side of the villa, cypress trees towering in the back. For once, Zoran was right. It is a beautiful, quiet setting. Behind this serenity and beauty, Keiran silently reminded himself, the storm was about to break.

Grayson had stopped his van when he saw that his colleague's was parked several meters beyond a large open wrought-iron gate. The modest black metal signs attached to the gate said, in script lettering, '*Villa Magico Pace*.' Underneath these words, in similar lettering was, '*Nessuno Violazione*.' Grayson's associate was waiting for him.

"Good Morning, Bob. Sign says not to go in. No trespassing. You think that means us?" His smile was wide.

"No. Not simple hikers like us," Grayson replied. "If they were serious they'd have the place crawling with guards. No guards means they don't mind trackers. Besides, I believe our host travels with security. Time to change and hike."

His associate opened the rear of the van and unzipped a large canvas bag. Out came jeans, weathered blue shirts, hiking shoes, and two backpacks. Quickly, he and Grayson retreated into the van, changed, and placed their discarded clothes into the canvas bag.

"Ready for our hike?" Grayson smiled.

"Beautiful scenery. Perfect day for a hike, sir."

"Agreed. The air is so fresh. Perks one up, wouldn't you say? Did you pack a lunch?"

"Yes sir. A heavy lunch."

"Good, I'm hungry. Put your hat on. Sun can get brutal this time of the year."

They both donned soft, floppy khaki hats that partially hid their faces, took hold of two long walking sticks and proceeded to stroll back toward the villa's entrance.

Simpson was waiting, his black suit jacket opened, his maroon tie flapping in the mild, cool wind. As Zoran's car approached, he walked down the steps from the entranceway and stood rigid until the car stopped, its rear door directly opposite him. He quickly opened it.

"Welcome Mr. Hemmrich, Mr. Hogan."

"Everything in good order, Alan?" Zoran asked.

"Yes sir. Mr. Ho-Lee and the group are waiting in the living room. They seem comfortable and are having tea."

Zoran looked at his watch. It was 9:00. "Fine. I don't suspect our meeting will take long. Roubier, bring the package with you; Chavez, stay in the foyer…just in case."

Both Roubier and Chavez nodded, with a smirk on his face as if he alone understood Zoran's code words 'just in case.'

"Keiran, shall we refresh a bit before we visit our customer? Would you like that?" Zoran asked, undoing his tie, and slipping it off. "Best day ever. Air is clear, fresh and cool."

As he turned, he saw in the distance two figures hiking along the gravel path. "Alan, haven't you posted the 'No Trespassing' signs? Hikers, probably English. They hike all over this area. The English invented private property, but never respect it."

"Yes, we've posted the signs, but none of these hikers pay attention," Simpson replied, holding the entry door open for Zoran and the rest. "They usually don't come close to the villa and will follow the service roads to the top of the hill and then go down to the village on the other side. Chavez can look after them. If they come close to the house, he knows how to shoo them away." Chavez grunted, his left hand patting the lower side of his jacket where he kept his weapon. Again his lips parted in a quirky smile, the kind of smile that tells an onlooker that he is a thug and likes being one.

Keiran looked in the same direction and he thought he recognized the peculiar gait of Grayson, who, because of some unexplained injury, would drag his left leg after his right had taken a step. He did this quickly, but it was still discernible. Silently, Keiran mused, no, not here. You're imagining things. God you're tired, Keiran. But that walk. Oh, shit! He can't be here. No. Get a grip on yourself.

Rather than continue on the gravel road, the pair soon, as Simpson predicted, slipped off into the dirt service road that ran between the rows of vines and disappeared among the ripening grapes.

"Coming, Keiran?" Zoran asked.

Without replying, Keiran followed Zoran into the villa, his mind now working on how he would respond when the package was opened and the material the North Koreans thought they had bought wasn't there.

"Alan, we'll go upstairs and refresh a bit and then meet our customer in a few minutes. Tell them we're here and will greet them momentarily." Turning to Keiran, Zoran pointed up the stairs, "Please, Keiran. I'll take you to your room. You'll fall in love with this place. A perfect spot for some peace and quiet. Anytime you wish to use this for a holiday, it's yours. Better in late summer and early fall—rather than now when the rains come. We had a sample of that just these past few days."

They walked into a stone-floored foyer and up the staircase; Keiran noticing the heavy, highly polished, wood banister, its surface covered with intricately carved concentric scrolls. The banister itself was held up by wrought iron rods, each of which joined the other by a moderately sized rooster formed of black iron. Along the walls were several tapestries of grape harvesting scenes. At the top of the stairs was a long, wide, soft yellow stucco hall. On one side, a series of oversize six-panel wood doors were closed; on the other side were open windows, curtainless, facing the vineyards, allowing the light morning breeze to come in and giving the house a cool and clean atmosphere.

"You're at the end, Keiran. Did you bring a change of clothes? No tie needed, dress informally. We're in the country. Time to relax."

"Okay," Keiran responded mechanically.

"Fifteen minutes sufficient time for you?" Zoran inquired.

"Sure." Keiran silently noted how solicitous Zoran was; his whole attitude had changed. Zoran was calm, serene and detached. Keiran knew it wouldn't last long

Keiran's bedroom was large and square, painted like the hallways. The various pictures on the wall were enlarged color photographs of the surrounding countryside. The room's windows were also open and on this clear day he could see the whole panorama of forests, vineyards, and hills extending into the horizon, broken only by the scattering of other villas and farmhouses. He welcomed the magnificent beauty. The scene had a soporific effect on his thoughts, which now turned to Jennifer. Again, in the swirl of events, he had not made his daily call to her, missing one day as he promised himself and her that he would never do. As he took in the view, reveling in the fresh cool air, he could see two men trudging along the dirt service road which looped around the back of the villa and then came parallel along its side before joining another service road directly in front of the home. He headed toward the bathroom, itself half the size of the bedroom to which it was connected.

"Yeah, I could stay here for a long time," Keiran said aloud to himself. He took off his shirt, brushed his teeth, then washed his face with cold water. The coolness took out the grogginess he felt from the ride and from the lack of real sleep the night before. Walking back into the bedroom, he began to collect his thoughts for the chaos he knew to be coming and which he knew would not be pleasant. He put on a cream polo shirt that went well with his dark blue slacks. Zoran had said the meeting would be informal, which was reasonable given the fact that the Koreans didn't wear any ties, let alone western-style shirts—their uniform was the Nehru style jacket, buttoned up to the top with a thin collar around the neck. All their suits were a dull gray and he didn't think the delegation would be wearing anything else, despite the informality of the venue.

"Keiran, are you ready?" Zoran shouted through the closed bedroom door, knocking loudly.

"Yes, sir. I'll be right there."

He opened the door to see Zoran and his two bodyguards, Simpson and Roubier. Zoran was in a casual dark blue polo shirt and dark gray pants; both guards were dressed similarly but with jackets—probably to hide the weapons they were carrying.

"A bit refreshed, Keiran? Great air, wouldn't you say? I could live here forever. Forever. I love this place."

"Spectacular view from my room, Zoran. You couldn't have picked a better place for a meeting. I hope this makes the customer more agreeable."

"I hope so too. But if not, well…we'll see what happens, isn't that the advice you gave me?"

"Good that you remembered," Keiran added.

"I never forget what my lawyers tell me," Zoran laughingly rejoined, then picked up his pace as he led the group quickly along the hall and down the winding staircase to the foyer, where he strode confidently into the living room. There, seated at a round table in the center of the room, under a wrought iron chandelier holding candles of various lengths from previous burnings, sat the three members of the delegation: Mr. Han, Mr. Ho-Lee, and Mr. Koo. Behind them were four bodyguards. As Keiran had predicted, everyone was dressed in identical dull gray Nehru-style suits. No one was smiling. Cups of tea were in front of the three delegates. Plates of breakfast pastries and fruit, also in front of each man, remained untouched. Not a happy sight. Zoran went directly to Mr. Ho-Lee, shaking his hand first, then the other two. Keiran followed suit.

"Well, now, did you enjoy your time here in the country?'

"It was peaceful. We appreciate your hospitality. Most enjoyable. Now, on to business. The documents and computer discs—you have them?" Ho-Lee said, a slight impatience in his voice.

"Roubier, please bring the package."

Roubier handed the package to Zoran, who turned it over to Keiran. "Please, Keiran, would you be kind enough to open this and distribute the material to our friends?"

Keiran rose from his seat, placing the package directly in front of him. Roubier had brought shears and a small knife Swiftly, he slit the tape that sealed the paper over the package, then carefully lifted the paper away, revealing a box that was taped along the top. He took the knife and slit open the top, lifted the flaps and took out a white envelope that was marked 'Computer Discs' and three other envelopes.

Keiran took them all out, placed the white envelope on the top of the three manila envelopes, and gave them to Zoran.

"Thank you, Keiran. Gentlemen, your material. I told you that I would have it by ten, and it is just about that time now. I am not the kind of businessman who doesn't perform. You should have understood that from the beginning. We had some problems getting this material here—weather and so forth—but here it is, what you have paid for. Please open it and see for yourself." Zoran spoke pompously, his jaw raised, the words coming out slowly and with great precision, like a man who wanted badly to say, 'I told you so.' Keiran had to admit his introduction was a good performance.

"Thank you, Mr. Hemmrich. We never had any doubts. We appreciate your good efforts to conclude our arrangement. May we open the envelopes in your presence? We would like your permission to verify what they contain." He spoke in a humble fashion, softly and almost inaudible, but his intention was clear.

"Certainly. Please open the sealed envelopes. They have not been touched since they left Mr. Farris' office in London."

The wind blew gently through the open windows, causing the flowers in a large brass bowl to sway back and forth and providing a light touch to the somber feeling that pervaded the room despite Zoran's optimistic announcement.

Mr. Ho Lee opened the white envelope first. He took out two discs and handed them to Mr. Han. "May we place them in our computer?" Ho-Lee asked Zoran.

"Certainly. You have a laptop? You can use one of ours if you need to."

"No, we have one of our own. Thank you." Mr. Han moved away the untouched plate of fruit and cup of tea in front of him, reached down, and brought up a small black canvas case from which he retrieved a laptop computer. Everyone watched silently as he opened its top, turned it on, placed the disc in its proper slot, then waited. After a few moments, he spoke to Mr. Ho-Lee in Korean. The expressions on their faces didn't change, but the tone of Mr. Ho-Lee's voice did.

"The disc doesn't contain what we need," he said brusquely. "It is simply the contract between us. Nothing else. It is not what we have paid for. You aren't treating us with respect, Mr. Hemmrich. This is not the manner in which we like to do business."

Zoran turned to Keiran, panic-stricken. "Keiran, did you receive this from Farris?"

"Yes, sir, and we brought it right here."

"I don't believe that what we want is in these either," Mr. Ho-Lee said as he opened the first of the three envelopes. He slid out several pages from it. "This is not what we paid for. These papers are blank. We are most disappointed. You have made fools of us, Mr. Hemmrich. We expect to have our funds returned to us promptly."

"Fuck you," Zoran said abruptly and loudly, his tortured face looking at Keiran mouthing silently, what the fuck is Farris doing to me? Do you know? He continued aloud, "We've tried our best. I don't know what has happened. Mr. Farris died of a heart attack just yesterday; perhaps his office sent the wrong material. I just don't know. You have to understand. His death has changed the circumstances. I'm sure his office in London is in disarray because of his unexpected death. You must understand the changed circumstances." Zoran's voice remained loud, his eyes remained fixed on Mr. Ho-Lee in manner that said 'Okay, you want a fight, you've got one.'

"Certainly these aren't the circumstances we had expected. And we regret Mr. Farris' death. But we told you that if the material wasn't here by 10:00 this morning, we would expect our money to be returned before we leave."

"Whatever is owed you, you shall have. You disturb me, my friends. Would I be here presenting you with this package in person if I knew it to contain the wrong material? Come now. Be reasonable. This has to be a mistake at Farris' office. The wrong package was sent."

"Your word is not enough to us now that you have failed to deliver what we have purchased."

Zoran lifted his hand in a signal. Roubier rose and moved over to the door and stood there with his hands in his pockets. Simpson went to the other side of the room and stood near a table that held the tea and coffee. The Korean bodyguards watched Roubier and Simpson move from their seats behind Zoran and Keiran. Two of them rose to go to the table, holding teacups in their hands. They placed the teacups and saucers down on the table near Zoran, who was watching their every move, and were smiling at him before one plunged his knife into Zoran's stomach. Zoran let out a painful scream.

Within seconds, the second Korean bodyguard turned and fired from his silencer equipped pistol, slamming Roubier against the wall with several bullets. Simpson yanked out his weapon and fired a fuselage of bullets at the Koreans, rapidly spraying Mr. Ho-Lee, Mr. Han and Mr. Koo before he was hit by their guards. Chavez came running in, firing his automatic at the ceiling before he realized what was happening, then shooting straight ahead at the Korean guards, killing or wounding them before being stopped himself.

The villa shook as the first explosion crumbled a shed that housed two tractors and assorted harvesting equipment. Pieces of metal flew in all directions, hitting randomly like untargeted multiple missiles. The building located about 100 meters from the main house collapsed in a ball of fire and smoke. The noise was deafening. Zoran lay on the floor, fatally bleeding from the hail of bullets fired at him when Simpson had targeted Mr. Ho-Lee and his colleagues. A shot had hit Keiran's shoulder, flinging him from his chair. Seconds later, a massive explosion tore into the back of the house. Screams were heard as the villa staff fled into the fields. Keiran crawled to the French windows and, not looking back, made his way onto the adjoining patio, where he collapsed near a border of shrubbery.

A short distance away he saw the two hikers walking quickly toward him, both with weapons. Oh, shit! It's Grayson. He's the one who is making hell for Zoran. Keiran tried to rise, but all he could do was crawl, one hand on his shoulder, trying to stem the flow of blood.

"Fancy meeting you here," Keiran said weakly as Grayson arrived on the patio. "Do you always blow up people's homes?"

"Not often. You look as if you need some help. We'll talk later. Come, let's get out of here before the police come—and they will come, we've called them. Can't get a decent hike anymore in Tuscany. I mean, look at this place. A mess. A real mess. Where's your client? Does he need help?"

"I don't think so. He couldn't deliver what he promised, so the customer took him out. I don't know how I'm still alive."

"Well, whoever survived will have a long story to tell the authorities." As he spoke, a fourth and final explosion blew up the three cars in the driveway, pieces flying in all directions. Then silence.

"Let's go, Keiran. We don't want to be caught in this maelstrom, now do we?"

"No, we don't. But who are you Mr. Grayson? Who...?" Keiran couldn't complete this thought as he passed out, his hand now bloody from holding on to his shoulder.

"Come on, mate," Grayson called over to his colleague. Give me a hand. We've got to get this young man to the airport and home."

Forty

Keiran would not be dazzled by the unfolding landscape of Tuscany as Grayson's speeding van approached Radda, a small town several kilometers from Gaiole di Chianti, where the remains of Zoran's villa still burned. He was in a fog of semi-consciousness, sufficiently alert, though, to direct a silent fury at Grayson, whom he now understood to be behind the trail of terror directed against Zoran. Shafts of sun pierced the early summer clouds. Maybe this was the most beautiful part of Tuscany, but he would not see it. The perfect landscape—the cypresses winding up the hills, the cut hay rolled in perfectly formed wheels, the plowed dirt, the vineyards—would be ignored. He knew that the only rush of joy here was Grayson's. He had accomplished his mission—the destruction of Zoran and, by happenstance, the North Koreans caught in a deal that wasn't only illegal but also probably dangerous for whatever the definition of world peace was at the moment.

He admitted that Grayson could have, but didn't, eliminate him and was now trying to have him treated—such an excursion wasn't part of his mission, but was an obligation, unspoken and unwelcome, but nevertheless there, committing him. Grayson was a stranger who had come into his life. It was time now for both to part for good. He'd be returning to London. Whether or not it would be to Kenton & Ward was another issue. Besides, with what he knew, why would Kenton & Ward keep him? His interest in joining Grayson's law firm was clearly over. Wasn't it Farris who said that he knew of no clients of Grayson's firm and had even wondered aloud whether the firm was, in fact, a law firm?

As much as he liked Grayson, the last few hours were convincing enough that he really didn't know much about him nor his real work. Keiran knew there would be conversations with the firm's partners about what had happened in Italy. Even that would pass. In all likelihood, the police would conclude that the fire, deaths, and destruction of the villa were the results of a deal gone sour and those inside were all 'bad guys' anyway. Besides, the North Koreans were probably in Italy illegally, so their own fatal ending just saved everyone time, energy, and the possible embarrassment that would have been involved in their deportation. For that matter, who in North Korea would admit that a few of their senior government members were floating around the world seeking impermissible stolen missile guidance systems? No, it was doubtful that anyone would complain; it was more likely that everyone would cooperate in covering up the true nature of the 'accident'—a web of deceit that would satisfy everyone involved.

Keiran, his brooding mind silently thinking, does anyone, other than an immediate family, ever mourn an arms dealer who is universally disliked and hunted? Maybe, in a perverse manner, some partners in the firm will miss the fees generated by Zoran and Farris, but even that would pass in a firm that had just last year celebrated the 160th anniversary of its founding. A portrait of Farris would probably be hung in the main conference room in the firm's New York headquarters and that would be about the extent of a memorial to Farris. His replacement was probably already on a plane for London. As for Farris 'crossing the line,' well, he did that without the permission of the managers of the firm, he had 'deceived his own partners'—that would be the line used, and used with excellent effect. It was clear to Keiran that he didn't belong in this kind of existence. It wasn't that he was unable to intellectually understand and absorb dishonesty. The simple truth was he didn't want to be that way. Honorable, yes. Stupid, no.

The angry thumping of his heart reminded Keiran of the sound of heavy rain on the front porch awnings of his parents home in Quincy, which was where he wanted so badly to be during this time of turmoil in his own life. The rules of life he had harbored since childhood had totally changed. He knew he'd head back to Quincy. Better to sort things out with family. But then, why would he burden them? And Jennifer? What will be her reaction to his heading home after such a short time? That did matter. It mattered more than anything.

There was no innocent delight in either Grayson's or Farris' character. Their deceit wasn't some quaint old-fashioned amusement in these times of world chaos—it was deadly serious. Everyone—Grayson, Farris, Zoran, and even Keiran, peripherally—delved in the realm of forbidden things. Betrayal is a part and parcel of life. Is that what I've learned? Is betrayal a shadow of trust and loyalty? Is life just a big game of betrayal with treason being betrayal on a grand scale?

Located on Radda's outskirts, the medical clinic of Dr. Antonio Galluzzo was impossible to miss from the road. It was a gleaming white two-story stucco building on which there hung a large white wood sign divided into four equal squares by a large red cross with the word '*Clinica*' spread across its center. Usually Dr. Galluzzo attended to the simplest of ailments: foot aches, backaches, sore legs, and other ailments associated with seniors who were taking their retirement tours by hiking the hills around the town, as well as the local population. His practice was easy and he didn't consider it mundane. On the contrary, he liked it just the way it was—quiet, simple, and, importantly, his patients paid him promptly, a far cry from his earlier stint as an emergency room doctor at Florence's St. Cecilia's Hospital Center. No, this is the kind of quiet medical practice he enjoyed. Nothing serious.

"We're here, brother Keiran." Grayson turned around to speak to Keiran, glancing at his face, noticing by the lines in his brow that Keiran was in some pain. "You'll be patched up in a jiffy. I know you're angry, but at least thank me for bringing you to a doctor."

"You're fuckin' crazy, Bob. That's my answer. I'm supposed to be happy that you nearly blew me away?" Keiran's voice was quiet but firm. "Everything in your way was destroyed, Mr. Grayson? Everything."

"Discipline, Keiran. Isn't that what your swimming coach taught you? Discipline. Don't comment about me until you know all the facts. Besides, I didn't ask what your emotions are. I just made a statement that we are here and you'll be attended to by a doctor."

Keiran fell silent, his cold blue eyes fixed on Grayson like the eyes of a trapped animal.

"Park in the back," Grayson instructed his colleague. "Wait here with our patient. Make sure he doesn't run away from his saviors." Grayson walked around to the building's front, past the sudden sharp scents of window boxes heavy with purple and yellow flowers. He had stemmed the flow of blood with a makeshift tourniquet, but he knew that Hogan needed a proper dressing and some antibiotics. He hurried to the front and entered directly into the waiting area, where he observed three other patients seated. One, a man in his sixties, had his boots off and was rubbing his stockinged feet.

"*Prego, parle inglese?*" Grayson inquired mildly.

"*Si, si.* Yes, yes, of course. What can I do for you?" The nurse, a middle aged woman, bland and unsmiling yet resplendent in her white uniform, a small red cross in her lapel, spoke with a heavy accent.

"I have a friend in my car and he needs the doctor's immediate attention. I've parked in the back and I'd like to bring him in through that entrance. Is that possible?"

"What kind of emergency? As you can see, we do have other patients who are waiting to see the doctor," the nurse asked, shrugging off his statement in an ill-humored fashion.

"I understand. But, my friend was on a hike with me and…. Well, he fell some distance and scraped his shoulder quite badly. These hills are so deceptive…you think the hike is easy and then, of course, it's more difficult than you can imagine."

"*Si, si.* Yes, yes," the nurse repeated. "We hear the same story so many times. Important to be careful. *Molto attento, molto attento, importante*. I'll see what the doctor can do." She rose and strode briskly through a swinging door, her air remaining as icy as well-water.

It wasn't very long before Doctor Galluzzo appeared, a gray haired, rotund man of medium height, his hands thrust into the pockets of his sparkling clean white medical coat, a pad and pen stuck tightly in a pocket. His left cheek trembled slightly as if a muscle had gone berserk. Thrusting out his strong hand, he had a look of a wounded man, his smile automatic.

"*Senori...?*"

"Grayson. Bob Grayson. Can you see my friend? It is quite urgent."

"Maria tells me your friend had a fall while hiking." Dr. Galluzzo stared at Grayson, his dark eyes contracting until they no longer expressed the doubt he had about Grayson's storyline.

"Yes, while hiking."

"*Prego*. Is he conscious?"

"Off and on—that's why I brought him here. He's in the van, out back."

"*Certamente*. I will meet you at that entrance." He then turned and spoke quietly to his nurse.

Grayson, left the waiting area and walked back to the van. There, he and his colleague tried to lift Keiran gently, whose face nonetheless grimaced with little jolts of pain.

"Bob, leave me the fuck alone. I can manage. And to think I trusted you, that I wanted to join your firm. Fuck you, Grayson."

"The anger of a youth who doesn't know the full tale," Grayson looked at his colleague who nodded his head in agreement. "Keiran, we're helping you to make sure you don't fall down. We're here to see a *medico*—you know, a doctor. He'll get you sewed up in a jiffy and we'll be on our way to the airport and on a flight to London."

"Fuck you. I don't want to be around you anymore. I can get to the airport without you."

Grayson laughed sympathetically, "Yeah, sure. We just want to make sure you get on the plane."

"Knock off the crap. The only way I'll get on the plane is if I do it myself. With you around, I'm not so sure I'll make it. Look at what knowing you has brought me—an incredible headache and a painful shoulder. Add a dead client to that list as well, among other assorted experiences, including drive-by shootings in Venice, not to mention the heart attack in Guernsey where your friend here was disguised as a telephone repairman. Why did he kill Leyden? He was an innocent man doing no harm."

"All in a day's work, Keiran. All in a day's work," Grayson responded, unsmiling.

Keiran remained silent. His eyes had a brittle darkness and he looked with bitterness toward Grayson. "What I know about you, I don't like. Just leave me alone." He walked unaided toward the open rear door of the clinic where Dr. Galluzzo waited with two nurses.

Dr. Galluzzo appeared annoyed and overhearing the conversation had annoyed him even more intensely. He had a prejudice against people who didn't tell him the truth and, just by the look of the injured young man, he knew his injuries had not been caused by a hiking accident. He held the door open as the nurses took Keiran directly into an examining room, and guided him to the treatment table.

"Some fall," Galluzzo commented as he looked at Keiran, whose face reflected continuing pain. "And you're...?"

"Hogan. Keiran Hogan. I'm fully awake and want to stay that way, doctor."

"*Si, si,*" Galluzzo replied. "*Prego*. Please get up on the table and lie down." Keiran, his face still writhing in pain, did as he was ordered. Swiftly, Galluzzo and his aides worked, removing the shirt and undershirt and swabbing the right shoulder wound clean. On examination, it was slight, only several inches of skin and flesh had been torn away.

"Your wound will require a few stitches. Otherwise, you're fine. Strange wound for a hiking accident. Looks more like a bullet wound to me. I don't believe this was caused by a fall. Looks like a bullet hit him…yes, a bullet."

"Really?" Grayson feigned surprised.

"Yes. I may have to notify the police. Rules and regulations, you know."

"Of course. But it's not a bullet hole. I don't see that."

Keiran said nothing as he stared intently toward the room's ceiling.

"You'll feel a short pin prick, Mr. Hogan. I'm going to give you a local pain killer and a dose of antibiotic to stave off any infection, although it appears there is none. This is being done as a precaution."

Galluzzo then, after a few minutes for the anesthetic to take effect, quickly placed antiseptic solution on the wound, sewed four stiches of self-absorbing sutures and bound it tightly with gauze and bandages. "I'm also giving you two sets of medication. One is for pain, Mr. Hogan, and the other is an antibiotic. I want you to take the pain medication now. You need it. The sutures will not have to be taken out, they will desintegrate over time." A nurse followed with a glass of water. Keiran placed the pill in his mouth and then drank the water quickly.

Turning to Grayson, Dr. Galluzzo handed him two small envelopes. "He should take one of these three times a day for five days. The pills in this yellow envelope are antibiotics; the white envelope has a supply of pain medication that he should take as required. Everything is labeled on the front of each envelope. I've given you the English translation. I suggest, however that he see his own doctor as soon as possible when he gets back to...."

"London."

"Yes. London. Will he be leaving soon?"

"Yes, later today. You've been most kind to interrupt your schedule Dr. Galluzzo. Please take this." Grayson handed over two thousand-dollar American Express traveler's checks. "You may make them out to whomever you wish. I've pre-signed them."

Dr. Galluzzo dismissed his nurses. "This is much more than I need for this service. Much, much, more. I still...."

"Certainly. The Police. Why bother? They probably have more important things on their minds right now. I'm sure you'll reconsider. You know, police reports and interviews can be so very messy and time consuming."

"Yes. Time consuming...."

"Takes time away from your practice. And you have such a lovely place here. Quiet and serene. You probably want to keep it that way."

"*Si, si.* Admittedly so. Now, you should be going. Your friend here will be fine and he is still awake, as you can see."

Keiran continued to be silent, shaking off any help from Grayson or the doctor. He rose slowly, pushing himself off the medical table, noting he was bare-chested, a large bandage covering his right shoulder.

"I need a shirt or something to cover this."

Dr. Galluzzo helped him down. "*Certamente*. Here, take this medical gown. It'll help until you can get to a store to buy a shirt. I don't need it returned."

"Thank you again, doctor. We appreciate what you've done. May I have his soiled clothing? We'll take care of discarding them."

Galluzzo retrieved Keiran's soiled clothing, which had already been put in a trash bin, and placed them in a white plastic bag, which he handed to Grayson. "There. That should do it." Turning to Keiran, Galluzzo said, "Good luck young man."

"Thank you, doctor. I appreciate your taking care of me." Keiran managed a slight smile as he spoke softly.

"My duty young man, my duty."

"Thank you again. We'll be on our way," Grayson added. "And, by the way, doctor, I never signed any admission form. It's not necessary, is it?" Grayson asked slyly.

"No. Not now. Everything is fine. Have a good trip."

Grayson and Keiran walked back to the van in silence. Keiran hoped that the pain medication would bring the sleep he needed. He hated to face Grayson again or even to talk to him. Now wasn't the time for more talk. The back seat had been reclined slightly, allowing Keiran to slide down comfortably. As soon as his head touched the headrest, he was sound asleep.

Grayson, now sullen and thinking silently, turned and looked at Keiran, knowing that he had a voice Grayson would not forget. A man worthwhile to save. Life brings the unexpected even when one tries to reduce it to vulgar fractions. Hogan is different. So different. He plays his game in his own particular way. The guy's a fierce one—believes in himself, a touch of arrogance, authentic, and original. What is this sentimentality? He's alive. That's all that matters. Today's events won't even make a footnote to history. The larger picture is yet to be written and I may not even be in it. Hogan…he's another story. He may be. Yeah, he just may be."

It was about two hours to Florence's Aeroporto Amerigo Vespucci. There, Grayson and his colleague drove directly to the terminal and were quickly waved to go directly onto the tarmac where a small jet, its tail emblazoned with a large red cross, waited.

"Keiran, wake up. We're here. Your private wings await you, my friend." Grayson leaned over, reaching behind his seat and shaking Keiran's leg vigorously. "Wake up, friend."

Quickly, two blue uniformed men came down the aircraft's steps and hurried over to where the van was parked. Grayson got out first; his colleague remained at the wheel. He slid open the van's side door, allowing Keiran to get up and off the reclined seat he had been occupying.

"Thanks fuckin' friend Bob."

"Ah, the anger of youth and no thanks for saving you from an ungodly inferno."

"For which, fucker, you're responsible."

"Keiran Hogan, listen," Grayson's voice was now soft and serious. "I won't be seeing you again. It's a very long story and it's not worth your time. I saved you because you're worth saving. The others were not."

"Fuck you. Get out of my life."

"Your anger will vanish soon. Someday, the true tale of this adventure will be made public, but not now. And hey, young man, who introduced you to Jennifer? Not anyone but me. Just remember that bit of luck. Take good care of yourself. No one will bother you. We'll take care of the police and the other aspects of this sordid mess. We have some influence. Goodbye, Keiran Hogan. And the best of luck, brother, the best of everything."

He reached over and gently hugged Keiran, who stood still. Despite his anger, a mist came over Keiran's eyes. He didn't know why, he really didn't know why. Who the hell is Grayson? Why can't he know everything? Why are so many of life's experiences so unanswered?

"Be kind to Jennifer. And name your first after me."

"You arrogant S.O.B. Okay, Bob. Goodbye. I don't know whether to believe you or not. Will you being going back to London?"

"No. Have to hurry. Safe flight. And hello to Jennifer."

After about two and a half hours flying time, the air ambulance Airbus jet was on approach to Gatwick Airport.

"Mr. Hogan, Mr. Hogan. We're about to land. Would you like to freshen up? We've laid out a change of clothes for you. Mr. Grayson suggested that you would probably want then." A woman in a blue uniform was staring down at Keiran, gently shaking his arm.

"Here, let me help you." She reached over and pressed a button on his armrest, allowing the seatback to quietly come forward. "Are you feeling better? Nasty fall you had."

"Fall? Is Mr. Grayson here?"

"No. He sends his regards and reminds you to get well enough to go to the Grovenor Hotel by 8:00 this evening. I guess you'll understand what he means."

"You mean he's not here?"

"No. Is there a problem? We'll be landing in about 30 minutes."

Keiran rose and in fact he did feel better. The pain in his shoulder was almost gone; his head was clear and he was starved—a sure sign he was well.

"Do you have anything to drink or eat?"

"Sure, I can get you a soft drink, tea, or coffee, and we have some great sandwiches on board."

"I'll have some coffee and a couple of your sandwiches. The bathroom...?"

"Straight ahead to the front. You need help?"

"No, I can manage."

Keiran slowly made his way to the lavatory. He noted it was much bigger than those he was used to on commercial aircraft. Hanging behind on the door's hook were clean shirts, slacks, and in a plastic bag on the counter were shorts and socks. Propped up against the counter was his briefcase—a bit scorched but otherwise its contents still intact. How in the hell did Grayson do this? What a mystery man. Shit. When I see him, I'll want to get to the bottom of all of this.

He slowly undressed, looking at his bandaged shoulder, raising his right arm to see if all was okay. He took a washcloth and vigorously washed his face and hands. This is where not having to shave everyday comes in handy, he reminded himself. Nevertheless, he splashed aftershave lotion from a small bottle placed on the counter. He put on the clean shirt, pants and socks, combed his hair and slipped on his shoes, which had been brushed cleaned. He had to admit he felt a great deal better. When he returned to his seat, the flight attendant had already set up his tray table, on it was coffee, two sandwiches, slices of oranges and apples, and a bottle of water.

"Is this satisfactory?" she asked.

"Great. Beautiful. Say, who owns this plane? Mr. Grayson?"

"No, no. He doesn't own it. One of his clients does. We're an air ambulance service. We transport people who are ill. Mr. Grayson believed this would be the best way to get you back to London for your evening appointment."

"My evening appointment?"

"Yes. Have you forgotten? Here's the note that Mr. Grayson told me to give to you." She handed him a small cream-colored envelope.

Keiran opened it quickly and took out a small folded piece of stationery:

Brother Keiran: By now you're probably wondering what the hell is going on. Well, brother solicitor, don't ask. Just enjoy the ride. Don't forget that Jennifer is getting an award this evening at the Grovenor Hotel. You should be there 8 sharp. I guess this is it, brother. I'm off to other things and other places. Take good care of yourself. Of course, she may miss the award ceremony and meet you at the airport. I've sent her a message. Be alert. Good luck. And brother, don't think of me as an evildoer, okay?—Grayson.

Don't ask? Fuck you, Grayson. What do you mean don't ask? When I see you, 'brother,' you'd better tell me everything. Blowing people up is not my idea of a friendly gesture. You almost killed me, you bastard! Keiran's thoughts raced as he munched his sandwich. Jennifer is getting an award? Of course, the award from Medill's company. How could she accept such a thing…and from him? Listen, Keiran. Don't be so proprietary. You know what happened before. She probably deserves the award—whatever it is.

Keiran's eyes were glued to the window as the plane came in for a smooth landing at Gatwick. He was at last on his way to his London home, looking forward to seeing Jennifer. It took several minutes for the plane to pass the commercial docking slots, taxiing to the private air terminal at the far end of the terminal building

The attendant stood by the exit door, her smile wide, her hand held out to shake Keiran's.

"Goodbye Mr. Hogan. You've been the best of patients, not demanding at all. Take care of yourself. I see you've someone to meet you. Good luck, sir."

If he could have run down the twelve steps of the plane, he would have. There, standing at its bottom, was Jennifer. Was it a dream? A mirage? Bob, you fink. You always…. You…. His words came to him all disjointed. He didn't know what to think. Jennifer opened her arms, greeting him, holding him gently, kissing him.

"Keiran Hogan. You've got to take care of yourself. Mr. Grayson called to tell me the strangest story…."

"Jennifer, it was more than strange, beyond strange. Another day to tell you." He kissed her passionately on the lips. She kissed him back, tears in her eyes.

"No award tonight?"

"They can mail it to me. I love you, Keiran Hogan. Promise you'll stay out of trouble?"

"There is so much to tell you, Jennifer. So much to decide. You really want to be with me always?"

"Always. You can't do this to me, though. What were you doing hiking?"

"Grayson told you I was hiking?"

"Yeah, he said you were taking a break from your client's meetings."

"Man…Grayson. Whew! A hike."

He held her hand tightly as they walked through the sparsely populated private aircraft lobby. He now knew that Grayson was a master of his art—that difficult and unsavory art about which he knew so little.

Joe Fontana